ASSAULT ON JUSTICE

Assault on Justice

MONTY MCKINNON

I dedicate this book to everyone who enjoys the suspense and fun involved in immersing themselves in a crazy mystery story.

I hope you enjoy the book and are thoroughly entertained.

Cover Design: Ken Steven
Author photograph: Peter McKinnon
Stock imagery: iStock

ISBN 978-1-7386509-9-6 (paperback)
ISBN 978-1-0690080-0-8 (eBook)

First Printing 07-2025

Chapter 1

Today the packed courtroom felt like an audience settling down before a concert, filled with anticipation as the performers took to the stage.

Whispers, packed with enthusiastic conversation, rippled through the room like white noise.

The prosecutors and defense lawyers sat in silence, eyes flickering between the jury door and the court clerk. Closed files sat idle on the table.

It wasn't a long trial, but it was unusual. That was the reason for the discreet conversation in the courtroom.

Detective Sergeant Borden and Detective Cross had made a point of arriving early after learning the jury had reached a verdict.

Both settled into their prearranged front-row seats. Cross scanned the room while Borden fidgeted with his pen.

"Do you think this will take long? We'll need to get back to the office as soon as possible."

"Why?"

"I guess you didn't watch John Mackie on CanWide News this morning."

"No, I don't turn on the TV in the morning."

"Well, according to Mackie, forecasters predict the storm they've been tracking all week will hit Toronto this morning. If the forecast is correct and it's as powerful as predicted, it will cause severe damage. We may even see some hail as well."

"I think I caught something about that on the radio driving in. Don't worry, we won't be here long. We'll hear the results and get out. Though, if the verdict goes our way, we might want to savor the moment."

"Good. The forecast says heavy winds and torrential rain. We don't want to get caught in it. If the storm hits us hard, there'll be flooding, power outages, and snapped branches. With no power, most of us will be on traffic duty. I imagine it's gonna be a long, stress-filled day."

"Oh, here they come," Cross said. The jury door clicked open, and the room fell silent.

Judgment day had arrived for Juan Estrada and Jason Madler. Six weeks of intense legal battles were about to end.

The shopping list of charges against them was extensive: drug smuggling and trafficking, possession with intent to distribute, operation of a drug manufacturing facility, and money laundering. They also faced charges of possession of illegal firearms and attempted murder of law enforcement officers.

As the courtroom filled behind the detectives, hushed whispers spread among the curious onlookers.

Borden leaned over to Cross. "Well, this is it," he said, his voice steady but mixed with excitement and expectation. "I'm sure justice will prevail here today."

Cross nodded, her eyes reflecting the same anticipation, hope, and nervous anxiety. "I think the Crown prosecutors presented a strong, unyielding case. But you never know with juries. Let's hope they understood the gravity of what happened when we raided the Mississauga warehouse and destroyed their operation. If I hadn't been wearing my Kevlar vest, I would have died during the gunfight with those monsters. Oh, and thanks again for pulling me to safety. I owe you one."

The noise level in the room diminished as the judge observed the jury.

The members in the jury box shifted in their seats, trying and failing to get comfortable. All eyes inside the crowded room followed each procedural step.

The jurors' poker faces revealed no hint of the impending verdict. A muted, dull roar from a swelling crowd of protesters outside the University Avenue courthouse was becoming louder.

As expected, the jury foreman stood. His hands displayed a slight tremor as he handed the verdict slip to the clerk.

In a detached, uncaring voice, the clerk read, "On the charges of drug smuggling and trafficking, we find the defendants, Juan Estrada and Jason Madler, guilty."

"On the charge of attempted murder of law enforcement officers, we find the defendants guilty."

Borden breathed a deep sigh of relief and satisfaction, low whispering, "Yes, thank you, Lord."

The courtroom was silent as each remaining charge continued to be read aloud.

Cross placed her hand on Borden's arm as a subtle reminder to stay calm and composed. The clerk continued to announce the final verdict, causing the courtroom to erupt in soft murmurs.

"The verdict is guilty on all counts," said the clerk.

Borden tightened his fists and forearms. Justice had finally been served.

The judge hammered his gavel, bringing instant silence and order to the room. He thanked the jury and dismissed them before turning toward both defendants with a stern face.

"Sentencing will follow in one week. Court adjourned."

People scrambled from the courtroom, hollering that it was a rigged trial.

Although the room was almost empty, Borden and Cross remained seated momentarily, turning toward the noise in the hall, wondering what was happening. The crowd outside began hurling insults at the police and the court system.

They both savored the victory. They knew the case was now closed. It was time to move.

"We did it," Cross whispered, her sense of relief turning into a broad smile. "This conviction officially shuts down the cartel's drug operations in Ontario and may disrupt whatever they were planning for the rest of Canada. But it still feels unfinished."

Borden nodded, understanding her sentiment. "I know, Cross. The ambassador is still out there. Diplomatic immunity shields him, but we'll find a way. This isn't over. Let's head back to the station."

As Borden and Cross made their way out of the courthouse, a sudden cold gust sent a chill through the air. Overhead, the sky had turned gloomy, with large cumulus clouds swirling.

As rolling thunder rumbled over the lake, the two detectives exchanged a glance, foreshadowing the approaching storm.

Despite the heavy clouds and darkening sky, the protesters carried on chanting, "No justice, no peace," "Free Juan Estrada," and "It's a rigged trial." A portable bullhorn amplified their voices up and down University Avenue.

Borden and Cross looked on as hundreds of protesters, angered by the trial's outcome, stood shoulder to shoulder. The angry protesters blocked the courthouse steps, spilling across the sidewalk and onto University Avenue.

Traffic came to a complete standstill. The crowd swelled, growing angrier by the minute.

Car horns blared, met with foul language and multiple rude hand gestures from angry protesters. Drivers stayed in their vehicles with doors locked and windows shut tight.

Bystanders leaving Hospital Row watched in disbelief, uneasy at the chaos in the city they called home.

One woman turned to her friend and asked, "Isn't this the city known as 'Toronto the Good'? What's happening?"

"Looks like we're in for a rough day," Borden muttered. Cross glanced at the storm clouds, then back at the crowd.

Navigating their way through the growing crowd, they headed to their car. Cross turned around and noticed a black limousine idling by the curb.

She pointed to the vehicle and commented, "Look who appeared."

Borden followed her gaze and saw Carlos Martinez, Mexico's ambassador to Canada, step out of the limousine, flanked by his security detail.

The crowd of protesters greeted his presence with a roar of approval and started chanting his name: "Carlos, Carlos, Carlos."

Martinez raised his hands, calling for silence. The crowd quieted to listen. Borrowing the bullhorn, he spoke in fluent Spanish, his voice calm and reassuring.

"I understand your frustration and your anger at this verdict," he said. "But let us remain peaceful. Justice will prevail."

Borden's hands tightened, his jaw twitched, his heartbeat quickened.

"The gall of that man," he muttered. "Orchestrating this whole charade, standing there grinning like he was some conquering hero. I'm surprised the people hang on to his every word."

Cross nodded, her eyes focused on Martinez. "They don't know he's the reason we were in court today."

As Martinez continued speaking, reassuring the crowd, he urged them to disperse quickly. Borden and Cross remained unimpressed.

Rain began falling on the pavement, and the two detectives took the hint and headed for their car.

A second black limousine sat idling in front of the courthouse, unnoticed. Inside, Sean watched the detectives drive away. He reached for his cell and hit a number on speed dial.

Miles away, sitting in a luxurious penthouse overlooking the lake, the call was answered with a single word.

"Well?"

"Forty or fifty constables out here trying to maintain order. The demonstration's bigger than anticipated. Right now, everything is going much better than we hoped for. I better get moving."

"Okay, and bring back some good Mexican coffee with you. Our meeting needs a caffeine boost."

A soft thank-you, and the call disconnected.

Sean eagerly arrived at the posh condominium to join the group planning session. Enthusiastic smiles greeted the aroma of the freshly brewed coffee he placed on the table.

During the coffee break, Tina pulled Sean aside, her frustration evident on her face as she stared first at Sean and then at the men around her table.

"Are these men ready? There is no room for mistakes. This raid needs to be successful. You know we won't have a second chance," she said.

"They're well-trained. They are the proficient recruits we taught. The camp was the perfect setting for this operation. They have the entire building layout memorized. Our team will enter through the rear entrance, avoiding cameras. They will overpower and subdue anyone they find. Then they will grab the keys. Half our team will destroy the video and computers. The others scramble to the basement and retrieve what is ours. They'll be gone from there in less than twenty minutes," Sean said.

"What if there are more officers still at the station?" Tina asked.

"We're prepared for that possibility. However, when we interrupt the power grid, all constables and detectives will be needed to monitor congested traffic."

"But will the power outages be enough to get everyone out of the building, or do we need more distractions?" Tina asked.

"I arranged for emergency calls to fire stations, shopping malls, even the local universities. They'll all be swamped. The station will be a ghost town by the time we move," said Sean.

"We're ready," Sean said.

"They know what's at stake," said Tina.

"Yes."

They nailed their rehearsals. No issues.

"Great!" Tina said.

"And I personally handled all the small explosives yesterday," Sean added.

The tension that had gripped the muscles in Tina's jaw relaxed, and a grin widened into a full smile.

"Good, and what about the retail stores? How many sites are we hitting?"

"Three malls. We scouted each location, mapped the exits and alarms, and timed their movement to the closest exit. The plan calls for parking close by, so it should work without a hitch. These distractions will provide excellent cover and generate extra time for the raid, should our team need it," Sean said.

"Get to Juan and Madler quickly. If Madler gives you any trouble or holds you up, then shoot him."

She leaned in closer. "Sean, understand, jail is not an option for Juan."

"We've discussed and reviewed the alternatives, but there's only one weak link," she said.

"I just caught the updated weather report on my way here. This rain's only getting worse. The report said to expect flooding, high winds, possible tree damage. It's likely going to continue for hours. The Weather Network even warned about the potential for tornadoes in some areas outside the GTA."

"A tornado would eliminate using the chopper."

"In that event, I'll see that the SUV grabs the package and heads straight to the camp."

"Power outage, heavy rain, high winds, that's a bonus for us and will add to the chaos. Every available constable will be out on duty."

"I also arranged for someone to report a stolen motorcycle which will add to the cops' workload. It'll tie up a few more officers. Depending on their response, we'll know how many stayed behind."

"The last thing before we move in is to assess the use of the parking lot. That will help us gauge what to expect inside. We've driven by four times in the last three days and made a note of employee and squad cars. We're more than ready," Sean said.

"I hope so, because I want payback for what they did to my family and my business," she said.

Chapter 2

The unexpected storm descended upon the down-town core with little mercy. The dark cumulus clouds now blanketed the city in a typical, dull gray haze.

Powerful wind gusts tore through the streets, expanding into the GTA, sending leaves, toys, and debris airborne. People dashing to the subway had their umbrellas blown inside out.

Buildings were damaged, trees toppled, and roads and sidewalks flooded by the relentless rain, forming large ponds of water.

First responders raced through the core, desperate to reach citizens in need. Reduced visibility obscured safe areas for both pedestrians and motorists. The roads became slick, treacherous surfaces, much like a skating rink or black ice, leaving people prone to accidents.

David Harper received permission to leave work early and get home before the storm. Heavy traffic tore away his lead, and now he was stuck in the middle of a treacherous drive home.

He worried about his children, hoping the school had closed early and sent the students home. They would be safe by now, he thought.

David was a big man. His large, muscular shoulders and strong hands allowed him to keep a tight grip on the steering wheel. He was excited to drive his new white Ford F-150 but wanted it parked in the garage, away from the storm.

He drove north on Willowdale Avenue. His hands tightened as he slowly approached the blocked intersection at Finch Avenue. He kept looking in every direction, inching into the intersection, careful to avoid a collision with other vehicles or pedestrians.

Having crossed through the intersection, he proceeded north at a painfully slow pace. He was a careful man and worried about his truck, especially if the rain turned to hail.

Harper strained his eyes as he squinted through the streaked windshield while the wipers thrashed in vain against the deluge.

David had left work early, hoping to beat the worst of the storm, but now he wished he had stayed at the office, where he would have been safe.

But the rainstorm had a mind of its own, and that was something he would soon understand.

Everywhere, traffic was a nightmare. His radio confirmed that cars were either stopped or crawling along Yonge Street and Bayview Avenue, their headlights barely penetrating the gloom. That was why David inched forward on Willowdale Avenue, his eyes darting between the road and the side mirrors, trying to avoid the unpredictable movements of other drivers.

He was shaking, sensing the danger around him. Everyone could relate to the accumulating anxiety of trying to navigate a safe route home.

Suddenly, blinding flashes of lightning lit up the sky and the interior of his truck. The flashes were followed by deafening crashes of thunder directly overhead.

David flinched and instinctively ducked inside the cab of his truck as his heart pounded louder than a rock concert. He held the steering wheel tighter, his hands sweating, his eyes glued to the road ahead.

He knew he was in danger, and without closing his eyes, he immediately started to pray.

That's when he saw it: a massive steel hydro tower, wires tearing away from its outstretched arms. The tower swayed in the wind, looming over the traffic opposite the Finch Subway parking lot.

"Oh no," he muttered.

Then, as if in slow motion, the tower gave way.

The metal structure buckled with a loud creaking sound before crashing to the rain-soaked grassy field. David watched in disbelief as one of the large gray support arms snapped loose, tumbling end over end toward the road. He lost sight of the metal arm as it hurtled toward him.

David instinctively slammed on the accelerator like a Formula One driver at the starting line, spinning his wheels on the wet road and fishtailing toward southbound traffic.

He yanked the wheel right, then left. The truck skidded.

A thunderous crash echoed in the cab as the rear window shattered. Harper screamed.

"What was..." David's words were cut off as the crushing weight of the tower arm tore apart the bed of his truck.

The impact jolted him. His head hit the frame above the door, sending pain down his neck and back. Blood trickled over his face as he lost control of the vehicle.

The truck slid across the road. The tires felt spongy as they lost pressure. David struggled to control it but failed. He was just along for the ride.

The truck slammed against a curbside lamppost, triggering the airbags to deploy. The blast knocked the breath out of him.

Harper was thrown back into his seat like a rag doll, stunned, trying to understand what had happened. Rain pounded the roof of the cab, matching the pounding of his newly acquired headache.

His hands still gripped the wheel. They trembled as he fumbled with the door handle. The twisted cab frame had jammed the door. Pushing didn't help.

He leaned his shoulder into the door, but it wouldn't budge. He swung around, lay on his back, and with both feet up, he kicked it. Once. Twice. Nothing. He slammed his feet again and again. Finally, the door cracked open.

He wedged himself out, staggering into the storm. Rain soaked his clothes instantly, clinging cold against his skin.

Wind pinned him back against the truck. He turned his head away from the driving rain, unable to assess the damage.

David steadied himself, then stepped away. He twisted back toward the truck. His eyes widened.

The cargo bed was crushed under the weight of the massive hydro tower arm, its twin lying in the road, blocking all traffic.

The impact had ripped the rear axle from the truck and crushed its sides and bed. The front end was wrinkled against the lamppost. Steam hissed from the radiator, and the windshield was cracked. The wipers jammed, grinding uselessly. A strange odor filled the cab from the damaged motor.

Heading south on Willowdale, David saw the glow of emergency lights through the darkness. Sirens wailed.

Still in shock, he walked away from the truck until he felt safe.

In the hydro field east of Willowdale, two more towers had collapsed. Twisted metal sprawled across the grass, live wires sparking on the soaked ground. The towers were now heaps of wreckage, blocking northbound traffic.

Homes across North York and the city core were without power. With no lights or signals, every intersection became a battleground. On Willowdale, cars crawled forward, inches at a time. Tempers flared, horns blared, and no one was getting through.

Dinner would be late tonight for everyone on Willowdale Avenue.

A few blocks away, it was worse. Debris-covered sewers had backed up, flooding streets and low-lying areas.

Firefighters and police worked frantically to direct traffic, secure the area, and guide people out of the subway lot.

David watched as two first responder's approached his truck. Their shock grew as they got closer.

"Are you okay, sir?" one called, his voice barely audible over the storm. "Is this your truck?"

"It was my truck," Harper murmured.

"Stay here. Help is on the way. We'll get you checked out and arrange for a tow truck."

"Thanks," was all Harper could whisper.

David leaned against the crumpled cab, rain dripping from his nose, and stared at what was left of his truck.

"I should have stayed home," he mumbled.

Chapter 3

Conductor Mike Connors frowned. A maintenance panel, usually locked and hidden from public view, hung open and unattended as he eased his train alongside the subway platform, just as he had done a thousand times in the past.

Before heading home early, Connors made his final walk-through. The intensity of the storm had gotten so bad that the Toronto Transit Commission shut down operations, announcing the closure of Line 1.

Flooding mixed with live subway wires was a disaster waiting to happen.

The platform and stairway lights flickered, then the train lights. Seconds later, darkness. A loud bang echoed, followed by a dim glow as emergency lighting powered on.

Rain and wind tormented the outside world, leaving Finch Station deserted. An eerie silence replaced the usual hustle and chatter of riders.

Mike walked through each car, checking that doors and windows were closed, peering into corners, ensuring no one had stayed behind. The dim lighting cast strange shadows across the floor and walls. It felt too quiet, too alone and too menacing.

He was nearly at the last car when something caught his eye. A white shopping bag, tucked far under a bench seat. A blue windbreaker was crumpled on the seat across from the exit.

Probably left behind in the rush, he figured. He leaned down to grab the bag, and his body cast a shadow. Then he stopped. His muscles froze.

Nestled between folds of plastic was a digital timer. One-inch-tall numbers flashing. Five minutes and 44seconds... 42 seconds.

Connors blinked. Then blinked again.

Inside the bag he saw wires. Nestled deep out of reach was a bomb.

His heart raced as he shot to his feet and stumbled backward. The train was empty. His instincts screamed at him to get out. Warn people.

So, he yelled. "There's a bomb!" as he made a dash sprinting toward the escalator. No power. Dead.

One option left. The stairs.

"Anyone here? There's a bomb! Run! Get out now!"

His chest heaved. Pain radiated across his shoulder. No one responded.

He ran harder, gasping for air, legs burning. He gripped the chrome handrail and hauled himself up, two steps at a time.

At the top, he stumbled and paused, legs shaking. Still no one.

Then he saw a man slumped against black garbage bags. It was a homeless man , barely conscious, propped against a yellow-tiled wall.

"Hey! You need to get up!" Mike shouted.

The man barely stirred.

Mike grabbed his arm and shook him. "There's a bomb!"

"A bomb?" the man mumbled, dazed.

"No time," Mike said, pulling him to his feet. Half-carrying, half-dragging him, they staggered for the exit, feet scraping across the tile floor.

Just a few more steps.

The floor rumbled beneath them. Tiles fell off the wall. The roar grew louder.

They pushed harder. Every breath hurt. Smoke rolled up behind them. A sudden burst of dust filled the air as electrical transformers exploded, scattering grit and insulation into a choking haze.

They reached the exit, pushed through the doors, and tumbled into the cold, rain-soaked street, gasping for air.

Circling the corner of the building, they collapsed onto a metal bench under a bus shelter. Cold rain plastered their clothes to their skin.

They trembled, shivering, still too stunned to speak.

Someone appeared with a blanket. Another handed them a plastic bag. They sat in silence as rain poured around them, mixing with the dust becoming a slurry and streaking down their faces.

After a few minutes, Mike finally spoke.

"Are you okay?"

The man nodded slowly. "Yeah... I think so. Thanks, man. You saved my life."

Mike nodded. "No problem. I just happened to be in the area."

They chuckled, a weak attempt to fight off the shock.

Mike stared back at the smoke-filled entrance and said nothing more.

Just beyond the shelter, news vans were already arriving.

CanWide News reporter John Mackie stood in the rain at the Yonge/Finch subway entrance in Willowdale, microphone in hand. Emergency lights flashed behind him. The air buzzed with sirens and officials shouting instructions.

"This is John Mackie reporting live from Yonge and Finch," he began, his voice firm. "We've just witnessed what may be the most devastating storm in Toronto's recent memory. And now, there's been an explosion in the Finch subway stop. Some are suggesting it appears that a bomb has gone off in the Finch subway train."

He turned toward the shelter behind him. "The two men rescued from inside the station are being checked by paramedics. One of them is TTC conductor Mike Connors. Sources say he discovered the bomb and raced to evacuate anyone nearby. He's a hero tonight."

Mackie turned again as another figure approached. "We're joined now by David Harper, a North York resident caught in the chaos earlier today when a hydro tower collapsed onto his truck. Mr. Harper, thank you for joining us. Can you tell us what happened?"

Harper stepped up, soaked through, still visibly trembling. "Yeah... it all happened so fast. One minute I was driving home, the next... the sky lit up with lightning. Then a hydro tower arm snapped. Came down right on top of me."

He paused, swallowed hard. "I thought I was going to die in that truck."

Mackie lowered his voice. "And you came here to see what was happening?"

"I didn't even know about the bomb until I saw the ambulances. But yeah, I wanted to see it with my own eyes. This city... I've never seen anything like this. Not in forty years. Storm, blackouts, explosions... it's unreal."

Mackie turned back to the camera.

"There you have it. Explosions underground, hydro towers collapsing, traffic lights dark, intersections blocked and terrified residents. Toronto is now in the grip of a storm and a threat far bigger than anyone imagined when they heard last night's weather report here on Can-Wide News.

Now, back to the studio."

He stepped aside as the camera light blinked off.

In the background, Connors and the homeless man remained huddled beneath the bus shelter, the shock of the day sinking in.

And above it all, the storm still raged. Out-of-control.

Chapter 4

The detective squad room was quiet. The few remaining staff gathered around, listening to the trial verdict.

Detectives Gibson, Kim, and Friedman reveled in the guilty verdict. For them, it was a moment of triumph, a major win for the team. After months of chasing down leads, the verdict finally felt like justice.

The verdict was especially meaningful for Gibson. His outstanding dedication in helping to find and arrest Juan Estrada and Jason Madler had earned him a promotion from police constable to detective.

Just then, the phone on Gibson's desk rang. He glanced at the caller ID and answered, his expression shifting from joy to concern. "You've got to be kidding me. All right, we're on our way."

He hung up and turned to Kim and Friedman. "We've got multiple robberies happening across the city at major mall locations. The caller said three malls have been hit. But here's the weird part: several jewelry stores were hit at exactly the same time in each one."

The detectives stared at each other in disbelief. Reaching for his car keys, Kim muttered, "It's going to be a long day." Friedman grunted but agreed.

Kim and Friedman each headed out to investigate.

Gibson stepped over shards of glass that crunched beneath his shoes. One of the stunned jewelry clerks pointed to a display case, emptied, with its plush velvet trays tossed across the floor. The clerk's hands trembled. Her eyes were red and puffy.

"The three men smashed our cases with hammers, scraped the contents into a black pouch, and disappeared in maybe three minutes," she said.

They knew the location of every security camera, every blind spot, and how to get to the exit without showing up on video.

It was a fast, in and out operation, but somehow, they managed to pull it off and leave many terrorized.

Before Gibson could say another word, his cell phone vibrated.

"It's the boss. I need to take this," he said.

"Gibson, what's going on?" Borden's voice crackled over the speaker.

"Sir, we've got reports of robberies at several malls. I'm at the Eaton Center now. Kim and Friedman are at the other two malls. All constables are out except for Baxter and Connelly at the front desk. Everyone is either directing traffic or responding to the flood of 911 calls. Once I'm done here, I'll head back to the station and help take some of the emergency calls. Baxter and Connelly can use some help. Right now, they're the only two holding down the fort, along with the admin staff. Oh no, the power just went out."

"Just when I thought things couldn't get any worse," murmured Borden. "Cross and I are still crawling through the heavy gridlock. We'll try to get back to the station as soon as possible. Keep me updated on the robberies."

"Will do, sir," Gibson replied before ending the call.

As Borden and Cross navigated the chaotic streets, they couldn't help but notice the storm's growing intensity. The traffic lights were still out because of the power outages near the station.

At almost every intersection, police constables braved the elements, doing their best to direct traffic and manage the chaotic gridlock.

When Detective Gibson finally concluded his investigation, he stared back at the shattered jewelry cases, glass littering the floor, and frantic store staff still feeling nauseated and trembling. He attempted to console them and suggested they leave everything as is until the forensics department had an opportunity to go over the scene.

Gibson approached the manager and suggested he send the staff home to preserve the scene. He agreed.

His work was done in this store. Gibson then headed to the next jewelry store. The story was identical except for one detail raised by a store employee.

The clerk thought she heard someone mutter something that sounded like Spanish to her.

Gibson made a note of the clerk's comment, as he thought it was possibly a valuable clue he could muse on later.

Every jewelry store in the Eaton Center was hit in a simultaneous smash-and-grab. Yet somehow, the criminals got away in under five minutes.

"How did they manage that considering the crazy weather and traffic?" Gibson wondered.

Chapter 5

A white Ford cube truck idled in the deserted police station parking lot. Rain battered its roof in steady bursts. The decals read, "Toronto Police Services," their vinyl edges curling slightly from wear.

No one noticed the faint hiss of the door sliding open.

The three men climbed out, wearing uniforms that were exact replicas that included their badges, name tags, utility belts, even the standard-issue boots and holstered sidearms.

They kept their heads down low, faces hidden under cap brims as they hustled toward the shelter of the rear loading dock, rainwater streaking off their jackets.

At the dock, the leader, a tall, broad-shouldered man, gave a passing glance at the security camera, turning away before it could catch his face. He set the timer on his watch for twenty minutes. That was all the time they needed.

Inside, Constable Connelly glanced at the monitor.

Nothing unusual.

Seeing the familiar truck and uniformed officers shielding themselves from the rain, he reached over and tapped a button on the control panel. The security door clicked and was instantly unlocked.

The three men slipped inside without a word. They nodded a brief acknowledgment to Connelly, dried their boots, and headed down the hallway.

They reached inside their coat pockets and immediately pulled on black balaclavas.

They moved fast, their steps becoming whisper quiet on the tile floor.

At the corner before entering the main lobby, the leader raised a fist in the air. Everyone froze.

No words spoken.

Just a glance, a nod, a hand gesture. They waited for a signal from the leader.

The leader counted down on his fingers. Three. Two. One. They burst into the front office, moving like clockwork, just as they had planned.

Two of them were on Connelly in seconds. A quick strike echoed when the butt of a pistol hit his head. He crumpled without a sound. The room filled with the ripping sound of duct tape being torn. In seconds, Connelly was gagged, blindfolded, and bound at the wrists and ankles.

His breathing was shallow. He wasn't unconscious, but very close. His head wound was trickling blood. One of the attackers dragged him against the front desk, where he lay like discarded luggage at an airport carousel.

The leader rushed to the front doors and flipped the deadbolt and security latch. He moved fast, cutting the power to the desk monitors and yanking the video feeds from their mounts.

The team worked methodically, disabling cameras and cutting wires. The station was blind and deaf to the outside world.

Inside, the sound of smashing equipment echoed through the empty halls. Computers were smothered in coffee and water, sparks jumping from keyboards.

The station's digital footprint was dead.

Down the hall, Constable Baxter paused.

He heard something unusual: dull impacts, glass shattering, a monitor crashing to the floor, but no voices. Something was not right. He moved fast, one hand on his sidearm as he turned a corner, dashing toward the lobby.

As he rounded the corner, he was met with the sight of Connelly, bound and barely conscious. He never got a chance to react. Before he could respond, the attackers rushed him from both sides. One yanked his gun hand down, another cracked his head with the butt of a gun, then slammed him against the wall.

The air flew from his lungs. He strained to get free when he heard the tearing sound of what he assumed was tape. In moments, he was on the floor, stacked beside Connelly with his arms and legs tightly secured.

Outside, a second white Ford cube truck coasted up beside the first truck. Three more raiders stepped out wearing the same uniforms, same masks. They covertly slipped past the security camera and through the rear entrance. Moving like ghosts, they joined their comrades.

The duty keys were tossed to the second crew as they dashed to the basement.

The first group burst into the administration area like a hurricane, catching the staff by surprise.

A chair was knocked over. Papers flew.

"Down! Get down on the floor!" one barked.

Instant panic erupted.

Screams.

A file cabinet slammed shut as a worker dove in behind it, only to be hauled out seconds later.

The women were held at gunpoint, then forced to the floor. The tearing sound sparked fear as they cried while their hands and feet were bound. The administration room instantly fell into a fearful silence. Only the low rumbling sound of distant thunder was audible.

The leader checked his watch again. Six minutes had passed. He nodded once, then turned toward the stair-well.

The team followed, boots thudding softly down the concrete steps. The hallway below was wide and sterile, the buzz from the failing fluorescent lights overhead barely alive with the depleting battery backup power.

The Evidence Room cage door stood at the end of the hall. A steel gate with reinforced mesh and three large deadbolts provided security. The gate surrendered to the duty keys they took from Constable Baxter. The heavy latch clunked open with ease.

The cage door swung open, revealing a varied arsenal of weapons, boxes of ammunition, bricks of narcotics, and thick bundles of paper-banded cash confiscated during police raids.

All of it boxed and labeled and destined for destruction in the incinerator. They moved fast, two men clearing shelves, stacking boxes and duffel bags onto flatbed dollies.

The elevator dinged, producing another man pushing a dolly.

The operation ran smoothly, each raider executing their role exactly as planned.

Once again glancing at his watch, the leader signaled for the team to hurry.

Three minutes later, both dollies were empty, and the station had been gutted.

The decals were removed. The attackers climbed back into their vehicles, peeled off their masks and gloves, dropping them into a sealed bio hazard bag.

As the trucks rolled out into the storm, the leader glanced back one time.

No alarms. No lights. No video. No evidence. And no one seriously injured.

He was satisfied they had left nothing behind, not even a fingerprint. It was a clean operation with time to spare.

The station was just another empty building in a city shrouded in chaos.

In the penthouse, a cell phone vibrated once. It was answered without looking and said, "Yes?"

A voice, calm and low, said, "It's done. We have everything. No witnesses. No trace. We were out with four minutes to spare."

She paused, then said, "You know what to do next."

Chapter 6

Borden swung the squad car into the police station's parking lot. "At last. I thought we'd never get here."

"I know what you mean. That drive was brutal," Cross said. "Feels weird not seeing the usual cruisers," Cross said. "Just a few personal cars in the back."

Borden nodded. "Something feels different. This lot's normally packed. I'm used to fighting for a spot to park."

"Well, at least that drive's over. I was impressed how you kept calling in those crashes and requesting assistance," said Cross.

"On the bright side, we won't have trouble finding a parking spot close to the door," Cross said.

"Maybe we might stay dry provided we hustle."

"You're right. We'll take another win after the morning we've had. Did I mention they were found guilty on all charges?" Cross nodded and gave a soft chuckle. "You did."

After a short dash from the car, Borden swiped his ID card, hearing the familiar click of the door unlocking. Inside they stopped short. Two flatbed dollies sat abandoned in the hallway.

"Strange," Borden commented. "Why are these just sitting here in everybody's way? Cross, find out who left these dollies, and tell them to put them both back downstairs where they belong."

"Okay."

"With all the 911 calls, maybe whoever had them probably got pulled off for an emergency, and didn't have time to return them to the storage area," Cross said.

"That makes sense," Borden replied.

As they moved down the hallway toward the front of the station, the chaotic destruction came into view. Connelly and Baxter were bound and gagged, their heads slumped forward, barely conscious. Blood pooled on the floor beneath them.

The hallway to the admin area was silent. No one else in sight.

Instinctively, Borden and Cross withdrew their weapons, scanning the area for any remaining threats. "Stay sharp," Borden whispered, moving swiftly forward through the station.

Arriving in the admin area, Borden was shocked to find his staff bound, gagged, and lying on the floor. He quickly cut through the tape, freeing Caroline and helping her to a chair. "What happened?" he asked as he cut the tape to release the others.

Caroline trembled as she spoke, "They... they came out of nowhere. We didn't see them coming. They had guns—and shouted at us to get down."

Cross freed Connelly and Baxter, tending their wounds with the first-aid kit from the wall. Both men were groggy, bruised and wincing with the repeated thudding of a splitting headache trying to process what had happened.

"They swarmed us," Baxter muttered, wincing as Cross dabbed his head with gauze.

Cross handed them Tylenol and water. "How many were there?" she asked.

"At least three or four, maybe more."

Baxter shifted in his chair and then stopped. No familiar rattle. "My keys!

They're gone," he said.

Cross replied, "What keys?"

"My duty keys."

"Oh no," Cross said, as she bolted for the basement. She flew down the stairs two at a time, her heart pounding as she gripped the railing.

At the bottom, her eyes went straight to the evidence cage. The door hung open. Her worst fears were confirmed.

The cage was empty.

Shelves bare.

Everything gone.

Cross took a deep breath, spun around, and charged back upstairs. Her jaw clenched, her leg muscles burning with a feeling of weakness. She continued the climb to the main floor. Her face flushed and eyes stinging with anger. "Borden, they cleaned out the cage. Weapons, ammo, drugs, cash... everything's gone."

Borden's expression changed instantly. His jaw tightened. His face flushed with anger.

"The keys were left dangling from the cage lock," Cross explained. "I will call forensics, ask them to process the scene. But with this weather, it'll be a while before they can get started."

"Do it," Borden said.

Back in the admin office, Caroline and her associates sipped some English Breakfast tea with trembling hands. "They won't get away with this," Caroline whispered. "How dare they..." she muttered under her breath.

Chapter 7

Rain hammered the windshield, and the wipers smeared more than they cleared. Visibility was almost zero.

Inside, Juan Estrada and Jason Madler sat shackled and anxious, their orange jumpsuits an ugly reminder of their future. Juan sat rigid on the cold metal bench. He remained silent, his body jolted by every pothole and bump. It was past the time for new shock's he thought.

He knew protecting Madler at Penetanguishene Penitentiary would be impossible. He'd heard that the prison held over 8,500 inmates, all waiting their arrival. None of them likely to roll out the welcome mat.

The prisoners' wrists and ankles were raw and bleeding. The rattle of their chains echoed in the metal confines of the box, giving Madler a splitting headache.

Juan leaned back against the truck wall, his mind swirling with thoughts of revenge. Outside, the storm mirrored the chaos in his mind. How would he get even?

He glanced at Madler, who sat across from him, hands clenched, his knees bouncing. He looked like he was on the verge of cracking.

"Juan, I don't want to be someone's girlfriend in prison. I'm scared," Madler muttered, his voice barely audible over the sudden crack of thunder.

Juan forced a grin to mask his own fear. "Don't worry, Madler. I'll have your back. Nobody will come near you. If anyone tries anything, I'll send them to the infirmary in small pieces or the morgue in a plastic bag."

Madler's eyes widened. "Juan... aren't you worried?"

Juan sighed and shifted. "Right now, I'm more worried about this bumpy ride and this horrible smell."

As the transport wagon crawled through the gridlock, the two men sat in silence, each afraid, neither willing to admit it.

They heard the occasional downpours on the roof and the rumble of thunder fading in the distance as they rode toward their destiny. The chains at their ankles rattled nonstop, and their echo seemed louder, making both men feel nauseous.

Juan's mind drifted back to the trial. The judge's voice still echoed in his ears. "I need to calculate the maximum sentence for you two criminals." One day, he mused, he would get revenge.

Juan Estrada was convinced they'd be in prison forever. Juan knew what prison meant.

No escape.

No parole.

No freedom.

No hope.

He glanced at Madler, who was at the edge of a complete mental breakdown. If that happened, Juan couldn't do anything for him.

For the first time, Juan felt regret set in. Maybe they weren't so smart or so tough after all.

Juan knew that going to prison was the better option than the alternative. Informing on the drug cartel would have meant certain death. Snitching on the cartel would be the same as suicide. That fate would also extend to their relatives and friends. The cartel had made that crystal clear.

He had no choice but to accept his fate, though it worried him. He thought the best course of action for survival was blending in, minding his own business, and making a point to have a good relationship with everyone.

His thoughts were shattered by a sudden blast, followed by a deafening squeal that dipped the nose and rocked the swaying truck back and forth with grinding metal squealing on the road surface sending sparks low and backward.

Up front, Jake, the driver, fought to regain control.

He yanked the wheel in the opposite direction of the skid. The truck rolled up on two wheels, then slammed down hard and rattled its' bones jolting everyone inside.

Wrong way.

He yanked it left.

Then Jake pulled hard to the right in a desperate attempt to gain control of the skid.

The wheel had a mind of its own.

The slick roadway offered no traction.

The wagon spun violently, pinning the prisoners against the walls. It twisted, fishtailed, and finally Jake lost all control. Both the guards and prisoners felt dizzy and queasy, thinking they would vomit.

Inside, Juan and Madler were tossed like tiny rag dolls and yanked back to their bench by the ankle chains which made them whine and moan.

The shackles tore at their skin. Their heads slammed against the wall, generating instant migraine headaches.

Up front, "Hold on!" driver Jake shouted. His partner, Sam, braced, grabbed for the dashboard with one hand while reaching for the door with the other.

The vehicle lurched, sliding backward as it zigzagged off the road. Front and side airbags burst with a violent pop, cushioning the impact but knocking the wind out of both Jake and Sam.

Jake's head snapped back from the force of the airbag, and he momentarily lost consciousness.

A sickening crunch of metal echoed in Sam's ears as the vehicle slammed into a sturdy, massive hundred-year-old oak tree, which brought the truck to an abrupt halt. The force of the impact twisted the wagon's frame and damaged the windshield, splintering it into a spiderweb of hairline cracks.

The crumpled hood hissed as white steam poured out, rising in a thick white plume. The front end of the wagon took the brunt of the impact. Twisted metal, shattered lights, branches embedded in and across the grille. The front tires were both flat, hanging off their rims and missing major chunks of rubber.

Jake groaned, his vision blurred. A throbbing pain radiated from his shoulder where the seat belt had dug in during the spin.

Warm blood trickled down the side of his face. "Sam... you, okay?" he managed to blurt out.

Sam didn't answer. He sat there limp.

Jake yelled out again. This time he yelled much louder.

"Sam! Are you okay?"

Sam slowly twisted his neck and looked over, feeling dazed, bleeding, barely able to focus.

Jake could see blood seeping from a cut above his eyebrow where Sam had hit his head on the dashboard before the airbag deployed. "I think so," he mumbled, trying to make sense of what just happened.

Everything fell quiet with the exception of the steam hissing from the engine compartment and the rain still dribbling on the roof of the wagon.

"Sam, let me get your head bandaged, then we'll check on the prisoners. They need to send a new transport wagon for all of us."

"What the heck just happened?" Madler gasped, as he rubbed the back of his head, eyes wide.

"Beats me," Juan replied, steadying himself.

They heard shouting outside.

"Did you hear that?" Madler asked, his voice shaking.

"Yeah."

"What do you think it is?"

Juan leaned in, listening. "No idea. But I'm sure we'll find out soon enough.

Seconds later, the rattle of a key entering the metal lock sent a chill down their spines. The deadbolt screeched, metal grinding against metal as it slid open.

The door was thrust open. Two men climbed aboard, dressed in black, with their faces hidden behind balaclava masks. One had used a key, taken from Sam, to free the prisoners.

Juan and Madler jumped out into the soft rain, their jumpsuits soaked instantly.

They twisted and gazed toward a large van, idling nearby. The side door slid open with a hiss, engine purring low.

"Who are you?" Juan shouted at the two men. "Where are we going? What do you want?"

The two masked men motioned Juan and Madler over to the van. Seconds later, the driver left the area. No one spoke a word.

Less than an hour later, as the storm eased, the van arrived at a heliport where Juan and Madler climbed aboard. Two different masked men were waiting. The chopper lifted off toward the northwest.

Jake tried to call out to Sam, but pain flared through his shoulder and shut him down. Just moments later, he and Sam were shoved into the back of the wagon.

Jake slumped, exhausted. Now he and Sam were the ones shackled to the floor.

Chapter 8

For the first time, Borden truly felt the weight and stress of his job and thought maybe it was time to hang it up and retire.

He had mentored Cross for a few years, and Borden thought she was ready to tackle his job. They had worked together on multiple cases, and she had an investigative mind that paid attention to every detail. Cross was originally selected because she was an outstanding leader with all the right qualifications.

He was certain the Chief would agree that Detective Cross was the right choice to take over. That had always been the plan since he recruited her as a respected member of the Police Academy leadership team.

Borden understood that his responsibility was the security of the station and well-being of his staff. The break-in was a major security failure and Borden alone was accountable. That didn't sit well with him.

He buried the emotional weight, of knowing his police station had become an active crime scene.

After 36 hours of turmoil, Borden had developed a throbbing headache that pulsed behind his eyes and pounded through his temples. It was not unusual for a headache to give him moments of pure frustration, but sometimes it could affect his thought process.

That bothered him.

Fortunately, he carried a small supply of pain relievers, which he swallowed immediately. He knew relaxation was what could help, but that would need to wait.

For Borden, the attack on his station was still fresh and raw. He was aggravated and thought how much he would enjoy two weeks at his cottage right now. It would be an opportunity to play, swim and enjoy Since that wasn't possible, he knew what he had to do next, and he dreaded it.

Taking a deep breath, he reached for his phone and hit the speed dial for his boss. The line rang once before the Chief's stern voice answered.

"Borden, good to hear from you. I was just about to call. My congratulations on the conviction of Estrada and Madler this morning. That was solid work by you and your team. Everyone in my office is impressed with your tenacity. Excellent job. You and your team put two of our worst criminals behind bars, probably for life. Well done. So, what can I do for you, detective?"

Borden swallowed hard. The praise only made the news he had to deliver more difficult.

"Thank you, Chief. You are correct in that it was a solid team effort. But I'm afraid I have some bad news."

There was a brief pause on the other end.

"Go on," the Chief said.

Borden took another deep breath.

"The station has been attacked. It happened just after we heard the verdict in court this morning. All of our staff were out on investigative duties given the chaos in the city. Constables Connelly and Baxter were here at the station alone. They were unexpectedly overpowered and subdued, as were our backroom admin staff. The attackers cleaned out the evidence locker.

Whoever struck our station took the weapons scheduled for destruction, as well as ammunition, narcotics, and a substantial amount of cash. Most of the material taken was confiscated when we raided the drug cartel warehouse in Mississauga six months ago."

"When did you say this happened?" the Chief asked.

"Just after my last three detectives were called out to investigate jewelry store robberies at the Eaton Center and two other shopping malls. That left only two constables and the admin team in the station."

"As the one responsible for the safety of our station and staff, I've decided to offer you my resignation and take early retirement. Detective Cross can assume my duties and she would be an excellent choice as a new leader," Borden said.

The Chief's voice was gentle and understanding.

"You're not going anywhere. I don't and I won't accept your resignation. You and Cross lead the best team I've got. That attack could have happened at any of our stations. You know what you need to do, Borden... go and do it."

"Thank you, sir."

"One more thing Borden, whatever resources you need, just let me know. I want you to find these guys. You'll have my total support with an unlimited budget as well," said the Chief.

Borden hung up. The Chief's final words echoed in his head:

"Whatever you need... unlimited budget."

The Chief of Police had just handed Borden the freedom to do whatever was necessary to apprehend and arrest these people.

Chapter 9

Borden reviewed the tidbits of information he had. As he shifted in his chair, his gaze drifted to the clock ticking loudly on his wall... click, click, click.

The ticking triggered a cascade of thoughts about the day's events. It couldn't have taken the attackers long, he thought. Maybe fifteen or twenty minutes at the most.

His mind was flooded with questions he couldn't answer yet. Did they have a schematic of the station? Could it be they were tipped off that everyone was out on calls? Did the storm have any part in the events of the day? And how did the attackers know the items in the cage were there, let alone scheduled for destruction in a day or two?

Who would have the resources, the motivation, and the audacity to pull this off?

He wanted answers!

A short two hours earlier, everyone was ready to celebrate, believing the department investigators as well as the Crown Prosecutors had finally put the drug cartel out of business in Canada.

Clearly, this assault was the work of a very sophisticated and experienced network of criminals. Whoever was behind this had to be deeply entrenched in both the criminal underworld and, disturbingly, possibly in Canadian and international politics through the Mexican Ambassador.

Ever since the former Prime Minister legalized marijuana, the Mexican cartel activity in the Greater Toronto Area, (GTA) had surged, increasing his department's workload dramatically.

The suspected involvement of the Mexican Ambassador to Canada, Carlos Martinez, would be particularly troubling for Borden's department.

Everyone in law enforcement knew the Ambassador's diplomatic immunity made him literally untouchable. It allowed him to break the law and laugh in the face of Canadian justice, slipping through cracks no one else could.

He was young, brash, arrogant, bold, and not afraid or concerned about Canadian law. He knew he could get away with anything. That made him dangerous.

Borden held onto the hope that one day, somewhere, the Canadian justice system would prevail and catch up to the Ambassador. He just wasn't sure how that would unfold.

But following his call with the Chief and knowing he would be supported, Borden began thinking he needed a Special Task Force.

He jotted some notes as he began to assemble a strike force to tackle the problem head-on. He wanted a tight-knit team willing to do whatever it took to dismantle these criminal networks piece by piece. Ever since his son

Mark had died from fentanyl, his mission was to dedicate himself to doing whatever it took to eradicate illicit drugs in Ontario.

The first names he recorded were Detectives Kim and Friedman. They brought years of investigative experience to the table, and Borden knew he would need every ounce of their expertise.

Gibson was a natural choice with his fresh perspective and unrelenting determination. He had already proven himself to be a valuable asset. He could be counted on to ask direct questions and challenge the status quo.

Cross, his trusted partner, had an uncanny ability to read people and situations, often seeing what others missed while providing clear, level-headed leadership.

He thought about asking Sergeant Rick Crawford of the RCMP to join the group. If this were indeed a cartel operation that attacked the station, he knew Crawford would definitely want in on the investigation.

Since the cartels were recognized as a terrorist group, Crawford brought critical powers to the unit. He was someone who could freeze bank accounts, seize the assets of terrorists, and be trusted. Not to mention, he was well-connected throughout law enforcement across Canada.

Borden made a mental note to reach out to him once he had more information and was ready to move forward. He knew he needed one more person who could advise and assist on the international front if necessary.

Experience had taught Borden that he could rely on Danielle Spade from CSIS, the Canadian Security Intelligence Service. She would be an outstanding asset.

Her insight into cartel-terrorist links and her global contacts might help find the missing pieces to crack this puzzle.

Although this may be a domestic problem, her insight and experience would prove invaluable as an advisor to any investigation.

He glanced over at his phone, hoping it would light up with updates from his team of detectives investigating the mall robberies.

Nothing yet.

The simple act of glancing at his phone sent Borden down another rabbit hole. He began thinking about the jewelry store robberies. They must have been part of the plan, but he needed evidence to prove that.

Those robberies raised one big question: Why would anyone go through the trouble of a smash-and-grab? It's reckless, destructive, guaranteed to get caught on video, and most of the time the merchandise on display are just decoys. Most watches and rings are fake, used for display only.

It didn't add up, unless it was purely opportunistic. But that's not logical either, because nobody would be seen walking around in a mall with a hammer prepared for a smash-and-grab on the off chance that the power goes out.

No.

This was no accident.

Someone had planned for this. That much, Borden knew for sure.

Just then, he heard the increasing sound of footsteps approaching his office. The door creaked open, and Cross stepped in, her face a mixture of concern and determination.

"You need some oil on those hinges, boss. I wanted to let you know the forensics team arrived," she said. "They've decided to process the cage first."

Borden nodded.

"Good. Let's see what they can find."

Chapter 10

The rain was letting up, leaving the helicopter window streaked with watermarks from the turbulence.

Juan shifted uncomfortably, his ankle itchy and throbbing from the chains in the police wagon. Madler sat still beside him, as though he was in a coma, pale as a hospital bed sheet.

Neither of them uttered a word. Below them, the world had vanished; they had no idea where they were headed.

The pilot kept his eyes focused on the instrument panel while the men who had freed them sat motionless, with their masks still in place, like a pair of department store mannequins.

Juan kept replaying the events of their escape from custody. If these guys were friendly, why hide their faces?

He glanced at Madler, the older of the pair, who looked like he was barely holding it together. His hands shook, and his right leg twitched nervously.

Juan leaned over and asked, "You good?"

Madler nodded, but his eyes didn't meet Juan's.

"Then knock off the twitching. It shows weakness and fear," Juan said.

The flight dragged on, the hum of the rotors the only sound. Juan figured they had flown for at least an hour, maybe more. His stomach churned and gurgled, hungry for food.

The helicopter banked steeply in a normal descending right turn. Trees came into view, rising fast toward the chopper.

Juan craned his neck, trying to see past the masks and the pilot, but all he saw was an endless expanse of green forest.

The landing was smooth, despite the bumpy ride. The chopper settled into a clearing, its rotors kicking up wind, dirt, and loose leaves.

One of the masked men slid the door open and gestured for them to step out.

Juan jumped out first, his legs stiff, his feet screaming in pain as he landed on the helipad. Madler followed, wobbling and light-headed as he jumped to the pad.

"Stay close," Juan muttered, glancing over his shoulder. He couldn't tell if he was trying to reassure Madler or himself.

The masked men herded them toward a narrow trail, still saying nothing. The path twisted through the forest, with large raindrops dripping from the trees overhead on the damp orange jumpsuits.

The trail opened into a clearing. Juan stopped, his gut tightening at the image before him.

Cabins. A dozen or so, scattered in a wide circle.

Most were small with a veranda and windows. They backed up against trees, their outlines barely visible in the dim light. But one cabin stood out from the rest. It was a much larger building positioned at the center of the perimeter. Its veranda swept around three sides of the building. It was wide with lounge chairs and tables. The dark windows seemed to watch them, following their every move as they walked past.

"Move," one of the masked men barked with a heavy accent.

Juan swallowed hard and stepped forward with Madler close by his side.

They mounted the steps of a smaller building. The door squealed as it opened, allowing the pair to be pushed inside. Juan and Madler found themselves ushered into separate rooms and bound by duct tape to an incredibly old, rickety wooden chair.

A cloth gag was tied around their heads, making it impossible to speak. Juan's mind blurred as he tried to make sense of what was happening to him and Madler.

One minute he and Madler had been in court, the next they were rescued, and now they were tied to old wooden chairs in the middle of nowhere.

Juan's head spun. He felt confused trying to understand.

Who had rescued him and why?

What did these people want?

Why go to the trouble of freeing him and Madler only to lock them up again like a prisoner somewhere in the wilderness?

Juan's body trembled as he took in his surroundings. He was concerned and that usually meant trouble. He needed some dry clothing.

The room was sparsely furnished; the air carried a stuffy, weird smell of old, damp wood. He was cold and shivered in his orange prison jumpsuit, which was still damp and clung to his skin.

Chapter 11

The door creaked open. A short, heavyset man shuffled in, meandering over to Juan. His face was weathered, marked with a scar running down his cheek. His two companions, tall and muscular, followed, their narrow eyes fixed on Juan.

With a thick Spanish accent, the man spoke. "Welcome, Juan Estrada. You are now my guest. I have many questions for you."

Fear swirled in Juan's gut, and his hands began to tremble despite his best efforts to stay calm. He knew these men weren't just criminals, they were cartel. He had faced worse before, but somehow this felt different.

Stay calm, he thought. Don't display fear or make yourself a target. One of the men used a knife to cut away the gag.

"What is this place?" Juan asked, trying to keep his voice steady.

The man responded to Juan, saying, "Shut up. I ask the questions. Tell me what you said to the police when they questioned you about the raid in Mississauga."

"That's old news. I didn't tell them anything."

After the next painful hour and with several blows to the head, Juan was beginning to think dying might be the better option.

"What did you tell them?" The interrogator's voice was low, almost a growl. "You might as well tell me. I'll find out sooner or later."

"I didn't tell them anything of value."

"What do you mean by value?"

"I told them nothing they could use against the cartel or me. I said we used burner phones, and we are instructed what to do by text message. I said none of us knew what the other cartel members were doing. We only know the part we are to do and nothing more. One person never knows the entire plan. That is all I told them."

"Now we're getting somewhere. What else did they want to know?"

"Well, they did ask about shipments of drugs. I told them that the shipments arrived in Mississauga by truck, and that's it. But I assumed they already knew that. Trust me, I would never squeal on the cartel."

"Here's the thing, Juan. I don't trust you. How did they find the warehouse?"

"You already asked me that. The cops followed Madler. It wasn't me. I was careful. No one ever saw me go to the warehouse or leave. I swear. No one."

The interrogator's anger flared. He took a step closer, his voice dripping with contempt, low and dangerous. "Did you tell them about the trains?"

For a split second, Juan felt panic. He had told the police about the trains, and how they were being used to smuggle drugs into the country. But he couldn't admit that now. Not if he wanted to stay alive.

"Of course not," he said, trying to keep his voice steady and controlled.

The interrogator's gaze bore deep into him, searching for any sign of deceit. Juan swallowed, wondering if he had said enough to be convincing.

"Maybe I should shoot you right now," said the interrogator.

"You could do that but shooting me would be a huge mistake. I know how the drug distribution network operates in Canada better than anyone," said Juan.

"Really, and why is that?"

"Because I was the one who created it. In case you haven't noticed. I make huge amounts of money for the cartel. And yes, that would be untraceable money."

Pausing for a moment, the inquisitor addressed his companions. "Take our guest to his cabin. The boss will decide what's next for him."

He winced when duct tape was ripped from his wrists and ankles. His skin was still raw where the manacles had scraped, leaving bruises that continually throbbed.

As the two captors dragged Juan to his cabin, his mind raced with worry for Madler. Juan knew Madler was weak possibly too weak to hold up under this kind of pressure. Would he crack? Was he strong enough to keep quiet? Or would these guys from the cartel break him?

Chapter 12

Borden and Cross sat in his corner office, quickly flipping through the pages of the forensic report one last time. Detective Cross sat across from him, waiting.

He closed the file and dropped it on his desk.

"Well," said Borden, looking at Cross. "It seems that turned out to be a dead end. The forensic team didn't find anything useful."

He leaned forward, his bloodshot eyes and clenched teeth showing the usual signs of exhaustion and worry.

"Cross," Borden began, tightening his grip on the armrest, "the attack wasn't a random act. Someone planned the events that occurred here. This was a deliberate attack. The forensic team did a thorough job and found nothing.

They identified smudges, which tells me they were all wearing gloves."

Cross raised an eyebrow.

"They didn't find anything. What about the keys hanging from the door lock?"

"Nothing. And not a single print on the duct tape either.

The storm was an anomaly. They couldn't plan that. But everything else was orchestrated. Think about it. Everyone left the building to untangle chaotic traffic, which alone could involve dozens of constables. Our detectives were dispatched to investigate robberies in several malls. The bomb squad and K-9 units were out investigating fake bomb threats and following up on the subway bombing at Finch Station.

I believe we were the actual target all along. The other events were staged to facilitate the attack."

"True, that is a possibility," said Cross. "I agree these intruders don't control the weather, and this storm was not expected. I checked with the Weather Network, and this storm wasn't in the forecast."

Borden nodded, his eyes distant as he pieced the puzzle together.

"What if the storm was a stroke of luck that snarled traffic and worked to their advantage?

The storm and power outages scrambled traffic, caused crashes, and blocked first-responder's. The storm just brought the chaos to a new level."

"Cross, it has to be the cartel. No one else has the resources or the precision to pull something like this off.

The evidence locker held all the drugs, weapons, ammo, and cash from the Mississauga raid. With the verdict today, all that evidence was scheduled for destruction in a few days."

Cross's eyes began to sparkle with clearer understanding.

"Are you suggesting the cartel planned this entire event as a way to reclaim what we seized during the warehouse raid?"

Borden waited a few seconds and then nodded with a grin.

"Exactly. And from the external video, the raid was executed with what I would describe as military precision.

Whoever it was had plenty of time to rehearse. They knew exactly where to go.

That's likely how they overpowered our constables and admin staff so quickly.

The Mexican cartel is the only group with enough experience to pull off something like this."

Cross let out a sigh, shaking her head.

"You've got to be kidding me."

Caroline's voice came through Borden's intercom with an urgent message.

"Detective Borden, there's a call for you from the booking sergeant at the Detention Center in Lindsay. He said there's been a very unfortunate and serious setback."

Borden reached across his desk and activated the speaker.

"Sergeant, I'm here with Detective Cross, and you're on speaker. What's this unfortunate situation?"

The sergeant's voice was clear, with an edge of frustration.

"The transport carrying Estrada and Madler hasn't checked in, and we can't reach them by radio or cell.

We dispatched a chopper from Durham Region to track the route and locate the transport."

"And did you find it, Sergeant?" Borden asked, leaning forward.

"Yes, sir. We did. And that's the problem."

"How so, Sergeant?"

"We found the transport southwest of our Lindsay detention facilities, off the road and partially hidden in a small grove of trees. The tires were shredded, likely from a spike strip."

"Did you say spike strip?" Borden's voice sharpened.

"Yes, sir. That's what it looks like. The tires were shredded, and the undercarriage appears damaged.

The driver's cab was partially crushed on impact when the vehicle collided with a large tree."

"What about the occupants? Are they injured?"

"We found the driver and guard inside the prisoner's quarters, chained to the floor."

Borden exchanged a look with Cross, his eyes wide.

"Did you say the driver and guard were chained inside the wagon?"

"Yes, sir."

"And the prisoners?"

"They were gone. I don't know how, but it looks like they got away."

The sergeant continued.

"The driver and guard told us they encountered a roadblock on the way to the detention center.

The blockade had multiple police cars, flashing lights, and barriers.

This happened about twenty-five minutes south of Lindsay. They were told to detour because of a multi-vehicle accident.

It didn't raise suspicion. They had taken the same detour in the past."

"One last thing," the sergeant added.

"Both the driver and guard had minor head injuries. They reported hearing a van or truck pull up behind the transport.

They weren't sure, but it arrived and left quickly, maybe within a few minutes of the crash.

They believe it happened three to four hours ago. I'm sorry, Detective, but your prisoners could be anywhere by now."

Borden's stomach dropped as the full realization hit him. Estrada and Madler were gone, and they were no closer to finding them.

"Thank you for the update, Sergeant. Let us know if anything new comes in," he said before ending the call.

Borden leaned back and dragged a hand through his hair.

"Cross, this week has turned into a nightmare."

Cross nodded.

"How could Estrada and Madler escape custody? They didn't do this alone.

Someone else was involved. Otherwise, there wouldn't have been a van or truck, and they'd still be chained to the floor."

"It must have been the cartel. I keep coming back to that because I don't know who else could make this happen.

Can you think of anyone else? They wanted back everything we seized from the raid.

They wanted Juan and Madler to return to business as usual.

Get Gibson and Kim out to the scene to investigate. I don't want to miss anything."

"And one more thing. Why was Martinez at the trial this morning?

He calmed that angry mob, but I don't believe that's why he was there."

Cross nodded slowly.

"Remember what Martinez said as we left the courthouse? 'Justice would be served.' Was that just a speech, or was it a message?

Maybe he knew Juan and Madler would be freed. Maybe Ambassador Martinez is the one who planned this."

"No way. What could he gain? If he's involved, he's throwing everything away. His career, his reputation, even his life.

Why would Martinez risk being tossed out of his posting and Canada in disgrace?

I heard he has political ambitions. A scandal like this would destroy him."

Chapter 13

The room felt small with poor air circulation, as Madler sat alone, motionless, in the dim light of his ancient cabin, his hands and feet bound to the wooden chair with duct tape.

He was close enough that the muffled shouts and blows from Juan's torture caused beads of sweat to drip down his forehead. He knew who would be next.

Every thud, every groan from Juan sent shivers down Madler's spine, making him swallow hard and tense his muscles. His overactive imagination painted vivid images of the punishment awaiting him.

Then, the voices stopped. He strained to listen. He heard nothing, just silence.

When the door to his room finally creaked open, Madler's heartbeat quickened. His leg twitched instinctively, but the tape held it in place. He sat there, waiting, wishing Juan were there to protect him.

A short, overweight man with thinning gray hair and leathery, wrinkled features stepped inside. He was flanked by two burly guards. The scar on his right cheek twisted grotesquely as he smirked at Madler.

"Jason Madler," the man said, his voice dripping with menace.

"My friends just call me Madler," he replied, trying to sound brave.

"What makes you think I'm your friend?" The interrogator's smirk vanished, replaced by a cold, hard stare.

"In a few minutes, I will take pleasure in ending your life. But first, I intend to inflict some pain. If you tell me what I want to know, I may decide to let you live another day. It's up to you."

"Who are you, and what do you want from me?" demanded Madler, his voice cracking as he struggled to hold back his tears.

Ignoring Madler's questions, the interrogator politely asked, "How did the police find the warehouse?"

"It was my fault. I didn't know I was being tailed when I left the Ford Hotel on Bay Street. I didn't see anything suspicious in my rearview mirror as I drove to Mississauga."

"So, am I to understand the loss of the warehouse, our drugs, our money, our weapons, it was all your fault?"

The interrogator's fist smashed into Madler's face, sending him reeling backward, his head crashing hard onto the floor. His head lay against the wooden planks, his eyes closed. He tried, but couldn't move, his body stunned and numb.

He felt the wetness of his own blood, his head pounding with a migraine that radiated through his temples and across the top of his head. His vision blurred. He was convinced he would die any minute.

The two guards righted the chair as Madler's head bobbled and fell forward onto his chest. His shoulders were on fire, the searing pain ripping through his muscles. For an instant, he thought prison would have been better than this.

The interrogator bent over and said, "Should I kill you now, or would you enjoy a little more fun? If you ask me, I prefer to inflict more pain before you die."

"What do you want from me? I didn't do anything!" Madler's voice cracked as he gasped for air, trying to hold back tears.

"Stop hitting me."

"What did you tell the police?"

"They wanted to know how many warehouses we had."

"What did you tell them?"

"I told them Mississauga was the only warehouse in the country. I didn't say a word about warehouses in other cities and towns. They have no idea at all about any of the other locations."

"Why did you tell them about Mississauga?"

"Because they already followed me there and knew what was going on. I simply told them what they already knew."

"You want to know what I think? I should kill you."

"No, you don't want to do that."

"Why not?"

"Seriously, not good. I know how to fraudulently obtain money the cartel needs to finance its operations here in Canada better than anyone else. If you kill me, that all goes away."

"So, you're telling me you have better ideas than the cartel?"

Madler took another blow to the face, the impact tearing the skin on his cheek.

"Much better ideas. That's why the man in charge handpicked me."

"Who?" The interrogator's voice was cold, disbelief creeping in.

Madler smirked through his pain.

"Ambassador Martinez. You know, the one who runs the show. You already know that. So why keep hurting me?"

The interrogator paused before answering.

"We had to be sure you didn't squeal. For now, I will spare your life. But if I find out you are lying to me, I will kill you in less than a second. Do you understand?"

"Now, it's time for you to get cleaned up. I'm sure the boss will want to meet you."

Chapter 14

Juan paced the floor of the tiny cabin, his muscles aching constantly, feeling as though his nerves were stretched to their breaking point.

He knew Madler was being interrogated and feared what his weak-willed accomplice might reveal. If their stories didn't match, they were both in serious trouble.

Since his interrogation, Juan had been left alone for what felt like hours, the silence broken only by the occasional sound of rain beating against the roof. He heard nothing from Madler's room, and that worried him. He didn't know if Madler was alive or dead.

He had no idea what time it was. Without a watch or clock, he could only guess. The day blurred together, and he had long since lost track of time. If he needed to escape, knowing his location and the time would be crucial.

His stomach growled, a sharp reminder of his hunger and thirst. He craved food and something to drink. His throat was parched. The thought of cool water nearly drove him mad.

But if offered anything, he would take it.

As he paced in front of the cabin's window, he caught sight of two men escorting Madler back.

"Okay, that's why I didn't hear Madler. We're both alive, so far, so good," he thought. "Madler didn't spill the beans."

Just as he began to feel a glimmer of hope that the worst was over, the door to his cabin burst open. The interrogator stormed in, his face twisted with rage.

"You lied!" he shouted.

A surge of terror flooded Juan's body, his heart pounding in his chest.

The trains, he thought, panic tightening his throat. They know I lied. They know.

The interrogator slowly unfastened his sidearm, his cold eyes never leaving Juan. He took a long, deliberate moment before speaking.

"I could end your life right now, but I want to see if you'll beg for mercy first."

Juan was ordered to sit, and he complied immediately. The cold metal of the gun dug into Juan's knee, the pressure escalating as the muzzle pressed harder against his skin. A sharp pain shot through his leg, and he clenched his teeth to keep from reacting.

"You have one last chance. One, not two, just one. You said you didn't tell them anything. But you did tell the police about Randy."

"I had no choice," Juan replied, his voice defiant.

"Well, maybe I have no choice, Juan." The interrogator pressed the gun deeper against his kneecap. "Why would you betray us like that?"

"I did not betray you or anyone else."

"Then why did you tell them about Randy?"

Juan screamed, "Because they'll never find Randy! Randy isn't a person! It's just the name we use for the hundreds of people we send. Randy is any person who smuggles drugs across the border for us. It doesn't identify anyone. If I didn't give the police something that sounded plausible, they said I would be shipped back to Mexico. They promised if that happened, they would drop a leak to the press that I had told them everything they needed to crush the cartel in Canada. They wanted you to think that I was a rat."

"You are the rat," the interrogator growled.

"No, that's not true," Juan insisted. "I had two RCMP officers standing outside the door holding my plane ticket back to Mexico. I saw the actual ticket. They planned to escort me to the airport, put me on a plane, and then they were going to notify some local TV reporter and have him do a newscast saying I told them everything about the cartel's business plans. They knew, and so did I, that the cartel would grab me the moment I landed, drag me home, and murder me in front of my wife and children. You and I both know that's exactly what would happen.

"What would you have done? Really, in my situation? You think I had a choice?"

The interrogator slowly lifted the gun from Juan's knee, sliding it back into the holster.

He stared at Juan for a long moment, then twisted around and walked to the door.

"That's all for now. You'll live at least for today. But if I catch you lying, I'll terminate your life in an instant. Do you understand?"

"I'm not lying."

Chapter 15

Borden sat in his quiet office, with the early morning light streaming through his single window. His coffee sat beside a stack of unopened files, nearly cold. His vision was slightly blurred from a restless night spent searching for answers to the bizarre events of the day before.

Every time he shut his eyes, a voice echoed in his mind. Even if he dozed off at his desk, he could hear it. A voice he knew well, repeating the same declaration. "Pay attention to the small pieces of an investigation because they are central to the solution," his father would say.

Borden's father, a successful former Toronto police detective, had drilled this advice into his sons over the years. Pay attention to the small pieces of an investigation. Those details are central to the solution of every case. Borden's instincts were telling him the same thing now. Minute details would lead him to the answer. He knew his dad was right.

Borden knew that insight had led his father to the capture of one of Toronto's most notorious bank robbery gangs in the 1950s. He agreed and understood that advice. His career benefited because he believed that the details would be crucial in solving this case, just as it had for him in so many other cases Borden solved.

He gathered his thoughts and prepared for the meeting with his team. Cross, Kim, Friedman, and Gibson were already assembled in the conference room when he stepped in.

Tension dominated the room as Borden took his seat at the head of the table.

"Alright, everybody," Borden began. "We need to piece together everything that happened yesterday. Let's start with what we know at this point."

Kim was the first to speak, breaking the silence. "I looked into the power outages. They weren't caused by the storm. Small explosive charges were strategically placed to bring down the hydro towers that supply power to the downtown core and surrounding areas in the GTA. Some neighboring areas and police stations still had full power. This was a deliberate act. Someone wanted to ensure that the traffic lights in the core of the city and those that served the courthouse and our station would be out."

Borden nodded. "So, this wasn't random. They knew exactly what they were doing. What about the jewelry store robberies? How are they connected?"

Gibson leaned forward, opening a file folder, his expression serious. "The robberies were not random acts of theft. They were executed with frightening precision and speed. My investigation showed that each jewelry store in the Eaton Center and other malls were all hit at exactly the same time. The thieves were dressed identically in black clothes, black gloves, and balaclavas in each mall. They didn't speak a word, communicating only through hand signals, just like those we saw on video who attacked our station."

Friedman spoke next, his tone serious. "Based on a hunch, I started looking into whether a helicopter was involved. But there was no flight plan filed for any helicopter north of the city. I'm investigating whether any helicopter was rented anywhere up to three weeks prior to the storm. I haven't checked with every heliport yet, but so far nothing. I'll also need to look into any privately owned helicopters purchased during the past six months by individuals or organizations."

"Friedman, why are you thinking about helicopters?" Borden asked.

"It's my military background. If I needed to escape quickly, I would leave in a van or SUV to avoid suspicion. The escapees would change clothes in the vehicle. Then I would rendezvous with a helicopter to fly me out of the area. I could vanish in minutes. With a full tank, a helicopter could fly Juan and Madler anywhere within a 300-mile radius of the escape scene. That would cover anywhere in Ontario, parts of Quebec, or even into New York State."

"Alright, keep digging and let the team know if you find anything. But be careful not to disappear down a rabbit hole," Borden said.

He gazed over the team as his hands leaned on the table. "If my theory about the cartel wanting their people and property back makes sense, then Juan and Madler, along with the stolen evidence, are likely still in Ontario. We need to focus our investigation here," commented Borden.

Cross set down her chamomile tea. "The attackers destroyed every camera inside the station, but they missed one recorder." She paused, glancing around the table. "They didn't know about the new building containing the backup generator, which also contains a recorder connected to hidden cameras, not the old domes they smashed."

She placed a folder on the table. "Our tech guys pulled footage from the cloud. No faces, but we got something else. They used two identical vans, both disguised as police vehicles. There were six men in total, fully dressed in police look-alike uniforms, black gloves, and balaclavas. There was no audio, just hand gestures." She looked at Gibson. "Exactly like the jewelry store crews you mentioned."

Borden instantly froze and set his coffee down. "We had the explosion at the Finch subway station and the threats of more bombs in the subway system or elsewhere in the city. Power outages. Multiple robberies in separate locations. So, this was all a coordinated effort. They wanted to pull every available police constable and detective out into the city and leave our station defenseless. Clever," said Borden.

"The demonstration outside the courthouse required us to send more than thirty constables to provide crowd control in the downtown core. And I think the ambassador was the architect of this entire plan. Why else would he show up for the trial verdict?" Cross said.

"I think we're dealing with an experienced strategist capable of coordinating an operation with multiple moving pieces. And yes, I suspect the ambassador was involved, but I'm not sure how at the moment.

His appearance at the courthouse was unexpected. We saw how the crowd reacted firsthand, so I don't believe his presence was anticipated. Besides, I don't think he's smart enough to pull this off on his own. Someone else was pulling the strings. I just don't have any idea who it could be," Borden said.

Chapter 16

Ambassador Martinez walked into a secluded barroom at the Fairmont Château Laurier, where a hint of stale cigar smoke lingered alongside the rich aroma of aged wood and leather.

The hotel, built more than a hundred years ago, still featured its original dark walnut-paneled walls and craftsmanship. This was the perfect setting for a clandestine meeting, offering the utmost seclusion and privacy among the shadows.

It was known as a sanctuary for discreet conversation. Here, the waiters served more as silent guardians, preserving patrons' privacy.

This evening, at a table concealed in the dimmest corner, sat Jonathan Winthrop, the Canadian Minister of Foreign Affairs.

He swirled a glass of his favorite Penfolds Quantum Cabernet Sauvignon, the deep crimson liquid catching the low light as he savored the taste, sitting patiently while waiting for his guest.

Carlos Martinez, Mexico's Ambassador, fresh from his morning courthouse visit on University Avenue, moved quietly toward the table and took his seat across from Winthrop.

He exchanged a brief nod as a waiter appeared, filled a glass, and retreated, leaving the two in solitude.

"How was your flight?" Winthrop asked, breaking the silence with a question that felt more like a formality than genuine curiosity.

"No problem," the ambassador replied. "They were late departing, and there was a little turbulence caused by a localized storm. Nothing serious."

"That's good," Winthrop murmured, leaning in closer. His eyes gleamed with something unsaid. "You made the news."

The reporter indicated that you were a huge hit with the demonstrators in front of the courthouse this morning.

"Nice public relations move," Winthrop commented, raising his glass in a mock toast. "You should feel exhilarated with all that local support and power. Were you effective in calming your countrymen when the trial verdict was announced?"

The ambassador's eyes gleamed with quiet victory. "Canada's civil rights are truly a blessing, allowing Mexicans to protest a fellow countryman's arrest.

It's reassuring to have such support here. As for your question, yes, I was able to calm the crowd. It could have easily gotten out of hand, and an international incident is the last thing we need right now."

Winthrop nodded, but his face tensed as his lips tightened into a straight line, and the corners of his mouth began to droop. "It appears it was all for naught. Juan Estrada and his Canadian associate, Jason Madler, were convicted on all counts. Was that expected?"

The ambassador's smile didn't change. "Yes, that was the anticipated outcome. But fortunately for us, this story has a happy ending. Both Estrada and Madler are free men now. The merchandise they lost about six months ago has been fully recovered with an extra inventory bonus."

Winthrop looked sharply at the ambassador. "Is there anything else you require from me or my office?"

The ambassador slowly leaned in, his voice dropping to a conspiratorial whisper. "Yes, there is."

"What more could I do for you, Mr. Ambassador?"

The ambassador's expression stiffened, and he leaned forward, locking eyes with Winthrop. His voice barely a whisper, he said, "I've heard my weak and ineffective president is considering launching a soft re-election campaign soon."

Winthrop's eyes sparkled with curiosity. "I've heard rumors about that. I believe he's already started."

"If I were to consider running against him, I'd need to uncover his vulnerabilities and gather as much dirt on him as possible. My desire would be to crush him and his campaign in a convincing fashion.

He's been ineffective in his role and has forgotten who got him elected in the first place. I will replace him, crush his chances for re-election, and assume his power. And I'll make sure you're more than compensated for your help, Winthrop. Of course, you already know my gratitude for any assistance would be overwhelming."

Winthrop leaned back, his eyes narrowing as he considered the plan. The silence stretched between them, heavy with unspoken tension. "You know that won't be easy," Winthrop said.

"Is anything easy?"

"Everything I've heard about him suggests he appears squeaky clean, giving the appearance of being above board in everything he does. I thought the people in Mexico liked him and his policies during the last election and saw him as an honest man. You do understand he'll be tough to beat."

The ambassador's smile turned cunning. "That's because we crafted that narrative for the electorate. He appears that way, but he was always ruthless during his climb to the top. He made plenty of enemies along the way. I believe you'll find quite a few bodies if you do a forensic scan of his clandestine activities."

Winthrop grew quiet, contemplating what could be done to help his friend and colleague.

"We know the charges don't need to be true, just believable enough to shift the news cycle and smear his reputation for a few days," said Carlos.

Winthrop nodded his endorsement and determination as he envisioned what Martinez had just told him.

Martinez continued, "Then, the following week, we leak another story. We keep the pressure on until he loses favor with the people. I intend to bring him down."

Winthrop's voice dropped again to barely a whisper. "You know he has the cartel's backing. They were the ones who got him elected."

The ambassador's smile didn't waver. "Unfortunately, I was partly responsible for that, which is why he made me the ambassador to Canada. He wanted me out of the way, knowing I would one day challenge him."

"Do you have enough money to challenge him?" Winthrop asked, his tone serious.

"Not quite. I need investors."

A slow smile spread across Winthrop's face. He leaned in slightly, lowering his voice. "Well, one suggestion comes to mind. What if the Canadian government were to invest forty or fifty million into Mexico's infrastructure, and should some of that money disappear during the transfer? Would that help your cause and career?"

The ambassador's eyes gleamed with excitement. "Immensely. Can you facilitate that?"

"Of course," Winthrop replied smoothly. "There are more than a few government officials eager to invest in Mexico's social services. The federal government loves funding projects and taking expensive trips to witness their progress. I can make those arrangements. Who knows? You may have overruns on your projects that could require extra funding."

The ambassador nodded thoughtfully. "Perhaps we could tie the money to a popular project in Mexico to boost my public profile and become a campaign promise. I'm convinced the voters would soon get excited and recognize who's responsible for their well-being."

"An excellent idea," Winthrop agreed. "I'll expect details from you in a few days."

"And with Juan Estrada out of jail," Martinez continued, "within the next two months, it should be business as usual, and we should see an increase in our cash flow. We must be careful of the authorities who are determined to locate and arrest all terrorist groups in the country, and we are listed as one of those organizations. And one last point, don't forget, that applies to anyone who assists or helps a terrorist group. They would lock the two of us up for a hundred years."

"I understand," said Winthrop.

"By the way," said Martinez, "I heard from Tina last night. She mentioned she was working on some innovative ideas for raising working capital and hoped to have some new suggestions soon."

"I like the sound of that," Winthrop said with a grin. "She's an amazing asset. Arturo Fernando made a smart decision where she's concerned."

The minister and the ambassador exchanged a sharp, knowing smile before raising their glasses, toasting their partnership.

Chapter 17

The Ambassador's plane landed smoothly in Toronto early the next morning, while the sky was still a pale gray. A black car waited, engine idling, and carried him away to the Omni King Edward Hotel.

His meeting with Winthrop had him smiling with excitement as he turned his thoughts back to the next steps in his journey to being elected the next President of Mexico.

The Victoria Café provided a warm atmosphere, inviting guests to "Discover the Art of Breakfast." The historical room boasted large floor-to-ceiling windows, and an enormous food buffet spread along the back wall as part of the new décor.

The expensive renovation created a room that offered several small, intimate seating arrangements for guests' privacy.

In one of those secluded areas, Tina was waiting for Martinez to arrive. She had tracked his flight and knew he would be on time. Then her phone chirped. His text indicated he was less than ten minutes away.

Two glasses of freshly squeezed orange juice were delivered to the table along with the leather-bound breakfast menu. The server returned and refreshed Tina's morning coffee.

As Martinez approached, Tina's eyes met his. She couldn't help but notice his sharp and widening grin.

"So, how is Winthrop treating you these days? Is he still stewing over the warehouse raid?" asked Tina.

"It's good to see you as well, Tina. Did you order breakfast?" Martinez asked.

"Not yet. I was waiting for you."

Martinez sank into the chair opposite her and leaned forward, a smirk on his lips.

"Yes, he's still on that. And soon everyone will know how weak and ineffective he really is. When I declare I am running for the presidency, he'll become very hostile toward me."

"So, it's official then?"

"Yes and no. I haven't made any public announcement yet, but it's coming soon. The time for waiting is almost over. The people of Mexico are ready for a change, and I will be the one to give it to them. I'm their future, and nothing will stand in my way. I'll just need to wait a while longer."

Tina leaned closer, lowering her voice to a whisper.

"I told you before, I can take care of that problem. Just say the word."

"I remember, but that could complicate things and spark a massive investigation."

"Not with me it won't. No one would see me coming and they wouldn't even know what happened."

"I'll keep that in mind. But if you ever need help, I can make sure it is done quietly. No one will ever know it was us, and it will be handled with precision."

Carlos Martinez took a sip of his coffee, his eyes narrowing, and asked, "What's the latest news on Juan and Madler?"

Tina's expression hardened.

"They gave the authorities minor information, nothing that would jeopardize us. They said nothing about the railroad or the magnetic boxes."

"Are you certain?" Martinez asked, with a bit of an edge to his voice.

"Yes," Tina replied. "They were interrogated thoroughly, and we don't believe either of them revealed anything."

"If they had, I would have taken immense pleasure in dealing with them. We'll conduct multiple test runs. We need to be absolutely certain before resuming full operations. The authorities won't get a whiff of anything unless someone betrays us. If that happens, they will be as good as dead."

Martinez nodded.

"I agree. Let's make sure the test runs go smoothly first."

He reached for his phone, his fingers poised over the screen. After a few moments, his phone lit up with a response from Winthrop.

"No worries, Winthrop's on it. He'll connect with his sources and see if there is any chatter on the fugitives. If there are any concerns, I'll let you know immediately."

"Good," Tina said, her eyes gleaming. "I heard from Señor Valdez who sent empty test boxes over a week ago under random passenger trains. They all went through without any interference."

Martinez leaned back, feeling quite satisfied.

"Excellent. Keep me informed. We have much to prepare in a short period of time."

Martinez said, "We need to ensure our supply chain remains secure."

"It will be, as long as we've addressed every vulnerability. Nothing, and I mean nothing, gets past me. I'll make sure we're untouchable," said Tina.

Chapter 18

Detective Borden was having another sleepless night. He leaned forward on the sofa, his elbows propped on his knees, staring at the case file spread across his coffee table. Nothing resonated.

The dim glow from the side table lamp cast shadows across the pages. His untouched coffee had gone cold hours ago. Sleep wouldn't overtake him for a while. Not tonight.

Just like his past restless nights, his father's voice continued to echo in his mind, as clear as if his dad were sitting across from him. Gather every detail. The insignificant things matter.

Borden exhaled sharply, rubbing his face. The mantra his father had drilled into him since childhood echoed through his mind. He never forgot that every detail matters. Even now, despite his father's slipping mind, those words were as sharp as ever.

"Follow every lead. Never stop looking. If you can't find anything, start over, because you missed something."

He ran a hand through his hair, eyes burning from fatigue. The irony gnawed at him. His father's mind, once razor-sharp, was now slipping away, lost in the cruel emptiness of Alzheimer's. But the lessons he taught would always apply.

Borden flipped a page, scanning it again. Something was missing. He could feel it, just out of reach.

He leaned back, staring at the ceiling, and closed his eyes.

The escape of Estrada and Madler rattled Borden and his team. Two days had passed since the jury's verdict, but it had only served to mark the beginning of their real nightmare.

Those two fugitives were still out there, free while Borden kept searching, feeling like the case was beginning to slip through their fingers.

Borden sat up, running a hand through his hair, his thoughts returning to Janet Cross.

He knew his partner had been through the wringer, especially after being shot. He worried about her. He knew she was strong, but didn't everyone have a breaking point?

He glanced at his list of options, each lead flickering through his mind, but none seemed to fit.

Each potential lead flickered through his mind like a slideshow. How did the attackers know where to go? Could someone inside the force have been involved? Had they overlooked a critical piece of evidence? Was there a new player in town orchestrating these events?

He closed his eyes, trying to piece together the puzzle. His father's voice only grew louder. Review your details. The answer is in the details. If you don't find it, start over.

For Borden and the majority of staff, the ransacking of the Police HQ felt personal, intensifying the need for answers.

The jewelry store heists were deliberate. He realized they were too coordinated to be a coincidence. The bomb threat at Finch subway was a distraction, but for what purpose? A lot of people could have been killed.

The evidence locker break-in was the key. He was sure of it.

The speed inside the station was concerning. Borden's team agreed that somebody had orchestrated this chaotic mess with pristine timing.

His cell vibrated unexpectedly, jolting him from his thoughts. He grabbed it, hoping it wasn't more shocking news. It was a message from Cross. If you can't sleep either, meet me at Police HQ?

Borden dressed quickly, slipping into his well-worn black leather jacket, a familiar source of comfort. He left a note for Lois and walked out into the chilly night.

The drive to headquarters was eerily quiet. As he looked around, the city was at peace, oblivious to the turmoil simmering beneath the surface and in his head.

At HQ, Cross was leaning against her car, her face illuminated by the dim streetlight. Her eyes were tired but determined.

"Couldn't sleep either?" she asked, her tone softer than usual, though Cross already knew the answer.

"You've been carrying this case hard, haven't you?"

"Not really," Borden replied. "We need to go over everything again. There's something we're missing."

They made their way inside, the building's silence almost oppressive. The evidence locker door hung open, a stark reminder of their failure. Borden's mind raced as they sifted through the events, looking for anything that might have been overlooked.

Cross paused, glancing at the evidence spread before them. "What was it your father always said to you? Something about the details, right?" She was looking at the case from a different angle, but she could feel the same nagging sensation Borden was experiencing.

"Every detail matters," Borden replied automatically. He could almost hear his father's voice, feel his presence guiding him.

The two detectives worked late into the night, retracing their steps, reviewing every piece of evidence.

As dawn approached, a thought struck Borden. "The bomb at Finch. What if it wasn't just a distraction like the hydro towers? What if it was a message?"

Cross looked at him, a spark of understanding in her eyes. "A message for who?"

Borden's mind raced. "The timing of everything was perfect. The heists, the bomb, the break-in. What if someone wanted us to know they were in control?"

They stared at each other, the implications sinking in. Maybe this wasn't about the Cartel. This was bigger. Someone was pulling the strings, and perhaps they wanted Borden and Cross to know it.

Borden's cell buzzed again, and for a moment, he hesitated. Another message, this time from an unknown number. His index finger hovered over the call as a light chill slithered up his spine. He tapped the button. And his blood ran cold, as he read, "Nice work at Finch. Too bad you're always one step behind. Better luck next time."

"Cross, how did someone get my cell number?" Borden asked.

"Nobody has access to this number unless I give it to them."

Chapter 19

Juan didn't need to be told twice. He was anxious about meeting with the person they called the boss. He moved at a steady pace, his anger still simmering over what they had done to him earlier.

Juan's strides were long and deliberate, masking the tight knot in the center of his chest. His escort struggled to keep pace, but Juan wasn't really in any mood to care.

The anger boiled inside of him, his fists clenching at his sides. He thought he could taste the bitterness of revenge on his tongue. Juan wanted to unleash his rage on the men who tortured him. He begged for the opportunity to inflict his revenge. His mind raced with what awaited him. Each step brought him closer to an uncertain future. But he didn't care, not right now anyway.

The man with no name was stubby, carrying a white handkerchief. His frame supported a large, round belly, and beads of sweat formed on his forehead and temples. Juan wasn't the least bit interested in him, as evidenced by the fact he barely glanced in his direction. His mind was too occupied by the little man's words, "The boss wants to meet with you."

"Who is the boss? I don't know your boss, and he doesn't know me," Juan said.

"The boss knows all about you," said the escort.

"How could that be?" thought Juan. That bothered him. He wanted to know exactly what all about you meant. And who was this boss? Where was he? Maybe he would get lucky, and it would be the interrogator.

Juan had no idea what was happening or what to expect. That uncertainty made him bubble with anger and filled him with huge anxiety. This meeting could be worse than he ever thought possible. He had to be ready.

Juan marched across the center square and approached the large wooden chalet. He wasn't worried. He was a street fighter who knew how to take care of himself. His eyes fixed on the ground as he tried to conjure up several believable stories, not knowing what to expect.

He allowed his mind to race to a scenario where he would be rewarded. Maybe even accepted as an insider and given a more significant role in the cartel hierarchy. Or maybe more torture awaited him. He had no idea at all, but he was ready for a fight.

Stepping onto the wooden planks, he entered the building and was immediately aware of the distinct scent of fresh pine.

He followed his escort into an opulently decorated yet deserted conference room.

The room had a warm, rustic feel, with wainscoted pine walls and a vaulted ceiling. Massive landscape photos adorned the walls, bringing the outdoors in.

A huge circular light hung suspended from the ceiling peak, positioned directly above a massive sixteen-foot wooden table surrounded with matching wood and leather chairs along each side and at the table's ends.

Two large, four-bladed fans hung from the ceiling at opposite ends of the room, facilitating air movement throughout the area.

Juan tried to ignore the comfort of his new surroundings, his thoughts racing. The plush furniture, the coffee, the pastries, he knew none of it mattered. Not until he knew who the boss was and what would happen to him next. He glanced around, taking note of how perfect everything looked.

Off to his right was a large bank of floor-to-ceiling picture windows overlooking the wraparound wooden porch with exit doors at each end of the room.

From one window he could see a small lake with a large wooden dock jutting out into the water. In the opposite direction stood men unloading packages from trucks and carrying them into a cabin with no windows.

He could smell the aroma of a large display of coffee on a long pine side table, which also contained fresh, warmed pastries.

His escort invited Juan to partake in any of the refreshments placed there for his comfort. With that said, his guide announced that the boss would be with him soon, turned, and promptly left the room.

Juan poured himself a cup of black coffee, savoring the warmth. The sound of a truck backing up outside broke the quiet. It was a reminder that this place, despite its comfort, was still part of a much larger operation.

He followed the sound emanating from the truck, which allowed him to spot a truck backing up outside to a nearby cabin. Glancing through the picture window, he examined the plush furniture and lounge chairs spread around the veranda. This cabin screamed comfort, and he liked it.

The smell of freshly poured coffee permeated the atmosphere.

He immediately began to feel important and allowed himself to relax as he sauntered through the room, examining the intricate details of local artifacts and paintings.

Juan thought to himself, nobody would put out fresh fruit, yogurt, pastries, and coffee for a man about to be killed—or would they?

The door creaked open slowly at the opposite end of the room. Juan's body stiffened. His heart began to beat louder in his chest. This was it. It was the moment he'd been anticipating and dreading. His breath caught in his throat, the magnitude of the moment crashing down on him. Whoever the boss was, everything was about to change.

He knew whatever his fate, whatever it would be, was about to unfold in front of him, and there would be no turning back now.

His senses indicated it was time to fight or run.

Chapter 20

Juan's jaw dropped as the woman entered, her confident stride commanding the room. It was the last person he expected to see.

This was not just any woman. It was someone he knew and loved.

Tina.

She had a wide, exuberant smile, her eyes filled with emotion as she stretched out her arms, reaching for him.

"What are you doing here?" Juan said, overjoyed, embracing her in an extended hug. "I'm supposed to meet the boss here."

Tina brushed away the tears flooding her eyes and said, "Juan, I am the boss."

"You're the boss?" he exclaimed, a surge of relief and disbelief sweeping over him. It felt like a dream.

The woman he had always trusted, now at the helm of this operation. Was she the same person, or had the power changed her? Juan wasn't sure.

"It was you. My treasured sister, you were the one who saved me."

Trembling with joy, Juan whispered how much he had missed her, refusing to let go.

With a wobbly voice, he mumbled, "Was it you who sent the helicopter for me?"

"Yes. The Ambassador and I couldn't sit by and let you rot in prison. You must remember, the plan was always for me to follow you to Canada. I was meant to head up operations here and naturally would involve you.

"After you were detained, I knew I had to do something bold to rescue you and that other fellow, Madler. I just moved up the timetable a bit.

"Back home, I had an excellent meeting with Arturo Fernando," Tina said.

"Wait, you met with Arturo?"

"Yes. And like I said, it was a great meeting. As you know, we have a long history with him going back to when we were children. He was eager and willing to invest in your freedom.

"I also met with Ambassador Carlos Martinez several times. When he learned Arturo was anxious for your release, he became extremely helpful. Now he wants to meet Arturo, but that's a story for another time.

"Together, Martinez and I plotted a strategy we both felt would work. And it did. In fact, it was better than perfect.

"This place where we are now is used to train our soldiers. I knew we would need a base of operations for our business and to free you and Madler. To me, this seemed the perfect location. But that's not all.

"Arturo told me the Cartel was still furious over the police raid in Mississauga. So, it was necessary to appease them before they struck back.

"I made Arturo a promise. I told him I'd get the drugs and money back that we lost in the warehouse raid if he helped me get you out. But more than that, I knew this was my last chance to rise even higher in the Cartel. I wasn't just doing this for you. I was securing our future, both in the Cartel and beyond. If I could rise to the top, I'd be untouchable.

"But I needed you to get there.

"After I made the suggestion to Arturo, there was a long pause as he thought through the idea. Then he told me to make it happen. I said I would, and here we are."

"That's impossible. The police have all our stuff. How could you possibly pull that off?"

"Well, it took a few weeks of careful planning. Once that was done, I accomplished what I promised to Arturo. But the good news is, I did much better than that.

"I also managed to retrieve all the cash that the police seized, weapons and ammo as well. Talk about a win-win plan. This was it. The Cartel is incredibly happy with me and pleased that you are free to help me reestablish our network.

"And the icing on the cake was when we acquired bags of gold and silver jewelry. We have jewelry including earrings, necklaces, diamonds, and rings, which we seized during a smash-and-grab string of robberies intended to confuse and otherwise occupy the police.

"We targeted high-end stores across the GTA during the chaos of that storm. It was the perfect cover, distracting the police while we moved in. The storm gave us the edge we needed, and we capitalized on it.

"The reason we have so much jewelry is we hit all the stores in multiple malls across the GTA, all at exactly the same time. That would have the police guessing for days, trying to sort out what happened. These occurred during the pandemonium caused by that crazy thunderstorm, which paralyzed the city.

"I have dozens of Rolex and Cartier items from the robbery. If you need a wristwatch, we have a room full of timepieces, rings, and other jewelry. So don't hesitate. If you'd like something, just help yourself.

"Our men enjoyed creating the distraction and were all back here safely in no time.

"We needed a strong diversion, and the robberies worked well for us. Oh, and the incredible weather was an unexpected bonus that made the entire day easier for us.

"While all the police were busy elsewhere untangling traffic, clearing roads, and investigating explosions, that provided the perfect opportunity for us to free you and Madler.

"So now that you are home and safe, I'll be able to resume our business as usual, only in a more creative way.

"Winthrop was on board with all of this, and he was the one who even found this location for us about eight months ago. He has proved to be particularly useful and surprisingly resourceful.

"We use this camp to receive and distribute drugs to various locations across Canada. It is not just to provide training for Cartel members. We use the recruits to distribute narcotics for us to and from other warehouses across the country, most notably in Vancouver.

"This place is a fortress, Juan. Every inch of the property is covered. Video surveillance, tripwires, motion sensors, you name it, it's all here. We're prepared for anything. And I'll show you the heart of the operation, which is the control room," said Tina.

The small room was a technological paradise. A wall of monitors displayed various camera feeds: an empty driveway, the front gate, a dock stretching from the shore onto the lake, a helipad, a parked fuel truck inside the open Quonset hut, the parking area, and several cabins.

"So, Juan, you are safe here. Nobody can get in or out of this property without our knowing they are here. And if that should ever happen, we'll be ready and waiting," said Tina.

Chapter 21

Tina and Juan sat quietly in a secluded corner of the camp, surrounded by tall trees whose leaves swayed in the gentle breeze.

The two sat side by side, staring up at the moon, its light barely penetrating the thick forest that concealed their camp.

They felt relaxed and safe as they gazed at the starry sky, reminiscing about their childhood as orphaned street kids in Mexico City.

Tina shifted the conversation. "Everything started when you and Madler were captured. I had no choice. I had to turn to Arturo Fernando for help," she said. "He still lives behind those tall, opulent walls in his secure compound north of Mexico City. He has armed guards everywhere.

When I arrived, he was busy playing tennis on his private court. Just enjoying his quiet life, I guess."

Juan nodded, recalling the ruthless drug lord who had clawed his way to the top, leaving a trail of bodies in his wake. "Arturo was always the most callous and cunning person from what I remember," Juan said.

"Exactly," Tina agreed. "His wealth and power are unparalleled. He has a group of mercenaries protecting him around the clock. Loyalty and obedience are everything to him. If you mess up, you're soon found dead in some alley."

Tina recounted her meeting with Arturo. "I approached his gatehouse, and the sentry rushed down some stone steps, dashed around a large, irregular-shaped swimming pool toward the tennis court. Arturo knew I was coming to see him, and the sentry took me to his office. The eight-foot double doors opened, and Arturo quickly entered as the doors clicked shut behind him. He took his seat behind a huge mahogany desk. I remained standing toward the left side of his desk, and he just stared at me.

"He didn't waste any time when he spoke. Arturo reminded me that I cost him millions in cash, weapons, and lost opportunities in Canada. I assured him I could get it all back and more."

"Really, what did he do then?" Juan asked.

"Nothing, he just stared at me," said Tina. "I told him I wanted to return to Canada and use you and Madler to expand our operations. I proposed to mastermind your release along with Madler and promised to deliver ten million dollars from the Canadian operation."

Juan listened intently as Tina continued. "I also had planned to use Ambassador Martinez and Winthrop, the Minister of Foreign Affairs, but Arturo refused. He had other plans for the ambassador.

"I told him that I intended to recruit and train a small military force with tech experts and individuals skilled in combat. This training campground provided the perfect place to set up a new hidden operation. He liked the idea of intensive training sessions focused on stealth operations, combat skills, and advanced hacking techniques to assist Madler in his fraud operations."

"What did he do?"

"Arturo sat there and said nothing at all. After considering my ideas, he said, 'You'll have my answer in the morning.' The waiting drove me crazy.

"The next day, I got a text that Arturo was impressed. He agreed to provide the funding for the new operation based on my reestablishing the business and delivering ten million dollars.

"We met later that afternoon, and he seemed more relaxed, almost informal. He walked me to the door, and that was when he said, 'Succeed, and you will have my full support. Fail, and there will be no place where you can hide.' The man is scary, Juan."

"So, I clearly must come up with the money or else. That's how I ended up running the business here in Canada. Let me show you around the encampment."

Juan watched as a truck was unloaded with precision. The men moved swiftly, their actions deliberate and silent as they carried the contents into the cabin. No one talked.

Tina approached the cabin, and the guards nodded, stepping aside to allow her and Juan to pass. Just the manner in which the men moved made it clear she was in charge. Juan noticed that all the windows were shuttered.

"Why is that necessary?" Juan wondered aloud.

Tina smiled slightly. "Security. We can't afford to take any risks."

As they stepped into the cabin, Juan's eyes widened and swept the room. He was shocked at the sight of the boxes of drugs, crates of weapons, ammunition, and stacks of money meticulously organized and accounted for.

"This looks just like our old warehouse," Juan said.

"It is," Tina replied. "We raided the police station at the same time we rescued you. The police still don't know what hit them."

"You what?" Juan exclaimed.

"You heard me," Tina said calmly. "We broke into the police station and took what was rightfully ours. I wanted what was at the police station, and I wanted you out of jail. So, I put a plan together. It's that simple."

She and Juan walked down to the lake by the water's edge, standing there without speaking. The moon still reflected off the calm water, creating a serene scene that contrasted sharply with their chaotic lives.

"I find this place peaceful, relaxing, and I enjoy the privacy," Tina said. "Sometimes I wonder if this is all worth it. I'm always running from the consequences of what we've done. If we could just stay here, free from all the chaos, maybe then I could find peace. But I know that can't happen, not for people like us," said Tina.

"What do you mean, different?" Juan asked.

"Well, for one thing, if no one was chasing us, I could stay here for a very long time and watch the seasons change. I would enjoy that. This would be a nice place to grow old."

"Tina, are you okay?" Juan asked, concern evident in his voice.

"Yes, I'm fine. Let me show you some of the training facilities."

They walked toward the gun range where men were being trained on the tear-down, and assembly, and use of various weapons in the darkness of night.

A narrow road led to a clearing where a black chopper sat silently, tied down with nylon rope. Next to the helicopter, in a small hut with the front doors open, a fueling tanker truck stood ready to refuel it.

As they walked, Tina shared more about the camp's operations. "This place is our fortress, our sanctuary. We have everything we need to continue our work and stay hidden from the authorities.

"The men are well-trained, and we have the best equipment money can buy. This camp isn't just a training ground, it's our Canadian base of operations. It is a secure place where we can prepare for the next phase of our plan. We're not just running a cartel. We're building an empire. We're prepared for anything."

"You've done an incredible job, Tina. This place is like a fortress."

Tina smiled. "Thank you, Juan. It's been a lot of work, but it's worth it."

At that moment, a sense of pride and purpose welled up inside Juan. Despite the dangers and the uncertainty, he knew working with Tina, standing beside her in this chaos, was where he belonged.

It wasn't just out of loyalty. It was something deeper. A sense of purpose he'd never felt before. He knew it was a feeling of contentment.

Chapter 22

Several short, stubby candles flickered, casting a warm glow over the former dining room in the main chalet. This soft lighting gave an illusion of security for tonight, at least.

The large pine table dominated the center of the room. Once the focal point for many disruptive schemes, tonight would be different. For a few hours, it would serve a different purpose: a private family reunion celebration.

Tina uncorked a bottle of rare red wine and lifted her glass. "To our freedom and future success," she declared.

Juan and Madler clinked their crystal glasses against hers. The sound provided a sense of security and invincibility in an otherwise silent room.

Juan sipped the refreshing liquid, savoring the rich taste before setting his glass on the table. "So, what's our next move, Tina?" he asked, leaning back in his well-padded soft leather chair.

Tina set her glass down and leaned forward. Her expression matched the seriousness of her voice. "The first thing, new identities for both of you."

"Madler, you're our forgery expert. How fast can you get new passports, driver's licenses, credit cards, and health cards for Juan and yourself?"

The question thrilled Madler, as it made him feel important and needed. "No more than a couple of days," he replied.

"Excellent," Tina said. "I need to remind you that these credit cards are for identification only. Do not use them for purchases. Use burner phones and replace them every two weeks or if you suspect they are compromised. We can't afford to be tracked by current technology. That means no emails, and do not use names in text messages."

Juan nodded, taking in the gravity of Tina's instructions. "And have you decided our roles in this operation?"

Tina twisted in her chair to stare at her brother. The muscles in her face relaxed, and her voice sounded soft. "Juan, you're going to be in charge here. You'll also train the recruits in hand-to-hand combat, mastering the use of our weapons. Make sure they're prepared for anything."

"You will be in charge of our camp," Tina said, her tone firm but kind. "Make sure it stays secure. You'll be responsible for everything here, training recruits, overseeing security, everything. All leaders and recruits will report to you."

Juan's jaw tightened, his resolve hardening. "I can handle it. You can count on me. I'll make sure the camp stays secure, no matter what."

"You need to know your interrogator wasn't convinced either of you were up to the task. He said Madler was weak, and Juan, he didn't think you knew what you were doing. But I am in charge here, and I ruled in your favor. I told him I had plans for Madler. He will leave for Mexico in a week or two. In the meantime, Juan, he will be reporting to you. He won't like it, so be careful. Can you handle that?" said Tina.

"Yes, I can manage that tiny tyrant."

Juan knew he was more than capable of providing security for the campground around the clock and was motivated by his top level of trust and responsibility.

Tina then faced Madler. "I need you to secure new locations for shipments, Madler. They can't be traced back to us, and they need to be hidden well. No mistakes. Find a place where nobody will suspect what we are doing. It should be large enough to sort the deliveries by product, repackage them, and have them ready to meet demand while being dispersed across Canada without detection. We have plenty of manpower at the camp, so it might be possible for some of that work to be done here. You and Juan can make arrangements for whatever space you require."

"That is not a good idea," said Madler. "If we use this site, the camp is exposed to various couriers, and Juan would lose control of people coming and going."

"You're right. I don't want any exposure," said Tina. "We must find an alternative location within a week. Is that possible? Our contacts in Mexico are breathing down my neck. They are eager to send multiple large shipments to us within a month."

He intuitively knew this was his chance to impress Tina, as Madler's face broke into a soft grin and his eyes sparkled. "I've got a better plan than using warehouses. What if we use residential houses instead?

Small, unassuming, no one would ever guess what we were doing. We buy them and use them as distribution points. If we lose one, we lose a fraction of our stock, not everything. Houses are less suspicious and can be conveniently located close to shipping facilities. We could use a different house for each type of product imported. Management would be the only ones who know the various locations. I think it is safer for us in the long run," said Madler.

Tina raised an eyebrow. "Interesting plan, Madler. I like it. Where exactly do you plan to get these houses? And do you have any locations in mind?"

Madler grinned. "Yes, I do. You won't need to worry about all the details. I'll take care of all that," said Madler.

Tina considered the plan, her mind racing with possibilities. "It's risky, but it could work. What's your timeline?"

"I believe it will take about three weeks to secure the first house and prepare it for business," said Madler. "I can start the search immediately. We'll need about fifty thousand dollars in seed money."

Tina nodded. "You'll have it. We can discuss the details later next week, but Madler, we don't have long to be operational."

Madler raised his glass again. "To our new beginnings."

Tina and Juan joined in, enjoying the silky taste of the red wine, consummating a new pact of goals and responsibility for the two escapees.

A prolonged silence settled over them as they each considered their future before retiring for some much-needed rest.

It had been a stressful day for Tina. She was tired, and even though she had a headache, she began reviewing everything she had to do the following day. She needed fresh air and some time alone.

The moonlight bathed the camp, casting long shadows across the glassy water. The only sound was the soft lapping of the lake against the shore as she stood in quiet contemplation.

Tina took this rare opportunity and had slipped down to the lake, unnoticed, for five minutes of personal privacy before getting some required rest.

She stood there, not moving, staring at the sparkling water and reflecting on the day's events, allowing the quiet of the lake to calm her racing thoughts.

She was enjoying the stark contrast from earlier in the day that was filled with tension when the waves broke on the shore and now seeing the water hardly moving, glimmering like a sheet of smooth, polished glass.

She relished her quiet time until an imperceptible rustle broke her solitude. Instantly alert, she tensed, wondering what predator was behind her: human, a bear, a coyote, or was it something else?

She swung around, her hand instinctively reaching for the gun holstered by her rib cage and shoulder strap. Out from the shadows stepped one of her night guards, his face drawn, pale, and out of breath.

"Tina," he whispered. "I've been looking for you. We may have a problem."

"What is it?"

"It's Sean," the guard replied, fear evident in his voice. "He's missing."

Panic gripped Tina for a moment, but she quickly suppressed it. "What do you mean, missing? Did anyone see him leave?"

"No," the guard said. "I think he is still here because his equipment is in his cabin. He should have been back here an hour ago. He was on a night training mission with a few recruits, and none of them returned."

Tina instinctively ordered the guard to gather the eight others and form two search parties. "We need to go and find him. Bring a first-aid kit and flashlights with you. Get back here in five minutes."

The guard rushed off. Tina stared into the darkness, her mind overcome with worry. Sean had to be found. He could be in trouble.

She needed him.

She depended on him.

He was her safety net.

Within minutes, two search parties were assembled. Tina led one group, her flashlight cutting into the thick forest in the direction where they thought Sean was headed with the recruits.

They slipped through the woods quietly, whispering Sean's name, their voices amplified over the stillness of night and across the open water.

Twenty minutes into the search, a faint groaning sound echoed from a nearby thick patch of towering trees and tangled underbrush surrounding a small clearing.

They moved cautiously toward the faint groans, their flashlights cutting into the thick brush and guiding their footsteps.

Sean used his leather belt and a broken tree branch, applying a makeshift tourniquet to the man's cut and broken leg.

Sean's face was etched with concern. His makeshift stretcher was ready, and he was about to lift the recruit when he heard the search party calling.

"Tina, I'm over here," Sean said. Tina and her two search parties arrived, and one of the men handed Sean the first-aid kit.

They found Sean still kneeling beside one of the recruits, injured after falling from a tree-climbing exercise during their night training.

As Sean tended to the recruit, he said, "He lost his footing when climbing and twisted his ankle, fell, breaking his leg in two places during training. His fall left cuts from rocks and branches. He'll need to see a doctor straight away."

Nobody spoke. They just looked at the swollen leg and deep cuts being closed with large bandages soaked in iodine and wrapped with adhesive tape and twine.

The recruit's face was ashen, with pasty beads of sweat beading on his forehead, his eyes narrow as he groaned barely audible sounds of throbbing pain. His leg was swollen, wrapped tight by an iodine-soaked cloth.

There was total silence from the trainees apart from the injured recruit. "I couldn't just leave him out here alone," said Sean.

Tina's heart, still pounding with increased anxiety, softened. "You did the right thing, Sean," she said, her voice quiet but firm.

She turned to the others. "Let's get him back to the camp infirmary. Contact the doctor. Tell him it's an emergency. See if we can get him looked at tonight."

Chapter 23

The warm scent of pastries, freshly baked by Borden's wife, filled the room, and despite the tension in the air, their stomachs betrayed them.

Morning light poured through the sliding glass doors, casting a golden glow over the weary faces of the team.

It was an unusual setting for an unsanctioned meeting, but Borden's ranch-style bungalow offered the perfect seclusion the team needed.

Borden was quick to pour a second round of coffee for everyone, except for Cross. Instead, he dipped a chamomile tea bag into hot water and handed her the cup. She nodded, appreciation showing in her eyes and smile.

"All right let's get to it," Borden said, his voice cutting through the comfortable murmur. "This operation is completely off the books. No one outside this room can know about our discussion.

The ambassador's diplomatic immunity makes him untouchable, on paper. But we know the truth. Any leak, and our investigation is over. The chief contacted me and gave direct orders: we can't go after Ambassador Martinez."

Groans rippled through the room before the silence settled in. Grim faces met Borden's gaze, none of them pleased with the situation.

Cross broke the silence, her voice steady, filled with resolve. "We can't go after the ambassador, but we can dismantle the cartel he's involved with. If we hit them hard enough, he'll have no choice but to retreat or head back to Mexico. So does anyone have any suggestions for how we make that happen?"

The mood shifted as ideas began to emerge. Borden passed around photos, each one more damning than the last. Images of the ambassador in compromising situations, meeting with known cartel members. The evidence was circumstantial, but it was compelling.

"We've heard rumors," Borden continued, "that the ambassador might run for president. If that happens, our window of opportunity is closed. So, we need to move quickly."

Cross pushed her chair back, setting her teacup down before wandering to the window, her gaze fixed on the serene garden outside. "What if we turn some of his associates? They might give us the leverage we need."

"How would you do that?" asked Gibson.

Crawford leaned forward. "I can look into collusion among the staff. It might lead us somewhere useful."

The discussion gained momentum as strategies were debated, each suggestion met with cautious optimism.

"What about Winthrop?" someone asked. "How is he tied to all of this? Or is he not involved?"

Borden's expression darkened. "We're not sure yet, but wherever Martinez goes, Winthrop isn't far behind. We need to keep digging. My gut tells me he's involved in this."

Spade, always the strategist, offered a solution. "I have contacts who could go undercover in Mexico. They can gather intel from the ground up. They're discreet, and I trust them."

The room hummed with energy as a plan began to take shape. They agreed the goal was clear: dismantle the entire cartel network. No small feat.

As the meeting wound down, Borden reiterated the importance of secrecy. "Caroline will keep us all in the loop. Stay ready for anything."

As the others filtered out, Cross lingered at Borden's request. He turned to her with concern etched in his features. "How are you holding up since your experience at the warehouse?"

She hesitated before responding. "I'm fine. More than fine. I want to nail these guys if for no other reason than to get justice for my sister."

Borden nodded, appreciating her resolve. "Just promise me, if you need a break, you'll take it. I don't want to order you to take time off, but I will if I have to."

Cross nodded, but her eyes burned with determination. "We're going to get him one way or another."

Just as they began cleaning up, Caroline rushed in, her face ashen.

"Borden, you need to see this," she said, holding up her iPad.

The screen revealed a live feed from a hidden camera placed near the ambassador's residence, authorized under warrant for security purposes.

The ambassador met with Winthrop, and the conversation clearly focused on their next move. They spoke in hushed tones, but Caroline had enhanced the audio to catch every word.

"They're planning something big." The team gathered around, listening intently as the ambassador mentioned a large shipment coming in from Mexico within days or weeks. Winthrop added that security would be tightened and that they would be watching for anyone who might pose a threat.

"We need to intercept that shipment," Cross said, her voice urgent. "If we can get to it first, we might have the leverage we need."

Borden nodded. "We need to move now. Caroline, can you trace their communications?"

Caroline nodded. "I'll see what I can do."

Everyone fell silent as the live feed revealed the ambassador's conversation. The significance of what they were seeing became clear, highlighting the urgency of moving forward. This could be their chance to act against the cartel, but it was risky. If they were wrong, it would expose everything.

Borden and Cross knew this could be the break they'd been waiting for, but would intercepting a large shipment of drugs be enough to disrupt the cartel?

Chapter 24

As expected, Monday morning brought its usual amount of anxiety.

Cross stepped into Borden's office, still processing the footage Caroline had shown them. She set her tea down and met his gaze.

"This whole thing stinks," she said, her tone blunt. "The break-in, the timing of the storm, the prison transport wasn't random, we know that.

Someone knew exactly what was going to happen, when it would happen, how it would happen, and in the case of the prisoner escape, where it was going to happen. Somebody had our station layout. They had the route we take to transport prisoners. This wasn't just luck."

Borden's expression darkened. "You're saying someone inside tipped them off?"

Cross nodded, leaning forward. "It's the only explanation. They knew too much and were too precise."

Borden, who had been flipping through a stack of files, stopped and looked up, his face hardening. "You think it was someone inside the force?"

Cross nodded, setting her cup of chamomile tea down.

"There's a connection, Borden. I can feel it."

Borden leaned back in his chair, studying her. He always tried to empower his team to follow their instincts, so his response was natural. "Go on."

"Think about it. The break-in at the station, the escape of Estrada and Madler, it's all too coincidental. Someone wanted our station cleared out, and the timing was perfect. The storm, the power outages. Only two constables remained. It was the perfect setup."

Borden frowned. "You're thinking that the cartel orchestrated everything? Even the weather?"

"No, but they sure took advantage of it. Only a handful of officers were on duty. The intruders had clearly studied our layout, knew where to hit, and they were in and out in about fourteen minutes, as we saw on the video."

Borden nodded slowly. "Okay, say you're right. That explains the station. But the escape, how did they know exactly when and where the police transport would be with the prisoners?"

"That's the crux of it," Cross replied, setting her cup down. "Someone tipped them off. Someone high up, with access to schedules and routes. The timing was too precise."

Borden's mind raced. "You're thinking it was the ambassador? Martinez?"

"Or someone close to him. Maybe Winthrop. They have the means and the connections. And let's not forget, the police transport always follows the same route. They could have tracked it for days or weeks."

Borden's eyes narrowed. "Even with the storm?"

"Especially with the storm. The detours might have changed the route slightly, but not the end destination. They intercepted it several miles south of the prison. If they used a helicopter, it was ready and waiting nearby.

I think Friedman is right about the chopper. Someone leaked all that information. This had to come from inside. Someone with access to our computer systems has betrayed us."

Borden stood and began pacing. "We need more than speculation, Cross. We need evidence."

"And that's why I'm heading to interview the guards again. There has to be something we missed. Their stress, the timing, the sounds. They might remember something new."

Borden paused, considering. "Do you think the guards were in on it?"

Cross shook her head. "No, but someone had to help the prisoners escape. Our driver and guard wouldn't know anything about the station layout. We need to dig deeper."

"Follow up on that. Check in with Kim and Friedman. They might have leads from the street."

Cross nodded, heading for the door. "I'll keep you updated. And Borden, breakfast at Emily's is on me when we crack this."

"Deal," Borden replied, a rare smile crossing his face. "Get moving, Cross."

An hour later, Detective Gibson found himself in front of a small costume shop Caroline had identified. From the outside, the store looked like a piece of history from downtown Toronto. Inside was no different. The shop represented a relic of the past, its narrow aisles packed with dusty old costumes, the air choking with neglect.

The owner, an elderly man with a weathered face, greeted Gibson with a wide smile.

"Detective Gibson," he introduced himself, holding up his badge. "I'm looking for information about anyone who rented a police uniform in the past two weeks."

The shop owner stood still, deep in thought. "Can't say I recall anyone, detective. But you're welcome to check our records."

Gibson spent the next thirty minutes scouring through the dusty logbooks and found nothing of interest. As he was about to leave the store, a thought struck him.

"What about custom-made uniforms? Do you know anyone who makes them?"

The owner's eyes lit up. "Ah, my wife! She's a seamstress, you know. She's made costumes for all sorts of events. I can ask her."

The owner's wife, a small woman with a sharp gaze, appeared from the back room.

"I understand you're looking for someone who might make police uniforms, Detective?"

Gibson nodded. "Yes, any leads would help."

She smiled faintly. "I haven't made anything in months. But it would not be unusual for people to have their own tailor. You may want to check stores that sell suits and dresses, or perhaps you could look for independent clothing alteration businesses. Any one of those stores may be able to help you."

Gibson's first thought was the task was nearly impossible. How many clothing stores were in the GTA? He thanked the couple and headed to the door.

Gibson's phone chirped as he left the shop. It was Cross, her voice sounding urgent.

"Meet me at the station. We might have something."

Gibson hurried back, his mind racing with possibilities.

Cross was waiting, a determined look on her face.

"You know, I've been thinking about the driver and the guard. Their stress, their reactions, they were under a lot of pressure. There has to be something we missed earlier. We need to re-interview the transport drivers. I have a feeling they may have forgotten something and maybe know more than they realize."

They spent the next few hours questioning the driver and guard, digging into every detail of the detour, who stopped them, the reason for the detour, and then the interception. As the pieces slowly began to fall into place, a clearer picture emerged. The timing, the coordination, the precision, it all pointed to a well-thought-out operation.

As the day drew to a close, Cross and Borden reconvened.

"No solid leads," Cross admitted, her bloodshot eyes showing exhaustion but fired up with determination.

"It's going to take time, Cross," commented Borden.

Chapter 25

Gibson left for work early, his mind already racing and flooded with questions. He could picture the transport driver and guard, their answers holding the key to the details he felt were missing.

As he navigated the morning traffic, the images of the prison escape replayed in his mind, each scene that was described to him more urgent than the last.

At Police HQ, Gibson and Cross met with the two transport drivers.

Their initial statements had been thorough, but Cross urged them to walk through the events once more.

"Don't leave anything out. The smallest detail could be important," Cross instructed.

Both the driver and guard nodded in agreement.

"Close your eyes and relax. Now, go back to the scene of the escape. Visualize everything that happened on the day of the storm. Tell me what you see or hear. Don't leave anything out," Cross said softly.

The older driver scratched his head, brow furrowed in concentration. Then he said, "No one spoke. They used hand gestures. It was all so choreographed, like watching an old-time silent movie."

Cross's eyes narrowed. "Hand signals…" She thought for a moment. "Military precision. Just like the station raid."

Cross found Borden pacing near the coffee maker, his expression tense. She relayed the details from the interview, and Borden stopped mid-step, pursing his lips as he processed the information.

"That suggests they knew our routines. Perhaps they've monitored us," he said, his voice low and frustrated.

Detective Kim's cell chirped with a text. One of his street informants sent a coded message.

"The alley, twenty minutes." Kim hollered to Friedman as he pocketed his phone and headed for the door.

Kim and Friedman slipped into a narrow alley, wedged between two crumbling brick buildings. The stench of rot hung in the air, and the ground beneath them was a quilted patchwork of cracked asphalt, deep potholes filled with stagnant, rancid water.

Overhead, a rusting fire escape swayed precariously, its anchors half-pulled from the wall. The smell of vomit and rotting food explained why no one would venture near here.

From the deep shadows, Kim's wiry informant emerged. He was thin, with a face weathered and streaked with lines like old shoe leather from a hard life on the streets. His wary eyes darted, unable to rest for long.

Kim slipped a couple of folded bills into the man's trembling hands. The crinkling sound of new cash seemed to spark his memory and sharpen his recall instantly.

"There's a guy from Mexico. Bad reputation. Nobody likes him. Loves knives. Word on the street is he carries more than one."

Kim's pulse quickened. "Where?"

Flustered, the informant rattled off an address. Before Kim could write it down, he vanished like a magician retreating somewhere into the underbelly of the city.

Kim wasted no time, entering the location into the squad car's computer. They needed backup and a warrant, and both were confirmed.

Within minutes, a team was dispatched. Kim and Friedman drove to the address, a seedy downtown hotel out on Dundas Street East, where unattended cars didn't last longer than an hour. The detectives parked, scanning the neighborhood.

Kids laughed and ran toward a park, oblivious. Nearby, a garbage truck groaned, its familiar mechanical growls echoing off the buildings.

Inside the hotel, the desk clerk nodded.

"Yeah, I remember him. He left earlier. No clue when he'll be back."

"Does he have a phone in his room?" Kim asked.

"Yeah."

"If he returns, call his room once, then hang up. After that, call 911 and tell the operator detectives require backup at this address. Got it?"

The clerk hesitated. "Are you allowed to do that?"

"Yes," Kim asserted, flashing his badge. "Thank you."

Walking to the elevator, Friedman reminded Kim that backup was dispatched.

"I know. A reminder call might move things along faster."

"Okay."

Upstairs, Kim knocked on the door of room 324.

"Toronto Police Services." Silence.

With a nod from Friedman, Kim entered first, guns drawn. The room was a mess.

A brown canvas duffel bag slumped on a chair. Kim pulled on latex gloves and rifled through it, finding a manila envelope stuffed with cash.

"Ten grand, easy," Kim muttered.

The phone rang once and stopped. Kim heard the elevator's telltale chime, followed by the metallic grinding as it slid open.

Footsteps echoed in the hallway. A key rattled in the lock.

Kim and Friedman took defensive positions as the door creaked open. A short, stocky man stepped in and sneered when he saw the detectives.

"Who are you? Get out!" he yelled, lunging at Kim.

Friedman slammed the door, knocking the man off balance. He recovered quickly, landing a punch that split Kim's lip. Blood trickled down Kim's chin, igniting his anger.

He retaliated with two swift jabs to the ribs, but the man twisted away, surprisingly agile for his stocky build.

Friedman moved to flank him. The suspect grabbed a lamp and swung it wildly. Kim ducked. The lamp smashed against the wall, shards flying everywhere.

The man pulled a seven-inch hunting knife from behind his back, the chrome blade gleaming under the harsh light.

"Surrender," Kim ordered, his voice steady despite the adrenaline surging through him.

"Never," the man spat, his eyes wild. He lunged, the knife flashing dangerously close to Kim's face. Kim dodged, feeling the blade graze the air near his cheek. Too close. Now Kim was angry.

Friedman shoved the man against the wall, his shoulder driving into the suspect's chest. They grappled fiercely, their muscles straining as the man used surprising strength to break free. He swung the blade at Friedman, who barely managed to block it with his forearm, the knife nearly cutting through his sleeve.

Kim shouted, aiming his gun at the man's center mass.

"Drop the knife!" The man hesitated, his eyes darting between the two detectives.

A loud banging rattled the door.

"Toronto Police Services, open up!"

Kim saw his chance and didn't hesitate. He lunged, twisting the man's arm hard. The man screamed, the knife rattling to the floor.

With a wild yell, he headbutted Kim, knocking him backward.

For Friedman, that was the last straw. He seized the moment, delivering a powerful spring-loaded punch to the man's jaw.

A sickening crunch followed as his jaw was crushed and dislocated, blood and teeth sent across the room from his distorted face. The man's eyes rolled back as he crumbled to the floor in an unconscious heap.

Baker and his team rushed in, eyes widening at the chaos.

"I take it your meeting didn't go as planned?" Baker quipped.

"You might say that," Friedman replied, a grim smile on his face as he rubbed the knuckles on his hand.

They yanked the suspect up and placed hand restraints on him. Friedman removed another knife strapped to the man's leg.

Kim wiped blood from his chin, wincing at the sting.

"Let's get this guy back to the station," he said, as he secured the evidence.

In the elevator, Kim turned to Friedman.

"How do I look?"

"Terrible. Change your shirt."

"This was new. Can I put it on my expense account?"

"Nope."

"Well, at least let me send it to the dry cleaners?"

"Nope."

"Figures."

As they rode down, Kim called in the arrest and requested an interview room, noting the suspect's need for medical attention.

Chapter 26

President Enrique Morales of Mexico sat in quiet reflection, concealed in a secure location deep within the Presidential Compound. His mind reviewed the alternatives for his next political move.

Morales had built his career on making impulsive decisions and acting on instinct, which caused him to frequently make political mistakes.

Some he regretted.

For the first time, Morales sat alone, deep in thought, unable to make a quick decision with the same degree of certainty that had guided him over the years. His problem, although serious, was unlike any he'd faced before, with too many variables and too many consequences. He had always acted instinctively, but this time, one wrong move could bring everything crashing down.

He was worried, and aside from Garcia, who might struggle with his potential decision, Morales had no one to turn to.

He was alone. This decision was his, and no one could help him.

A seasoned military veteran, he had risen through the ranks and was an individual who was more comfortable making snap judgments and dealing with the consequences. If he was wrong, he ignored the circumstances and moved forward, never looking back. His instinctive military decisions were usually right. But he knew this time was different. The fallout from a wrong decision could be catastrophic.

He was known for his spontaneity, yet he now thoughtfully weighed how his decision would play out in both his private and public life, and he wanted to avoid blow-back in both areas.

Once the command was given, there would be no going back.

His reputation was one of integrity, strategic brilliance, and an unwavering resolve against corruption. But those who knew him best harbored no illusions. Only one of those traits actually applied to President Morales.

Behind closed doors, Morales was callous, cunning, and unyielding in his pursuit of power.

A soft knock on the wooden door interrupted his concentration. "Enter," he commanded. General Garcia stepped inside.

Morales had appointed General Garcia to be his intelligence director due to his long, loyal service and sharp insight, qualities Morales valued above all else.

Growing up in Mexico, they had supported each other on numerous occasions, and Morales trusted Garcia more than any other friend.

Morales tossed a dossier back on his desk as Garcia approached him.

"Mr. President, you asked to see me?"

"Yes." Morales pointed toward a leather chair, extending an invitation for the general to sit. Morales twisted the file and pushed it toward Garcia.

"You've reviewed this dossier, I trust?"

"Yes, sir."

"It points out the ambassador's fondness for luxury, women, parties, along with other extravagant indulgences. It seems our charming ambassador to Canada is enjoying his lavish lifestyle and gaining popularity both in Canada and here. His impressive speeches would indicate that he is considering a run to challenge me for the presidency of Mexico," said Morales.

"Really," said Garcia.

"People see his youthful appearance, hear his charismatic speeches, and assume he's the next man for this office."

"I understand how that could be a potential problem for you, Mr. President," said General Garcia.

"I assume you have studied this dossier?"

"I am familiar with the contents, yes sir."

"We have everything we need to bury him. His ties to the cartel, the drug routes he's established through Canada, the money-laundering schemes concealed beneath layers of real estate deals... it's all here."

Garcia nodded slowly. "Yes, Mr. President. But if we release this, Martinez won't hesitate to reveal that the cartel funded your winning election campaign."

"That's possible," said Morales.

"What if the RCMP received an anonymous tip to investigate Ambassador Martinez? I could arrange to forward untraceable evidence of his involvement to discredit him and smear his reputation. You can be sure the Canadian government would not waste any time formally requesting that you recall him. He would return in disgrace, destroying any hope of a bid for this office."

"I like that," said Morales.

"The dossier shows us the ambassador enjoys his many luxuries, including women, parties, and expensive indulgences." Garcia's expression darkened. "As insurance, I'll arrange for an international scandal to surface, something that will shock the electorate and cripple his chances before he even announces his campaign. A mistress with photographs, or a party that gets out of hand and involves the Canadian police."

Morales leaned back in his chair, a slow smile forming. "You're right, General," he said slowly. "A scandal, a smear campaign, those are possibilities that would weaken his foundation, perhaps even make him question who he can trust. I believe that would sink his chances."

"Would you like me to proceed, Mr. President?"

"I will need some time to evaluate all of the options before I move forward. I will let you know my decision soon. That will be all for now, General. Thank you."

"Yes, Mr. President," said Garcia, as he stood up from his seat and withdrew from the room.

Alone again, President Morales reached into a locked desk drawer, dropped the key on top of the file, leaned over, retrieved his secure cell, and tapped a number, the magnitude of his decision settling into his bones.

There would be no turning back now.

Chapter 27

Gibson struggled with the confines of the makeshift workspace he occupied while the station underwent renovation. He fidgeted, shifting positions in a futile attempt to find even a sliver of comfort.

His bloodshot eyes, heavy with exhaustion, scanned the loop of video footage for what felt like the hundredth time. Maybe it truly was.

A bottle of eye drops had become his best friend against the unrelenting blur of the video screen. He believed that his tedious search, frame by frame, held the clue that could crack this case wide open.

Occasionally, a passing colleague cracked a wise remark. Gibson's lips broke into a grin, but his gaze never left the screen. He was locked in, driven by a dogged determination that had earned him his recent promotion.

The relentless grind was taking its toll, and when his vision doubled, he knew he had to step away.

He pushed his chair back and reached for the eye drops again, the cool liquid offering instant soothing relief as he leaned back.

Across the room, Detective Kim remained immersed in his own work, quietly sorting through case files and logistical data, crosschecking arrivals, property use permits, and warehouse rentals. Gibson could tell from his posture that something had caught his interest.

"Find anything?" Gibson asked, more to break the silence than out of curiosity.

Kim didn't look up. "Hard to say yet. Still pulling threads."

Gibson nodded. It was enough for now. Kim had a habit of staying quiet until he was absolutely sure.

Meanwhile, in his office, Borden was reviewing the forensic report from the transport escape. No prints in the cage. Just another dead end. His thoughts drifted to the spike strip used during the hijack.

"Friedman, see if you can find out where that spike strip came from," Borden ordered. "It might lead us to something. See if any other jurisdiction lost a strip. It's also possible it was homemade in a warehouse somewhere."

No sooner had he hung up than Cross knocked and stepped into his office, her expression unreadable but focused.

"Kim's digging through activity logs, shipment routes, unusual movements tied to known cartel areas. He's onto something, but it's not ready to share just yet," she said.

Borden nodded. "Good. Keep him on it."

Just then, Gibson knocked and entered, his face flushed with a mix of triumph and exhaustion.

"I believe I found something," he announced, dropping some photos on Borden's desk. "I caught a clear image of the driver and passenger in that F-250 from a glass reflection. We've got faces, and the truck has a license plate."

Cross leaned in. "We need to cross-check these with nearby surveillance. Check all retail, commercial, traffic cameras. Whatever we can find."

"We're running facial recognition on the occupants as we speak," Gibson added, the excitement clear in his voice.

Borden studied the images. "If we can put a name to those faces, it'll confirm we're getting closer."

Less than an hour later, Gibson's phone pinged with a message from a close friend at the courthouse. His heart skipped as he opened the attached photo. It was a clear image of the woman seen with Ambassador Martinez. Finally, a real lead.

He forwarded the image to Cross, who showed it to Borden.

"This might be our, "person of interest," she said, her voice sharp with anticipation.

Borden examined the image. "I remember her from the courthouse. Run it through facial recognition. I want a name and address."

Before they could dig further, Borden's phone rang again. It was Jonathan from tech.

"Borden, I've analyzed the system crash during the storm. It wasn't hacked as we suspected. We believe the network was just overwhelmed by the volume of emergency calls. Multiple calls were made on a loop from a dozen or more IP addresses."

"But not the fire alarms?"

"I believe the fire alarms were triggered manually at multiple locations. Three sets of alarms, each followed by the same number of pulls fifteen minutes later. My conclusion is the chaos that consumed the city and snarled traffic was a deliberate, coordinated assault."

"And the downtown power loss?"

"Electrical issues, mostly. But the timing of the outages and the traffic light failures is strange."

"In what way?" Borden asked.

"It's too coincidental. Someone had to orchestrate these events."

"Wow. Okay... keep on it," Borden said, his voice low as his mind weighed the implications.

"Will do. We'll talk later," responded Jonathan.

As Borden ended the call, the squad room buzzed with a faint sense of momentum, or maybe it was just hope.

Cross tapped lightly on the door and stepped inside, a coffee cup in hand, scanning the desk for a clear spot.

"I thought you could use this," she said, her voice gentle.

"Our team is contacting every informant we have. I expect something definitive will surface soon."

"That would be great. Let me know immediately if you get a hit," said Borden.

As the door clicked shut behind her, Borden's eyes drifted to the clock on the wall. A shadow of doubt crept in.

Chapter 28

Detective Gibson walked into the squad room, his eyes scanning for his boss, Detective Cross. She sat at her desk, taking a much-needed break, her hands wrapped around a mug of chamomile tea, savoring the solitude.

Her moment of peace vanished as Gibson approached.

Without a word, he pulled a chair to the side of her desk, nearly spilling his coffee. Cross remained silent and waited for him to settle in.

"Cross," Gibson began, "do you think the Cartel operates nationwide?"

"During our interrogation, I remember Madler mentioning possible warehouses in key cities across Canada. But it could have been a diversion or just a small-time crook trying to impress us."

"Maybe," Gibson conceded. "Friedman had me check with Vancouver PD. I just got off the phone with them. Two months ago, they reported a stolen spike strip, and its serial number matches the one we found at the escape scene."

Cross continued listening, her mind working through the implications.

"How does a stolen spike strip from Vancouver end up at a crime scene in Ontario?"

"That's a long way," Cross said. "If it's true, this operation might be bigger than we thought."

"Oh, it's true all right. Otherwise, the serial number wouldn't be a match."

"If this is all connected, we might be looking at a nationwide syndicate," said Gibson.

Cross nodded slowly, her mind already racing. "If it's that big, Borden's calling in the RCMP, CSIS, maybe even Vancouver PD. This case is about to get a whole lot bigger."

Gibson took a sip of his coffee, adrenaline surging through him despite the coffee's bitter taste.

"Speaking of expansion, Friedman's been mapping out potential helicopter refueling points."

Cross's focus shifted to the set of grainy photos Gibson laid out. He then played the video of the station raid on his phone.

"They never spoke so there's no audio but check the hand signals." He stopped the video. Then he tapped the photo, drawing Cross's attention from the video to a barely visible tattoo on the leader's wrist.

Cross studied the image, squinting. "What am I supposed to be looking at?"

"A tattoo associated with senior members of a Mexican Cartel," Gibson explained. "Ran it through our system, and I got three probable matches. One of the matches flew into Canada four weeks ago, and we caught him on camera at the luggage carousel and again going through security."

Cross leaned back, absorbing the information. "And?"

Gibson handed her another photo, a close-up of the man's face.

"It's him. The same guy who attacked our station, seen at customs, and picked up his luggage."

Cross's lips pressed into a thin line. "So, what's our play?"

"We've got surveillance on the address from the customs form," Gibson said, his voice quickening with excitement. "One of our detectives staked it out. Hours went by, nothing. Then two guys showed up, both unknown to us. They knocked, looked around, and disappeared inside."

"Did we get anything from the surveillance?" Cross asked, already calculating their next steps.

"Two clear photos before they went in. We tailed them afterward and followed them to a post office where they dropped off several parcels. Friedman got in line behind them, and after they left, Friedman produced his badge and had the parcels set aside."

"And?" Cross's voice was sharp now, on the edge, waiting for Gibson to reveal what he and Friedman discovered.

"We've got three addresses," Gibson replied, his eyes gleaming. "We're certain the parcels contain narcotics. We're ready to raid, but we need warrants and approval."

Cross exhaled, her mind spinning. "We have to move fast. If they catch wind that we're onto them, they'll vanish."

Gibson nodded.

"I'll brief Borden," Cross said, already rising from her chair.

"Oh, and there's something else," Gibson added, pausing for a beat as he pulled a folded schedule from his coat pocket. "Spade contacted me earlier and told me she accessed the ambassador's calendar and sent this over to me by mistake. It should have gone to you, and she asked me to pass it on."

"Cross, Martinez has meetings set with the Minister of Foreign Affairs, the Justice Minister, and a woman named Tina. Most of the meetings are happening at the King Edward Hotel."

Cross's eyes narrowed. "The Minister of Foreign Affairs? What's Winthrop's involvement?"

"Danielle Spade noticed Winthrop has planned trips to D.C. and Mexico with Ambassador Martinez. The ambassador's calendar shows he has a meeting with Miguel Valdez, the head of the Mexican National Railway, and possibly others."

"Miguel Valdez. He's the same guy we tied to those black boxes of cocaine," Cross muttered. The pieces of the puzzle had started to come together in her mind. "So, Valdez is also deep into this smuggling operation as well?"

Cross stood up, her expression hardening. "I'll bring this to Borden myself. We'll need eyes on Valdez and the Minister, but I'll leave that decision to him."

Gibson nodded, watching as Cross finished her tea with a single, deliberate sip. The mug clattered against her desk in one final and resolute motion.

Cross thanked Gibson, who retreated to his desk. She slipped through the squad room, her pace quickening with the weight of what Gibson and Spade had uncovered. She knocked on Borden's door.

Chapter 29

The Omni King Edward Hotel, a historic landmark in downtown Toronto, had hidden over a hundred years of its secrets behind its grand facade for both staff and patrons alike.

Carlos Martinez was a flirt and an impeccable diplomat. He maintained his public persona with effortless charm. His schedule of greeting dignitaries, playing golf, and attending high-profile meetings was a well-crafted smokescreen. Tonight, however, was different.

He had arranged a secret, off-the-books meeting with Tina Estrada and Johnathon Winthrop, the Minister of Foreign Affairs, in the concealed confines of the Deal Maker Bar on the hotel's mezzanine.

The mezzanine floor usually hosted seminars and retirement parties, but tonight's meeting was neither.

The Deal Maker Bar was known for its exclusivity and privacy, the perfect setting for such a covert gathering.

Tina arrived first but hung back, choosing to observe from a distance, watching, analyzing, ensuring she identified the fastest escape route. Her mind continually calculated, always prepared and never relaxed.

Sean, once a member of an elite special unit, carried the weight of a mission gone wrong. This trauma, coupled with his deep-rooted disillusionment with the violence he once justified, drove him into the shadows, where his tactical brilliance and resolve found a new home within the Cartel.

A tech-savvy operative loyal to Tina sat at a small walnut table with a clear view of the Deal Maker Bar entrance.

His audio connection was discreet and crystal clear. The laptop recorded every word spoken during the meeting fifty feet away. The computer produced a soft glow as Sean scanned the schematics, having already hacked into the security cameras.

He scanned the Deal Maker Bar, the kitchen, and the surrounding mezzanine meeting rooms for any threats. He noted the exits and verified that escape routes were clear, just in case.

Only when he was satisfied that the area was secure did he give Tina a discreet nod, indicating that it was safe to enter.

Carlos Martinez, ever the charmer, greeted Tina with a broad smile.

"Tina, always a pleasure," he said warmly, though his eyes remained watchful as he scanned the room.

"Thank you for meeting with us," Winthrop added, his tone distant yet respectful.

"Did everything go smoothly for you?" Martinez asked, his curiosity evident.

"Splendid," she replied coolly. "We had some urgent Cartel business that couldn't wait. Just a couple of annoying situations needed to be resolved."

"And they were taken care of?" Martinez asked, his interest piqued.

"Everything was laid to rest quietly," Tina said, her words carrying a quiet double meaning.

Martinez nodded, though a hint of skepticism lingered in his gaze. "Good to hear."

Sean's fingers danced over his keyboard, maintaining surveillance.

"Let's get to it," Tina said, her voice adopting a firm, businesslike tone. "Remind me, what was the reason for this meeting?"

Martinez ordered snacks, cheese, and wine, attempting to create a more relaxed atmosphere.

"Tina, your recent rescue operation was reckless. It could have backfired on us worse than the Mississauga incident."

Tina's expression hardened.

"Or what, Carlos? The operation was meticulous. The police are clueless. We recovered our narcotics and weapons, and a significant amount of cash. We're now investing this money for a high return. You should be praising me, not threatening me."

Winthrop stepped in, hoping to defuse the tension.

"Let's change the topic. We discussed test shipments by rail with Miguel Valdez of the Mexican National Railway Company. He suggested running a few empty shipments first."

"Valdez is eager to resume deliveries," Martinez said. "He's built larger magnetized boxes painted to match the color of the undercarriage of the rail cars. A cell signal demagnetizes the box, dropping it flat onto the rail bed. The container and its contents are retrieved, and the empty box is sent back to Mexico on a southbound train. It's foolproof."

Winthrop nodded. "Why not use the pipeline instead?"

Martinez shook his head.

"The pipeline involves more people, which increases our exposure risk. Fewer people involved, fewer problems. Plus, we might want to use the pipeline as a decoy later on."

"Are we all in agreement?" Martinez asked.

Tina and Winthrop nodded.

Tina caught Martinez off guard with a direct question.

"Have you decided whether to give up your position and run for President of Mexico?"

Martinez, briefly caught off guard, recovered quickly.

"The idea was discussed a month ago, but I've made my decision."

"So, you've decided to run, then?" Tina asked.

"If you do run, you'll have to step down as ambassador, won't you?" she pressed.

"That's what we discussed," Martinez admitted. "Yes. I am going to remove Morales from office and will publicly announce my campaign in a couple of weeks."

Tina turned to Winthrop. "Have you had any progress recruiting the Minister of Justice?"

"I had a meeting scheduled last week, but he canceled last minute," Winthrop replied.

"I assume you set up a follow-up, right?"

"Yes. Next Monday. If you're interested, join me for lunch at the Parliamentary Restaurant in Ottawa. I can introduce you to a few politicians."

"We need a way to persuade him," Winthrop said. "We need some leverage, dirt preferably."

"We're working on it," Tina said. "Sometimes it's enough to leak things, which will smear his reputation. It doesn't need to be true. If you want, I can arrange that for you. It's the way things are done. Politicians lie all the time. It's expected."

Tina handed a small black leather case to Winthrop.

"Here's a little something to help the Minister of Justice get on board. The more politicians we buy, the smoother things go."

Winthrop opened the case and smiled at the sight of bundles of cash inside. Martinez grinned, nodding at Tina.

Before this meeting, Tina and Sean had recorded and photographed the serial numbers of the money contained in the case. Tina now had blackmail insurance on both men.

Tina explained, "The plan is for narcotics to be sorted by type in one central facility. From there, they're sent to various houses for packaging and re-shipment. Smaller amounts per site mean smaller losses if a location gets compromised."

The group shared a quiet laugh and sipped more wine.

Martinez asked about other provinces.

"The same system is running out west," Tina said. "Vancouver is our most lucrative market outside Ontario. We're already acquiring property there."

As the meeting wrapped up, Tina was the first to slip away. Sean had arranged for a video recording of Tina entering the meeting with a black case, and later, Winthrop leaving as Martinez carried the same case.

More insurance, she thought.

Winthrop and Martinez exited the Deal Maker Bar, unaware Sean's camera had caught everything.

As they stepped into the hallway, Winthrop asked Martinez, "Can we really trust her?"

Martinez's reply was short. "She needs us, and for now, we need her."

Winthrop nodded, though a hint of doubt crossed his face.

"We'll keep an eye on her just to be sure,"

Martinez added. "We can't afford any surprises."

Chapter 30

Tina Estrada stepped through the revolving door of the Omni King Edward Hotel in downtown Toronto. The cool night air marked a sharp contrast to the warmth of the hotel interior she'd just left.

Distrust was second nature to someone who grew up in the streets of Mexico City. Tina glanced back through the glass door. No one was there. No one approaching. A good sign, she thought.

Tina's eyes were missing the usual sparkle, and her face looked tired. She fiddled with the twisted leather strap of her Louis Vuitton handbag, amplifying her unease.

She knew more downtime and rest were needed, making the decision to head south to Harbor Square. This was her hideaway in a posh condominium overlooking Lake Ontario. It was time to relax, giving her a few minutes to think about nothing at all.

It was a short ride from the King Eddy Hotel, and her meeting had left her feeling powerful and in control.

She liked that.

As usual, before sauntering toward the waiting limo, she took a careful look out both King Street East and West, then twisted back to check the hotel lobby.

Using the reflection from the glass door, she saw no one across the street. No one inside. Sean was idling the black limo about ten paces from the lobby entrance, his eyes tracking her approach, making sure she wasn't followed.

As soon as she slammed the door closed, Sean pulled into the light traffic without saying anything.

No greeting. That was odd, thought Tina. They had worked together for years, and his loyalty was never in question.

Sean was like family and trusted by everyone. Tonight, something was different.

She sensed a tension in his eyes, shifting between mirrors, changing his speed, and tapping on the wheel as he followed a longer, more indirect route to the condominium.

"What is it, Sean?" Tina asked, her voice edgy and direct.

"Just a second." Sean glanced between the road and the rearview mirror, then over at the side mirror, worried they may not be alone. "I noticed someone who seemed to be hanging around outside the bar entrance during your meeting," he began, his tone quiet and methodical. "Whoever this was seemed to be loitering, walking past the bar a few times. I thought at first he was searching for someone. Maybe another hotel guest. But when he noticed the three of you at the table..." He stopped and scanned the street again.

Tina's eyes narrowed. "And?"

"That's when something changed," Sean said. "He stopped glancing around and then zeroed in on your table. The bartender noticed him, and that's when he moved along. Sure enough, he walked by again. I'm sure he was watching your meeting, Tina."

"Really," said Tina, absorbing the information. Her exhausted mind snapped into high alert. "You're sure he was observing us, not just killing time or people-watching? Maybe he was meeting someone, and they were late?"

Sean's jaw and teeth strained, his lips grew tight, and his face flushed up to a brilliant red with a feeling of anger and lack of control. "No, I don't think so. After the third pass by the door, I knew. His continued phony glances were too specific since he stopped and stared at your table. He wasn't just interested. I think he was studying all of you. From my angle, I couldn't tell if he was taking photos. My direction was off a bit. But his hand was in his pocket as he walked away."

"If someone is watching us, I need to disappear for a while," Tina murmured. "I can't jeopardize our operation and potentially risk leading someone back to the camp. Although we could bury an intruder there and no one would ever know."

Sean nodded his agreement. "Exactly. If there's even a slight chance you're being tailed, you need to disappear. I will find out who it is. Then you can decide what happens to him."

Reaching for her handbag, she pulled out her phone and stabbed Juan's speed-dial number. After a few rings,

Juan's voice came through sounding uneven and alert. "What's up?"

"Listen carefully, Juan," she said. "Someone may have been watching our meeting tonight at the King Eddy. Sean saw a guy hovering around and focused on our table."

"Do you think someone recognized you?"

"I can't say for sure, but we can't take any chances," she replied. "For now, I want you to take charge of the camp and handle all contact with Madler. I'll keep my distance and stay off the grid for now."

Juan grunted. "No problem. I'll handle everything."

"Good. If they're watching me, they might be watching others, too. Make sure everything at the camp is safe, and make sure you know everyone coming and leaving. Be careful and don't trust anyone you don't know. You know how to reach me."

Exhaling slowly, Tina tossed her phone back into her handbag.

"Well done, Sean," she said, glancing over at him. "We can't afford any slip-ups. Not now."

Chapter 31

Back inside the King Edward Hotel, RCMP officer Carl Burke sat quietly in a street-level bar, watching King Street through the massive windows, undetected. He kept a low profile, blending seamlessly into the hotel's late-night crowd.

Burke, dressed in black jeans, a sport shirt, and a very well-worn old leather jacket, was on a quiet, off-the-books assignment. With years of clandestine experience, Burke instinctively knew when to be seen and when to vanish. His unique skill set was why he'd been handpicked by Sergeant Crawford himself. No one handled this kind of surveillance better than Burke.

While his vantage point behind a large marble pillar offered a good profile of the front door and lobby, he knew it was time to move to a better location.

The instructions he received were clear: photograph Martinez's every movement and document everyone he met. Every face, every conversation. Nothing was to escape his notice, and nothing was to be disclosed outside of Crawford's inner circle.

Get close.

Stay invisible.

Standing concealed in the shadows of Toronto Street opposite the hotel, he maintained a perfect view of the front door, undetected.

As Burke scrolled through the photos on his phone, which he'd taken earlier of Martinez and Winthrop during their meeting and exiting the bar, he couldn't quite make out the conversation, as the pair were talking in low voices, unaware of his presence.

Then he paused on her. The woman at their table.

He replayed the video of her exit. Her gaze seemed deliberate.

To Burke, she appeared to be a woman who radiated confidence and calm self-assurance, and one who was in a hurry. Burke couldn't help but wonder why she swung around looking back into the lobby.

Did she forget something?

Did she know he was watching her?

His next instinct...trouble.

Burke focused his eyes, studying her face. "Who are you?" he whispered. One thing was for certain. We're going to find out, he thought aloud.

Without hesitation, Burke messaged Rick Crawford and attached photos of Martinez, Winthrop, and the woman, labeled as Mystery Woman. The note read: Ambassador Martinez and Minister Winthrop with an unidentified female tonight. She left moments before they did. Possibly worth a closer look.

He hit send and pocketed his phone. Uncovering her identity was now his top priority, and he knew exactly what to do.

Moments later, his phone buzzed with Crawford's response: Understood. Keep her in sight if she reappears.

Burke allowed himself a small smile. Whoever this mystery woman was, she was now on Crawford's radar, and Burke wouldn't let her stay hidden for long.

Chapter 32

Detective Janet Cross parked in front of a Starbucks on King near Bay, her mind swirling with doubt and determination.

She walked into a nondescript building, the weight of her decision growing heavier with each step. She glanced at the office directory, searching the tiny white plastic nameplates and office numbers.

She traced her finger down the list and found the name she was looking for.

The elevator ride to the fifth floor was agonizingly slow, her heartbeat pounding louder with each passing floor.

At the door marked "525," she paused, taking a deep breath before turning the handle and pushing it open.

Relief washed over her at the sight of the empty waiting room. No need to explain herself, at least not yet.

She sank into a well-padded swivel chair, glancing around the room. The soothing ambiance clashed with her racing thoughts.

A Keurig sat in the corner beside a selection of teas. Chamomile. The familiar sight brought a faint smile to her face.

The flat-screen TV on the wall rotated silent news stories. She left it muted. Her eyes flipped to her watch. "One more minute, then I'm out," she thought. If the door to the inner office didn't open, she was gone.

Just as she shifted to stand, the door eased open.

A well-dressed woman in her forties stepped out with a warm, inviting smile. She extended her hand.

"Detective Cross, please come in."

Cross could feel her body relax and her breathing slow.

The office was modern and inviting, with a glass desk, a black swivel chair, and a separate seating area with four leather chairs around a low glass table, fresh flowers, and a box of tissues.

Faint jazz guitar played familiar tunes from the ceiling speakers, helping Cross feel a rare sense of relaxation and safety.

As she glanced around the room, she couldn't help admiring what she saw and thought her office could definitely use a renovation.

They sat side by side in comfortable swivel chairs. The woman engaged Cross in easy small talk—daily routine, exercise habits, vacations, and hobbies.

Cross felt her natural guarded demeanor slip as her level of comfort increased.

"So, what brings you here today, Detective?" the woman finally asked.

Panic surged. Her hand trembled, face flushed, and every instinct told her to run.

She took a deep breath and said, "I'm having recurring dreams about being shot in a warehouse raid several months ago."

"Would you feel comfortable telling me about the incident?" the woman asked gently.

"I think so," said Cross.

Cross's eyes glazed over. Her breathing became shallow, her memory in overdrive.

"We surrounded the warehouse. Special forces came in hard and crashed through the mezzanine windows. At the same time, we entered through a side door and a large overhead roll-up door. Lots of loud noise. Gunfire. Screaming. Flash bangs exploding. Tear gas. Smoke bombs. Glass shards filled the air. It was hard to see. I moved to take cover.

I spotted two shooters, caught the muzzle flash. They turned, aimed their automatic weapon in my direction. I fired at both of them. Both men screamed something. Their guns crashed to the concrete floor. Later I learned they were two cartel gang guys I had shot.

There was so much noise. Everyone was moving. I momentarily lost track of my assault team in the chaos. Everything happened so quickly.

I looked around and couldn't see anything. I wasn't sure if I was alone or not. More rapid gunfire coming at us from up on the mezzanine walkway. They were taken out quickly.

As I turned to move, I saw the muzzle flash, then nothing. My eyes opened. I was on my back staring at the roof, gasping for air. I thought I would die in that warehouse.

It was like an elephant sat on my chest and I couldn't move. I wasn't sure if I was alive or dead. I felt a hand at the back of my neck. My body was being dragged along the floor. Someone pulled me away from the direct line of fire.

I remember the EMS attendant saying something about how lucky I was to be wearing my Kevlar vest."

The woman nodded, her expression understanding and soft.

"That's traumatic. How often do you keep reliving the moment?"

"Almost every night," Cross admitted, her voice trembling. "I keep seeing the flash of the gun. Then I'm falling, staring at the ceiling. I remember the floor felt cold."

"Did you make a mistake during the raid?"

"No, I don't think so. We had a plan, and I executed my part perfectly. Or so I thought."

"Were you careless?"

"No, I was careful. It was just bad luck, I guess."

"What happened to the man who shot you?"

"My boss, Detective Borden, took him down. I was told he risked his life when he crossed the floor under heavy gunfire to drag me to safety."

"Did you take time off after the shooting?"

"No. We're too busy. There's always something happening."

The woman leaned forward slightly.

"Could you describe a typical day for me?"

Cross laughed bitterly.

"Crazy. I supervise detectives, provide training, write and read reports, meet with my boss and others, go to the gym, do target practice, go out on calls, attend court, and work with the Crown Prosecutors. I also do performance reviews and investigate crimes."

"That sounds intense. How many hours do you work each week?"

"Around 70 to 80 hours."

"Are you married?"

"Yes and no."

"What does that mean?"

"I'm married, but my husband and I have separated."

"How long have you been apart?"

"Several months. We're both busy with work. He thinks my job is too dangerous and that I work too much. He worries he will get a knock on the door saying I was dead or in a coma."

"Is he right to worry?"

"I hope not."

The woman paused, considering her next words carefully.

"Detective, I can help you, but you need to listen to me. You need time off before you burn out or make a fatal mistake. Can you take three weeks off and go on a vacation with your husband?"

"Possibly. It depends on when I can get away and if he can leave his job as well, or if he even wants to."

"Can you get a friend to go with you somewhere?"

"That's a possibility."

"What about going away now?"

"Now's a bad time. Too much is happening. Maybe later, when things slow down."

"Does your work ever slow down?"

"No, not really."

"Do you have any family?"

"I had a sister. She died from an overdose. I didn't even know she was hooked on drugs."

"What would you have done if you'd known?"

"I'd have gotten her into rehab. Then I would've hunted down the dealers and either killed them or totally destroyed their operation."

"What does that mean?"

"I would have arrested them or killed them."

"Do you think you didn't know about your sister because you were working too much?"

"Probably."

"What's probably true?"

"That I work too much."

Cross let out a slow breath, the weight of regret and responsibility settling over her. She reached for a tissue.

"During that last big thunderstorm, someone broke into headquarters. Stole weapons from a secure cage. It was a stain on the department. And now those weapons are back on the streets. Someone is bound to get hurt."

"Did you tell anyone about this visit today?"

"No."

"What would your boss do if he knew?"

"Worry. Then stick me behind a desk."

"Would that be so bad?"

"For me? Yeah."

"Talked to any friends about this?"

"I don't have any."

"Have you talked to your husband?"

"Not really. We've talked. Mostly about divorce. I wouldn't tell him about my job. He'd leave for sure."

"Detective, if I prescribed some medication, would you take it?"

"No."

"Why not?"

"I can't afford to have impaired reactions or clouded judgment. Not in my line of work. I need a clear mind when I'm in life-threatening situations."

Cross felt her phone vibrate. She checked the screen.

"I need to take this."

"No problem."

She thanked the doctor, who nodded.

"Consider another visit?" the doctor asked.

Cross hesitated then nodded, understanding that her job might pull her away.

Cross slid into her squad car on King Street. She collected her thoughts and called Borden. His voice came through, steady and clear.

"We have a name."

Chapter 33

The team gathered in Borden's family room, eager to hear progress reports. Borden shut the door, cutting off household noise and distraction. He stretched across the edge of the table, dragging his hot coffee within reach.

"We've chased this rabbit long enough," he said, his voice low and steady. "Tina Estrada. It's her."

Borden paused a moment, letting her name settle over the group. "I think we'll find all our evidence will lead us straight back to her. We don't have conclusive proof yet, but I am convinced we will have what we need soon."

Janet Cross looked up from the file in front of her. She stopped writing and twirled her pen as she waited to jot a note.

She shifted in her chair. "And what about Sean Fergus?" she asked, her tone inquisitive, her eyes narrowed. "He's not just muscle. I'd bet my paycheck he means more to her than that."

Rick Crawford leaned forward, the chair creaking beneath him. He raised an eyebrow, smirking. "That's a leap, Detective. You sure those dots connect?"

Borden stood up, shoving his hands into his pockets. "I don't see her as reckless. Getting involved with Sean would be a careless mistake on her part. I don't see that happening. It could get messy.

Everything was planned. Coordinated.

If Tina Estrada was the one behind the activity of the last few days, she was incredibly careful," he said, pacing back and forth. "Every move was calculated. And every time we got close, we hit another dead end."

Borden stopped and looked at the team. "I don't believe that's luck on her part. That's control. We need to get ahead of her. We need to stop playing catch-up."

Cross stopped fidgeting with her pen and closed the folder in front of her. "And what about Fergus? He might be the one who keeps the wheels turning," she said. "Intimidation. Distractions. Murders. Whatever she wants, is my guess." Her voice was calm, but frustration was beginning to edge in.

Rick Crawford exhaled and leaned forward. "So, what's the next move? We can't afford to sit around hoping she slips up. Based on what I've heard here, I don't think that is likely. That doesn't sound like your style, Borden."

Borden didn't waste time. "No. The escape and the raid at the station must've cost a lot of money. Look into possible shell companies, property purchases, and unusual cash movement. Someone left a money trail. We just need to find it and see where it leads us."

He leaned on the table, looked at the group, and stated, "I am convinced it's Tina Estrada. I'm sure of it. Use every resource and every informant we know.

As I mentioned earlier, I have no proof yet, but I suspect she planned the station break-in too.

Knowing her brother was in jail, she created a plan to help him escape custody. I'd bet my vacation that she's the brains behind the transport escape and maybe even the cartel warehouse in Mississauga."

"Well, at this point, and without evidence, why do you think she's behind all of this?" Cross asked.

"Fair question. As I mentioned, with her brother in jail and occupied in a lengthy court trial, he had no opportunity to plan anything, let alone help her to plan his escape."

"She had help," Cross said firmly.

"Absolutely," Borden said. "The question is, who?"

Janet Cross glanced up from the case file in her lap, her brow furrowed. "Fergus is her enforcer. He's always close. That's not a coincidence."

Crawford leaned forward. "Are we sure about this?"

Borden nodded. "It lines up. The escape, the drug routes, even the timing of the cartel shipments through the GTA. She's not a player. She's the one pulling the strings. Tina Estrada is the boss."

"Then why haven't we grabbed her? Shouldn't we bring her to the station and question her?" Gibson asked. His voice carried an edge of frustration.

Borden pressed his knuckles onto the table, his voice edgy with determination. "We don't move until we can take the entire operation down. You hit her now, she disappears, sets up somewhere else, and we're back to square one. Another problem is we don't know where she is at the moment," said Borden.

Crawford quickly commented, "Fair point. But let's not get ahead of ourselves. What's the plan to find her and keep our eyes on her without tipping her off? Does CSIS have an informant inside the cartel?"

Danielle Spade cleared her throat. "Yes, but I can't talk about that. We haven't been looking for Estrada, but I can get someone on it. I have no idea how long it might take to locate her.

Our tech guys are picking up movement on the train routes previously used by the cartels. Small shipments of narcotics are still coming in. I suspect they may be testing the method to determine if it is safe or not. We intercepted one, but we are allowing others to slip through to make the importers feel untouchable.

Eventually, they will get greedy and want to expedite larger shipments. We just need to wait for the right moment and seize the larger bulk. The upside is bigger shipments will involve more cartel members to handle the larger quantities. When that happens, we'll arrest them all. Every last one."

"False sense of security," Cross murmured, looking over at Spade. "It's risky."

Spade shrugged. "So far, it's working. They think we're too busy chasing the ghosts to notice."

"Speaking of chasing after shadows," Crawford said, "This encampment I heard about up north. Do we know if it is real or just a rumor?"

"Some of us believe it's real," Spade replied. "But finding it? That's the hard part. Our intel is vague at best."

Gibson leaned forward. "I know I'm the new guy, so help me understand. What exactly are we looking for? A training ground? A warehouse? A clearing with a couple of tents?"

"Could be all of that or none," Borden said. "We don't know yet. But a camp makes sense if it's out of the way and somewhere the cartel could create another warehouse facility."

Crawford sat up. "With help from CSIS, we'll keep following the trains. They are the main supply line, and because they run on time, it will make our job a little easier. Our surveillance will eventually lead us to an interception point. We can't afford to lose the trail now. Oh, and one other point. The use of trains could be a decoy. If so, they might be inclined to use trucking companies, so we've increased security and inspections."

"Good decision," Borden said, turning to Spade. "Any pattern to their shipments? Will you have eyes on the next shipment?"

"Yes. We're already operational," Spade replied. "But if they catch on, we'll lose them. We can follow the runner after the pickup. That's not a problem.

One of the magnets used to secure the metal boxes to the train undercarriage failed. It fell to the track. Hikers found it and called the police.

Since some of the drugs went through, the importers will be confused and worried why their shipment came up short. We left the box on the track, hoping they come looking for it. If they do, we'll be nearby and follow them after pickup back to their packing or distribution facility."

"They won't catch on?" Cross asked, her voice calm but firm.

"Not if we're vigilant. And patient."

"Patience is great," Gibson muttered, "but what happens if they decide not to show up?"

Borden felt tense and his jaw tightened at the comment from Gibson. In a stern response, Borden replied, "We leak a story to John Mackie at CanWide News saying that drugs were found by hikers on a train track, not mentioning the metal box. He'll jump all over a story like that, and the drug importers will think the police are not clued in to the frequency of shipments."

Silence settled over the room.

Crawford broke the quiet. "I'll make sure our team's ready. When I hear from Spade that another shipment is moving, I'll arrange for undercover agents to board the train, watch for a drop, and have CSIS back it up via satellite."

"Okay, we all have work to do. But no one moves," Borden said. "Not until I'm sure we have the whole picture."

Spade stood and smoothed her jacket. "I'll update you when we've got new intel.

But for now, the place up north, if it exists, is still a mystery."

As the others gathered their things, Cross looked at Borden. "Can I have a word when everyone's gone?"

"Of course."

Chapter 34

Detective Cross stood with her hands on her hips. "Are you okay?" Borden produced his usual grin. "I'm fine, just a bit tired."

"Tired isn't one hundred percent," she replied, her voice and tone softer. "I'd say you've been running on fumes for days."

He gave her a tired smile. "Really, I'm fine."

Before she could counter, Borden's phone vibrated. He glanced at the screen. "It's Kim. Let's see what he's got."

They leaned over the screen as Borden scrolled through the message.

Detective Kim, Stakeout Summary:

Target is active. Couriers in and out all day.

Neighbors confirmed constant deliveries for several weeks.

Two individuals just entered.

Borden whispered, "That's it. We're not waiting any longer. If Madler's using this place as a warehouse, we need to shut it down now."

Cross nodded. "Calling backup."

Within the hour, they stood a block from the target house, their team in position. Officers in plain clothes were scattered along the perimeter. An unmarked van hummed quietly nearby.

Borden and Cross watched from their vantage point. Couriers, some on bikes, others in cars, trickled in and out with their packages clutched tightly.

"They're moving something big through here," Cross muttered.

Borden's gaze locked on the front door as two more men approached, then entered through an unlocked front entrance.

The first was lean and nervous, his eyes darting up and down the street as if expecting trouble. The second, short and broad with wild hair, struggled to carry a heavy duffel bag.

Borden's radio crackled. "Strike team ready on your command."

"Hold," Borden said. "Let those two inside first." They watched as the men disappeared inside. The door slammed shut. Quiet dominated the neighborhood again.

Borden gave a single nod. "Go."

The team moved in silence, quick and precise. Officers surrounded the house, blocking every possible exit. Cross and Borden flanked the front door with the breach team.

The door blew inward with a deafening crack. Shouts of "Toronto Police Services !" filled the air as constables stormed in.

Inside, chaos erupted. A chair was hurled through a back window, sending shards of glass flying. Men were yelling and making a dash for the side door. Furniture toppled. A table stacked with small white packages crashed to the floor. White powder in plastic bags spilled out. One man bolted toward the back of the house, another toward the basement.

"Runner!" Cross shouted.

Borden gave chase but struggled to keep up, his heart pounding as he burst through the kitchen to a back door. The suspect threw a lawn chair in his path, but Borden vaulted over it, the adrenaline obscuring his exhaustion.

The runner dashed through the short backyard and leaped the wooden fence with ease, disappearing into the laneway lined with old wooden garages with broken doors in need of repair facing each other. The odd car parked outside the wooden structure.

"Suspect fleeing westbound in laneway," Borden barked into his radio.

Behind him, Cross was with the strike team as they subdued the others. Ramirez, the bigger man with the duffel bag, was cuffed and dragged to a squad car, demanding to see a warrant.

Borden stood in the yard, bent over, catching his breath as he watched younger police constables fan out into the night, flashlights cutting through the darkness in pursuit of the laneway runner. He looked back. Cross was emerging from the house.

She caught up to Borden, saying, "We got the one in charge. He hasn't said anything except mumbling about a warrant. We checked his duffel and it's full of cash and ledgers. If my hunch is correct, these items may belong to Madler. If so, we might have cracked this thing open."

Borden nodded at Cross, then glanced toward the alley, still hearing the distant shouts of his constables. "If they catch the runner, we'll know for sure."

Cross nodded. "Let's hope he doesn't get too far."

A loud, unexpected engine roared to life down the alleyway in the distance. Borden and Cross snapped their gaze toward the sound.

"Sounds to me like he had help," Borden said.

"Is that a bike?" Cross asked.

Cross's eyes narrowed as she slipped into the laneway.

She saw a motorcycle, one rider, blow past the corner out of sight. No plate, no helmet, just noise and speed.

"He's gone," Cross said, as she watched the constables walking back, looking around them to see if the suspect had dropped anything.

"This job never gets easy," said Cross.

Borden looked at her and said, "That's for sure."

Chapter 35

Tina received a call from Madler, his voice booming through the speaker with unusual excitement.

"We won't need two weeks. I've already located and toured a farmhouse. We can move in immediately if we want. I knew the moment the agent showed me the listing that this was the ideal location for our enterprise. It has the perfect space for storage or repackaging. It's remote. This is a farm situated northeast of the city. The owner wants to sell, but the agent said he is open to renting it if the price is right. I told her I would submit a rental offer. Just waiting for the owner's response."

"When do you expect to hear back?" Tina asked.

"It shouldn't be long now," Madler replied, his tone exuberant with confidence.

"Lying to the agent was easy. I told her the house was for me and my family, said I wanted a place close to a public school for my kids. She bought it. She even drove me to the town of Leaside. Told her I was looking for a property for my cousin Frederick."

Madler continued, "The hobby farm I want to rent is about a forty-five-minute drive northeast of the 407. There's a metal gate off the main road. A long dirt-and-grass driveway leads to the barn and house, where there's ample parking. Trees line the entire driveway, blocking the house from view.

"Lots of trees surround the building, giving total privacy. It's spacious, secluded and a typical farmhouse with three bedrooms, a kitchen, and a dry basement. So, it's perfect for storing and packaging product.

"The barns near the house are big enough to park inside. The barn is dry, with a few shuttered windows in case of a storm.

There's a small tool room and a trapdoor in the floor with a space to stash weapons, cash, or product. No one would suspect anything unusual. The floorboards are thick, no hollow sound or echo when I walk on them. That area could be used to secure anything we want down there.

"I think you'll like it. I'll send some photos. If you're okay with what I found, I'll lock it in for a year with options to renew."

"Sounds perfect. But Madler, if the owner stalls or gets cold feet, I want to know about it immediately. Don't say anything to the agent or owner other than you'll check and get back. I'll want the address and contact info of the owner. I may need to make the owner a direct offer no one could ever refuse."

The call ended with a hard click.

Tina stared at her phone, thinking.

A farm was a smart idea being private, practical, and in a location no one would suspect.

Yes, a farm was an excellent idea, especially since Tina could bury many things there that would never be found.

Chapter 36

At Police HQ, Detective Cross stepped into Borden's office just as he unlocked and opened his gun drawer.

"Going out for coffee, boss?" she teased.

"Get your gun, Cross. We're taking a ride," Borden said, handing her photos of several people who had entered Canada from Mexico two weeks ago.

"Kim got a tip, a name and a location. These are possible suspects tied to the crew that broke into the station. I was about to head out solo, but there's a strong possibility this guy isn't alone. Backup might be wise on this one. We'll get Gibson and a couple of others to join us."

"I'll grab my vest and be right behind you," Cross said, adrenaline already kicking in.

Borden's team approached the target house in Rexdale using an unmarked car, no lights and no sirens. The small lot held a two-story building, each floor with a large plate-glass window. The white aluminum siding was weathered. The windows were grimy. A van sat in the driveway, its front bumper nearly touching the concrete porch.

Constables confirmed movement inside. Lights flicked on and off. Then an unexpected car pulled into the driveway behind the van. A lanky young man jumped out, grabbed a large bag from the back seat, dropped it on the porch, and rang the bell. Cross snapped a photo of him and his license plate as he pulled away.

A man in his twenties opened the door, grabbed the bag, and disappeared inside. Borden guessed multiple people were inside, judging by the size of the bag, assuming it was a food order.

There were no signs of children. No toys. No bikes. No kids playing outside.

The street was eerily quiet in both directions.

Cross approached a neighbor, flashed her badge, and asked about the house. The answers confirmed that at least two men lived there, took frequent deliveries, and shipped boxes daily via FEDEX, UPS and Purolator.

Borden ordered his team to surround the house. The license plate confirmed the van belonged to the man who had retrieved the package.

Before the police could close in, a man stepped through the front door carrying a parcel. He unlocked the van with a remote and started the engine.

As he prepared to pull away, Gibson jerked open the door, slid into the passenger seat, and leveled his gun at the driver.

"Who are you? What do you want?" the driver demanded.

Gibson's reply was cold. "Drive."

The driver obeyed, circled the block, then rolled to a stop.

An unmarked car eased in behind the van.

Gibson ordered, "Out. Hands on the van where I can see them." Looking confused, the driver complied.

That was Borden and Cross's cue. They moved in.

Cross yanked his arms behind him, snapped handcuffs onto his wrists, and spun him around.

The driver trembled, sweat beading on his face. Panic flickered in his eyes. He avoided eye contact, breathing heavily. He had no idea what was happening.

The questions came rapidly.

"Who... who are you?" the young man stuttered.

"I'm Detective Borden, Toronto Police Services. This is Detective Cross. How many others are inside the house?" Borden asked.

There was no hesitation.

"Two others are inside. They're armed to the teeth."

The two men sat at a worn Formica kitchen table near the back of the house, feasting on their Uber Eats delivery. They had pistols holstered on their hips and knives strapped to their backs.

Borden asked the young man about the pistols.

"I don't know anything about guns, Detective. I can't help you," he said.

The team was notified that the house was loaded with weapons. The informant fidgeted as he rattled off where he had seen the guns located. The suspect was placed in the back of a squad car and taken to HQ.

Borden decided to split the team. He and Cross would breach the front door. Gibson and another team member would take the side door. The rest were to cover the back-yard.

The teams took their positions and waited.

On Borden's count, two, three, they moved.

Borden kicked the front door open, gun aimed toward the kitchen. Cross pivoted, covering the staircase. Gibson barged through the side door, moved up the steps to the kitchen entrance, and held position.

Gunfire exploded from the back of the kitchen. Borden ducked to his right into the living room. Cross dropped to the floor at the foot of the stairs. A steel chair hurled from the kitchen blasted through the back window.

They returned fire. Gibson leaned around the wall and joined in.

Gunfire blasted again from the kitchen. Another chair crashed into the dining room. Two detectives in the yard raised their guns and took aim at the kitchen window. Borden yelled for the suspects to surrender. More gunfire was the answer.

Borden dropped low, rolled, and squeezed the trigger, hitting one of the men in the leg. The man screeched. His gun jerked upward, spraying the ceiling with bullets as he collapsed.

The second man fired blindly into the backyard and then toward the front door. He yanked his wounded part-ner into the kitchen and ducked behind the overturned table. Cross fired, hitting the second man's thigh. He dropped. His gun skidded across the floor.

Gibson pounced.

"Don't move a muscle," he shouted, leveling his gun.

Bleeding and breathless, they didn't argue. They complied.

Gibson kicked the gun aside and secured both men.

Cross moved upstairs, instincts sharp. She cleared each room. All empty. Gibson bolted downstairs and found a stash of weapons.alongside empty shipping containers.

Minutes later, the paramedics arrived, quickly turning the chaos into order.

"Minor flesh wounds. Nothing serious," a paramedic reported. "We'll transport them. Your officers are welcome to ride along and start questioning them."

Cross and Borden locked eyes. Answers couldn't wait.

"Go with them," Cross told two officers.

As the paramedics tended to the suspects, Cross and Borden swept the house again. In the basement, they found crates of stolen guns and thousands of rounds of ammo, including weapons taken during the station robbery.

Most of the guns still had plastic ties around the triggers, rendering them useless.

Upstairs, Cross's eyes froze.

Two envelopes lay open. Each held over five grand in US cash, a flight itinerary, and a Mexican passport.

Cross intuitively knew each item was a piece of the puzzle. The mystery was coming into focus.

A brown UPS truck pulled up to the curb and stopped. Right on schedule.

Borden stepped outside.

"We're not ready. Come back in an hour," he said.

The detectives snapped photos of each package and address.

Borden dispatched teams to stake out the pickup, then tail the courier. Each address was logged.

Tension spiked.

A second team staked out the drop-off locations.

Back at HQ, word of the shooting spread. The squad buzzed with excitement.

Cross and Borden wasted no time, launching a relentless interrogation of all three men. Questions came fast. There was no time for lies.

The youngest suspect had no real information. He was new.

The focus turned to the wounded men.

Separated and shaken, each man fixated on his wounds. Dehydration rattled their thoughts. They began to crack. Names. Addresses. Gang affiliations.

One muttered about a campground up north.

"Some idiot called it a resort," the suspect grumbled.

Cross and Borden pushed harder. Their voices sharp. Eyes locked.

The suspect fidgeted, mumbling half-truths. His words became jumbled, tangled in contradictions.

But the break-in and the hint about a campground held their attention.

His eyes scurried left and right. He stuttered through answers, stumbling from one sentence into the next. He couldn't keep up.

"Where were the guns and ammunition taken?

Who orchestrated this?

How did you reach the campground?

Who drove the truck?

How many men were involved?

Where was the stolen property stored?

Still in the city?

What became of the drugs?

Do you wish to spend your life in prison?

Who took the money?

Who called the shots?

Who planned the break-in?

Where did you meet?

Who tipped you off about the campground?

Where's Juan Estrada?"

After forty-five minutes, they removed the cuffs and tossed him back in his cell to stew.

Cross watched from the viewing room behind the mirror.

When Borden entered, she asked, "How did your update go with the chief?"

"Absolutely no problem. He is solid in his support for what we're doing," Borden said.

Twenty minutes later, Detectives Gibson and Kim pulled the suspect out for round two.

Borden's gut told him they were close. Too close to stop now.

"We're close, Cross," Borden said. "No letting up now."

Cross didn't blink.

"I agree with you. We finish this. I owe it to my sister Karen to break these guys and demolish their drug empire. I'm sure you feel the same about ending this for Mark Junior as well?"

Borden didn't answer.

Chapter 37

After the initial interrogation, the two wounded suspects were returned to separate cells. The police had confiscated their passports, ensuring they weren't going anywhere.

Crown prosecutors had to decide whether to put them on trial or deport them to Mexico, where they might avoid custody.

Rick Crawford confirmed the passports were issued seven months earlier in Mexico City.

So, these three bewildered men, like the others, had likely been lured by promises of quick, easy money.

They had no known cartel background, which likely explained why they stayed silent during the break-in. Yet, they turned extremely violent the moment police confronted them.

The interrogations, while intense, yielded only low-level intel. The detectives debated continuing the questioning and decided to apply more pressure.

It worked. The suspects squirmed in their seats, desperate for escape. Their eyes darted between the detectives as they silently prayed for the questioning to stop.

It didn't take long to confirm that they had transferred most of the stolen property, including the jewelry from the smash-and-grab robberies to another vehicle after leaving the city.

The prisoners bellyached about not being invited to some campground. They were angry, clearly feeling rejected, even though they had five grand in their pockets.

The prosecutor told Cross they had offered a reduced sentence for names, but the men didn't really know each other or even who hired them.

Recently, Gibson discovered something useful during his tedious hours of video research.

In the video, one of the suspects had a wrist tattoo that became visible as he pointed out instructions to others.

Further research confirmed the tattoo as a gang initiation mark given to their leaders.

The internet revealed the gang's identity, and the suspect was confirmed through a posted graduation photo on a gang-affiliated website, which was not a smart thing to do.

The picture portrayed a cocky young man with attitude and disdain evident in his eyes for rules and authority. He wanted the world to know he was a tough guy, one to be feared, based on his pose showing off a weapon slung casually in one hand. He was now officially a person of interest.

His passport photo was a match. He was identified as Ramirez, who entered through Vancouver, where he caught a connecting flight to Toronto.

One of the suspects offered additional information when he saw the photo.

"I know that guy. I think he is staying at Sheraton Parkway Hotel in Markham. He's bad news. Nothing but trouble. Mean to the core of his being. I would be careful around him."

Cross immediately issued a BOLO for Ramirez as a person of interest in the break-in and robbery of Police HQ.

The second captive said he remembered seeing him in the van and stated that Ramirez was definitely involved in the station robbery.

The third man didn't really know his name. Didn't want to. He avoided him because he thought the guy was crazy and violent.

Crawford confirmed Ramirez had already booked his return flight to Mexico, where he would make a connection at LAX, then on to Mexico City.

Once again, Borden's group was on the move.

They were joined by the York Region Police, who surrounded the hotel and confirmed which car belonged to Ramirez.

It was immediately immobilized.

The front desk verified Ramirez would be checking out after lunch and had ordered room service.

The food order was delivered by a York Region detective who posed as hotel staff. Detectives flanked both sides of the hallway outside the door to Ramirez's room.

The detective knocked on the door and called, "Room service." One hand held the tray, just plate covers and cutlery. The other held his gun.

Nobody answered.

He knocked again and still nothing.

The detective set down the tray and used his passkey, calling out, "Room service." When the detectives slipped into the room, the sliding patio door was cracked open. Ramirez was gone. The room was empty.

A middle-aged man burst into the hotel lobby, panting and wild-eyed, his right arm flailing toward the ceiling.

"Help, I need help! Somebody, anybody, help!"

He stumbled mid-stride, crashing to the floor with a huge thud, then scrambled onto his knees. He was gasping for air like he couldn't breathe. A few drops of blood spotted the floor from where he cut his chin when he toppled to the floor running to get help.

Chapter 38

The hotel guest gasped, "Some little twerp had a gun, pointed it at me, screamed he'd kill me, and put the gun to my head and yanked me from my SUV. I tripped and fell.

He drove away in my brand-new Explorer! He headed north on Leslie Street in my SUV. Somebody, please call the police!"

The front desk clerk said in a calm voice, "Sir, the police are already here."

Amid the shouting, Detective Kim rushed into the lobby to assess the situation.

He radioed in the Explorer's description and sprinted to his car. Siren wailing, lights flashing, he sped off in pursuit.

In the distance, he saw the SUV veer east on Major Mackenzie Drive before accelerating onto the cloverleaf and merging north onto Highway 404. Other detectives joined from the southbound lanes as the suspect's SUV cut off and tore east along Elgin Mills.

The suspect weaved recklessly through traffic, endangering lives at every turn. He swerved past a transport truck, nearly skidding off the road at a dangerously high speed.

Reaching Highway 48, he blew past stopped cars, swerved into oncoming traffic, and fled north, accelerating.

As he neared Vivian Road, and without warning, he jerked the wheel right, sideswiping a car and sending it spinning into the ditch. He barreled toward Port Perry, no idea where he was headed or what he'd do next.

Detective Kim contacted Durham Police. They were ready to intercept and apprehend the suspect upon arrival at the edge of town.

Ignoring oncoming traffic, he continued to rip along Vivian Road, going airborne in some places. In the distance, he spotted a Durham Police barricade looming large in front of him.

Adrenaline surged through his veins as he foolishly stomped down on the gas pedal.

The SUV roared forward, tires shrieking against the asphalt, leaving a trail of smoke. It swerved violently as it lunged toward the police barricade. He tightened his grip, bracing himself for impact as he aimed for the center of the blockade, thinking it was the weakest point.

The SUV slammed into the first police car with a thunderous crunch, spinning it sideways before its momentum died.

The front tires exploded on impact with the spike strip, shredding the rubber. The once-powerful machine wobbled violently.

Metal screamed against metal at a deafening pitch as the SUV flipped into the air, somersaulting like a rag doll tossed in the wind.

Each roll felt endless. The world beyond the windshield was a dizzying blur of dirt, dust, and glass.

The vehicle slammed hard to a rocking halt in a wide ditch, debris and glass raining down like missiles. Officers dove for cover behind their cruisers, shielding their heads from the deadly shower. The air was thick with choking dust and smoke. Steam hissed as it hid the wreckage below.

Silence. The SUV lay on its side, two shredded tires spinning lazily, creaking like a dying beast. Dust hung in the air. For a moment, the world stood still, the aftermath of chaos settling in like a movie filmed in slow motion with no sound.

A faint click. The driver's door creaked open painfully slow. The door pointed skyward, pushed there by a blood-soaked hand. No one said a word.

Ramirez's hand latched onto the doorframe as he strained to maneuver his body free.

His breathing labored. He gasped as he twisted, choking on the dust and smoke.

With throbbing muscles, Ramirez leaned against the doorframe and gradually hauled his body out of the wreck.

Instinct screamed at him, run now, fast. His panicked mind raced instantaneously in search of another car, but that thought evaporated.

Four officers stood with their guns drawn, pointed directly at him. No one spoke. The officers stood waiting for him to drop down.

"Get down! You're under arrest!" one officer barked.

Exhausted, terrified, and overwhelmed, Ramirez complied and dropped to his knees.

The officer turned to a colleague, saying, "Read him his rights, cuff him, and lock him in the squad car. And get a tow truck for the Explorer."

Durham Police notified Detective Kim. Already in pursuit, he arrived two minutes after Ramirez's failed escape.

The commanding officer ordered Ramirez pulled from the squad car and handed over to Detective Kim.

Back in Toronto, Ramirez grew belligerent before deciding not to cooperate. Toronto Police Services had seen that act a thousand times before.

Borden entered the interview room, unamused that Ramirez had become speechless. He was done playing the nice guy.

When Ramirez heard Borden tell Cross to book a return flight to Mexico, he panicked thinking about what could happen at the airport. He was no longer feeling like the tough guy, knowing he would never leave the airport alive.

His future was likely winding up stuffed into a duffle bag and shoved inside a pay locker somewhere in the underbelly of the airport. He knew he wouldn't leave the airport alive. That's when the tough guy act evaporated.

He spoke English fluently and chose not to answer Borden's questions. He revealed nothing about the raid at the station. Ramirez claimed he knew nothing about weapons, or any shipments headed north to some place in Muskoka.

Borden stepped away and spoke quietly with Cross, asking her to assign someone to investigate resorts or campgrounds with foreign ownership. Too many people had mentioned a campground. He wanted to know if it was real.

Cross learned that Ramirez had been paid $5,000 and told to return to Mexico whenever he wanted.

In just a few more days, he would have vanished for good.

Cross told Borden, "When Ramirez was shown a photo, he identified Ambassador Martinez and Winthrop, the Canadian Minister of Foreign Affairs, in Mexico City. The third person in the photo he thought was an evil, sadistic senior Cartel boss. He wasn't certain of his name, thought it was Art or something like that."

Cross wasn't convinced. "I want another crack at him," she said. Borden agreed.

Cross entered the room. "You should know," she said in a calm voice, "you're a prime candidate for terrorism charges based on your activity during your brief time here."

"My office has already started the paperwork to charge you with terrorism and attempted murder."

The word "terrorism" rattled him. A chill crept down Ramirez's spine. Cross continued to explain, "That means you will spend the rest of your life lost in a Canadian prison somewhere."

That comment distressed him. Ramirez started to fidget, and beads of sweat formed on his forehead. His left hand showed a slight twitch.

Gibson stepped into the dim interrogation room, a thick folder under one arm. He didn't speak. Just slid the folder across the table toward Ramirez. The man's eyes flicked to it, then froze as Gibson flipped it open to reveal photos of Ramirez's wife and two small children.

They were candid, joyful shots, his daughter on a swing, his son blowing out candles.

Ramirez's breath caught. "How did they get those pictures?"

"They look happy," Gibson said quietly, his voice calm but edged with something darker. "Beautiful family. Shame if they never see you again."

Gibson sat silently, letting his comment sink in. "Maybe your wife will marry someone else."

Ramirez's gaze shot up, his fists clenched.

The door creaked. Borden stepped in, his presence like a dark cloud.

He didn't waste time with pleasantries. "Listen," he growled, leaning over the table, his voice low but dripping with menace. "The Cartel doesn't take kindly to loose ends. If you don't start answering our questions, they'll assume you've already spilled your guts. You know what happens then, right?"

Ramirez's lip trembled, but he said nothing, his eyes darting between the two detectives.

Borden straightened, turned toward the door, speaking like it was over. "Ship him back to Mexico if he clams up. And tell the reporter it's okay to run the news clip on him. And be sure CanWide News runs a close-up of his face. Let the reporter know Ramirez talked, gave us everything we needed."

He paused, casting a side glance at Ramirez. "And have the reporter thank Ramirez, on behalf of the Canadian authorities, for his assistance."

The color drained from Ramirez's face. It was over, and Ramirez knew it.

"You can't!" he choked out, his voice barely above a whisper.

Gibson leaned in, keeping his voice soft but pointed. "The Cartel's everywhere, Ramirez. They'll hear. They'll know.

You'll be dead within a week." He tapped the photo. "And they'll go after them next. You know how this works. Talk to us, and maybe, just maybe, we can keep them safe."

Ramirez swallowed hard.

His chest heaved as panic set in. The room felt like it was closing in on him.

"You think they won't find out anyway?" Borden's tone was dismissive. "You're already in deep, Ramirez." He nodded to the photos on the table.

Ramirez's hands trembled as he reached for the pictures, his voice cracking. "What do you want to know?"

Gibson exchanged a look with Borden. Now, the real interrogation could begin.

He claimed he didn't know anything, but Borden was willing to let him stew over his predicament.

Borden notified Crawford about the picture of the ambassador and the Minister of Foreign Affairs in Mexico. He wasn't at all surprised by the photo, as he had several in his dossier.

Crawford confirmed they were aware of his activities and monitoring the Minister, and that Agent Spade of CSIS had an undercover agent tracking Cartel activities in Mexico.

Chapter 39

A burner chirped softly, answered on the first ring by a low, emotionless voice.

"Where did you get this number?"

"The dark web. It said you offer guaranteed special services. I'm in need of such skills."

"In certain situations, discreet special opportunities may be arranged for a price. What's your problem?"

"A high-profile individual to retire permanently from a position of responsibility."

"People retire from positions of responsibility every day. That's not unusual.

Understand, once a contract is engaged, it cannot be stopped. There will be no further communication until the contract is completed.

If we agree, this number will vanish. The phone destroyed. There will be no way of contacting me again unless you follow the same steps that you took to get here. I'll study the retiree's habits. After the party, there will be no trace of anything. Nothing left behind, no one will ever link this contract back to you or me."

"I understand. But if someone were shot, could a bullet be traced?"

"No. I make my own. It can't be traced."

"You certain this is what you really want?"

"Yes. An accident is preferred, but murder is acceptable if there is no alternative."

"My terms are simple. Payment in full before I proceed."

"What's the retiree's name, when's the retirement party?"

"Can the timing of the party be altered?"

"Yes."

"Will there be guests? Security?"

"Yes, security is twenty-four-seven. Will the security be at the home of the retiree?"

"Most likely. The target will be home, with his butler and one maid. Both off duty by six."

"When exactly do they leave?"

"At six."

"There's an additional fee for security complications or unexpected collateral damage," the assassin said.

"That's not a problem."

"Is the target high profile and likely to draw media attention?"

"Absolutely."

"Is this a rush surprise party?"

"As soon as you're ready."

"Planning the retirement party may take several days to get everything needed in place for the get-together."

"Understood."

"Is this to be a public or private retirement party?"

"Private is best."

"Understood. But you're not opposed to a public retirement?"

"No, not really, but as I said, private is preferred."

"With high profile and tight security, the cost of this retirement package is three hundred thousand, plus one hundred thousand for rush execution. Wire half the money within fifteen minutes to show you're serious. The remaining half should be paid within three hours. Stay on the line to confirm transfer and answer a few last questions."

"Why three hours?"

"That's when I'll be back from dinner."

The line remained open. Six minutes later, a voice returned. "The full amount's been transferred, plus a bonus of one hundred thousand if you can arrange the surprise party quickly or almost immediately."

They exchanged details about the retiree's fortress-like home and its tight security.

The caller weakly expressed a preference for avoiding collateral damage but left the decision to the assassin's situation and discretion.

"The environment will dictate the timing," the assassin said. "I remind you, no trace of my existence will be left behind, understood?"

"Understood," said the caller.

The location and schedule of the target were forwarded. Proof of completion was deemed unnecessary.

A contract was set.

The retirement party would be featured on CanWide News, a public sign the contract was completed.

The burner phone was destroyed, and a new number was placed on the dark web for future business.

The assassin spread a map of downtown Toronto across his desk, meticulously plotting three alternate escape routes to vanish without a trace. No rehearsal was needed. He had everything on hand he required and understood the plan by heart.

But a drive-by to time everything was essential.

The party was scheduled for the following evening or shortly thereafter. That would allow for recon tonight and tomorrow.

He selected his favorite untraceable Glock 9mm, loading custom-made rounds from a hidden cache of weapons behind a heavily reinforced wall.

He never entered the address into the car's GPS. Instead, a handheld device displayed a large, back-lit map of Toronto, the target area clearly marked.

The assassin knew the streets well and how to avoid any digital traces of his presence.

He cruised the neighborhood, noting trash schedules, mail routes, gardeners, video cameras, delivery habits, parked cars, gridlock, pedestrians, dog walkers, parks, and construction zones.

He logged every detail: public transit, community speed limits, red light video cameras at intersections, community speed control cameras near schools.

He counted stop signs, mapped dead-end streets, observed parking options. The escape routes were analyzed for bottlenecks and choke points, timed meticulously to vanish clean into the night.

The recon provided valuable intelligence, reinforcing his expectations. Everything was falling into place.

He examined photos of neighboring houses, finding no external cameras. Only one post had a camera aimed toward the target's property, which he correctly assumed was government surveillance. Most driveways were secured with closed wrought iron gates.

A business acquaintance and specialized hacker supplied an app to override the target's mansion security system and control the government surveillance camera. It was loaded onto the assassin's smartphone and worked flawlessly.

He observed the butler and maid leave at 6:05 PM. The quietest time in the neighborhood was determined to be 9:40 PM.

A final drive-by confirmed which residents parked on the street, in driveways, or inside garages. Nothing was left to chance.

He noted a security detail parked near the lower third of the driveway and the frequency, direction, and time taken during his walkabout. The target's limousine sat closer to the house than usual.

In mere minutes, a retirement party would begin, and one that people in the neighborhood would talk about for years.

Chapter 40

The soft clink of coffee mugs and idle chatter faded as Borden entered, his heavy footsteps a prelude to the anxiety that challenged the group.

The team sat in his family room, their faces reflecting a quiet determination and fatigue.

Borden remained standing.

He paced the room, then took his place at the head of the table, his expression grim.

Borden scanned the room, making eye contact with each of them. A silent acknowledgment of the storm ahead.

"We've learned more from our interrogations," he said, his voice cutting through the stillness. "I've heard the Cartel is pushing harder than we expected. While my next comment hasn't been confirmed yet, we're thinking this isn't just about drugs. It might be about political control."

The unspoken truth settled in. The threat was bigger than anyone had anticipated. Even the most seasoned officers felt a chill.

The drug trade threatened to dominate a larger part of their caseload, a reality that none of them found acceptable, especially Borden and Cross, who were both still carrying personal losses to drug trafficking.

"This can't be allowed to happen," Borden continued, reaching for his coffee. "We need to act, and we need to act fast."

Rick Crawford leaned forward, his jaw set with resolve.

"We need more manpower. More help from local law enforcement. The Cartel's going to escalate, become more violent, unless we confront them now and end this. I can arrange for the RCMP to switch out the ambassador's security detail or slide in one of our own onto his protection team. I have someone in mind who is young with an extensive background handling personal security."

Danielle Spade nodded. "Operation Shadow must be airtight. We'll need someone undercover, tracking Martinez and other officials with Mexican ties in Ottawa."

The group nodded in grim agreement.

They knew the risks and understood the importance of keeping their operation concealed. Caroline was tapped again to coordinate comms, track feedback, and generate exclusive reports. She was more than ready to do whatever was asked of her.

Crawford took the front of the room, clicking through a series of grainy photos that filled the screen. The team leaned in, their eyes narrowing as the images sharpened.

Sleek, cylindrical cameras were tucked discreetly into the stone bed lining between the railway tracks.

"These," Crawford began, twisting toward the screen, "are high-res cameras concealed in custom metal casings.

They're equipped with pressure sensors and motorized covers. When a train hits a sensor about one hundred yards out from the camera, the protective cover slides back and these action cameras start recording."

He flipped to the next image, showing a train's under-carriage caught in crystal-clear detail. "The live feed and video go straight to us via satellite."

The group shifted in their creaking seats. The team murmured as the implications sank in.

"If a drop box is in play, we flag it and send the train's route to local law enforcement." His voice carried a sharp edge of confidence.

"CSIS is stepping up too. They've got satellites tracking heat signatures from the drug pickups. Couriers can run, but they won't get far."

He turned back to the team, letting the weight of the new plan stew. "We'll not only catch them, but we'll be able to trace the entire distribution network and shut it down at the source. That is assuming they use this method for transporting drugs across the border," Craw-ford said.

The group murmured with excitement, exchanging glances. Crawford's plan had impressed everyone.

They broke for a quick coffee break, their minds racing with the possibilities of what this technology could do to help them. After their break, a brief discussion followed, then everyone departed.

An hour later, back at HQ, Borden called an impromptu meeting with Cross, Gibson, and Kim. The urgency was evident on all their faces.

"We need to locate these drug distribution facilities fast," Borden said.

"We need someone to go undercover using our informant list to pinpoint their operations. We've got some leads, but we believe there are more distribution centers out there. We need to find and shut them," said Borden.

Cross and Gibson immediately volunteered, but Detective Kim interjected. "I think I'm the best choice. I wasn't seen at the warehouse raid, and I have a solid network of informants on the street."

Everyone sitting around the desk knew Kim was right. He was well-connected, and he might be their best hope.

Kim hit the streets, connecting with his informers, buying drugs to keep up his cover while checking with old contacts and street friends.

The buys paid off.

Using petty cash, Kim made several buys, gleaning more about packaging, drop locations, and local distribution networks than he had anticipated.

His sources provided him with insight into types of drugs and quantities, revealing key parts of the Cartel's urban setup.

Kim returned to HQ, his pockets lighter but his mind loaded with valuable intel.

"We've got leads on key locations," he reported. "But as usual, these distributors and pushers change locations often. I need to get back out there, lock in addresses, and nail down specifics before we make a move," Kim said.

Chapter 41

Detective Kim's heart pounded as he ducked behind a row of parked cars, his eyes locked on his informant, Joe, who was deep in a hushed conversation with a known drug runner he called Marco, not likely his real name.

Kim quietly snapped photos and recorded video, hoping to pick up audio.

The sun had just slipped below the horizon, casting long evening shadows that provided perfect cover for Kim. Tonight, he would follow Marco to the source of the drugs he sold Joe. His gut told him this was a terrific opportunity.

Joe nodded, signaling Kim the deal was done. As Marco turned to leave, Joe casually slipped away, heading in Kim's direction. Kim caught up with him a few blocks away and slid two hundred dollars into Joe's hand.

"Nice work, Joe," Kim said, watching as his favorite informant melted into the night. A small smile played on Kim's lips as he mouthed thank you, friend.

Kim's phone vibrated with a message from Borden: "Keep me updated." He quickly typed back a response and sent the photos and video taken earlier. He pocketed his phone and resumed his pursuit. Marco was cautious, and Kim needed to stay sharp.

For the next thirty minutes, Detective Kim trailed Marco through a maze of side streets in East York, his senses on high alert.

Marco stopped occasionally, checking his rearview mirror to see if he was tailed, but Kim was experienced and stayed undetected. The thrill of the chase pumped adrenaline through his veins, each step bringing him closer to what he thought might be the heart of the cartel operation in Toronto.

Marco finally pulled up to a modest bungalow in lower East York near Woodbine Avenue. Kim noted the address, parked, and observed from a distance. He forwarded a photo of the house and the address back to Borden.

The house was nondescript, blending effortlessly into the neighborhood. But Kim knew better. He was sure it was a front, a crucial decoy in the drug distribution network.

Kim watched Marco interact with a few individuals, exchanging packages and envelopes. The flow of narcotics through this single house appeared to be staggering. Kim pulled out his phone, capturing more photos and jotting down notes. He knew the department team needed evidence, and every detail counted.

Kim saw Marco prepare to leave. His mind raced, knowing he had to follow him to acquire more actual evidence. He tailed him to the next location but knew it was crucial that he did so without getting spotted. He hung back and waited until Marco had driven off before following in his unremarkable squad car.

Kim stayed several car lengths behind.

The pursuit led Kim north to an industrial area on the outskirts of Markham. Marco parked outside a large warehouse and entered through what appeared to be an unlocked side door. Kim parked a safe distance away and watched the building, wondering why the door was unlocked.

A chain-link fence topped with barbed wire surrounded the warehouse. It screamed stay out, but Kim wasn't going to back down just yet.

Undeterred, he waited until total darkness before making his move. Marco never left, or if he did, Kim didn't see him.

Time ticked by slowly, the darkness amplifying every sound. Finally, as the area fell silent, Kim approached the warehouse, careful to stay in the shadows.

He scouted the perimeter, found a broken section of the fence, and slipped through. Staying in the shadows, he made his way to the side door.

He cracked the door enough to peek inside. The warehouse was a hive of activity. No one paid any attention to the side door area. Workers moved with precision, packing drugs into wooden crates and loading them onto pallets. The scale of the operation was immense. Kim carefully moved through the stacks of crates, capturing photos and recording conversations with his video camera.

As he moved deeper into the warehouse, Kim stumbled upon a small office. Inside, a man was talking on the phone, his voice low but urgent. Kim strained to hear, catching snippets of the conversation.

"Yes, everything will arrive as scheduled. No, we haven't had any issues with the police or anyone else. The next batch will be ready by tomorrow night."

Kim's heart pounded. This was it, the intel he needed. The moment the man left the office and rejoined his co-workers, Kim slipped inside, snapped a few photos of the documents scattered on the desk, and ducked back out without anyone spotting him.

Kim quickly made his way back to the car, snapping photos of license tags in the parking lot. He had enough to blow this case wide open, but before he notified HQ, he needed to quietly slip away.

As he started his drive back to Police HQ, Kim's phone vibrated.

"Kim, did you find anything?" Borden asked.

"Boss, you won't believe this. I tailed Marco to a large warehouse. It's a massive distribution hub. They're moving a huge quantity of product. I've got photos, recordings, and shots of some documents on a desk. I haven't checked them yet, but they should be in your inbox. Oh, I also sent photos of cars and trucks in their parking lot. Thought we should track the owners."

"Great work, Kim. Get back here safe. We need to analyze everything you've got," Borden said.

Kim ended the call, his mind still spinning from the night's events. At Police HQ, he was greeted by Borden, Cross, and Gibson. The group was bursting with excitement in anticipation as Kim laid out his findings.

"We've got addresses, photos, recordings, the works. This is the mother lode. It's the breakthrough we've been waiting for," Kim said, spreading the evidence across the table.

Borden nodded, his face a mix of relief and determination. "This is it. I will notify the chief. Cross, Gibson, get those warrants ready. Kim, get some rest. You've earned it," stated Borden.

As the team dispersed to prepare for the next steps, Kim headed straight for home. He couldn't help but feel the adrenaline rush from his discovery.

Sleep would not come easy for him, not tonight anyway.

He parked in his usual spot just after nine. The street was quiet. A breeze moved the trees. He locked his car, tucked the evidence folder under one arm, crunching a piece of paper sticking out from the folder. He ignored it and headed toward the entrance of his building.

He paused for a second before inserting his key. Something was off. Not enough to trigger an alarm, but just enough to make him glance over his shoulder.

Nothing.

He pushed open the door and stepped inside.

The lobby was modern in style, well-lit, and exceptionally clean. There was a bit of a shadow caused by one of the overhead lights that had blown again. Kim was annoyed that both elevators were out of service. Repairs, he thought. He turned and walked toward the stairwell.

As he hit the second flight, the stairwell door opened in front of him.

He heard it too late.

A figure came out the door and lunged into him from the landing, slamming into Kim with full force, knocking him off balance.

Kim staggered back. The folder slipped from his arm. He tried to brace himself but failed. When a second man appeared, he knew this was no accidental mishap. The second attacker came from below, driving a shoulder into his ribs. Kim fought to stay on his feet.

A punch caught him under the chin. Another snapped his head sideways.

He lashed out, caught one man in the thigh, but it wasn't enough. He felt a searing pain as a heavy object cracked into the side of his skull. For a moment he couldn't see anything.

Kim crashed to the floor, his knees buckling as the stairwell spun, making him feel nauseous as his vision blurred.

He collapsed onto the landing, gasping. One boot pressed against his chest.

A voice muttered, low and certain. "Message delivered."

A second figure stepped in and checked his pulse.

"I think you killed him. I can't feel a pulse. We'd better get out of here."

They bolted the stairs, balancing their downward momentum with a tight grip on the handrail.

Kim lay motionless, eyes flickering and opened just once more before his world slipped to darkness.

Jordan Jones, the night janitor, was pushing his mop bucket toward the stairs. He enjoyed the late shift because it was always quiet, and no one was around to bother him. That usually allowed him to finish early and go home.

Just then, as he looked over in the direction of the stairwell, two men burst through the door, slamming it hard against the concrete wall. The metal door created a loud, jarring crash as the pair darted toward a car parked nearby. They jumped in and sped up the ramp into the night.

Jordan just shook his head at the lack of respect for private property and thought he should check the door when he got there. So he carried on with his work as he hummed his favorite church hymn.

Partway down the corridor, he noticed some keys sprawled on the floor and leaned over to gather them. As he straightened, he saw a blood smear on the floor which trickled from the head of a tenant he recognized. Detective Kim's body lay face down, motionless. The janitor reached for Kim's walkie and radioed security to call for the paramedics and the police.

He stooped down, careful not to touch anything, and began to pray for Detective Kim.

Chapter 42

The outdated overhead speaker crackled to life, its voice sterile but insistent.

"Code White. Trauma Unit. Dr. Clark, urgent. Dr. Clark, Emergency Trauma Unit."

The words bounced off the tiled walls. A metal tray clattered to the floor as a young Dr. Clark bumped the edge of the gurney, already running toward the trauma bay.

Kim didn't move. An IV fed him fluids. His motionless body was tethered to various monitors. The heart monitor beeped a slow, steady rhythm. His eye was swollen shut. Skull and ribs were heavily bandaged. His face was beginning to show obvious bruising.

Detective Cross stood outside the trauma bay, arms folded, eyes fixed on the floor, her jaw clenched tight.

She could hear the annoying hum of the fluorescent lights. Behind the curtain, Detective Kim fought to breathe. His chest rose unevenly under layers of gauze, wires, and a thin blanket. The constant beeping from the monitor was a grim reminder of the risks police officers face every day. Now one of her own was in a fight to stay alive.

Beside her, Borden stood silent, haunted by his own terrible memory of being shot on duty as a young constable. His phone vibrated, unanswered, in his pocket.

"He went out there alone," Cross said. "That's on me."

"No," Borden said quietly. "That's on whoever set him up."

"But I knew he was excited, proud of the intel he'd pulled in for us."

A nurse pushed past but paused just long enough to say, "He's stable. But the next twelve hours are always critical. He's lucky to be alive."

"Thank you," Cross said.

"Borden, someone hit him with a pipe, cracked two ribs and gave him a concussion. They dropped the weapon and ran. It rolled about four feet from where Kim was found. The forensic team has checked for prints on the pipe, the door, and the railing leading from the first floor. I'm amazed he's alive. The evidence shows he didn't have a chance to defend himself. There's video at the door and in the garage. We'll have answers soon."

"I'll need to pull his phone records and retrace his steps to piece everything together," Cross said.

Just then, a doctor pulled back the curtain and stepped out.

"He's conscious," he said. "If you want to speak to him, now's your chance. He's not critical at the moment. While his vitals are stable, he needs plenty of rest. Don't stay long."

Cross and Borden stepped to the side of the bed. Kim's face was pale, swollen, and bruised. His eye was swollen shut.

Cross leaned in. "Kim... do you know who did this?"

In a soft whisper, "They knew... I was coming home. Power off... stairs..."

He drifted off before either of them could respond.

Cross's phone vibrated. She stepped aside, answered quietly, then nodded. "Okay, got it."

"Borden, Kim didn't use his phone after our meeting broke up and he headed home for the night. There was a call on his phone, but that was from the janitor who called 911."

The paramedic confirmed that Kim had been found unconscious in a stairwell below the first floor. His badge was clipped to his belt, his gun missing. His shirt was soaked in blood. He had been struck with a glancing blow to the side of his head with a lead pipe and sustained multiple blows to his core and back. Kim had two cracked ribs.

The paramedic added, "He was fortunate to be alive, barely hanging on given the blood he lost. Our initial impression was he was gone, when we first arrived and saw him."

Outside the trauma unit, the stairwell door slammed open. Detective Friedman stormed down the hall, tie askew, badge clipped to his belt, eyes narrowed, lips pursed with rage boiling just beneath the surface.

"Why didn't anyone notify me?" he barked, eyes locked on Borden.

"You were in North York," Borden said calmly. "We just got the call less than thirty minutes ago."

Friedman yanked the curtain aside. One look at Kim's battered face stopped him cold. He stepped back, jaw twitching.

"They came after him?" he said. "Seriously? After what he just gave us?"

Cross nodded. "Looks like they knew where he was going. Someone might've tipped them off."

"You think we've got a leak?" Friedman asked, voice sharp.

"We're not ruling anything out," Borden said. "But whoever did this had to know he was a cop. And they wanted him quiet, or dead."

Friedman clenched his fists and turned to Cross.

"Boss, I want in," he said.

Chapter 43

Carl Burke thrived in the shadows, where danger lingered and secrets often came to light. In just eight years with the RCMP, he had built a successful career record most agents only dreamed about, always one step ahead of his targets.

His knack for slipping in and out of criminal networks unnoticed made him one of the country's top undercover operatives.

Yet even for him, there was always the feeling that something darker loomed ahead, the ultimate challenge that would push him to the brink. Burke never allowed himself to dwell on negative thoughts. He always stayed focused on positive outcomes.

Today felt different. As he walked through the familiar halls of HQ, he wondered why Borden had requested a meeting with him.

His gut told him this wasn't just another meeting. Whispers in the ranks had him on edge. Something different was coming. Colleagues said they heard this assignment had the potential to trigger an international political incident. But for now, those were just rumors, and Burke ignored gossip.

Borden and Cross were waiting in a private room, their faces shadowed by the low light. They drank tea and coffee while they discussed how Burke would be the perfect operative for this covert assignment.

Burke's pulse quickened as he approached the door and entered the meeting room. He knew it was the excitement and danger that he lived for, that thin line between hunter and prey. He had been warned, although nobody knew for sure.

So, an invitation to join a clandestine operation would come as no surprise.

Burke's heart raced with anticipation because he loved the thrill of working undercover, and perhaps this operation might be particularly challenging.

As he approached the table, Borden looked up and smiled. "Carl, thanks for coming in. We have a delicate situation and need your expertise."

Cross handed Burke a file. "If you agree, you'll be keeping tabs on the Mexican Ambassador, Carlos Martinez. We believe he is actively involved in running drugs from Mexico to Canada. Obviously, this needs to be discreet. He must not know he's being watched. He has a security detail assigned to him twenty-four seven."

"An ambassador. I've had a few of those before. They all love using their immunity. No problem," Burke said.

Closing the file, he tossed it on the table. "I've dealt with enough dignitaries. I know how they think and how they feel superior to everyone around them. I'll soon discover exactly what he's up to. What's the context?"

Borden leaned in, lowering his voice. "We believe Martinez could be engaged in some drug smuggling activities with a Mexican cartel and a federal MP.

We need to gather convincing intel without tipping either of them off. We need to know who he is meeting, where he goes, and generally what he is up to.

He will be surrounded by his security detail, so you may need to operate from a distance. Can you manage that? His security rotates throughout the day, so he normally has one bodyguard with him at all times, and there is one or two stationed outside his home each night. Ambassadors have immunity, and while we believe he is a criminal, we can't do anything about it.

But there may be someone or several other associates of his that we could shut down, thereby destroying his side-hustle."

Burke's eyes twinkled with excitement. "Let me at him. I'll get started right away."

Shadowing Martinez came naturally to Burke. He could dissolve into the background and turn invisible at will. He was always aware when to be seen and, more importantly, when not to be seen or when it was time to vanish.

His first order of business was to secure a detailed background on the ambassador and his security. Using his extensive network of contacts, he started documenting information on Martinez's associates, cronies, golfing friends, and enemies. He knew people in positions of power like the ambassador always had enemies.

He aspired to know everything about the man. Where he lived, worked, and played, as well as his weaknesses and any trouble that might follow him. Burke pondered the ambassador's playboy image, knowing it was a weakness and a perfect opportunity that could be exploited.

Carl Burke spent hours diving deep into government databases, obtaining the ambassador's calendar, airline travel plans, hotel reservations, as well as searching for anomalies. His persistence paid off when a vibration from his phone signaled a call from one of his contacts.

"Got something for you," the voice on the other end said. "Martinez has regular meetings at a private bar downtown called The Deal Maker. It's located in the King Eddy mezzanine level, and the meetings never show up on his official schedule."

Burke's heart quickened. "Thanks. Keep digging."

Now, his search narrowed, Burke focused on the ambassador's free time and off-book activities.

He scrutinized every detail, looking for that weak link in the chain. And then he found it. A recurring name in Martinez's off-hours activities, one that didn't fit the usual pattern.

That evening, Burke staked out an exclusive hotspot where Martinez was set to rendezvous with a contact around nine thirty PM. The area was upscale, filled with high-end cars and well-dressed patrons. Burke blended in seamlessly, his attire and demeanor matched the surroundings.

He watched as Martinez greeted the doorman with his usual warm smile, pleasantries, and a generous tip. Burke noted the ambassador's relaxed demeanor. It was a stark contrast to his public persona. If Martinez was here to unwind, that made him vulnerable.

As the night wore on, Burke's patience paid off. Martinez slipped out of the main lounge, moving toward a private room. Burke followed at a discreet distance, his every sense on high alert.

Burke waited, but no one answered his gentle knock on the adjacent door. Using his discreet pouch of tools, he slipped inside and used a small listening device to capture the conversation.

Voices murmured through the device, and one name stood out, one Burke recognized from his research. In the room with Martinez was the Minister of Foreign Affairs, Jonathan Winthrop. Winthrop mentioned an imminent shipment.

Burke's pulse quickened as he grasped the significance. He carefully shut down his recording device and slipped away unnoticed.

The next day, Burke met with a tech-savvy colleague and friend to help him analyze the recording. For several hours, they analyzed the recording, not just for what was there, but for what was missing. It was this meticulous approach that led them to a startling discovery.

"Can you explain a gap in Martinez's travel records, one that just happens to coincide with a mysterious shipment?" his friend said.

"Somehow I need to find out what he's transporting and who's involved," commented Burke.

His associate nodded. "We need more. I can dig deeper if you bring me more data or recordings."

Burke maintained his surveillance, piecing together Martinez's web of deceit as he monitored him relentlessly.

The ambassador's activities revealed a complex network of transactions and meetings, each one adding to the growing dossier of evidence. But none of it was enough.

Burke shadowed Martinez, who at times chose to travel without his security detail, to a secluded warehouse on the outskirts of the city. The secluded location was a perfect place for clandestine operations.

Burke's heart raced as he watched Martinez meet with a group of men, all talking simultaneously, their conversation appearing intense. Raising his arms, Martinez tried to calm the agitation.

Burke crept closer, slipping into the shadows beside a black truck, his presence swallowed by the cover of darkness. Burke bent down and crawled under the truck and moved quiet as a mouse toward the front wheel, which provided cover and brought him closer to the conversation.

He caught snippets of their discussion. Someone mentioned the arrival of a special shipment, some mundane security details, and some coded references to drugs. This was it. Burke's camera clicked silently, capturing every detail, including video.

Back at Police HQ, Burke stood in the briefing room. The hum of computers and distant office talk faded as he presented his report to Borden and Crawford.

Borden leaned over the table, his eyes focused on the mounting evidence. Silence lingered for a moment before he spoke, his voice low but filled with intensity.

"This is bigger than I thought," Borden muttered, the weight of the revelation sinking in. "Martinez isn't just a player. He's pulling strings at levels I didn't realize."

Crawford's jaw clenched, his usual calm replaced with urgency. "We need to move. Stay close to him and live in the shadows."

Burke's heart raced as he explained various shreds of evidence pointing directly to Martinez. But the question remained. What to do, knowing Martinez has total immunity.

Chapter 44

Each morning, Friedman visited with his partner, Detective Kim, before heading to work. He gauged Kim's mood and raised the subject of the attack only if Kim wanted to discuss what happened. He encouraged his partner, often updating him about the ongoing investigation into the attack.

"The janitor who found you saw the two guys who assaulted you and identified their mugshots in our system," Friedman said. "They're from the Ottawa area and have extensive rap sheets. I can't wait to get my hands on them."

"How is your new partner working out?" Kim asked.

"He's great. Detective Porter is on loan to us until you're back on your feet, then he'll return to the Specialized Criminal Investigations Unit. He's an excellent choice. I'm sure you remember him since he has worked with us before."

"I do remember him."

"He's experienced and smart and wants these two guys behind bars like the rest of us. We put the word out on the street and issued another BOLO. It won't take long. I'm sure someone will contact us with a lead.

"How are the headaches?"

"Not as intense as yesterday, but my movements are restricted by the bandage around my rib cage."

"Good. They'll heal faster that way. Don't try to get back to work anytime soon. Best-case scenario is you'll eventually return to half days for a while, but not active duty until you are ready.

"In the meantime, Porter and I have work to do. You might be interested to know that both the Chief and Borden ordered us to find these guys and make the arrest. They've expanded our departmental access, so we have all the help we'll need.

"I should head to the office. Get some rest and I'll contact you later."

"You know where to find me."

"I do!" Friedman said as he left.

Detective Borden stared out his office window, surveying the squad room as his eyes moved back and forth.

He watched the detectives, each moving with purpose. Concern for their safety was a heavy burden. Borden turned and spotted Detective Porter hunched over Kim's desk, photos spread before him.

Porter looked up, made eye contact with Borden, and nodded. His photos and recordings revealed clear patterns. Unsuspecting couriers were unwittingly leading the team right to individual supply houses, which the team suspected to be central repackaging facilities.

Borden smiled and gave a small nod of approval, a spark of excitement evident in his eyes. Fifteen minutes later, Porter and Friedman hit the streets again, gathering additional drug samples from sellers and informants.

The goal was simple: raid every facility they could identify in the city simultaneously.

After Porter and Friedman left on assignment, Borden turned to Cross and Gibson. "Prepare the warrants for the addresses we have," he ordered.

This operation was gearing up to hit all locations at a moment's notice.

Cross contacted the legal department, her voice firm and decisive. Gibson typed rapidly, pulling up the necessary forms and data for the warrants.

Hours later, Porter and Friedman returned, their faces flushed with excitement over their latest discovery. They had spent much of the day navigating Toronto's underbelly, connecting with informants, following leads, and acquiring narcotics from various sellers. Their work had paid off. They had discovered additional suspected sites.

Porter spread out the latest photos of each location. "These are the recent sites we've confirmed," he told Borden.

"Each one matches the profile of a supply depot or possibly a repackaging facility," Friedman said.

Borden studied the photos, noting the steady movement of traffic in and out of each house. "Good work. This is coming together. We need more eyes on these locations. Cross, assign more detectives to stake out these places."

Cross nodded and made the call to assign additional personnel.

Borden's mind raced with possibilities, knowing each newly discovered facility brought them closer to their goal of shutting these operations down.

The facial recognition software processed the images and generated profiles which flashed onto the screen.

Each identified individual was cross-referenced with the department's criminal database. The search revealed a network of players deeply embedded in the underworld and linked to Cartel operations.

"We've got names," Borden said, a hint of achievement in his voice. "Friedman, run background checks on each one. Let's find out everything we can about them.

"Good work, everyone."

The detectives compiled profiles, pinpointing key players within the Cartel's distribution network. The pattern of activity sharpened with each new piece of information. Borden felt the parts falling into place. But with all his experience, he knew the prosecutors would need more evidence before they could secure a conviction.

Undercover detectives documented everyone who visited the houses, snapping photos of couriers, suspected buyers and sellers, and recording timestamps. The data revealed a steady flow of packages leaving each house by UPS, FedEx, and Purolator, further evidence of a well-organized operation.

Borden oversaw his team as they meticulously logged every detail. The sense of urgency grew with each discovery. The Cartel's trafficking network was more extensive than they had initially believed.

Energized from his meeting, Borden left after updating the Chief on his investigation. Both men agreed the time to dismantle Toronto's criminal networks had finally arrived.

With the necessary warrants secured, detectives embedded themselves in courier trucks, tracking the destinations of packages collected from the houses.

Courier drivers were interviewed, then temporarily replaced by undercover officers who completed the deliveries. Hidden cameras captured each transaction, received and signed for at the door. The evidence continued to mount, each piece building toward a future coordinated take-down.

Borden's phone vibrated, an update from Special Agent Burke. He confirmed the Ambassador, Martinez, was deeply involved in the operation. Burke's investigation had uncovered shipment schedules, payment transfers, and links to high-ranking contacts within the Cartel.

Burke's message was direct. "Martinez is a key player. I don't see how you'll be able to move on him, given his diplomatic immunity. Not sure about Winthrop. The two of them meet frequently."

Borden relayed the information to his team. "Burke's got more on Martinez. He is connecting the dots for us. We're so close, so we need to stay focused."

Caroline's memo provided additional context, outlining the progress of the investigation and the raid on Police

HQ. She included an update on the healing progress of Detective Kim, who was now up and walking in his neighborhood and feeling stronger by the day. Her updates provided encouragement for the tight team and ensured nothing was overlooked.

At the weekly meeting with the Chief, Borden laid out their findings. The Chief listened intently, excited by the progress.

His experience told him this was dangerously close to the end, and he couldn't afford any blowback from politicians or the public. He looked directly at Borden and said, "We have some evidence, but we'll need this to be airtight. I trust your judgment on this. I want you to keep me updated on every move."

As the team finalized their tactics, the sense of expectancy grew. They understood the risks but were certain they were ready. The moment of action was near. Then, at the last minute, Borden made a change.

Borden's team would hit one Cartel location, and the other teams stood down to observe their targets to monitor the effects of one site being destroyed.

If the Cartel attempted to move a large quantity of drugs or showed signs of panic, the other teams would move in quickly.

If the Cartel believed they had only lost one house, they might dismiss it as an anomaly and continue operations, possibly even setting up a new location.

If they attempted a massive drug transfer or their activity increased, the other teams would strike fast and hard.

The convoy of police vehicles cut through the darkened streets, headlights off, engines low, like wild wolves closing in on their prey.

They reached their target location and waited for further instructions.

The night was deceptively calm, masking the storm that was about to break. Borden's team was in position, their movements synchronized and precise. As the clock ticked down, he took a deep, steady breath, his mind focused on the task.

His hand hovered above the radio for a brief moment before he issued the go command.

"This is it," he murmured, his voice steady. "Let's move."

At Borden's command, they cut Internet and power.

The team surged forward, battering the door open with a ram, then stormed through the building with swift, calculated precision. Men scrambled for their weapons and froze mid-stride when they saw assault rifles pointed directly at them.

Little shouting, but no hesitation to comply. Just the sharp, controlled chaos of professionals dismantling a criminal stronghold piece by piece.

Each room was swept clean, every corner cleared with methodical ease in seconds. The suspects, one by one, were pulled from the house, placed in handcuffs, and escorted into the waiting police vans.

It almost felt too effortless.

Chapter 45

Ramirez was in trouble, and he longed for his freedom more than anything. Walking away from money his family depended on felt like a small price to pay.

Maybe he could strike a deal. If he told the police everything, they might change his identity and relocate him and his family.

He was terrified and confessed everything he knew and had overheard to the police.

He wanted his freedom, but the Cartel was never forgiving. Word got out quickly. Ramirez had betrayed them. He was a dead man, and no amount of protection could save him.

When Tina learned what had transpired during the jail interrogation, she was furious that Ramirez had mentioned the campground to the police.

She knew this needed to be handled quickly.

Tina had Sean set up a bar fight in downtown Toronto, ensuring Samson was arrested and held overnight for a hearing in the morning.

Ramirez believed that by tomorrow afternoon, he would be a free man, untouchable and invisible.

Samson recognized Ramirez, but to Ramirez, Samson was just another stranger. While sitting in lockup, the two bonded over their mutual hatred of the police and the unfair justice system.

Samson whispered, "I'm really worried, man."

"About what?" Ramirez replied.

"They're interrogating me first thing tomorrow morning."

"You too," Ramirez said.

"I was told it's a brutal experience. I'm scared," said Samson.

"Oh, no need to worry. The interrogation was easy. Just tell them whatever they want to know, and you'll be set free right away."

"No... really?"

"Yeah, I'm getting out tomorrow afternoon."

"How's that?"

"If you don't know the answer, make stuff up. Lie to them."

"I'm scared to do that. They'll keep me here."

"I told you, no need to be scared. They asked me about a campground up north."

"What did you tell them?"

"I said, yeah, there's a campground up north. But I'm not sure where. Some of my friends went there for more training after we broke into the police headquarters."

"You broke into a police station?" asked Samson.

"Yeah, me and some other guys," Ramirez said.

"They kept pressing me for more information on the campground, and I told them everything I knew. After that, I just made stuff up. You know what I mean?"

"Wow, you actually lied to the police. That's so cool, man."

"Yeah, they're so dumb, and I get to go home tomorrow," Ramirez said.

"Good for you."

The guard entered the cell area and called, "Samson."

"Well, here we go. See you around," Samson replied.

"Okay, friend, see yeah," Ramirez answered.

After the interview, Samson received a visit from an old friend. He was bailed out, and he and Sean left the local jail. Sean connected the speakerphone, allowing Samson to speak directly to Tina.

"Did you find out what he told the police?" Tina asked.

"Yes, he confessed and told them everything about the break-in, including details about the campground. Ramirez revealed everything, including his role in the police station break-in."

"Are you sure about that?" Tina asked.

"Yes, I am. That's what he told me. The police kept pressing him, and he admitted to making things up."

"Sean, do we have anyone who can handle this situation?" Tina asked.

"I can make arrangements within the hour," said Sean.

"Do it."

"And Sean, Samson has been a loyal soldier. Take care of him," Tina said.

"Certainly."

Two homeless men rested quietly against a concrete wall beneath the overpass, out of sight. They talked about the weather and where they might find a hot meal. They watched as a car rolled to a stop beside the curb beyond the support columns. Two flashes of light flickered inside the automobile before it sped away.

The car entered a wrecking yard, passing crushed vehicles and metal cubes stacked up beside a massive wall, beyond where a noisy machine hissed steam like a dragon. Sean stepped out without a word, slid into his spotless limousine, and drove off.

A gigantic industrial magnet, supported with chains, hoisted the car, dropping it with a thunderous clang into the wide and deep crushing chamber. The pneumatic pistons roared to life as metal grinded against metal, creating a high-pitched squealing sound.

Tina was visibly shaken with rage and anger. Her face flushed a color similar to crimson red, and she clenched her fists. She paced the condo searching for clarity after learning that Ramirez had revealed key information, including the campground. In her world, giving up Cartel information was not only unacceptable, it was unforgivable.

For the first time, she felt vulnerable, exposed, out of control, an unbearable sensation. But regardless of how she felt, Tina was the boss, the one in charge. She had to take care of business. That was her job. When her call ended, she began to relax, sat down, and reached for the remote.

A brief time later, a meal cart wobbled down a vinyl corridor, distributing small cardboard boxes of unidentifiable substances resembling food to inmates awaiting their court appearance.

Before his interview, Ramirez's guard arrived to pick up his tray. He banged a metal cup against the steel bars to announce his arrival.

He called Ramirez's name, "Bring me your tray," but Ramirez ignored him and didn't bother to turn around. The old guard called again. Silence followed.

"Don't make me come in there, Ramirez. If I do, it won't be pretty. Do you hear me?" the guard said.

Ramirez remained still with his back to the cell door. Frustrated, the guard grew angry and signaled his colleague down the ramp to unlock the cell. As the door unlocked, two more guards arrived.

Ramirez sat motionless on the lower bunk, facing the toilet, as dead as a stone. No one saw or heard anything.

His death was a mystery. How had this happened? An autopsy was ordered to determine cause of death, but the results would take some time.

Chapter 46

At the campground, Juan trained his recruits in advanced close-up combat and tactical offense, skills for both defense and attack.

Juan's life began in the gritty underbelly of Mexico City, where the streets were a battleground and survival meant adapting quickly. As a boy, he learned to navigate the maze of alleyways and marketplaces, honing a street-smart instinct that kept him always one step ahead of danger.

Orphaned by violence, his only protector was his older sister, Tina.

Like his sister, Juan found himself drawn into the world of the drug cartels. At first, he was a runner, smuggling illicit packages hidden in the folds of his ragged clothes. His fierce determination and cunning caught the attention of higher-ups, and he quickly ascended through the ranks.

By his teens, Juan was managing operations, his reputation forged through ruthless efficiency and steadfast loyalty to the cartel. His rise was driven by raw ambition and a desperate need to escape the squalor that once defined his life. Yet the violence and betrayal that marked his ascent left scars that would never heal.

The recruits had heard the stories, tales of Juan's brutal upbringing on the streets of Mexico City. They knew better than to cross him.

The campground graduates were assigned to various repackaging houses or as cartel protection specialists, stationed to safeguard drug shipments.

Others were sent to guard drop zones where train shipments were scheduled to arrive. Once the drugs were retrieved from the rail-bed, couriers transported them to predetermined locations.

The rail shipments ran smoothly, silent, unseen.

Nobody saw a thing, and no one heard a sound.

Juan's reputation for toughness was unshakable. A well-known and well-trained assassin, he was eager to pass on his skills.

On a cloudless day, Madler waltzed into the campground. Pressed for time, he planned to return to the city to train his next handpicked crew.

The campground was his recruitment ground, ideal for finding the best candidates to work at his drug repackaging facilities.

His methods varied depending on the task, each one meticulously chosen to impress Tina and the cartel leaders.

The unforgiving streets of Toronto shaped Madler. His lack of physical prowess was rivaled only by his inflated self-image.

As a child, he was often mocked for his waddle and lack of strength, yet he clung to an unshakable belief in his own brilliance.

Despite his frequent failures and average intelligence, he was drawn into the drug cartel immediately after high school, eager to prove himself as a mastermind.

Madler's misguided ambitions and delusions of grandeur led him to idolize Tina, seeing himself as a vital figure in her world while romanticizing the idea of a relationship with her.

His need to impress, combined with his naive belief in his own arrogance, made him easy to manipulate, forever a small-time player.

Madler considered his identity theft scheme genius, and to his credit, he successfully generated a steady stream of operational cash for the cartel, resulting in public praise from cartel leaders. Madler thrived on the praise, believing it made him important.

With his hands-on coaching style, the recruits learned how to buy and sell property, exploiting homeowners on vacation, turning their absence into easy profits.

The real estate fraud bolstered Madler's status, enhancing his reputation as a dependable key player within the cartel. The lavish wealth and praise from cartel leaders were intoxicating, and Madler craved more.

At times, he was torn between loyalty and self-preservation. Skimming a little untraceable cash here and there could build quite a nest egg, enough to disappear with a new identity he could easily create.

But he knew thoughts like that could get him killed in a flash.

Madler eagerly prepared his report for Tina, highlighting the latest house acquisition and growing cash flow.

He thought that if this didn't impress her, surely requesting a larger drug shipment from Mexico would. His sales were already outpacing projections.

He was eager to tell her they had the capacity to package and ship many more drugs, with every house fully engaged in transporting inventory.

Tina was content, although nagging doubts seemed to linger, especially about Madler's place in the cartel.

Chapter 47

On the surface, the task seemed simple enough: find and dismantle any facilities involved in drug trafficking and mercenary training.

They needed to search over 200,000 square miles to identify any abandoned campgrounds which might serve as a terrorist training facility.

Detectives Borden and Cross met with their colleague, Detective Friedman, a retired military pilot with extensive flight experience, along with their police drone pilot, Detective Allan Bruce.

Although the group initially favored using a drone for surveillance, Friedman objected. "The drone would be easy to spot in a quiet area," he explained. "The buzzing sound would give us away." Detective Bruce agreed.

Friedman suggested using a high-altitude airplane, as it was quieter and covered a larger area in aerial photographs. This approach could expedite the search and likely pinpoint potential targets.

Two additional aircraft were considered. Detective Bruce pointed out that no one would pay any attention to an Ornge air ambulance or seaplane, common sights up north. They would attract little attention whether flying north to cottage country or south to the city.

A grid pattern was created and integrated into the flight plan to prevent redundant coverage.

They decided to exclude areas immediately surrounding the cities of Barrie and Orillia, along with the towns of Gravenhurst, Bracebridge, and futher north to Huntsville.

Borden tasked two constables with researching real estate records for any resorts, campgrounds, or logging facilities registered in the past 10 years.

Aerial photos revealed a possible campground, an open clearing surrounded by a few buildings that might be the site Borden was looking for. He ordered a thorough search of the facilities to make a conclusive determination whether this was the camp they sought.

The early morning rain faded into a foggy mist that clung to their gear, making them invisible in the forest's eerie haze.

Constables Wilkes and Cooper moved cautiously, their boots softly crunching on the damp foliage as they followed their GPS coordinates.

As they pushed through the thicket, the campground came into view, a forgotten relic consumed by nature.

The once-bustling logging site lay eerily still, its machinery and structures smothered by creeping vines and moss. A rusted, broken saw blade, with missing teeth, lay discarded nearby.

A few yards away, a decaying truck stood silent, its frame corroded by years of neglect and rust.

A wooden cabin, once a house for workers, sagged under years of decay. The walls were scarred by rot, and its splintered windows rattled in the gentle breeze.

The enormous logs that had once been proudly stacked lay scattered and forgotten, their bark peeling beneath layers of thick, greenish mold, alive with crawling insects.

As they ventured deeper into the abandoned site, remnants of its past emerged in eerie detail.

Rusted axes, hooks, and other logging tools were discarded haphazardly, half-buried in the overgrown brush.

Another cabin, now little more than a skeletal frame, held remnants of its past, faded photographs pinned to peeling cork-board, a yellowed map, and personal items abandoned in haste with ants crawling about.

As they searched the facility, the disappointment began to set in. It was a dead end. They captured the site on their cellphone cameras and forwarded the photos to Cross. It was a bust.

Back at HQ constables combed through real estate records, searching property sales and rentals from the past decade. They found nothing.

Still, Borden and Cross found encouragement in the discovery of the old logging camp. Borden reasoned that if one abandoned camp existed, others might too. He explained that the logging camp had likely made wooden planks and logs for buildings, not campfires.

The two constables searched databases, looking for retreat centers, children's campgrounds, fishing lodges, or sports camps the size of Muskoka Woods Children's Camp, anywhere within a radius 100 kilometers north of Barrie.

One abandoned campground from the 1950s surfaced. It was quite large but surrounded by dense forest and underbrush.

The authorities assumed the owner didn't have the funding to support a substantial renovation, which led to declaring bankruptcy twelve years earlier. The consensus was that the site would require deep pockets to fund such a major renovation, and it remained unused for over a decade.

Several years after the bankruptcy, ownership was transferred to an Ontario numbered corporation. Nothing seemed unusual, except the registration indicated the property was unoccupied and inactive. There was no renovation taking place and building permits issued.

That raised suspicion. Property taxes were paid annually, and a monthly hydro bill was automatically paid by credit card. It was situated just a few hours from Toronto.

The property spanned over 25 acres and contained several buildings. The condition of the buildings was unknown, although given the years of neglect, they were likely beyond repair.

The Ornge Ambulance flew above the area, capturing photos of several buildings, open spaces, and water access points.

Much of the road into the facility was obscured, likely buried beneath dense forest growth and untamed brush.

The police drove past and spotted an opening that likely served as a driveway. An old, rusted tubular gate, once used to keep out unwanted visitors, lay partially discarded beside the roadway.

The local hydro crew arrived on site to trim branches near the power lines with a chainsaw. The noise provided cover for the police to deploy their quietest drone.

The drone navigated the winding road, bringing it to the edge of the property where several buildings were located. It then reversed course and returned to its handler.

The video quality was excellent, and it was immediately forwarded to Borden for his review.

The drone video did not reveal any signs of hidden cameras along the road heading in or out of the campsite.

However, the video did reveal a clearing large enough to land two helicopters simultaneously, with sizable steel Quonset huts at the edge of the clearing for protection. These structures could serve as heliport enclosures for each chopper, protecting them from the elements.

The police constables tore through records searching for building permits. The only permit issued for any property in the area was for a residential double-car garage.

Borden read the report twice, trying to determine the purpose of the site shown in the photos.

Perhaps he or Cross could get some answers if one of them were to squeeze the prisoners awaiting their hearings.

Detective Cross eagerly took on the assignment and about an hour later, returned with more answers.

During her interrogation, Cross confirmed that a rented cube truck transported most of the weapons up north.

She believed the manner in which the information was revealed suggested it was credible.

Detective Cross instructed Porter and Friedman to contact rental companies and locate the cube truck.

Detective Porter got a break at the second rental company he contacted. On the day of the storm, a large Ford truck was rented for two or three days. The agent didn't recall who rented it, but he had a copy of the receipt on file.

The agent showed the detectives where the truck was located in his secured compound. They found the truck, and Porter requested that the forensics team examine the vehicle.

While forensics was scouring the truck, Detective Porter obtained the starting and ending mileage from the dealer. Using the mileage data, he plotted a search radius on a map of Ontario that closely matched the one they had drawn earlier.

They now had a clearer idea of where the weapons had likely been transported.

Armed with this information, Detective Borden realized that the most recent campground fit within the search radius. He ordered a targeted search of the area surrounding the potential campsite.

The search uncovered that one customer had purchased an unusually large supply of hunting ammunition along with gun cleaning supplies in the past month.

The owner remembered the transaction clearly because the bill was paid with cash, and one fellow asked about assault rifle ammo.

Investigators contacted local food stores, inquiring about any unusual or large food orders, hoping to determine delivery locations and dates.

The constables gathered addresses, and one stood out, flagged by the manager of the grocery store.

The manager recalled his staff assisting the drivers of a large F-150 in loading their supplies into the truck bed. The unusual thing was they always paid with cash. It was great business as they became regular customers, showing up every two weeks.

The manager anticipated another visit later that day. The manager agreed to allow one of the investigating officers to join his staff and work the store through the afternoon.

Undercover officers, dressed like cottage hikers on electric bicycles, explored the area, eventually finding the dump where the campground men disposed of their trash. Rummaging through the garbage, they uncovered empty ammunition boxes along with spent brass casings. They also found blood-soaked bandages and empty beer cans, which were tagged and bagged as evidence.

Two undercover constables, dressed as hikers, quietly entered the area, navigating their way along the length of the road searching for any booby traps or cameras installed.

They had agreed that if they were discovered by any-one, they would ask directions to the main road, claiming they got turned around and were lost.

The two officers arrived at the edge of the forest. From there, they saw a large square opening surrounded by cab-ins.

They stopped to observe the activity, men engaged in hand-to-hand combat training, others performed push-ups under the direction of an instructor who looked like he could use some exercise himself.

Cabins lined the perimeter, with a large central cabin facing south. Off to the west, they caught a partial view of a parking area with trucks parked facing outward. Re-maining hidden, the officers took photos and sent them back to Police HQ.

The scene resembled a military training camp. The two officers froze, sitting still, holding their breath as three men passed by, barely 20 feet away. One of the men stopped, turned, and removed some cigarettes from his pocket, lighting up before moving along, chatting. Once the men were out of sight, the officers quietly retreated toward the road.

Chapter 48

Tonight, it would happen. One final reconnaissance trip to ensure no detail was overlooked.

He glided through the area surrounding a predetermined address programmed into his handheld GPS. He couldn't help but admire the serene, upscale Toronto neighborhood known as Rosedale.

Large, opulent homes, undoubtedly staffed with maids and butlers, stood a midst meticulously maintained gardens. Their wrought-iron gates, underground sprinkler systems, and turn-of-the-century streetlights underscored the timeless grandeur of the neighborhood.

This was the quiet, exclusive domain of Toronto's elite and powerful. Soon, it would be washed with red and blue flashing lights and yellow tape, shattering its tranquility.

The overcast afternoon draped a misty blanket over the lush lawns, sidewalks, and roads, muting the vibrant colors of flowers bursting from the weedless garden beds.

No one took notice of him. Why would they? In this crime-free community, security was assumed. Danger and violence were unthinkable. That was about to change.

Unnoticed, he perched in his car, watching, memorizing every detail. Preparation was everything. Soon, he would strike and vanish within minutes, swift and precise, like a falcon diving at lightning speed on unsuspecting prey.

At this time of year, many in this community had either returned from the annual trip to open their cottages or had just arrived home from vacationing in the sunny south.

The nearby Eaton Center shopping mall was a favorite destination for discerning Toronto shoppers.

After a gourmet dinner in Yorkville, he returned to scour the neighborhood once more, retracing his selected exit route. Everything appeared textbook for an undetected visit and murder.

The mall was now near closing for the evening. Soon, the day would wind down and people would secure themselves indoors for the night.

Shoppers and retail clerks would make their way to the subway and ride the Red Rocket back to the comfort of their suburban homes.

Rosedale's residents appreciated the seclusion, their enormous homes shielding them from the city's noise, congestion, and dangerous elements. It was the true quintessential enclave of the city's historical families.

But tonight, no one was walking their dog. No one was out for a stroll. No one was seen anywhere in the empty streets. The silence seemed unnatural. The setting was ideal for completing an undetected contract.

Rosedale, the epitome of urban luxury and privilege, lay hidden in its usual serenity. But tonight, the stillness carried a weight, an unseen quiet threat lurking in the shadows.

A few sleek cars lined the narrow streets, their polished surfaces catching a weak glow from the streetlights. Some cars rested in private driveways, while others sat quietly behind grand metal gates or tucked away in carriage houses.

But one vehicle stood apart. A dark sedan, positioned just far enough down the block to escape notice, yet close enough to be significant. It had remained in place for an hour, undisturbed. Its presence raised little curiosity, yet in a neighborhood like this, at night, it felt wrong. Unsettling.

Beneath the comfortable warm glow of mansion windows, all appeared quiet. Residents, secured in their homes, remained blissfully unaware of the unseen eyes that watched from the protected shadows.

The sedan remained motionless, blending into the night, biding time, waiting for the perfect moment to strike. Swift and silent. Ten, maybe fifteen minutes. Just enough time for an unnoticed visit.

But with every step planned, there was always the risk of something more. Collateral damage was a mere detail.

Irrelevant unless something went wrong.

Tonight, Rosedale's silence would not be as quiet as it seemed or as residents hoped.

No one would see or hear his arrival or departure, because a ghost doesn't make any noise. In moments, he would instantly vanish like a magician's final illusion.

If by chance someone did catch a glimpse, they would certainly have regrets. The response needed to remedy the situation would be swift.

He glanced down the street and saw an elderly couple carrying packages from their parked car into their home.

The urge to offer help crossed his mind, but he resisted. The couple paid no attention to him. Doubtful they had noticed his car idling, as they never once glanced his way.

Thirty seconds later, the elderly couple switched off the outside porch light. It was time to watch their prerecorded documentary.

The street was dark again, covered by heavy dark clouds and towering trees, some blocking the streetlights. The timing was flawless.

As a precaution, he drove away and returned an hour and a half later. Nothing had changed. The streets were empty, the houses silent and dark.

He replayed the recording drummed into his head. Success was all about paying attention to the trivial details. It was a lesson he never forgot.

A quick mental run-through of the details of the night confirmed he hadn't missed anything.

With the ceiling light switched off, he twisted and reached for a black duffel bag.

He retrieved a pair of quality black latex gloves. He blew in them, expanding the material before he stretched them over his muscular hands, honed by years of experience.

He examined his hands carefully. No tears, no holes, and no fingerprints would be left behind. Perfect.

He reached deeper into the soft-sided leather pouch, retrieved a black case, opened it, and withdrew his favorite well-worn Glock 9mm and suppressor.

He inspected it carefully to ensure it was ready for work. A quick trigger check. It worked flawlessly. He screwed on the suppressor and secured it.

As a precaution, he wiped down each custom bullet and loaded his clip. Then, he inserted the loaded clip into the gun, placing it in his custom-made holster.

The clean backup magazine he slipped into his black jacket's breast pocket. Reaching back into the leather bag, he retrieved a small case containing a syringe and a small vial. The needle cap was removed. Just the right amount of liquid entered the tube. Cap replaced. He took a deep breath, releasing it gently.

He paused for a minute and glanced at his Rolex. It was time.

The well-lubricated car door slid open with ease. He exited in silent darkness, apart from the soft click of the locked door.

Dressed in black, he paused, momentarily scanning up and down the street, then in the direction of the target.

He knew where the house was and slipped through the neighbor's yard into the backyard of the target.

No sounds. No dogs. No people.

He saw no sign of the tiny green dot that would signal a video camera in a window or doorbell. He was careful to avoid the typical surveillance points.

Ian Webber had recently joined the security detail and, as the new guy, was assigned to night security. He sat in his car, absorbed in reading a book on his smartphone while parked in the lower driveway with his window open. A warm breeze filled the car, and he felt comfortable. He exited the car, beginning his hourly sweep of the grounds. He checked the side and back door of the mansion.

As Webber walked about, he recalled the arguments he had over the past few days about Martinez's lifestyle exposing himself to a variety of possible dangers. The butler and maid had to leave the room more than once while the two quarreled.

Martinez blew it off, saying it was Webber's job to protect him. So do your job. The resentment between the two was increasing. Webber returned to his government-issued sedan, slid in, reaching for his phone to continue his reading.

In soft-soled shoes, a predator stepped behind the car. Using it as cover, he glanced around one last time.

The lone parked car had gone. The street was empty. Just him and the security guard.

The security camera, mounted high, covered the front of the house and part of the driveway. He melted into the shadows, unseen.

He saw that Webber's window was open and removed the plastic tip of the syringe. He plunged the needle into the carotid artery, and Webber was unconscious without a fight. The plastic cap was replaced, rendering the weapon harmless.

Lying slumped over onto the passenger seat, he reached in and hauled him upright behind the wheel. He pulled back his jacket, slipped his gun into his hand, and screwed on a suppressor. Webber sat lifeless, secure in his car.

He circled back to the house, slipping past the gate and around a black limo sitting locked and idle in the driveway. He pressed a gloved hand on the hood. It felt cold to the gloved touch.

Good. The limo hadn't moved in hours. The driver was gone for the night. If not, collateral damage.

Stepping quietly into the backyard, he scanned the house. The curtains remained tightly drawn.

He turned, sweeping his gaze over the neighboring houses. Dark and silent. Earlier, he had noted the dark houses lining the street where he parked. Perfect. Either the occupants were asleep or away.

The backyards lay still and shadowed. No dogs. No barking.

A shadowed figure peered in through a sheer curtain, searching for his target. He saw nothing. Experience had taught him patience.

Maybe the target had gone to bed, he thought. But if that was the case, then why was the light still on? Was that normal?

All was quiet, and there was no apparent movement inside.

He considered leaving, coming back another night. But that posed a problem. The security detail sat unnaturally still. This wasn't how the evening was planned. Had something gone wrong?

Then he froze.

He twisted around. A sound? It couldn't be the guard. That sedative would have him out for at least another twenty minutes. No one. No animals. Just a slight breeze.

He stood as still as the shadow. A phantom in the dark. Someone was watching. Admiring.

Everything remained quiet. Nothing moved. Nothing stirred.

He crept toward the backyard then stopped.

Inside the elegantly furnished room, a silhouette emerged. A coffee cup in hand.

Target acquired.

Where were the maid and butler? He'd seen them both leave earlier. Had they returned? No. They would have served the coffee. The target had to be alone.

The coffee rested on a side table. Then he could faintly hear the jazz guitar music gently drifting through the silence.

He slipped to the side entrance and waited. He was ready. His moment had arrived. Silent. Perfect. Undetected.

This was the ideal setting. In approximately three more minutes, he'd be gone. Unnoticed. Wealthier. And have another satisfied client.

With the display dimmed, the signal jammer remained active on his smartphone.

The alarm system was glowing red. Security disabled.

He keyed in his hacker's code and slipped through the unlocked door. Undetected.

He waited for five seconds. Silence. The soft hum of jazz guitar must have masked the lock's faint click. The target reached for a dossier sitting on a nearby table then turned.

Who the...

Two muffled shots. The target crumpled. The dossier beside him.

The shell casings were retrieved. No powder, smudges, no telltale burn marks on the carpet.

A quick scan. No changes. No video. No security. Nothing touched. He glanced at the folder. It was irrelevant. Left it where it fell.

No footprints. No soil. No water stains on the floor. He eased through the door and reactivated the alarm.

The light was now green. Without touching anything, the video system was fully reactivated, and the door was relocked, sealing the corpse sprawled on plush carpet.

Back at the car, he reached in, replaced the agent's gun, and secured the dome button to the holster. He wiped some gunshot residue on Webber's hand. He dropped one shell casing beside the driver's door, another outside where it would naturally fall as if the agent entered the car and dropped it by accident. He watched it roll under the car.

He vanished into the shadows, knowing he had one more task that needed his attention.

He slid into his car, retrieved his black duffel bag, and secured his gun, suppressor, and syringe. Silently pulling away from the neighborhood, he headed for his chosen exit route, passing no one on the street or any other cars, disappearing like a wisp of smoke.

As he drove away, the mansion's pristine façade remained untouched. Inside, chaos waited to be discovered.

His departure was as seamless as his arrival, leaving behind a scene that would soon be drenched in flashing blue and red lights, shattering the tranquility of Rosedale.

He was tired, as the time was approaching the end of another busy day for him. The push of a button on his burner phone enabled his call.

The second ring answered with one word.

"Yes."

"It's done. The fall guy asleep in his car."

"Understood. Goodnight."

"Goodnight."

The line went dead. Soft jazz played as he vanished into another Toronto night.

Chapter 49

Detective Cross's phone vibrated with an urgent call, pulling her attention away from pressing police work. She was irritated by the interruption, wishing she had silenced her phone.

Ramirez was found dead in his cell, his lifeless body discovered by a guard collecting food trays. The shock pierced her, disbelief hitting like a punch in the gut.

"How is that even possible?" she whispered.

Cross's voice remained steady and firm as she called Borden. "Ramirez was found sitting on his bunk this morning, staring at the back wall. The guard entered the cell to collect his food tray and found him with his back to the cell door. No signs of a struggle. No violence. Just him, dead in his cell."

Borden's response was incredulous. "How could this happen? He was awaiting a court appearance, not in any position to make a grand escape. It's not like he was a star witness in the trial of the century."

"That was my question," Cross replied.

Cross's frustration simmered just beneath her composed exterior. "I'm with you on this one. The coroner is on her way and will likely order an autopsy, but it'll take time to determine the exact cause of death. Right now, we have no answers."

Borden's mind churned through the implications. "Given how hard it was to capture him, Ramirez must have been important to someone, or somebody wanted him dead for some strange reason.

What did he know that was worth killing him? Obviously, whoever did this didn't want him talking to us. I can't help but wonder what more he knew, or did he know anything at all?

Have a detective review everything he said since he got here."

Cross considered the possibility. "Could this have been a suicide? We need the coroner to look into that angle too. It's too suspicious to rule anything out just yet."

"Absolutely," Borden agreed. "While you wait for those answers, we've made some headway with the drug houses. We intercepted parcels being shipped from one location. Friedman got onto a FedEx truck and confirmed the packages contained fentanyl. I've sent you the address. Check it out if you're able. Our stakeout team is tailing the courier, so stay sharp. You may need to join them momentarily."

"I'm on it," Cross said. She hung up, feeling the weight of the case pressing down on her.

Cross pulled up to the address Borden had given her, a modest house tucked away in a quiet neighborhood.

The street was quiet, bathed in the soft light of early morning. She parked a few houses down, taking a moment to survey the area through her car's tinted windows.

The house was unremarkable, blending seamlessly with its surroundings. Yet as Cross studied the two-story building, something felt off.

The house stood in silence, its windows darkened, its front yard meticulously maintained but eerily deserted. "Why?" she wondered to herself.

No cars. No movement. The peace of the urban setting felt almost too perfect, a stark contrast to the turmoil she was feeling in her gut.

She waited, but her thoughts wandered to her husband and their strained marriage. She thought of her recent therapy session, the things she had said, the truths she needed to face.

Bill wanted her to quit her job and work with him. That didn't appeal to her. She relished the excitement of being a detective and wanted justice, especially for her sister.

Cross was confused, trying to evaluate their relation-ship from both sides. The back-and-forth thoughts tormented her.

She loved being a detective, and she felt fulfilled in her job. The idea of separation crept into her mind, and she wondered if that was the right thing for them. The ques-tions kept coming one after another. Those thoughts she needed to stop.

Without noticing, she had dragged her personal life across the line into her professional pursuits. That was dangerous. Hesitation could affect the necessary instantaneous decisions a police detective must make every day.

She understood Bill worried about her, but she also had the skill and experience to survive. She'd proven that many times in the past.

Bill was an entrepreneur. She knew he needed to focus on his business and realized self-employment wasn't easy. She was out of answers or just making excuses. She wasn't sure anymore.

Cross was torn. Their lives were drifting apart, two roads splitting into different directions. Which was the right path for her?

Bill loved his work. She loved hers.

"Stop," she said aloud in the squad car. That's when the decision was made to defer these issues to her next appointment on Bay Street. But for now, the case and her investigation came first. It was her job.

Cross slid out of her car, her movements smooth and controlled like a seasoned detective. Her footsteps were measured and quiet as she crossed the street, unconsciously staying close to the morning shadows.

The exterior gave no immediate clues, but Cross's instincts whispered whatever was happening, it was inside that house.

She checked her watch. The neighborhood was beginning to stir with human activity. Dog walkers on the sidewalk, lawnmowers springing to life.

Cross took a deep breath and approached the front door. Her gloved hand found the handle, twisting it carefully. Her other hand hovered over her weapon. The door was unlocked, a detail that set her nerves on edge and spiked her pulse.

Inside, she announced herself as Toronto Police Services while she looked around. The house was pristine, almost sterile. The living room was methodically organized, every item in its place, but there was an unsettling stillness that felt unnatural. Cross moved cautiously, her senses on high alert. She made her way through the rooms, her footsteps muffled by the thick plush carpet.

The kitchen told a different story. She knew someone had been there, recently. A half-eaten breakfast sat abandoned. The coffee mug was still warm to the touch. But no one was in sight. She didn't feel any immediate danger. She continued, each room revealing nothing but an unsettling calm.

Finally, she reached the basement door. Her heart quickened as she descended the stairs, the darkness enveloping her. The basement was a maze of storage and clutter, but Cross's trained eye quickly picked out anything that seemed out of place. The faint hum of machinery caught her attention, and she followed the sound to a small room in the back.

Inside, a makeshift operation unfolded. Tables cluttered with packaging materials. Cardboard boxes stacked neatly in rows, labeled and ready for shipping.

The air reeked, a chemical scent of fentanyl. Cross examined the scene, noting the organized chaos of the drug operation. The evidence was clear. This had to be a distribution hub. She took photos and sent them back to Borden.

Her phone vibrated with an update from the stakeout team. They had lost the courier. He was gone. The tension in Cross's shoulders tightened immediately. The missing courier. Gone.

The house. Deserted. This seemingly abandoned bungalow, and the courier, were pieces of a puzzle she had to solve.

As she prepared to leave, she heard a distant siren, a reminder that the calm of the neighborhood was not what it seemed. Cross knew that while the house might appear to be a dead end, after what she saw, that didn't seem to be the case.

The threads of the case were still tangled, and the discovery of the fentanyl cache was just the beginning.

She slipped from the basement and back into the sunlight, her mind ablaze with a multitude of questions. Who lived here? Where were they? How long had this been a drug factory?

Why no car in the driveway? How many people live or work here? Who owns the house? Is this part of the cartel they were seeking?

The silence of the house was broken only by the faint echoes of her footsteps as she left. The basement find was significant, and she knew Borden would be all over that when he saw the photos. But Cross knew she wasn't done, at least not until she unraveled this mystery first.

She hesitated as her brain considered whether she should call in for backup. That would be the smart thing to do.

But who needs backup for an empty house?

She moved cautiously, wandered down the driveway, peering into the garage.

Empty.

She thought, a half-eaten breakfast, a warm coffee mug, no one here, the house and garage both empty. What is going on here? Why did someone leave in such a hurry?

She walked into the backyard and looked around. Nothing stood out or captured her attention.

She decided to take one last look, peering through the backyard sun-room window. She logically concluded, the place was deserted.

Then, a sound she knew too well. A click. Right behind the back of her head.

Her body tensed. She recognized it immediately.

Trouble.

Her instincts took over, and she decided the best thing to do was to turn around slowly.

She acted in an awakward and clumsy manner, to peer nonthreatening and turned, words ready, hoping to talk her way out.

Chapter 50

Before she could turn, a gun muzzle was jammed be-tween her shoulder blades, pushing her forward.

She wondered how she had been so careless. How had she not seen this coming? The warm mug on the table, the unlocked door. Those were signs she had ignored.

For a seasoned detective, she had been far too casual. Oh, for a do-over, she thought.

Facing the sun-room window, she caught the man's stubby reflection in the glass. Slowly, she raised her hands, thinking, I need to get out of this. What now?

Through the poor-quality glass, his distorted image came into focus. He was bald and short, and she caught a clear glimpse of a scar on his cheek.

"You're trespassing, lady. What do you want?" the man said with a deep heavy accent.

She could catch him off guard, spin quickly, disarm him, force his weapon to the ground, and drop him like a sack of birdseed.

But this time, she wasn't wearing her Kevlar vest. If she wasn't fast enough and he got a shot off, it would go straight through her heart.

She would be dead in an instant. Not the best option.

"Last time, lady. Who are you?" the man demanded.

Silence. Then darkness.

Cross blinked, her head throbbing with a relentless, dull, but growing ache. Her vision swirled in cloudy circles before gradually settling into focus. The spinning stopped.

She slowly registered her surroundings. She was sprawled on a cold, uneven floor, her wrists bound behind her with rough, frayed rope.

The single overhead bulb flickered intermittently, its dim light casting long, sinister shadows across the room's bare brick walls. Cross had not seen this room when she walked through the basement. Was it the same house, she wondered?

The low hum of an old radiator or fan underscored the muffled, unintelligible voices coming from beyond the door.

Cross's mouth was dry and tinged with the metallic aftertaste of the brutal punch that had knocked her out. She strained against the ropes, but they only tightened, biting into her wrists and drawing a wince with each attempt to move.

The lone door in the far corner of the room was slightly ajar until a hand suddenly slammed it shut.

Low murmurs filtered in under the door, punctuated by occasional bursts of laughter. The room resembled an abandoned living space. Sparse, worn-out furniture was covered in dusty white sheets. A creeping chill settled over Cross, making her shiver. Her body trembled with sporadic jolts of pain.

She had been abducted and brought... where? Cross could only guess.

The disorientation from the blow to the head threatened to consume her until she heard footsteps approaching.

The door creaked open. A broad-shouldered man, short with a face concealed by a mask stepped inside. A handgun casually dangled at his side as he walked in circles. He glanced around, his gaze locked onto Cross.

"Wake up." His voice was raspy, thick with anger. "We've got plans for you."

Cross's heart raced. Her stomach twisted. She felt nauseous.

Plans?

What kind of plans?

Information maybe?

Perhaps leverage of some sort? She had no idea but didn't want to hang around long enough to find out.

She fought to push through the fog clouding her thoughts. Escape was the only option. But how? Her gaze darted around the room, searching for anything she could use. A weakness. A weapon. A chance. A way out.

Nothing. Not yet, anyway.

The man turned and stepped out, locking the door behind him, leaving her sealed in.

Cross heard muffled voices drifting through the crack beneath the door. Maybe they were talking about her. She wasn't sure.

They murmured about the next phase of their plan, about a shipment and making sure there were no loose ends.

Cross had no doubt. She was one of them.

Time slowed, each minute stretching into what felt like hours. Cross strained to listen, trying to piece together any scraps of information. Her location. Her captors. Their plan.

She felt weak, tired, vulnerable and alone.

A key scraped in the lock.

Cross tensed and froze, staying perfectly still. She hoped for a sliver of opportunity, but instead, the door swung open to reveal three men.

Their faces were obscured by masks. Their movements were brisk and deliberate. One of the men made a move to touch Cross inappropriately, and the one in charge hit him across the head with the barrel of his gun.. He glared at the man with a stern voice.

"Try that again, and I'll kill you," he barked.

The man backed away like a wounded dog, head hanging low and cowered in the corner crouching on his heels.

The leader, a wiry figure with a scar running down his cheek, approached Cross, muttered a weak apology, then lifted her with surprising ease.

He slung Cross over his shoulder and carried her through a series of dark hallways like a small sack of raw potatoes. The faint light from above provided fleeting glimpses of their grim expressions.

Cross noted every detail. The echo of their footsteps. The hum of distant grinding machinery. She bounced on the man's shoulder before he dumped her into the back of an SUV.

She wasn't sure, but with the distant hum of traffic, she thought they were somewhere north of the city.

Eventually, they rolled to a stop in front of a nondescript house. Ordinary from the outside, but likely full of grim secrets within.

They moved her. She was sure this wasn't the same house. she had seen before. It took too long to get here. This was somewhere further out of the city. Colder. Much colder. And likely isolated.

They shoved her into a basement room that was better organized than the last one. A bed sat in one corner, and high near the ceiling, a small window hinted at a potential escape route.

They cut through the ropes, using Cross's own handcuffs to secure her.

As they left, a key chain slipped from one of the captors' grip, dropping to the floor. The faint clinking sound didn't register, but Cross's sharp eyes caught the glint of a key among the other items.

Her hope sparked. This might be her chance.

One captor hesitated, sensing something was off, and slipped back into the room. He spotted his key chain on the floor.

He scooped it up and rejoined the others.

Cross felt her last hope of escape vanish. The key to her freedom was gone.

If she wasn't rescued, this basement filled with stale air and strange odors was where she would die.

Meanwhile, Borden hurried to his car after thanking Caroline, who said she would notify him when she heard from Detective Cross.

He found Cross's abandoned car parked at the curb, near the address he had given her.

A neighbor told Borden he saw her leave and gave a vague description of the van and the men who left with her.

Borden's mind raced as his hand tightened its grip on the wheel.

Urgency drove him as he scrolled through his list of contacts in his on-board computer.

"This is Borden. I need your help tracking down a missing officer. It could be critical."

A flurry of responses offering to assist poured in, as different departments scrambled into action. Every available officer was now searching for one of their own. The tension in a situation like this doesn't go any higher.

Borden scanned the neighborhood, his gut telling him there was more to find.

His phone vibrated, jolting him. It was one of his contacts.

The first response landed in less than ten minutes.

"I've got an address for you. We tracked the SUV from the address you provided via satellite imagery to an area north of the city at Lake Wilcox. I'm certain this is where the van's located. It's at a small house on the northern outskirts of the city. It may be heavily guarded, judging by the number of cars and trucks parked at the house. I've forwarded the address to you."

"Thanks for your help," said Borden.

His face flushed, his pulse pounding. He knew time was of the essence.

There was no room for mistakes. Every second mattered.

The atmosphere was intense as he evaluated speed against caution while searching for the quickest way to find Cross before time ran out.

His team of Gibson, Friedman, Porter, and Kim, who had just returned to work half days, mirrored Borden's tension, everyone shattered, concerned and sharpened by anger.

Friedman, in particular, looked ready to crack skulls with his bare hands, just for the pleasure.

Back at the safe house, Cross stared at the spot where the key had fallen.

She felt sick to her stomach, her shoulders strained by pain and her skull throbbed with a relentless pounding headache. If she could escape the headache, things would be be different. But, not really. Cross was weak, face flushed and swollen, fatigued and she knew it.

Her vision blurred.

She twisted and strained to maneuver herself to reach it, her wrists burning and bleeding, refusing to surrender her hope of escape.

Her heartbeat pounded with adrenaline and hope faded fast as the room seemed darker now.

The door closed with a porcelain white doorknob that hadn't been seen or washed in years. The vanish on the door peeling away, revealing cracks in the door and frame.

She heard what sounded like kick boxing with some banging against the wall and a loud thud just before the dry door split apart in multiple pieces. A small body tossed through the air, crashing to the floor cracking his skull in a lifeless heap directly in front of Cross.

She thought their could be two bodies in the hallway lying one on top of the other. She wasn't sure. They were motionless, arms dangling finger tips touching to the floor with blood pooling everywhere beneath them.

There was no sound. No movement. No weapons. Nothing!

She wondered if she was dreaming.

A large shadow stepped onto and over the bodies then entered the room without a word.

She couldn't make out a face.

Nothing. The form didn't speak. Cross on the verge of tears and pain said nothing, and tried but failed to focus.

Her headache continued to pulse and push down her neck between her shoulders. Her hair felt dirty and her head was itchy.

She felt her arms release, and fall to her sides but she couldn't move..

She struggled to gain any movement in them, although in her weak stage it was best to wait and see what might happen. She had to focus. To make a plan of escape, Her brain ached for rest. She was out of energy and knew it!

The numbness and aching from the tingling in her shoulder to her hands, intensified. She gasped for air, relief, something to help her.

The shadow crossed in front of her placing a burner on top of the incapacitated body in front of her chair, along with the weapons her captors had been carrying earlier. He knelt down behind her and removed the restraints that had been holding her in so much pain.

"Who are you?" Cross asked, unsure if she was dreaming.

There was no response. The ghost of a man said nothing and then seemed to just vanish as quickly as he had arrived.

She drew a steady deep breath. Escape was her only option as she reached for the burner.

What she did in the next few minutes could seal her fate. Every sound, every shadow was a threat or maybe an opportunity.

Her muscles began to relax and the screaming pain began to give up it's hold on her with their inflamed muscles began to find minimal movement.

Chapter 51

Borden's blood pressure soared with urgency, his heart pounding as he prepared for immediate action. The gravity of the situation pressed down on him in unison with the rest of the police force who were in a manhunt for one of their own. Time was a luxury he couldn't afford to waste.

Every muscle in his body tensed, ready for action. His head pounded for purpose with an intensifying anger.

For now, the steady tap of his fingers on the laptop schematic was the only sound breaking the silence as he plotted his next move. The tension was suffocating every-one around him.

Borden ordered a team member to reach the basement window and capture video of the room and verify if Cross was there.

Outside, the high humidity clung to them like water in a morning shower.

The overcast sky was needed to protect the force and provide the element of surprise.

Borden's team gathered one final time near the target house. Their eyes burned with adrenaline and fury. They inhaled slow, steady breaths.

The house loomed ahead, a dark sentinel with shrouded windows and a lifeless yard. Only rustling leaves and the occasional distant call of a bird swept by the wind disturbed the silence.

Clad in tactical gear, the team moved with surgical precision, their footsteps whispering over the leaf-strewn ground.

Borden checked his watch. He pressed his radio to his lips, voice low but filled with authority. "All units, radio silence. We breach on my mark. No unnecessary noise. I lead."

The EMS teams stood ready at strategic points, their vehicles hidden in the dense foliage. The medics scanned the surrounding area for any signs of trouble. They were poised to respond.

Borden and his team had encircled the house undetected. Borden signaled, his eyes fixed on the darkened windows.

They moved as one, their steps crunching silently on wet grass as they approached the side of the house. Borden's mind raced as he readied for the breach, every sense tuned to the task at hand.

Borden's team advanced, their movements fluid and deliberate. The locked doors and blank windows seemed to taunt them, concealing whatever waited inside.

Borden's gaze snapped to the side door as it creaked open. A man stepped out, a satchel slung over his shoulder. The team froze, their breath catching in their throats. The temptation to remove this obstacle was overwhelming.. A sharp blow to the. head, or a choke hold would render the individual useless. The man cast a wary glance around, lit a cigarette before slipping back inside. The door banged shut.

"Stay sharp," Borden murmured into his radio. "We have movement inside."

Inside, Cross was in a desperate fight for survival. Her wrists, raw and bleeding from the rope burn earlier, did nothing to weaken her resolve. Surrender wasn't an option.

Ignoring her throbbing headache, she began to focus and scanned the room. She reached for a weapon on the chair, checked the magazine. Fully loaded.

She was ready.

Her pulse pounded as she snatched the burner phone off the back of the body in front of her. Her fingers trembled, but her hands stayed steady. She'd done this countless times before. Her heart steadied as she took a deep breath and rubbed her wrists, willing the numbness to fade.

Footsteps thundered from above. She had only moments.

Cross dragged the bodies into the room and softly closed the door. She texted Borden, who replied he was nearby.

Defeat wasn't an option. The odds had shifted.

Now, it was Cross who had the upper hand.

Every creak of the floorboards, every shifting shadow across the wall, signaled a possible threat. Her heart pounded, each beat counting down the seconds. She crouched, trembling with a raw mix of fear and adrenaline.

A key scraped inside the lock. The door creaked open. A thin blade of hallway light cut into her darkness. Heavy footsteps approached, louder with every breath.

Cross's pulse spiked at the unmistakable voices of her captors.

"Where are the others?" someone asked.

"I think they're outside having a smoke. Should be back any minute."

"Okay."

The door hung slightly ajar. Shadows moved beyond it back upstairs without anyone noticing it wasn't shut.

She braced herself.

Borden raised his fist, and his team moved with practiced precision.

The side door was breached with a quiet, controlled force.

Borden's team slipped inside, their movements as precise and stealthy as shadows. Borden led the charge, adrenaline sharpening his focus. His eyes swept the darkness, hunting for any sign of Cross having been moved from the basement.

She froze when one of the captors' voices sounded too close. She held her breath, spine pressed against the cold wall behind the door. If someone entered it would be the last thing they did.

Borden's team advanced methodically, clearing room by room, tension mounting with every step.

As they neared the room where the heat sensors had detected a single occupant, assumed to be Cross, Borden's pulse hammered with urgency.

"Cops!" someone shouted.

Automatic fire erupted upstairs, thunderous and wild. Bullets chewed through door frames and spit splinters across the hallway. Glass exploded from light fixtures, raining shards in every direction. Screams echoed, loud and frantic. Men running for cover.

Borden's team sprang into action, weapons up, engaging the captors head-on. The sharp staccato of gunfire bounced off the walls. One of the captors overturned a table for cover, but it splintered, proving useless as rounds punched through.

The back door crashed open, more reinforcements surged into the chaos.

Cross's pulse thundered. Then she saw him, Borden, leading the team through the smoke and noise. Hope surged, but her grip on the weapon didn't loosen. One captor lay groaning nearby. She wasn't taking any chances. She assisted his continued sleep.

She bolted from cover, darting toward Borden just as more rounds slammed into the walls around them.

Their eyes met. His expression shifted, relief locked with urgency. He reached out, shielding her with one arm, guiding her behind the cover of a collapsed bookshelf. The house rocked with gunfire and the noise of shattering glass.

Cross crouched low, her hands trembling but steady as she covered Borden's flank. For Cross, the moment was raw excitement, fear, and relief converging in every breath. She was very much alive and excited.

Borden gave the signal.

A flash bang rolled across the floor, then detonated with a blinding burst and a bone-rattling crack.

The captors screamed, weapons dropping from stunned hands. One stumbled to his knees, one banged against the wall clutching his ears, while another collapsed, disoriented and reeling. Their resistance shattered in seconds.

The room fell into silence, just the ringing aftermath and the rasp of heavy breathing and unrecognizable language.

Cross, still armed, trembled with exhaustion and relief. Borden's team swept the room, securing the last of the captors.

The nightmare was ending.

Borden's team secured the area, their movements slowing now that Cross was safe. The house, once a prison, had become the scene of a successful rescue.

As the last of the captors were taken into custody, Borden turned to Cross, his face a mixture of concern and relief.

"You're safe now," he said, his voice steady despite the chaos around them.

Cross nodded, gratitude and exhaustion dulling her eyes. The ordeal was over, but the emotional toll was still sinking in.

"I must look a mess," Cross said.

"You do," Borden replied, and they both chuckled. As he led her outside, she glanced back one last time.

This nightmare was over.

But what about the next one?

The EMS team checked her over, noting some bruising and clearing her for rest.

The house, now quiet and subdued, was a stark reminder of the danger that had lurked within its walls. Borden's team began processing the scene. The captors were separated, the first round of questioning underway.

The violence of the night had left its mark.

Community Policing Services put themselves in harm's way every single day. Their hidden heroism, dedication, and bravery are beyond words. And only a handful ever know the full true story.

As Borden and Cross drove away, the weight of the events settled heavily on their shoulders.

"There's something I need to tell you," Cross said.

"Can it wait till later?"

"No."

"What if I said chamomile tea?"

"No, this is important."

"What is it?"

"I'm sure I saw him. He was there," said Cross.

"Who was there?"

"My arms were handcuffed behind me when I was in a wooden chair. I couldn't move. Borden, a body was thrown right through the door onto the floor in front of me. There was more low-volume noise in the hallway. The door creaked open and two other guards were on the floor, very much out of it, their arms dangling in blood.. A big shadow of a man slipped in, stepped over them, quietly. He set me free and left a cell phone and a weapon on the back of the body nearest me."

"Who was it?"

"I don't know. I didn't really see his face. Call me crazy, but I think it was The Ghost."

"Really?"

"He was careful. Knew exactly what he was doing. He never spoke a word. And then he just vanished, before you arrived."

"Cross, when was the last time you ate a meal?" Borden asked.

"Borden, there was another person in the room, I swear it.

He took out three guards with ease," Cross said.

"We're both famished and in need of a comfort meal. It'll be on me, Cross," Borden said.

Borden's dashboard phone vibrated, instantly changing their focus.

He hit the button. "This is Borden."

The shock of what the two detectives heard in the next few seconds was beyond alarming.

"We're on our way."

Chapter 52

Detective Cross, visibly drained and aching from her recent ordeal, agreed to let Borden drive while she rested in the passenger seat. The day's stress had carved lines of fatigue into both their faces, their eyes betraying exhaustion despite their resolve and determination. Another investigative call was the last thing either of them needed.

"I never expected anything like this," Cross murmured, her voice low but filled with an edge of bitterness. "But looking back, I'm not surprised. So, he gets away with it?"

Borden's jaw tightened. "It's not over. There's more to this than we realize. We need to focus on what's next. The crime scene might have the answers we need."

Borden slowed the car. "This is it," he said, gesturing toward the posh Rosedale neighborhood as it came into view. "This might be our breakthrough."

As they neared the address, the striking contrast between the opulent surroundings and the gritty reality of their work became more pronounced.

The homes in this area embodied affluence, their manicured lawns and grand facades testifying to the owners' wealth. Yet today, beneath the pristine veneer, a dark secret waited to be uncovered.

Borden parked the squad car. Both detectives stepped out, their movements deliberate and slow with the weight of their task.

Their footsteps were absorbed by the eerie stillness cloaking the neighborhood. They approached the front door of the ambassador's residence, each step echoing the gravity of the situation they would encounter.

The young constable at the entrance looked visibly shaken. His uniform was immaculate, but his face bore the strain of witnessing violent death, perhaps for the first time. "Detectives Borden and Cross," said the officer, his voice quivering. "I've been instructed to brief you."

The constable led them into the foyer, a space so pristine it seemed untouched by violence.

The grandeur of the room with its lofty ceilings, intricate moldings, and elegantly appointed furniture stood in stark contrast to the horror that had unfolded within its walls.

The only sound was the faint rustling of the breeze through the open windows, doing nothing to ease the oppressive sadness.

"Sir, ma'am," the constable continued, his voice shaking. "The butler reported the homicide. He found the ambassador dead in his sitting room. No signs of forced entry, no disturbances inside."

"The ambassador appears to have been alone last night. The security detail was outside, parked at the foot of the driveway. The agent on duty has no idea how the ambassador was killed. His name is Ian Webber. No one can explain why he was in his car. Maybe he was just taking a break."

Cross's brow furrowed. "The security detail? How did he not hear anything?"

"I don't know the answer to that, Detective," the constable said, his expression growing more somber.

"He was sleeping in the car when the butler called him, but there was no response. He then ran over and banged on the side of the car. His body was found slumped in the car with his head on his chest. No one saw anything, no witnesses, no clues. The driver's window was up, and the door was locked."

Borden's eyes narrowed. "You said the ambassador was found inside?"

"Yes," the constable said. "He was in the sitting room. He was shot in the forehead. No struggle, no overturned furniture, no witnesses. Everything's in place."

Cross and Borden exchanged a glance of suspicious realization, knowing this was unusual. The meticulous nature of the crime scene suggested a level of precision and cold calculation that was chilling.

Their initial impression reminded them of one name: The Ghost. A killer who left no clues, made no mistakes. No traces. Just a trail of bodies.

Borden turned his attention back to the constable. "Have there been any preliminary updates from the forensics team?"

"Not yet, sir," the constable replied. "They're still processing the scene. So far, there's been nothing out of the ordinary. No fingerprints were found. It's like the killer was a magician who just vanished into thin air."

Borden's frustration was evident. "Alright, let's start from the beginning. We need to know everything the butler saw or heard. Where is he now?"

"He's in the kitchen, sitting at the table. He's been in a state of shock since he found the body," the constable said. "I'll take you to him."

The detectives followed the constable to the kitchen, where the butler sat, his face ashen and eyes glazed over. The room, like the rest of the house, was impeccably clean, almost serene. The weary man looked up as they entered, his expression a mix of confusion and fear.

He stood to greet the detectives, impeccably dressed, well-groomed, a dignified gentleman.

"Mr. Thompson," Borden began gently. "Can you tell us what happened here?"

The butler's shaking voice was barely above a whisper.

"I... I didn't see much. I went to check on the ambassador, like I do every morning."

"When I arrived, I found him in the sitting room. He was... he was already dead. I immediately called 911 for help. I then hollered for the security guard and there was no response. I hurried over to get the security guard and that's when I saw him in the front seat," Thompson said, choking on the words. "I called him, but there was no movement. I assumed he was dead as well, but fortunately, he was sleeping. I have no knowledge of what happened here."

Borden nodded, taking note of the butler's distressed state of mind. "Did you hear anything before you found the body? Any noises? Anyone near the house?"

"No," Mr. Thompson said, shaking his head. "I didn't hear anything. It was... quiet. Too quiet."

Cross, observing the butler's demeanor, noted the man's trembling hands and the hollow look in his eyes. She approached him with a reassuring tone. "Mr. Thompson, I know this is difficult, but we need any detail you can recall, anything at all. When you left work last night, was the ambassador stressed or worried?"

"No, he was in a good mood and wanted a quiet evening at home, listening to music and reading."

Mr. Thompson's gaze seemed distant, as he appeared to be lost in a cloud of shock and fear. "I... I saw a car slowly drive by yesterday when I was outside retrieving the newspaper, and the driver was staring at the house. I thought it was odd, but I didn't think much of it because this is a beautiful house with well-maintained gardens and a lawn. Many people take pictures of the house."

"Did you get a good look at the driver?" Borden asked.

"Not really."

"Would you recognize him if you saw him again?"

"Possibly."

"Can you give us a description of the person?"

"No, I didn't get that long of a look at him. Let me think about it. I wasn't really paying attention to him."

"Do you know what color the car was or the make of the car?" asked Borden.

"No, sir. I don't know much about cars," he apologized, saying, "I wish I could be more help."

"No problem," said Borden.

Borden handed the butler his business card and asked him to call if he thought of anything.

"I'm sorry I couldn't be of any help, Detective," said Mr. Thompson.

Borden exchanged a look with Cross; their unspoken understanding was clear. This crime was executed with a chilling precision that hinted at a level of professionalism and callousness that was unsettling.

The detectives knew a crime scene this clean meant no clues. The pristine murders, no answers, only certainty that The Ghost had struck again.

As they left the kitchen, Borden's mind raced. "Cross, we need to dig into the ambassador's recent activities, his meetings, his contacts. Anything that might give us a lead."

"Got it," Cross replied, her voice steady despite her exhaustion. "I'll start with his schedule and contacts. We need to find out who might have had a motive or a reason to get close to him."

"Something doesn't add up," said Borden.

"How so?" Cross asked.

"Well, first of all, every window and door was locked from inside the house. Yet the ambassador was shot in his sitting room. What happened here? When was the ambassador killed? Was the ambassador killed first? Where was his security guard at the time of the shooting? And Cross, the security guard on duty last night was Ian Webber, he's one of us."

"If the ambassador was murdered first, wouldn't Webber have heard the shots?" Cross asked.

"Maybe, but what if a suppressor was used? Would Webber have heard that? If he did hear a suppressed shot, wouldn't he have called 911?"

"I see what you mean," Cross said. "Borden, could it be a weapon we're not familiar with? Maybe a homemade gun of some kind?"

"Interesting thought. We'll follow up on that once we get the autopsy report. Why not check our records, see if any other murders involve a homemade gun. There must be something on that in our database."

Meanwhile, Borden asked the forensic team if they could expedite their work on this particular case. "I need a full report ASAP. No detail is too small. We're looking for anything that might give us a clue, anything."

Borden asked the constable to escort Ian Webber to the kitchen.

Chapter 53

Borden motioned for Cross to close the door, then the three of them sat at the kitchen table. Borden turned to Webber. "Can you explain what happened?"

"Each hour, I left my car, walked around the house, and checked the doors for anything unusual. The doors were locked. I walked to the backyard but saw no one. I stopped, looked back at the house, then up to the second story. Silence."

"When I reached the front of the building, I scanned the street as usual. No one. Not even a dog barking. When I got back to the car, I opened the door, sat down, and thought I heard something. I can't be sure. Then I fell asleep," Webber said.

"Did you go inside?" Cross asked.

"No... I don't think so," Webber said.

"You don't remember if you went inside?" Cross pressed.

"Did you and the ambassador get along?"

"Most of the time," Webber said.

"What do you mean by that?" Cross asked.

"We argued," Webber admitted.

"You argued? About what?" Cross asked.

"He liked going to bars and clubs, the party scene. That made protecting him difficult. I told him he needed to stop or at least cut back and let his detail check these places first. He hated being told what to do."

"How did he respond?" Cross asked.

"He got angry and shouted at me."

"What did you do at that point?"

"I shouted back at him, and then we argued."

"Did anyone ever see you argue with him?" Cross asked.

"Yes, a few times. Others in the security detail had shouting matches with him as well."

"Anyone else witness your arguments?"

"Yes. We argued in the house a couple of times, and the butler and maid overheard us. Once, they were in the room when he ordered them to leave. He was impulsive and moody."

A knock sounded at the door. Borden stepped into the hallway, closing it behind him.

The forensics officer held up a plastic bag. "We were checking the car, and we found these." Inside were two brass shell casings, each sealed in its own bag.

"Sir, these match the caliber we use in our handguns. I should check Agent Webber for gunshot residue and inspect his weapon."

Borden exhaled sharply. "Great. Just what we need." He turned to the forensics officer. "Bring in your kit. We'll do it now."

"Yes, sir."

Borden returned to the room and sat across from Webber. "I need to see your gun. Hand it to Detective Cross." Cross instructed Webber to place the gun, still holstered and secured, into a large, heavy plastic evidence bag.

"Has the gun been fired recently?" Borden asked.

"No."

"Have you lent it to anyone?"

"No."

"One of our forensics team members is going to test your hands for GSR. If there is any gunshot residue, we will find it," Borden said. "You okay with that?"

"Sure, I've got nothing to hide. What's this all about, Detective Borden?"

A forensics technician arrived, swabbed Webber's hands for GSR, then left the room. The results came back a short time later and were forwarded to Borden. His eyes widened when he read that Webber's gun had been fired twice and had GSR on it, along with his DNA. The magazine was fully loaded, except for two missing bullets.

Another forensic technician tapped on the door, and Borden stepped into the hall.

"What did you find?" Borden asked.

"Sir, Agent Webber's fingerprints were found both inside and outside of the side door. We have a second set of the agent's prints on the door, slightly smudged, as if the door had been slammed at some point."

"We also found a half-full cup of coffee on a table in the mudroom with his fingerprints on it. We are testing the liquid for DNA now."

"One last thing, sir. We found some dirt on the car's floor, and it matches the dirt in the flower bed located by the side door entrance. We're also checking the floor of the mudroom and the hallway leading to the family room," the technician said.

"Thank you. Keep digging."

"Yes, sir."

"I'm John Mackie reporting live for CanWide News from the scene of a shooting here in the posh exclusive residential area of Rosedale Toronto. Police have not ruled out a possible murder. Sources tell us the victim was Ambassador Carlos Martinez of Mexico, who was shot and killed. Reports indicate that police already have a suspect in custody, and murder charges may be imminent. So far, there has been no official response from the Mexican government. We'll break into our regular programming with updates as soon as they become available. Reporting live from Rosedale this is John Mackie for CanWide News."

Chapter 54

As the forensic team continued their work, Borden and Cross combed through the house, scrutinizing every detail.

The sitting room, where the ambassador had been killed, was impeccably maintained. Nothing appeared out of place. Nothing seemed to be missing or broken, except for a bloodstain on the carpet.

The lack of clues and the many unanswered questions were eerie, and the silence felt almost oppressive. It was as if the house itself held its breath, waiting for the detectives to uncover the truth.

Meanwhile, outside in the lower driveway, the crime scene investigators continued examining the car where the security sentry's body was found asleep.

"What do you think happened here?" Cross asked.

"It is too early to tell. I can only speculate, and that could easily send us in the wrong direction."

As Borden spoke with Cross, his phone buzzed with an incoming call from one of his contacts.

"Borden, we may have something. A woman called in, saying she saw a car driving around the area then parked for about 30 minutes. She didn't get a plate number and doesn't know the make of the car. I'm sorry it isn't much of a lead, but maybe it's worth checking out."

Borden's pulse quickened. "Where was the vehicle spotted?"

"Apparently it was near our shooting address. We used satellite imagery, backed up the time stamp, followed the car and found it at a warehouse south of you at the edge of Lake Ontario. I don't have any more details, but I thought I'd pass it along."

"All right, I'll check it out. Can you send me the address?" Borden said, ending the call before relaying the information to Cross.

"We may have a lead. We'll check out this warehouse, then go home and get some much-needed rest. Who knows, it actually might point us to something."

The two detectives headed out, leaving the ambassador's residence, their energy and excitement renewed by the prospect of a potential lead.

"So, what do you think will happen to Webber?" Cross asked. "There's a mountain of evidence against him, and I believe he's facing an uphill battle. It will be rough. Our internal investigators will probably arrest him. He'll likely go to trial. If that happens, my guess is he'll end up in prison for 20 or 25 years.

The prosecutors need to establish a solid motive beyond just one or two arguments. The results of the GSR test pretty much makes this an open-and-shut case. Gunshot residue doesn't lie. The Crown will want to resolve this quickly to avoid an international uproar with the Mexican government."

"That's insane. Why would he kill the ambassador and use his department-issued gun? That's just plain stupid if you ask me," Cross said.

"We don't know everything yet. But you're right. It's stupid for him to use his department-issued gun and I'm sure the defense will raise that point at trial. Using that gun is like saying I'm guilty, come and arrest me," Borden replied.

"We're here, Cross. I know you must be exhausted by now but stay alert. No telling what we may find," said Borden.

The warehouse was a dilapidated structure with filthy, broken windows, rusted corrugated metal, poorly fastened and moving with the wind. Barely standing, it was situated along Lake Ontario waterfront, a few hundred yards below the expressway. The building emerged on their right as they approached from the north. The place appeared abandoned, its perimeter obstructed by overgrown vegetation.

A rusty chain-link fence enclosed the property. A weathered sign dangling by one wire on the front gate read: "CLOSED. NO TRESPASSING."

Borden and Cross moved cautiously, their footsteps crunching on loose gravel as they neared the entrance.

The warehouse's corrugated metal siding was corroded and battered everywhere, and the windows were either shattered or partially boarded up. A sewer stench lingered in the air inside the building. The empty structure magnified every step, echoing their arrival.

As they wandered cautiously through the damp building, their flashlights sliced through the oppressive darkness, revealing rows of empty crates and discarded cartons. A couple of tables, covered in dust and grime, sat in the middle of the area.

The space was eerily silent. The only movement was the shifting shadows cast by their lights and the occasional scurrying mouse.

"This place gives me the creeps," Cross whispered, her voice barely audible. "It's like a ghost town."

"Stay sharp," Borden murmured, his nerves on edge. "We don't know what we're walking into. I'm surprised we haven't seen a number of homeless people in here."

They continued, the tension mounting with every step, wondering if this could be a trap. The warehouse appeared abandoned, but they knew appearances can be deceptive. This wouldn't be the time to let their guard down, not now.

As they reached the rear of the warehouse, the dark outline of the Toronto Islands stretched across the water, distant and silent. Borden twisted around, his breath visible in the cool air. The place was empty. Lifeless. Their hope had run out. What they yearned to find wasn't here. It was never here.

It was time to get some rest before his special meeting tomorrow.

Chapter 55

The restaurant was located at the corner of the community of Islington Center Village West. It is a sought-after community of the younger generation with trendy restaurants, computer tables and not so comfortable. leather chairs., but it was one of the city's cherished affluent neighborhoods.

It was the sort of place that seemed to share whispered secrets, and keep them hidden.

The aroma of freshly brewed coffee blended with the low murmur of conversation, creating a comforting and inviting atmosphere.

A favorite among the trendy crowd, attracting patrons who enjoyed sitting close together at communal tables, pounding away on the latest laptop computers while sipping a five-dollar latte topped with whipped cream.

Borden arrived early and claimed a secluded table in the back corner, giving him a clear view to observe the entire café. He gazed out the window to a lonely, empty street, his thoughts entwined with the day's events. His partner's brush with death, the unraveling cartel investigation, and the two incredible murders pressed down heavily on him.

He needed to unwind, maybe venture to his cottage for the weekend, play a round of golf with his daughter.

When his brother arrived, he looked much as Borden remembered, graying slightly, a few extra lines around the eyes, but still carrying the same easygoing demeanor. His eyes scanned the restaurant, spotted Borden, and made his way over to the secluded corner. As he took his seat, a faint smile appeared on his face.

"Why are we meeting here?" he asked, his tone laced with curiosity and some confusion.

"This place is a little... quaint. And it's been ages since we last caught up. What's going on? Are you okay?"

"Good to see you too," Borden said.

He was used to giving orders, asking questions, and laying out plans. Today felt like a rare moment of vulnerability.

He looked at his brother, the one constant in his life, and sighed. "I almost lost my partner today," he began, his voice steady but tinged with a hint of emotion.

"And it hit me hard. I realized how much I've missed you. Maybe we could change that, see each other more than once a year."

His brother nodded, his expression softening. "I had no idea things were that bad. What happened?"

Borden hesitated, searching for the right words. "We had a narrow escape with a Mexican cartel moving drugs into Canada. It's possible they were the same ones whose product contributed to Mark Jr.'s death. It's messy. It's dangerous."

"Wow." His eyes focused on Borden. "That's serious business. I'm sorry to hear about your partner. Will your partner be, okay?"

"Cross is a tough woman and the best partner I've had on the force. Remember how Dad used to say he needed to trust his partner completely? That describes Janet Cross. I can trust her that much."

"That's a good thing, but you said on the phone you needed advice. Is that why we're here?"

"Exactly." Borden nodded. "We've been working a case that's hitting too close to home. I've always respected your insights. Sometimes, it feels you know more about the city than I do."

His brother leaned back, thoughtful.

"And you think I've got a police scanner hidden somewhere? Maybe in my car?"

Borden chuckled. "Something like that. I've wondered if you're working undercover or if you just have a knack for knowing things before, they hit the news cycle. I think you know more than you ever let on."

His brother's face remained mysterious, but there was a flicker of something, guarded maybe, with a hint of caution. "I've always had a good sense of what's happening around town. It's not so much insider knowledge and more about paying attention, and I'm well-connected."

The conversation drifted as Borden reminisced about their childhood. "Remember how Dad used to drill us about paying attention to the seemingly unimportant things? How could a small detail crack a case for him?"

His gaze grew distant. "Yeah, Dad was always big on that. The devil's in the details, he'd say. He had a way of turning everything into a high-stakes game."

"I remember Mom scolding him and telling him to stop, and he'd smile and say, Yes, dear, before continuing right on."

"Dad always said that minor details were key to solving any mystery."

Borden nodded. "Yeah, he believed that the smallest oversight could spell disaster. He hammered that into us every single day. Sometimes, I focus so much on the big picture that I miss those insignificant details right in front of me."

His brother's eyes narrowed slightly as he studied Borden. "You've always been the one to see the big picture, Mark. I guess I've always been more about the subtleties, the quiet whispers of the city."

Borden studied his brother, admiration and curiosity flickering in his eyes.

"Be the best at what you do, son," their father used to say. "Pay attention to your teachers. Find the obscure facts. Write them into your essays, and they'll know you were paying attention."

Borden asked, "Do you think Dad ever misses the job?"

"Dad loved his job, and everyone respected his dedication," said his brother.

Borden turned to his brother and asked, "So, what are you doing now?"

"Me? Still self-employed."

"You said that the last time. Doing what?"

"Mostly consulting."

"What kind of consulting?"

"Mostly helping CEOs, presidents, and CFOs solve staffing issues and restructuring plans."

"What companies? Any I'd recognize?"

"Can't say. Probably not."

"What's that supposed to mean? Why not?"

"Non-disclosure agreements or NDAs are all about corporate espionage. Lawsuits. The business world's cutthroat. That's the nature of business today."

"I'm a cop. You can trust me with this."

"I know I can. But my clients might not. I wish I could, but I made a promise. Can't talk about it. That's why clients seek me out, they know I won't say anything. They trust me. Knowing what I know? Someone could make a fortune if they knew what I did."

"I've noticed that. You catch what others miss. What's your take on the city's rising violence? Any insights?" asked Borden.

His brother took a slow sip of coffee, weighing his words carefully. "The most dangerous players? They stay in the shadows. Slip through the cracks unnoticed. Cover their tracks so you'd never know they were ever there. Sometimes, they've been around forever, working in the background, like ghosts, I guess."

A shadow of uncertainty crossed Borden's face. "That sounds like someone we've been chasing for years. We call him The Ghost."

Their eyes locked, Borden's filled with a steely resolve.

"The Ghost, huh? Interesting name. If he's real, there's a reason he's a ghost. I suppose a ghost is like the wind, you feel it, but you never see it coming or going. A real ghost wouldn't leave evidence. Wouldn't slip up. He thrives on being invisible."

"That's him, all right," Borden said.

His frustration was evident. "And yet, here we are, with a high-profile case, and no leads. The ambassador's murder was a precise execution. Chillingly efficient. No mess, no clues. It's like the killer wanted us to see his work but left nothing to chase after."

His brother's eyebrows lifted slightly. "The ambassador? Wait, are you talking about Carlos Martinez?" His tone shifted, tinged with shock. "I saw that on the news this morning. I didn't realize that was the case you're working. That's horrible."

"Ambassador Carlos Martinez. Mexico. Shot in his home. No clues at the scene. And to make matters worse? Looks like the killer was an RCMP officer," Borden said.

His brother stayed calm, but his gaze held an unreadable intensity.

"Sometimes, the best way to hide is to make the scene so clean that it becomes its own puzzle. Your so-called Ghost? Sounds like his MO, if it was him. But why an officer?"

"GSR showed up on his hands. When gunshot residue is on the hands, it's pretty much over. Shell casings were found in and under his car. We are testing his gun, but it's probably the murder weapon," Borden said.

"Oh man, I'm so sorry to hear that. That's a nightmare scenario."

Borden's phone vibrated, snapping him back to reality. He glanced at the screen, his expression hardening. "I have to take this." He pushed back from the table.

His brother watched him with a mix of curiosity and concern in his eyes. "Don't be gone too long. We haven't really caught up yet."

Borden nodded, the weight of his responsibilities clearly visible in his demeanor. He stepped aside and answered the call with a curt, "Borden."

The conversation was brief but urgent. As he ended the call and turned back to his brother, Borden's face was tense with the strain of his demanding role. "New developments. I need to get back to the scene."

"Aw, what's so important that you need to head back to work?" his brother asked.

"The ambassador's butler thought he saw someone driving by slow, staring at the house the day before the shooting."

"Can he ID the driver?" his brother asked.

"No idea. We'll bring him in, show him some photos. He might recognize someone. It's our only break, and I have to chase it."

"Hope it works out." His eyes softened, a rare moment of vulnerability. "Be careful, Mark. And remember, no matter how tangled things get, the details always matter."

Borden nodded with a faint smile. His mind raced with the implications of his brother's words. "Thanks. I'll keep that in mind."

As he walked away, unease settled in. Borden couldn't shake the feeling that their conversation had revealed more than just family connections. The insight his brother offered, though cryptic, seemed to hint at something deeper, an understanding of the city's darker undercurrents. Then again, maybe Borden was only tired and wished he'd be heading home, rather than following up with the butler of Carlos Martinez.

But he understood, this opportunity could be the one small detail that mattered most.

Back in the restaurant, Borden's brother sat alone, staring into his half-empty coffee. A faint trace of a smile crossed his face, his expression unreadable. It was as though he contemplated a mystery he had to solve. Then he murmured under his breath, "Better get back to work."

When Borden left his brother at the coffee shop and started driving, his thoughts became a whirl of unanswered questions.

The ambassador's murder, none of it made sense. Were there hidden motives he hadn't uncovered yet? These were pieces of a complex and growing mystery. His mind drifted to memories of his father, how he would struggle with a case, constantly reviewing every fact until everything clicked into place.

Friends and colleagues often told Borden he was just like his father, always chasing every clue, believing that every detail mattered. Borden took those comments as a compliment since he had always admired his father and the clever work he did.

As he drove back to HQ, he couldn't shake the feeling: the answers were closer than he realized.

Night had closed in, burying the city's secrets, making them more elusive.

For Borden, the search for an answer to his investigation was far from over. Then there was the matter of his brother's vague refusal to explain his consulting work. There was something off about it, something too carefully guarded.

He understood that in the cesspool of crime and intrigue, even the smallest clue could unlock everything. And maybe, just maybe, the key wasn't buried in evidence, but in conversations, silences, and instincts he'd learned to trust.

He thought back on the meeting with his brother. Their brief time together had been enjoyable. He just wished he'd had more time to dig deeper.

Chapter 56

Detectives Cross and Gibson entered the station just past 10:00 am and were greeted by a boisterous chorus of cheers and applause.

The normally busy squad room briefly fell silent in celebration of her return. Cradling a box of assorted pastries, Cross offered a weary but grateful smile. The sight of her colleagues' faces, reflecting genuine relief and happiness, was a bittersweet reminder of the dangers they faced.

As she made her way through the crowd, Cross felt as if she were in a whirlwind of gratitude and exhaustion. The office's familiar warmth felt oddly comforting after her harrowing ordeal. Her fingers trembled as she lifted the pastry box, the aroma of fresh-baked goods mingling with the rich scent of brewed coffee.

Gibson gave her a gentle pat on the back. "You look like you could use a dozen of these," he said, his tone warm but sincere.

Cross chuckled, the sound a rare escape from the anxiety of the ordeal she had experienced.

"Thanks, Gibson. I just might take you up on that," she said, offering him a pastry.

After the brief celebration, Borden and Cross stepped into his office as the squad room's cheerful commotion faded behind them. Borden's office, usually a cluttered maze of paperwork and case files, now felt like a quiet refuge. His worn wooden desk and leather chair were a testament to countless hours spent solving crimes and today would be no different.

As the door closed tightly behind them, Borden's expression hardened, shifting from relief to focused intensity.

"It's good to see you return, Cross. I know things were... rough."

Cross nodded, meeting his gaze. "Good to be back. But there's still a lot to unpack. What about our major case?"

Borden leaned back in his chair, steepling his fingers under his chin, lost deep in his thoughts.

"Let's get into it. The shooting at the ambassador's residence was clean. No mess, no signs of struggle. Everything inside remained undisturbed. The ambassador was killed while standing, caught off guard. No sign of forced entry. The security detail asleep. That makes no sense to me."

"We've been trying to bring down the ambassador for months," Borden continued. "And now, the lack of evidence at the scene suggests something familiar. This has The Ghost's signature all over it. We've been chasing after this guy for over a decade. This case feels eerily similar to cases involving The Ghost. Always meticulous, always vanishing without a trace."

Cross looked surprised. "The Ghost? I thought that was just a myth within the force."

"No legend," Borden said, his voice firm. "The Ghost is real and elusive. Whoever this is, they operate with an almost superhuman ability to remain unseen. No physical evidence. No witnesses. Just precise, efficient hits, and then gone. We are no closer now than we were ten years ago."

"So, what's our strategy? Recheck the house? The car? The grounds? We had to have missed something."

"I doubt we'll find anything new at the scene," Borden said. "The ambassador's residence was scrubbed clean. We canvassed the area extensively. Turned up nothing. But there's another angle I've been considering."

Cross leaned in. "What angle?"

"Jonathan Winthrop," Borden said, lowering his voice. "Our Minister of Foreign Affairs. He and the ambassador met often at the King Eddy Hotel, but no one seems to know why or what they talked about. There could be something significant, but we don't have anything solid yet. Maybe the two of them met with someone else. Maybe not. Right now, it's just speculation."

Cross's eyes flickered with curiosity. "So, you're suggesting we dig into their hotel meetings? What's the connection?"

"Strictly off the record," Borden continued, "CSIS has an undercover agent embedded in the cartel. We don't know whether they're in Canada or Mexico or what they're doing. We don't ask because they will deny every-thing and acknowledge nothing."

Cross absorbed the information, her mind racing. "And how do we get intel?"

Borden continued, "We patiently wait for the agent to send something. If they do, it could be big. It's possible this agent could tip us off to something significant, so we just need to wait. But, Cross, not a word to anyone."

"Crawford's combing through the hotel's records for leads," Borden explained. "Meetings, rented rooms, bar-tenders, anything unusual. Meanwhile, we gather what we can."

Cross nodded. "If you're okay with it, I'd like another look at the crime scene. You never know what we could find. We might've missed something."

Borden stood. "Good. We're not letting this slip. Not again."

They were about to leave when Borden's phone rang. He answered it quickly, his eyes narrowing as he listened. After a brief conversation, he hung up and looked at Cross with a grave expression.

"Crawford," Borden said. "Roadblock. The hotel staff are tight-lipped, and someone's messing with the security footage."

Cross's eyes brightened. "Interference? How?"

"It means someone is actively trying to block our in-vestigation," Borden said. "We need to push harder, find alternative sources of information. There's a chance that whoever is behind this knows we're getting close."

"Maybe I should change my plans and hit the hotel. Nobody knows me there. And sometimes waiters, well, they like to impress a woman," Cross said.

"Do it."

As she exited the office, Cross felt a renewed sense of urgency. She was well aware that persistence and attention to detail paid off eventually.

Chapter 57

The next morning, the sunlight cast long shadows over the Toronto skyline as Cross and Borden met in his office.

The atmosphere was charged, the previous day's revelations hanging heavy in the air. Borden stared through bloodshot eyes at a pile of documents on his desk, wishing he had gotten more sleep. He sat hunched over the files, rubbing his forehead in deep concentration.

Cross knocked firmly before stepping in. Her face was pale, her expression determined.

"You wanted to see me?"

"Yeah, have a seat," Borden said, nodding toward a chair. "The more I think about yesterday, the more unsettled I become."

Cross sat down, her eyes scanning the room, cluttered case files, a half-empty coffee cup on Borden's desk, a chair buried under paperwork.

"Do you know who did our department this big favor?" she asked, her tone guarded but hopeful.

Borden leaned back..

"The fact that the scene didn't produce a single hair, not even a boot print, it's almost like a calling card. This was no ordinary hit. We're dealing with the same elusive figure we've been hunting for the past decade, as I mentioned yesterday."

Cross's eyes lit up.

"You're suggesting The Ghost was behind this?"

"It fits the pattern," Borden said. "No mistakes. No evidence. No witnesses. Just a body."

"So, what's our next step?" Cross asked, leaning forward. "Revisit the scene? Re-examine the house, the grounds, the car?"

"Actually, I asked Gibson to sit down with Webber, see if he could notice anything during their conversation. The evidence against Webber doesn't sit right with me. Honestly, I don't think he did it."

"That's fine. Maybe something will come of it," Cross said with a nod.

"But going back to the scene won't help," Borden added, shaking his head. "The one thing we know is this guy never leaves a mess."

Cross frowned.

"What about Winthrop? He's the next logical lead."

Borden's gaze hardened.

"Winthrop's role is still murky. His meetings with Martinez at the King Eddy looked routine on paper. But if that's true, why the secrecy?"

"What exactly do we know about those meetings?" Cross asked.

"Nothing concrete," Borden admitted. "It's possible they were discussing sensitive government matters, but speculation won't get us anywhere."

He paused, massaging his temples.

"What I'm about to tell you must stay between us. Someone's life depends on it."

"I understand," Cross said.

"CSIS has an undercover agent embedded in the cartel. We don't know whether they're here or in Mexico, but we've got some inside information."

"Wow. That's good news. I hope."

"We need someone to dig around the King Eddy. Someone who can blend in, maybe talk to the staff. They'd be the logical source."

"I agree," Cross said. "And Crawford?"

"He's our main point of contact for now. He's handling the political side."

"What about Spade?" Cross asked.

"Her sources say Winthrop moved a large sum into a numbered account in the Cayman Islands. Martinez did the same just days before his death. That's troubling. I keep wondering, was it a payoff for the hit? And if so, who ordered it?"

Cross's mind raced.

"And Winthrop? What's his connection?"

"We're tracking him closely. He's set to travel to Mexico next week to meet the President. One more thing, Crawford says Winthrop has a new chauffeur. RCMP. Undercover. He'll report directly to Crawford."

"Who else was close to Martinez?" Cross asked.

"That's the problem," Borden said. "He had ties to so many people it's hard to pinpoint anyone. Maybe Webber's a fall guy, like Lee Harvey Oswald, if you believe that story."

"Do you think Martinez was involved with other ministers?" she asked.

"Maybe. Crawford's looking into it. We've got plainclothes officers and uniformed patrols watching Winthrop and his associates. It's a big operation."

A knock at the door interrupted them. A young detective entered, holding a folder.

"Sorry to interrupt, sir. We've got something from the King Eddy."

Borden flipped through the pages.

"What do we have?"

"A staffer remembers seeing a man matching Winthrop's description meeting with Martinez several times. Always on the mezzanine. No one knows what was discussed."

Cross glanced at Borden.

"It's a lead, but it doesn't explain much."

"We'll dig deeper," Borden said. "Right now, let's stay focused and keep pushing forward."

After the detective left, a quiet tension filled the room. Cross leaned back, her mind racing.

"If Winthrop's involved, we need to find out what he's planning with the President. And if The Ghost is still in play, we need to be ready for anything."

"Absolutely," Borden said.

Cross's phone buzzed. She checked the screen.

"Spade just sent an update. She has a lead, a possible connection between Winthrop and a foreign diplomat."

Borden's eyes lit up.

"That could be the break we need."

The mystery around the ambassador's death and Winthrop's possible involvement left them with more questions than answers.

Back in the squad room, Cross spotted Gibson approaching.

He looked serious.

"I just finished speaking with Webber. His story hasn't changed, and honestly, I'm starting to believe him. But one thing keeps bothering me."

"What's that?" Cross asked.

"Why would anyone break into a house, kill someone, then return to their car with the murder weapon along with shell casings, sit down, and fall asleep? I just can't believe anyone is that stupid."

"Interesting point," Cross said.

Chapter 58

The confines of the condominium and her self-imposed quarantine closed in on Tina.

She felt claustrophobic and wanted to break out of the condominium her self-imposed prison. Shadows danced across the walls, tugging at her concentration. She paced back and forth, anxiety building into a storm of uncertainty in her mind. The trappings of the condominium did nothing to calm or satisfy her agitated personality.

The suite, once adorned with expensive art and luxury furnishings, now felt unattractive and worthless. She no longer cared about those trappings that once represented comfort.

The colossal sum, over ten million, perhaps closer to fifteen or twenty, had become a double-edged sword. While it provided immense power and control, it also cast a blatant spotlight on the cartel's operations and her role in them.

The very wealth that was supposed to secure her future now felt more like a liability, something she'd never anticipated.

Madler's voice echoed in her mind: "It's in the millions... easily over ten to fifteen million, maybe more."

Those words served as a constant reminder of the inherent risks at play. But the money wasn't her immediate concern. The threat was the betrayal from within. She wouldn't let that stand. If there was someone, she'd find out who and bring it to an abrupt end.

Her phone buzzed, jolting her from her thoughts. Tina snatched her device from the table, her fingers trembling as she answered. "Sean, what's the latest?"

Sean's voice rumbled through the line, steady and clear but edged with tension.

"I've been monitoring Madler closely. So far, nothing out of the ordinary. But with this much cash in play, there's always a risk someone might be tempted to help themselves."

Tina's jaw tightened. "You think we've got a mole? Are you saying one of our own is leaking information?"

"I'm not accusing anyone yet," Sean said cautiously. "But with an operation this size, we have to consider every possibility. Remember the old saying: trust no one and verify everything."

The weight of Sean's words settled on Tina's shoulders. The hidden safe beneath the floorboards, once a symbol of their success, now felt like a disadvantage. If there was a traitor among them, the fallout could be devastating.

Tina's mind raced through a series of calculations and potential scenarios. She knew that any breach in their security could unravel everything she and Juan had built. That wouldn't please Arturo, who expected a healthy return on his investment. Everything surrounding her now seemed tainted by the potential for betrayal.

"Step up surveillance," Tina ordered, her voice resolute. "Watch everyone handling the cash. Report any irregularity, no matter how small, immediately."

Sean's voice remained steady. "I'll make it happen. I'll keep an ear out for gossip or unusual behavior. We've got to stay ahead of this."

As Tina ended the call, she stood still for a moment. The silence in the room gave her space to think clearly. She stared at the concealed safe, a vault of cash and gold that now felt like an obvious target. She knew she couldn't afford any slip-ups.

The possibility of a traitor was not just a hypothetical. It was a real and immediate danger.

Thankfully, she had Sean. He was loyal, relentless, reliable, and smart and ready to find the traitor.

Her thoughts circled back to Winthrop, the Minister of Foreign Affairs, and whatever hidden role he might be playing in this dangerous game. Just thinking about him unsettled her. She'd always kept a close eye on him, but now, more than ever, she wondered if he was part of the bigger puzzle. Was he the traitor?

Tina's decision was clear. She needed to reassess the entire operation. She dialed Sean's number again, her mind stirring with fresh concerns.

When he picked up, she got straight to the point. "Sean, I want intel on Winthrop. Find out if he's been in contact with anyone who could be competition. Hack into his computer. Look for anything that links him to us. Maybe he is the mole."

Sean didn't hesitate. "I'm on it. Anything else?"

"Keep it quiet," Tina warned. "We don't want anyone catching wind of this."

As she hung up, her eyes returned to the safe. Urgency clawed at her. The enormity of their situation compelled her to consider every consequence before making a move.

The money, the mole, and Winthrop's motives all wove a dangerous web that threatened to trap her. She wasn't going to let that happen.

Determined to regain control, Tina planned to visit Madler's safe house that evening. She needed to see for herself. Any sign of compromise, and she'd act.

With purpose renewed, she left the condominium, her mind locked on the challenges ahead. The night was dark, the streets empty, and Tina's resolve unshakable. She understood the only way to protect her empire was to stay one step ahead.

Chapter 59

The sun slipped below the horizon, casting long shadows across the landscape as Tina's car pulled up to the unassuming farmhouse.

Tina stepped out of the vehicle and scanned the area with practiced precision. The farmhouse, surrounded by fields and dense woods, seemed an odd choice for hiding such a considerable sum of cash. Yet the isolation made it an ideal location for Madler's operations.

Tina's concern about the security of her cash wasn't unfounded. The barn, where Madler had claimed the money was stored, felt vulnerable.

She made her way to the barn with purpose, her footsteps echoing off the wooden floorboards as she entered. Madler met her at the entrance, his face calm and unreadable. Tina studied him with a piercing gaze, searching for any signs of deceit. She found none.

"Show me," Tina said. Her tone left no room for hesitation.

Madler nodded and led her to the corner of the barn, where a large, reinforced safe was tucked away behind bales of straw, inside a horse stall. The sight of it did nothing to ease Tina's concerns. Despite the precautions, the spot was far from ideal for holding millions in cash.

As Madler began to turn the dial, Tina's eyes swept the barn, observing every detail. The former horse barn was cluttered with agricultural tools and hay bales, a seemingly mundane setting concealing a dangerous secret. The tension rose as the safe creaked open, revealing stacks of cash and neatly arranged gold bars.

Tina inspected every detail, the condition of the cash, how it was packed, and scrutinized the safe's lock. Madler lingered nearby, his anxiety obvious despite his attempts to fake a controlled exterior.

"This is a significant amount of money," Tina remarked, her voice cold and calculated. "And this place isn't nearly as secure as it should be."

Madler shifted. "It's the best we could do under the circumstances. We needed a place discreet and out of the way."

Tina didn't respond. Her mind was already racing through backup plans. If the money had to be moved, it would require absolute precision. Relocating such a hefty sum presented a new set of challenges.

Outside the barn, Tina tapped speed dial. "Sean," she said, "I want you to conduct a full review of our security protocols immediately. We can't afford any slip-ups."

Sean's voice answered right away. "What's going on?"

"We need to tighten security at the farm," Tina said. "We need to explore new methods to move cash to Arturo. I don't like this setup. It's too exposed," said Tina.

"I'll be heading back to the city. Convert most of the money to gold. It's heavier, but smaller and easier for us to hide. Keep me updated."

As Tina drove away, her thoughts were filled with the complexity of her situation. The protection of their assets was only part of the equation. The bigger concern was a traitor inside their organization. She had to make sure no one would interfere with her plans. She also needed to find the turncoat and dispose of him.

Back in the city, Tina met with Sean to plan their next moves. They met in a discreet, secure location where they could speak freely without being overheard.

"Have you found any intel on Winthrop?" Tina asked as soon as they were settled.

Sean nodded. "Yeah. I sure have. He's been involved in high-level meetings with foreign officials. His schedule's tight, but there are more than a few unexplained gaps."

"Unexplained gaps," Tina repeated, her mind working swiftly. "We need to find out what he's doing during those times. There might be something we're missing."

Sean hesitated. "Could be that Winthrop is using these gaps to coordinate with our competition. We'll need to dig deeper into his movements, note, and track his contacts. I'll keep a closer tail on him. There's something about Winthrop. I don't like him, and I certainly don't trust him."

Tina nodded. "And what about our money? We need to consider unusual ways to move it without drawing attention. Can we push the schedule up?"

"I've been researching options," Sean replied. "We could run it through shell companies and offshore accounts. Or we could use existing ops to slip the gold and cash into Mexico. Another option is to cross wasteland from Texas or California and move lesser amounts, so no one is suspicious."

"I'm nervous about those options," Tina said.

"Well, there is another option, and that involves purchasing short-term certificates from various branches of BBVA Mexico in the US. Being such a large bank in Mexico, no one would be concerned if we bought 30-day or 60-day certificates in the US and cashed them in Mexico.

We could use the same method of buying certificates from a Canadian bank and cashing them at a branch office in the US. That would get the money out of Canada to Mexico."

Tina considered the suggestions, her mind racing through the potential implications. "I want to move forward with both options, using lesser amounts to be sure it gets through. Start setting up the shell companies and explore secure networks. We need to act quickly and be careful. I think we should break up the money and send it in separate shipments on different days. Ship it directly to Fernando and be sure he knows when it was shipped. Keep him in the loop on all of this."

"I like your banking option, so let's test it as well," said Tina.

"Got it," Sean said.

The meeting ended, and she left with a sense of relief and a new determination. With the threat of betrayal looming and the task of safeguarding her wealth, Tina knew that every decision had to be calculated, precise, and triple-checked.

This wasn't just about protecting her money but ensuring the survival of the cartel in Canada. And as always, Tina intended to come out on top, no matter the cost.

At Police HQ, a call came in from EMS, reporting a domestic accident at a home in Rosedale.

Ambassador Martinez's butler, Mr. Thompson, was found dead, resulting from an apparent fall down a flight of stairs to the basement. The scene suggested he'd tripped, tumbling down the basement steps and striking his head on the concrete floor. A toppled box of produce from the weekly courier service lay scattered around him.

The coroner ruled it an unfortunate accident, a slip while carrying too many supplies down to the basement cold storage closet.

The report found its way to the desk of Detective Cross. She was shocked and read the report again.

She found it suspicious, too much of a coincidence, just days after the death of Carlos Martinez.

She needed to take a closer look. Something didn't add up.

Detectives Kim and Friedman headed to the home of Ambassador Martinez to investigate the circumstances surrounding the death of the butler. The pair of detectives weren't gone long. To them, it seemed straightforward.

Back at the station, they told Cross that they agreed with the coroner's conclusion, that it was an unfortunate accident. They speculated the butler had been distracted, maybe grieving the ambassador's death, and he was simply not paying attention when he attempted to carry a box of items to the basement when he lost his footing.

There was no sign of forced entry. No struggle. His shoes were scuffed, likely from slipping on whatever he'd been carrying as he stepped down onto the first stair and lost his balance.

A murder and one accidental death, all occurring at the same address within a week, was too much of a coincidence. Borden and Cross were convinced that there had to be more to it, and they wanted to be sure of what had happened.

"This is just too much of a coincidence," Borden muttered. He turned to Cross. "You buy the coroner's report?"

"I'm not sure. Why do you ask?"

"When we talked to the butler, he didn't strike me as a man who was careless. He knew exactly what he did that morning, so he wasn't forgetful. Why would he lug a large box to the basement?

And why didn't he break up the box of vegetables into smaller portions, especially if it was heavy or awkward? Sad as it may be, he struck me as someone who was highly intelligent, reliable, responsible, and most importantly, I felt he was careful," commented Borden.

"You're right about that. So, what's your gut telling you?"

"I think someone killed him."

Chapter 60

It was a large sprawling compound located beyond Tepotzotlán, nestled out of the way among the surrounding hills of the countryside.

This was the perfect setting. Seventy-five miles from Mexico City, the secluded location was a hidden epicenter of clandestine operations.

The compound, surrounded by high fences and watchful guards, hummed with practiced efficiency that concealed its underlying tension, just the way Arturo Fernando liked it.

Inside, the air was heavy with the dangerous, lingering stench of chemicals and dust, the perfect recipe waiting for a spark.

Dozens of workers moved with an eerie, almost mechanical precision. Their faces were hidden by wide-brimmed hats, and their conversation was sparse.

The rhythmic clatter of machinery, begging for grease, and the distant roar of generators created a relentless noise that the workers had long since tuned out.

Trucks parked haphazardly were being loaded with metal containers, bulging with their illicit cargo, destined for cities far beyond Mexico's borders.

In the midst of this chaos stood Señor Valdez, president of the Mexican Railway Company. His immaculate suit stood in stark contrast to the sweat and grime of the compound. Valdez's eyes tracked every movement. Each container bore a discreet identifying number.

His cell phone buzzed. He answered with a curt, "Sí?"

A tense, authoritative voice bellowed through the line. "Is the shipment ready?"

"Almost," Valdez said. "The last of the containers are being loaded now. I'm watching it happen. Trust me, I've got a close eye on everything."

He turned, gazing at a rundown shack. Inside, the workers were immersed in a blur of frantic efficiency, sorting and repackaging drugs with meticulous care.

A sudden commotion shattered the operation's steady rhythm. Two workers, exhausted from long hours and miserable conditions, exploded into a violent scuffle. Their bursts of anger fueled shouts and curses that cut through the otherwise muted hum and ambiance of the compound. The workers' faces were flushed with rage, their bodies straining against each other.

The guards swarmed in, yanking the fighters apart with practiced effectiveness.

One worker was pinned to the ground, his face grimacing in pain, while the other was pulled away, his shirt torn and his breathing ragged.

Valdez watched from a distance, his expression unreadable. His phone buzzed again. He ignored it.

The two men were quickly separated and forced back to their work. Their tempers were subdued, but the tension lingered.

Valdez's eyes darted between the workers and the containers, his patience thinning as his irritation increased. Another disturbance could jeopardize the shipping schedule.

Valdez directed his attention back to the metal containers being loaded onto a few canvas-covered trucks.

The process was simple, and each container had to be rechecked to ensure it was secured properly to avoid any spillage during transit.

As the final container was secured, Valdez's radio crackled to life. "The train is ready."

Valdez relayed the order. Trucks, their canvas covers flapping in the wind, rumbled toward a remote corner of the railway yard.

The metal containers were carefully lifted into place under each train car. The magnetic plates, custom-made to secure the containers, were fitted with precision as Valdez watched intently.

His phone buzzed again. This time, he snapped, "Sí?"

An impatient voice on the other end cut through the static. "I need an update on the shipment. What's the delay?"

Valdez's jaw tightened. "We've encountered an issue with one of the magnetic plates. We're working to resolve it now. I'll update you as soon as we're ready."

"I trust you understand the importance of this shipment. Don't make me wait."

The line went dead. Valdez's face was a mask of resolve as he turned his attention back to the workers. "Hurry up! We don't have all night!"

As the repair continued, the night deepened, and the atmosphere grew increasingly tense. The workers, drenched in sweat and grime, removed the plate with a sense of urgency.

Amidst the flurry of activity, Valdez's mind raced. He knew the immense value of this shipment. He had to get it right.

After what felt like an eternity, the final magnetic plate was in place, the fit secure and precise.

Valdez took a deep breath, his shoulders relaxing slightly as he surveyed the completed work. The train, now fully loaded, stood ready to depart.

He dialed Tina's number, his fingers tapping the screen with a mix of frustration and relief. When she answered, he kept his voice steady. "The shipment is ready. We've faced some delays, but everything is in place. The street value is close to twelve to fifteen million."

There was a pause on the line before Tina's voice came through, calm but with urgency given the situation. "Good. Keep me updated on any further developments. And make sure the shipment arrives on time."

Valdez nodded, even though Tina couldn't see him. "Understood. I'll inform you as soon as the train is on its way."

He ended the call and turned to oversee the final preparations. As the train began to move, he felt relief but knew the risks were far from over.

The train gently rolled out of the yard, bound for the terminal where it would load hundreds of passengers before departing north toward Detroit.

As silence and darkness slowly reclaimed the yard, the coolness of evening crept back in.

Valdez's thoughts were already on the next phase.

Tina's phone vibrated. She glanced at it.

The text simply stated, "It's moving."

Chapter 61

Tina's fingers glided over her smartphone as she sat at a small round mahogany table in the Deal Maker Bar, waiting for Winthrop's arrival. The dim lighting, soft jazz, and polished leather chairs created a setting of quiet elegance, but her thoughts were anything but calm.

Sean sat in a corner booth nearby, his laptop open, a recorder discreetly tucked beneath the table. He wore an ear piece. People would assume he as listening to music not a private conversation, if they noticed at all. He kept his head down, pretending to work, but his eyes were alert.

Winthrop entered with practiced ease, his designer suit flawless, his smile polished. He gave the bar a quick glance, before locking eyes with Tina. She stood to greet him, cool and composed.

"Winthrop," she said, extending her hand.

"Tina," he replied smoothly, shaking her hand before sliding into the seat across from her. "Always a pleasure."

Tina wasted no time. "Now that Martinez is out, it's time we reassess our strategy."

Winthrop gave a shallow nod, folding his hands on the table. "I'm listening."

She leaned in slightly. "We've tested an alternative to the train system. If it works, it could completely change how we move product."

Winthrop raised an eyebrow. "I assume you're talking about the pipeline."

Tina gave a slight smile. "Exactly. Minimal risk. We have access points at both ends and a team inside the maintenance department. We schedule shipments around official inspections."

Winthrop nodded, impressed. "And the trains?"

"Still in use. But they're the decoy now. If the authorities grab a small load on a train, it's a loss we can write off. Meanwhile, the real volume keeps moving through the pipeline."

Sean typed quickly, noting every detail.

At the bar, an undercover operative adjusted a small device clipped beneath the table ledge. His eyes stayed on his drink, but his ears were open.

"And the distribution on your end?" Winthrop asked, his tone casual.

Tina kept her expression steady. "Western warehouse network is operational again. From there, product is broken down and moved east by truck. We avoid using trains unless absolutely necessary."

Winthrop sipped his drink and paused. "What about upcoming political changes? Both here and in Mexico."

Tina's jaw tightened slightly. "We're monitoring the situation. If your re-election goes smoothly, we're solid. I'll fund your campaign discreetly. That keeps you in place regardless of who wins."

Winthrop's gaze darkened briefly, but he smiled through it. "Always two steps ahead, I see."

"Arturo still supports us," Tina added. "He's staying in the background for now, but he's invested. I spoke with him two days ago."

Winthrop nodded slowly. "And what does he want in return?"

"Money. Power. Loyalty. The usual."

Winthrop leaned back, his voice lowering. "And you trust him?"

Tina didn't answer right away. "I trust that he values the business and since I manage the business, that's enough."

A moment of silence passed. Winthrop's phone buzzed on the table. He glanced at it, then tapped the screen without unlocking it.

Tina caught the flicker of tension in his jaw. "Is there something I should know?"

Winthrop shook his head. "Just pressure from a few parties south of the border. Arturo has been nervous lately. He's worried you might become a liability."

Tina's eyes narrowed. "That's a lie. Arturo and I understand each other. We've worked too hard to let nerves get in the way."

"True," Winthrop replied. "But if he ever changes his mind, that could bring undesired trouble our way."

Tina didn't flinch. "And what would you do with that information?"

Winthrop smiled faintly. "Protect the operation, of course."

Behind them, in a booth near the bar, a man with short hair sipped an espresso and read the newspaper.

His name was Burke. He was a quiet observer these days, but his eyes were sharp. He had been tracking Winthrop ever since the ambassador's death. Something about the man didn't sit right.

Too many gaps in Winthrop's history. Too many unexplained associations.

Burke took a mental note of the exchange, especially the tension in Winthrop's face as his eyes narrowed and his forehead displayed crevices. He had a growing suspicion that Winthrop wasn't just a partner. Maybe he might be angling for something more.

Tina stood and offered her hand. "Let's keep the lines open."

Winthrop rose to meet her. "Always."

As Winthrop walked out, Sean joined Tina. "He's lying," he said under his breath.

"I know," Tina replied, watching the door close behind him. "But let's give him just enough room to hang himself."

Burke remained seated, casually folding his paper. He had heard enough.

It was time to dig deeper into Winthrop's past.

Chapter 62

Winthrop eased his car down the ramp into the underground garage beneath his luxury condo building on Sheppard Avenue, just across from Bayview Village Shopping Center. The car's headlights skimmed across freshly painted lines and polished concrete. He pulled into his usual spot, killed the engine, and stepped out, his polished shoes clicking faintly against the cement.

Burke, was parked at the mall across the street, and watched Winthrop's condo through binoculars. From where he sat in his sedan, partially obscured by a delivery truck, he could see the condo's glass exterior, entrance and the underground ramp. He lowered the binoculars and picked up a folded copy of the day's newspaper. It was the latest edition. The bar he'd just left didn't keep old ones lying around.

Inside the condo, Winthrop entered his suite and tossed his keys on the marble counter. The place was sleek, modern, quiet. He poured himself a glass of wine. He set it down untouched. Winthrop reached for his phone and selected a secure number.

It rang once before Arturo picked up.

"Winthrop," he said flatly.

"I have a concern," Winthrop said, lowering his voice. "Tina's getting reckless. If she draws too much attention to herself, it puts everything we do here at risk."

There was a pause.

"What are you suggesting?" Arturo's voice was cold.

"Maybe it's time to cut her loose."

Arturo didn't respond at first. Then came his measured reply.

"No. I have plans for her. Do not suggest this again."

Before Winthrop could speak, the line went dead.

Frustrated, Winthrop gripped the edge of the counter. A second later, his phone buzzed again. A message from an unlisted number. It was short.

Leave the building. Now.

His gut clenched. The timing was too precise.

He grabbed his wallet and phone and left the suite, locking the door behind him. The elevator was descending two at a time down to the parking garage.

A man in a maintenance uniform stepped out of the stairwell minutes later, calmly closing the door behind him. He walked to the exit, dropped something metallic into a trash bin by the side wall, and kept walking.

Burke watched Winthrop's car pull out of the garage and cross Sheppard Avenue toward the Bayview Village Mall lot. Winthrop parked a few rows down and walked direct toward the west entrance.

Burke waited, then stepped out of his vehicle and followed him inside.

Winthrop walked slowly, visibly rattled. He entered Il Fornello, a mid-range Italian restaurant, and asked for a table for one.

The hostess seated him in a corner. He ordered a sandwich and a glass of water but touched neither. He kept glancing at the entrance, to the mall hallway, and then to his phone.

Across the street, inside the condo tower, an explosion shattered the silence at 6:32 p.m.

A deep, muffled boom reverberated through the building. A ball of flame burst through the shattered window of Winthrop's penthouse suite. Fire alarms blared. Residents screamed and ran for the exits.

At Il Fornello, no one noticed right away. The condo was several hundred yards away. No heat, no rattling windows—just a distant thump.

Burke didn't react. He was too focused on Winthrop, who now sat stiffly in his seat, eyes darting toward the mall entrance. He checked his phone again.

Ten minutes later, it vibrated.

A text from Tina: Explosion at your building. Are you okay?

Winthrop didn't reply.

On the large screen in the mall's central rotunda, a breaking news alert flashed from CanWide News.

John Mackie stood on location, microphone in hand. Smoke billowed behind him as emergency crews worked to contain the fire.

"We're live at the Bayview Residences on Sheppard Avenue, where a powerful explosion rocked the upper floors of this luxury condo tower just moments ago. Fire marshals suspect a natural gas leak may have triggered the blast, but the investigation is ongoing. Officials say the explosion appears to be contained to a single unit, and there are currently no reports of injuries."

The camera cut to footage of firefighters entering the building and others cleaning up shards of glass.

Tina, watched from her condo, and didn't move.

She stood in front of the TV, eyes locked on the screen, one hand gripping the edge of the kitchen counter. She didn't call. Didn't text again. Just watched.

Burke slipped out of the restaurant quietly and returned to his car. He pulled out his phone and typed a quick message to Borden.

Explosion at Winthrop's condo. He's alive. Spooked. Watching him now. Will report back.

Inside Il Fornello, Winthrop paid his bill without touching his food. He walked out of the restaurant, looking around the mall as if trying to spot someone tailing him. He didn't see Burke. Didn't see anyone.

He left the mall climbed into his car and drove south, heading toward downtown.

By the time he checked into a boutique hotel near the financial district, his hands were still shaking.

That night, he couldn't sleep.

The next morning, he went to his Toronto office early and opened the hidden storage cabinet behind the fake wall panel. Inside were several neatly stacked metal brief-cases.

Cash. Gold. And something else.

He closed the cabinet and locked it.

Whatever came next, he'd be ready.

Chapter 63

Borden and Rankin met to devise a comprehensive strategy. Maps and area surveys were sprawled across the table as they discussed tactics to ensure precision, minimize risk, and prevent friendly fire.

Reports and photos from the hikers matched additional intel, estimated approximately 60 to 70 or more individuals at the campground. Shocked by the campground's scale, Borden and Rankin realized that a standard raid wouldn't cut it. They needed an unconventional strategy if they were going to pull this off.

Meanwhile, Cross returned from her medical checkup, her bruises and stiffness a stark reminder of her recent ordeal. Despite lingering pain, she'd been cleared for duty.

Borden, Cross, Rankin, Crawford, Spade, and Gibson gathered around the boardroom table, their faces etched with resolve.

They pored over maps and strategy sheets, building a meticulous plan to dismantle the rebel encampment with precision.

The room hummed with energy as the team considered each of their next moves. Borden paced, his eyes scanning a crude map stitched together from drone images, each detail a potential key to their success. Flash bangs, smoke bombs, and explosions dominated their debate.

Creating a massive diversion involving multiple remotely detonated explosions was on the table, as well as the potential pitfalls.

The discussions were filled with gestures toward the map, pointing out spots to plant explosives and possible fire zones. The team weighed the benefits of creating chaos as cover against the risks of placing and triggering multiple devices.

The plan would demand precision. Flash bangs and smoke bombs had to be hidden in dry containers as near as possible to the campground to avoid the grueling task of hauling them at the last minute when they would be under the most pressure.

Cross, her forehead furrowed in concentration, scrutinized the makeshift map. Her eyes darted between the entry points and the terrain, searching for the most effective strike zones. Each entry point was evaluated for its effectiveness in launching a surprise attack and the ability to seal off all escape routes.

As the debate escalated, Cross's voice cut through the noise. "We're looking at a dangerous situation that feels more like a suicide mission than a surprise attack," she said, her tone both serious and engaged. She leaned forward, her fingers tracing a path across the map.

The room fell silent as Borden turned to her. "What's your idea, Cross?"

She drew a slow breath before continuing. "We know their food delivery schedule. We've seen what they discard at the local dump. It tells us what they're eating. What if we taint their food or water supply with something that'll knock them flat on their backs and leave them bedridden, unable to respond to the raid? Think about it. If they're sick, weak, dehydrated, and stuck in the toilets, they'll be in no condition to fight when we hit them with flash bangs and smoke bombs."

She locked eyes with Borden, her suggestion hanging in the air. "We could use the confusion to our advantage. While they're incapacitated, we could breach the cabins and most likely secure the site with fewer casualties and less risk."

The room fell silent as the team absorbed the implications. The plan, while unorthodox, began to bring smiles to a number of faces.

For a moment, everyone stopped and stared over at Cross, thinking she was joking. Then, when the team realized she was serious, the room erupted in outright laughter.

The map lay sprawled across a large table, every detail marked, from the cabins to the vehicles parked in a grassy clearing, tucked away from all the cabins.

The vehicles, potential escape options, had to be disabled before any surprise attack. The team studied the images in silence, each person's gaze lingering on the vulnerable spots. Each one knew the way in and the way out.

Helicopter video showed figures moving through the training zones, running drills with sharp, disciplined routines. The reality hit hard. This was really happening.

These weren't just a bunch of new recruits lacking discipline. These were well-trained fighters. Any misstep could cost lives.

Rankin was the first to speak, his voice cutting through the nervous silence. "We'll need to close the highways," he said, still staring at the map. "My constables can handle it, and we'll evacuate any nearby cottagers. We can't risk civilians somehow getting caught in the crossfire by accident."

Gibson nodded thoughtfully. "Hospitals, too," he added. "They've got to be ready for casualties. Gunshots, trauma, everything. Let them know what's coming. Maybe we could get the medical staff to the staging area ahead of time?"

The team exchanged glances, the weight of the operation settling on them. Borden and Rankin knew it wasn't just about disabling the vehicles or securing the campground. The raid's logistics were a tangled mess, and time wasn't on their side. They had to strike fast when no one expected it.

Rankin spoke again, his tone grave. "We don't have the luxury of time to rehearse. We can't simulate this. We'll have to rely on the photos and video we have. We'll get a last-minute update just before we move. Look out for one another. If you see something potentially dangerous, shoot it."

A hesitant murmur of agreement rippled through the room. The team knew the risks of going in somewhat blind, but there was no alternative.

Borden stood, his facial expression tightening with concern. "We need a cloudy night, and it looks like we're expecting a short thunderstorm," he said, motioning toward the meteorological reports scattered across the table. "Moonlight could expose us. We'll need the cover of darkness, so the weather has to cooperate."

Silence returned as they processed the plan. They had to move fast, hit hard, and leave nothing to chance. Every team member memorized the layout of the campground, knew their role, and was ready to act without hesitation.

"Operation Whirlwind," Borden said, locking eyes with each member of the team. "We move out as soon as the weather gives us permission. And remember, nothing is left to chance. When in doubt, shoot to kill."

A quiet, unspoken tension settled over the room as the team nodded, understanding this was not a rehearsal.

Every detail, every move, had to be flawless.

"To ensure success, Commander Brad Smith, who most of you know, has joined us and will take charge. He has led many of these raids before. All successful. Never a single casualty. Don't spoil his record. He will take over from here," Borden said.

"Without an opportunity for practice, I want to remind everyone: there will be no second chances. Not for us, and not for them. If they fire on you, take them out. No hesitation," Smith said.

"Our tech support will cover us via satellite, but there could be the possibility of rain fade which would prevent coverage on the ground. They will be our eyes in the sky and alert us if there is no coverage for us. We'll try to use their live video feed before we engage in the attack. They'll be on comms, as will Borden, Cross, and me."

"Step one: we'll eliminate their power. The blackout should provide time for everyone to get into position. There could be gas-powered generators to restore the lighting, limiting our time in darkness. Now, it is time to wait for the meteorologist to indicate the best attack window," Smith said.

Outside, the clouds began to shift. Distant thunder rolled low across the sky. The promised storm was moving in, just enough to delay the operation by a few critical hours.

The sheltered team would wait. They knew their window of opportunity would come. And when it arrived, they'd be ready.

Smith gave permission to move out. They'd relocated to the staging area near the camp to await the go-command.

When the weather permitted, they'd hit hard. Until then, they'd just sit tight and wait.

Chapter 64

Rain flooded the windshield of the command truck as lightning danced on the horizon and surrounding forest. The team reviewed the details of their plan as they waited patiently in position at the staging area. Packed into vehicles or crouched under makeshift covers, no one complained. Nobody was bothered by the storm that had stalled their window of opportunity because everything was ready.

Inside the command trailer, Cross paced between monitors. She was still chasing something else.

The flurry of activity intensified throughout the room as the team grew anxious to commence Operation Whirlwind. Extra packs of ammunition were secured on belts and in pockets. The mood was upbeat, filled with laughter and determination as each personal weapon was checked twice and kit-bags were packed with extra supplies.

Each member of the team knew their role, mapped out, the operation meticulously planned. It would soon be time to crush and dismantle the cartel's network. Everyone understood the dangers, but the excitement of working with Brad Smith, a legend in law enforcement, fueled their drive. When the moment arrived, they would move fast, the gravity of the assignment pushing them forward.

Detective Cross paced the command trailer, her patience fraying. Her eyes darted between piles of evidence and a wall of flickering monitors. Each screen flashed with data, faces, phone numbers, scraps of conversation. Cross felt the sting of nerves, knowing she was walking into the fire, still slightly traumatized by the events of her recent past. She understood the risks, but this time she was ready. Cross wanted this opportunity.

She had a flashback to Winthrop, who was firmly in her cross-hairs. Cross was convinced he was deeply entangled in the drug business. But exactly how entangled was he?

She spoke with Crawford, her voice low and urgent.

"We need to get those warrants," Cross said, her tone cold and firm. "We need to hear everything the Minister of Foreign Affairs is setting up. Winthrop is up to his neck in this, I'm sure of it. If there's even a hint of corruption or betrayal, we need to know."

Crawford's voice crackled through her phone. "We're pushing hard. The judge is close to signing off, but it's a tough sell. We still need solid evidence."

Cross's gaze sharpened as she glanced at the mounting evidence on the table. The red tape, the political games, it all had to be cut away. Crawford's voice returned, taut, frustration and grit.

"We've got the pieces, we just have to convince them that the threat is real."

Hours of waiting blurred together until Federal Judge Parker finally gave the green light. It was a limited warrant, specific targets, specific conversations only. The focus was clear: the Minister of Foreign Affairs, and by extension, any calls to the President of Mexico.

Cross nodded in appreciation, her mind racing through the implications. Eavesdropping would commence soon, but the evidence had to be airtight. There was no room for error.

Meanwhile, across the command trailer, a cold chill seemed to swirl in the air, heavy with the shadows of recent events. Danielle Spade of CSIS, her face drawn with fatigue, delivered a bombshell.

"We've got solid intel suggesting Winthrop might have been tipped off about the assassination attempt on the ambassador. It's unsettling."

Cross's fingers tightened around her coffee cup. "Winthrop? That's a major lead. But how solid is this intel?" Cross asked.

"Pretty solid," Spade confirmed. "There's chatter that the Minister's close Mexican officials, they're the people who might have tipped him off."

"And Winthrop did nothing with that intel? Did he want him killed?" Cross asked.

"It's possible," said Spade.

The announcement of the ambassador's death from the President of Mexico was broadcast with raw anguish, his grief echoing across television screens around the world.

He condemned the Canadian government for failing to protect Ambassador Carlos Martinez, his voice seething with a mix of grief and rage. His words hung in the room, each syllable landing like a heavy hammer blow.

"He's not pulling any punches," Cross murmured, her eyes fixed on the screen as the Mexican President's fury built. "He's turning this into a political firestorm."

The President's face was grim as he announced three days of national mourning and ordered the lowering of flags to half-mast.

"A formal state funeral," he declared, his voice filled with sorrow and pride. "Our ambassador will be honored, and the Canadian government will answer for this atrocity."

His words struck like a hammer blow, and the fallout was immediate. The Mexican President's fierce rhetoric threatened to fracture the fragile diplomatic ties between Mexico and Canada. The implications were dire, extending far beyond the ambassador's assassination.

Watching the eighty-five-inch television in the privacy of their five-star penthouse, Tina and Juan watched the broadcast in silence, their concern growing. The flickering images of the President's broadcast alarmed them, underscoring the gravity of the situation. The announcement of a state funeral, the outrage, the political condemnation, it all spelled potential trouble.

Tina's eyes were cold as she processed the newscast. "Everything just changed. The pressure is on us now. We need to move fast and more carefully than ever," said Tina.

Juan nodded, his expression tense. "If the political tension between the countries gets any worse, it could jeopardize or destroy everything we've built. I'll do my best to keep our movements to a minimum so that we're invisible."

Chapter 65

Madler's truck rumbled down the winding dirt road, its tires churning up a cloud of dust that feathered into the gray, overcast sky.

The air outside was abundant with the scent of pine and earth, a stark contrast to the sterile concrete spread of Toronto's streets the pair had left behind.

The countryside swallowed both of them, casting long shadows as the last hints of daylight filtered through the canopy of trees.

Juan's mood spiraled. He felt sad and alone, a feeling of desperation, a growing sense that his future was slipping away.

He rarely showed emotion, but tonight his face seethed with pent-up frustration. The urgency of this clandestine meeting had pushed them from the city, where the walls were closing in.

When Madler finally parked and cut the engine, the silence of the forest swallowed the last remnant of sound. They stepped into the damp chill, the cold creating bumps on their skin as they moved toward a small clearing wrapped in dense foliage.

Here, beneath the sprawling canopy of an ancient oak, they would talk. Maybe even confess to each other.

Juan kept fidgeting with his hands, his eyes darting as though the trees were listening to his conversation. His lack of focus was an obvious reminder of his heightened paranoia.

The meeting was arranged in haste, and he had insisted that he and Madler meet far from any place that could be bugged or watched. He had seen the brutal side of their world many times, but this felt different. Something had rattled him.

Madler led the way into the clearing, each step slow and deliberate, muffled by the spongy forest floor. He glanced over his shoulder to ensure they weren't followed, trusting the precautions he had put in place.

The spot was secluded, providing the perfect cover for their conversation.

As they sat on rough-hewn logs that served as makeshift benches, Juan's frustration boiled over. He cracked.

"You know what, Madler?" he said, his voice low and intense. "I can't shake the feeling that everything's coming apart. The interrogator had me tied down and continued beating on me."

Madler nodded, his expression tight with understanding. "Tell me about it."

Juan's fists clenched as he spoke, anger burning in his eyes. "They were relentless and didn't stop. Blow after blow until my face was swollen. It felt like hours of questioning, no mercy. I thought I'd lose my mind before he let up. I wanted to rip him apart, no hesitation. But I couldn't. Too risky. He's got connections. He's got eyes everywhere. In a fair fight? He wouldn't stand a chance. I'd have killed him in less than two minutes, tops."

The words poured out like venom from a snake bite, and Madler saw the toll it was taking. Juan's rage felt alive, a living entity pulsing with every beat of his heart. Known for his brutality, Juan was accustomed to holding power through fear, but this was now personal.

"Listen," Madler said, keeping his voice calm. "I get it, you want revenge, but you've got to be smart. Charging in without thinking of the consequences could come back to bite all of us."

Juan's jaw tightened, his anger and rage simmering under the surface. "I'm supposed to be training new recruits, but I'm pushing that back. I need time to cool off. Maybe I'll head back next weekend. Right now, I've got to clear my head."

Madler caught a flicker in Juan's eyes, a dangerous mix of frustration and resolve.

He could tell Juan was close to the edge, and it made him all the more dangerous. He had to keep him focused, had to keep the plan from unraveling.

"If that guy comes at me again, I swear I'll drop him on the spot," Juan said, his voice cold and determined. "But you need to be careful too. If he hauls you in, watch what you say. You know how dangerous that can be."

Madler's expression grew tense. He understood exactly how risky this could be. "I'll be careful. You have my word."

The conversation shifted gears as Madler glanced up at the darkening night sky. The stars began to pierce the sky, and the forest came alive with the sounds of nocturnal creatures.

An abrupt rustling in the brush made both Juan and Madler freeze, heads swiveling fast in the direction of the sound. Juan instinctively reached for his gun, but Madler stopped him with a firm grip on his arm.

"Relax," Madler whispered. "Probably just a raccoon. Still best to stay sharp."

Juan eased off the grip on his gun, but his eyes remained focused on the trees.

"I caught the news about Martinez," he said abruptly, a grim edge to his voice. "The Mackie guy on CanWide News said Martinez didn't see it coming. I wonder how he knew that."

Madler nodded. He had seen it too, the news still fresh in his mind. "Yeah, it's all over CanWide News. They're running it nonstop. They initially reported no leads and no suspects. Just a mess. Now they're reporting his security guard killed him, then fell asleep in his car."

Juan let loose a dry laugh. "Some friends think I pulled the trigger. Can you believe that? I wasn't even in the city. Whoever did it... they did a heck of a job. No fingerprints. Nothing."

Madler studied him, speaking slowly. "So, you're saying you weren't involved? I'll take that, but there's always room for doubt, you know." They both chuckled.

Juan's expression tightened. "Madler, I promise you, I'm innocent. I didn't squeeze the trigger, I'm clean this time. Thought about it, yeah. But I didn't do it."

The forest closed in as night took hold, the hoot of an owl breaking the silence.

"I've been thinking," Madler said, shifting on the log. "If things keep going sideways, we might need to rethink our strategy. This isn't just about dodging bullets anymore. It's survival."

Juan's eyes flashed cold. "Survival? You think I don't know that? Every move we make, it's a dance with death. But we have to keep planning. And if we need to, we'll strike back, hard."

Madler nodded as the weight of his comment sank in.

"Right. We'll keep our heads down, stay alert. The last thing we need is to walk into a trap."

As the night deepened, their conversation grew more subdued but remained intense, their voices blending with the forest's nightlife. The dangers were real, and in their world, trust was paper-thin.

Madler spoke again, quietly. "You're unhappy, Juan. You said you're tired of training recruits. Why don't we take some money from the stash I have? Disappear, start fresh. Go somewhere different where no one knows us. If you were to ask, maybe your sister would join us."

Juan chuckled, murmuring, "That's a sure way to die young. The cartel doesn't stop hunting. They'd find us, kill us, along with everyone we know. That's how they send a message."

"I guess you heard that Ramirez was found dead in his cell?" Juan said.

"What happened?" Madler asked.

"Not sure, but Tina said it had something to do with peanuts."

"Oh, wow, that's crazy. Who do you think did it, or was it an accident?"

"Cartel, man. That's what I'm saying. They'll find us and kill us."

Madler pressed on. "We're dead either way. But maybe we can vanish, create new identities. If we tip off the cops about the location of the encampment and drug houses, they'd raid them, and the cartel will think we were either arrested or killed in the crossfire. We could fake our deaths, be remembered as cartel heroes. Let's move to England, Switzerland, just somewhere different."

Juan considered the idea, his mind racing with various possibilities. This could be the perfect setup for a double-cross.

"Okay, Madler," he said. "If you think you can pull this off without getting us caught, I'm in."

The two men plotted to grab as much money and gold as they could from the cartel's stash, then vanish. Madler's adrenaline surged at the thought of breaking free with millions, but one detail nagged at him: how, when, and where would he kill Juan without getting caught?

Madler also planned to leak the names of government officials on the cartel's payroll, to trigger a scandal. Can-Wide News would love a story like this, Madler thought to himself.

Juan displayed no outward sign of the disgust and anger as he listened to Madler's explanation of how his plan would take shape. As he smiled and laughed with Madler, his own agenda was secretly forming in his mind.

Minutes ticked by, heavy with unspoken fears and shared intent. Finally, Juan stood, his face hard with resolve.

"Partner, we need to move. Stay sharp, Madler. This isn't over."

Madler watched as Juan disappeared into the darkness, his silhouette swallowed by the trees. Alone with his thoughts, Madler knew the fight ahead would be more dangerous and deadlier than either of them imagined.

The sound of the truck's engine faded into the distance, leaving only the haunting silence behind in the clearing.

Chapter 66

Juan met with Tina, his mood as dark as midnight, fists and teeth clenched tight. He exposed Madler as a man who couldn't be trusted.

Tina immediately screamed at Juan as he replayed the conversation he'd had with Madler, making sure to emphasize the millions Madler claimed to have amassed for the Cartel.

"Where is the money?" Tina demanded.

Learning that Madler planned to steal the money sent her blood pressure soaring, and she knew it would do the same to Arturo Fernando. The repercussions of this betrayal would rip through their world with the force of a hurricane.

She appreciated Juan's loyalty, but the thought of Madler thinking he could double-cross the Cartel made her seethe. It wasn't just the betrayal. It was the threat to her well-being and her standing within the Cartel.

Tina's fury intensified as she thought about everything she had done to free both Juan and Madler. Juan was blood. Freeing him was justified in her mind. But now, knowing Madler's treachery, she wished she had ordered him tossed from the helicopter.

She stormed out of the room and slammed her bedroom door. Sean looked surprised but knew better than to question her when Tina gave him clear and direct orders. He knew exactly what to do and headed toward the car.

Tina's thin, trembling finger jabbed at the elevator button as she fought back a rush of emotion. She tried to stop thinking about the betrayal, knowing the solution was just hours away.

Tina used her Uber app and arrived at the Eaton Center for some mindless shopping. As she wandered the upper concourse, her thoughts kept drifting back to a massive trainload of drugs inching closer to Detroit to split east to Toronto and west to Vancouver.

Juan's phone buzzed, snapping him out of his thoughts as he plotted his ultimate revenge. The message from Tina glared at him.

"Madler's a liability. It's being handled."

There was no ambiguity in her words.

Juan had always known Madler was ambitious and reckless, but he hadn't anticipated betrayal this deep. In their world, disloyalty was normally rewarded with a crushing, violent end. The treachery left Juan deeply unsettled. It threatened him, Tina, and their standing in the Cartel. That was unacceptable.

Tina held her phone, knowing it would vibrate. She was already planning to appoint a replacement from Madler's trainees, someone who would keep business running smoothly as expected by Arturo Fernando.

While wandering aimlessly in the Eaton Center, Tina walked past some jewelry stores replacing shattered display cases under the watchful eyes of armed security. She didn't stop and join the crowd watching but continued moving. She kept glancing at her phone, anxious for a message. Heading to the west entrance of the mall, Tina waited for her Uber to transport her back to the condo.

Meanwhile, Sean tracked Madler using the GPS units Tina had secretly ordered installed in all the Cartel vehicles months earlier. It was a clever move. Tina could track everyone without them knowing.

For Madler, it could prove fatal.

Tina watched as Madler hit each of the drug houses, just as Juan had told her he would. He scooped up all available cash and drugs, then left in a hurry.

With each stop Madler made, her anger and blood pressure spiked, which was why knowing what she planned for Madler thrilled her.

This situation reminded her of the time Madler drove up the Don Valley Parkway and out to the Mississauga warehouse with the police right behind him, completely unaware. Obviously, he hadn't learned much from that experience, she thought. It was time to clean up this mistake.

Once Madler hit Highway 404, heading out of the city, he felt a sense of freedom driving a car stuffed with Cartel money.

He would help himself to millions at the farm, then in just a few more hours he would kill Juan and disappear with the money.

The text Madler sent said the police were going to swoop in on the houses and shut down the Cartel.

Great plan. I'll meet you at the farm soon.

To Tina, Jason Madler was a traitor, and he'd get the justice a turncoat deserved.

Madler kept calling Juan, but there was no answer. At first, he thought it was odd, so he kept trying, over and over, with the same result. Even then, Madler wasn't suspicious. Why worry? In a few hours he would be gone.

Naively, he thought he had flipped the brother of the most ruthless, cunning drug-smuggling trafficker in the country. All in an effort to steal the proceeds from her Cartel empire.

Juan was smart to ditch his old phone, Madler figured. He was using a new burner. All he could do now was wait. Either Juan would show, or he'd call. Perfectly logical, Madler told himself.

It had been a hard day, accumulating cash, stashing a few drugs, and preparing for the trip out west. Madler struggled to stay awake. He knew it was time to crash. But first, he had to condense the cash and gold and stash it in the barn safe until they were ready to move out.

He neatly stacked the bills, banded them tight, and cut the load of cash down to three stuffed portable bags.

The gold stayed separate. He was all set.

Still, no sign of Juan, and that began to worry Madler. What if the cops had arrested him? Had he changed his mind? Should he bolt without Juan? After all, he was going to kill him anyway.

He decided to try to grab some sleep before he and Juan took off with the money, assuming Juan showed up. In fact, it would be better if Juan grabbed the cash from the barn, giving Madler the perfect opportunity to shoot him when he was holding the money.

He would bury Juan behind the barn and drive west with the money. Nobody could trace him. They wouldn't know where he was or where he was headed. In his mind, it was perfect.

Madler headed to the barn and hid three loaded pistols in different locations so he would have quick access to a gun when he needed one. Everyone would assume Juan took the money. As for Madler, he'd vanish without a trace.

The farm's exterior looked unremarkable and forgettable. A couple of lights flickered in the distance, casting jagged evening shadows. Sean parked a discreet distance away, scanning with the eyes of a man who had done this before.

Nothing moved.

The surveillance gear hidden in the Cartel cars was working flawlessly. Live footage popped up on his laptop, the images bright in stark contrast to the darkness.

Sean waited. Listened to the wind stirring the trees as he eased from his car and stood quietly. A light, cool breeze brushed across his arms and back. He pulled out his phone and silenced everything, its ringer, vibration, and alerts.

Dry leaves and twigs crunched softly underfoot as he crept to Madler's car and peered inside. Empty. No cases, no bags, and no boxes. The hood was cool to the touch.

He vanished in the shadows, making his way toward the barn, allowing his eyes to adjust to the dark interior. No movement. No sound. He pivoted and crept quietly up to the back door and waited.

The hinge squealed as the door was gently opened and clicked behind him. He froze. Everything was quiet, except for the grating snore falling down from upstairs.

Sean saw the empty bags. Madler had organized and condensed his haul into a few bags for easy travel.

His eyes adjusted to the interior darkness. All he could hear was the disgusting noise of some idiot snoring, so loudly, Sean could hardly wait to stop that train with a bullet.

Sean climbed the stairs, slow, careful, one tread after another.

On the second floor he stopped, surveying what was before him.

A hardwood hallway stretched out in front of him. All of the doors were closed except for the one with the human foghorn inside.

He checked the hallway again, then removed the safety from his Glock and breached Madler's room. He froze, waiting, his gun trained on Madler.

Hearing the click of a gun snapped Madler's eyes open. A 9mm Glock was hovering three inches from his forehead. He didn't move. Paralyzed by raw terror.

Sean said, "I will only ask this once. Listen carefully."

Madler was beyond terrified. He nodded his head fast, his eyes wide and gleaming like silver dollars, ready to agree with anything.

"Where's the money?" Sean snarled.

1...2...

Chapter 67

After his meeting with the chief, Borden dropped a file on his desk and leaned back in his chair. The conversation had been encouraging, but tension lingered as Borden wondered how the prosecutors would take his comments.

There was no trial date set, and from all the evidence the prosecutors thought they had, a trial would not take up much time.

The ambassador's shooting involved one of Crawford's agents and was considered an open and shut case. The agent would be found guilty, and the potential for an international crisis would be quietly avoided. He'd go to prison for twenty years, the politicians in both countries would be satisfied, and the killer would soon fade from memory.

Borden kept reviewing the case, feeling something didn't make sense. Where was that one small detail, Borden wondered?

Cross knocked and stepped into Borden's office.

"You wanted to see me?" she asked.

"Yes. Have a seat.

"My meeting was focused on the ambassador's murder. Politicians are pressuring us to go to trial looking for a guilty verdict, hoping to avoid an international incident."

"I've thought about the case too. Honestly, I'm sorry he's dead. I would have preferred to arrest him myself and see him go to prison," Cross said. "Had I done that, I believe my sister Karen would be pleased."

"I get it," Borden murmured quietly.

"Cross, something's gnawing at me. This case feels too perfect. I'm beginning to doubt the evidence."

"If I remember right, you're friends with the prosecutor, aren't you?" Borden asked.

"Yeah, we've known each other for about fifteen years. We grab dinner once in a while and get caught up."

"Could you call their office? See if they'd be willing to meet with us here, or their office, and go over the case?" Borden asked.

"I'm on it," Cross said.

An hour later, Cross tapped on Borden's door and said, "We've got a meeting first thing tomorrow. Probably two of them coming over. My friend Todd Jefferies is the lead."

"Good. Let's meet later today to prep. Contact Crawford and invite him to the meeting. I'm sure he will want to be here."

At 9:00 a.m., everyone gathered in Borden's meeting room next to his office. Following the introductions, Borden asked the prosecutor if he'd decided to move to trial.

"The case looks solid based on the evidence," said Todd Jefferies. "We have the murder weapon, and the lab confirmed it's the gun that killed the ambassador. We also found gunshot residue on the agent's hand and in the holster. His prints were on the side door handle, and we recovered two shell casings, one in his car and one under it."

Detective Cross glanced at Crawford, and then over at Borden, who gave a slight nod. The evidence was compelling.

Cross said, "I received the forensics report, and there are some things that don't line up for us. If the agent is innocent, we drop all the charges. If guilty, he should go to jail. I think we can all agree on that, right?"

Everyone around the room nodded their agreement.

Cross continued, "For over ten years, we've had multiple flawless crime scenes, perfect, no mistakes. We believe they were all the work of the same individual. We call him The Ghost. He never leaves a trace. He has never made a mistake. No weapon. No shell casings. No prints, no witnesses. Nothing stolen, nothing broken. Not a single slip. Absolutely nothing. He commits the perfect crime," said Cross.

"Okay, that's a nice history lesson, but what's it got to do with this case?" Jefferies asked.

"Well, when we review this case, it's eerily similar. No damage inside the house, no footprints, no casings, no witnesses, no prints," said Borden.

"Not so fast, Detective Borden. We have his prints on the side doorknob," said Jefferies.

"Yes, that's true, but if you check all the doorknobs, his prints will be on every single one. He does hourly rounds and checks each door to make sure it's locked, even including the garage. Not only that, but he also pushes on all ground-level windows to be sure they are locked as well," Borden said.

Cross spoke up and said, "What bothered me was the accused in his car asleep. Who'd return to his car after killing a high-profile target like the ambassador, and then fall asleep in his car, which happens to be parked at the murder scene?"

"Doesn't that seem weird? No one could possibly be that stupid," said Cross.

"I'll give you that, Cross," said Jefferies.

"The gunshot residue on his hand is very convincing," Crawford said. "But if you go by the forensics report, why wasn't there any gunshot residue, GSR, on the sleeve of his shirt, wrist, forearm, or chest? There wasn't any on the front of his shirt, his jacket, or his pants. And the kicker is, there wasn't any DNA evidence anywhere on his clothing, not even his shoes."

"You're right, Crawford, that doesn't make any sense," said Jefferies.

Borden commented, "It was a warm evening with a breeze according to the Weather Network. The agent said his car window was open when he was taking a break and waiting for his next walkabout. But the butler reported calling to him in the morning, and going to his car, he found all the windows were closed and the door locked.

"Sure, he could've closed the window. But I don't think he did, and he doesn't remember doing it, and honestly, I don't think he did.

It cooled off during the night, but it was still a very mild night, so he would have at least cracked the window open. You need your keys to access the car accessory panel. The panel was off, no radio left on because the keys were in his pocket and he apparently was using his phone, yet it was found on the passenger's seat.

"I invited you here because of our thoughts on this case. There are too many unanswered questions. Agent Crawford can confirm this man's a highly respected officer. There is not a single blemish in his record. I really don't think this man should go to trial, but that's your decision. I assume there would be no objection if we were to provide his defense team with a transcript of our conversation?" Borden said.

"Not at all," Jefferies said.

"It's time for us to wrap up for today, as I heard the weather is about to change. Thanks for coming over and hearing our thoughts on the case," said Borden.

"You have raised some interesting and valid points, and I will be sure our team gives your concerns a fair hearing. I'll get back to you as soon as I know more," said Jefferies.

Chapter 68

The sky faded from a dull, thick, rain-filled gray to a lighter shade, casting a somber hue across the pine forest as moonlight peeked from behind cumulus clouds intermittently.

Scattered rain gently fell through a misty fog while thunder rumbled softly, preparing to blanket northeastern Ontario. The air was heavy with the promise of a gentle rain as wind stirred the leaves high in the treetops of the surrounding forest.

The pungent scent of pine needles mixed with damp earth hung in the air, amplifying the tension as men scrambled to move machinery to safety and get to shelter for some rest, far away from the tender overhead storm.

Borden read the silent "go-time" text from Smith, his jaw tightening and his heart pounding. He knew many men would be killed or wounded today, and he silently prayed for mercy and protection for the strike force.

This was it.

Finally, Operation Whirlwind was about to begin.

Beside him, Detective Cross double-checked her gear, her sharp eyes scanning the forest. She was always ready, always precise. Her meticulous nature ensured there was no room for error. She knew today wasn't a simulation or computer game. This was real. She touched her backup gun, her ammunition, her combat knife, securely fastened to her belt. She was more than ready.

After what felt like an eternity chasing justice, having dealt with shootings, courtrooms, criminals slipping from custody, months of surveillance, kidnapping, planning, and significant preparation, it might finally end today.

The thunder was farther away now. A light mist continued to fall, clinging to their uniforms as strike teams readied themselves by quietly shuffling into position.

Around them, the forest seemed to hold its breath, patiently waiting. No one spoke. They didn't need to. Crouching low against the underbrush, weapons at the ready, the team leaders communicated in hushed tones, splitting into smaller attack units as they vanished in separate directions deep into the woods.

Only soft rustling leaves and the occasional snap of a twig broke the stillness.

Borden and Cross had met Commander Brad Smith at a staging area north of Orillia. Camouflage paint darkened their faces, allowing them to blend seamlessly into the shifting shadows dancing across the forest floor.

The strike force had been briefed. They needed to be quick, decisive, ruthless. The plan: hit hard, hit fast, neutralize the mercenaries before they had a chance to react.

At Cross's suggestion, tainted food had done its job. The mercenaries were either passed out or scrambling to the latrine. This left most without access to their weapons.

The pending danger wasn't even a thought as many of them ran back and forth to the washroom to vomit. All they could think about was sleep and a speedy recovery from what they thought was flu.

Nearby, medical teams waited in a makeshift tent, prepared for the worst. Everyone knew there would be casualties. The reality of their mission weighed heavily on everyone's mind, but none of the officers let it show. There was no room for doubt or second-guessing, only forceful action.

The teams checked their weapons one last time. Extra ammo. Flash-bangs. Smoke grenades. All the tools they would need for war. Borden glanced at Cross. She gave him a sharp nod. They were ready.

The mist clung to their faces as the paint began to trickle down their foreheads and over their cheeks. They slipped deeper into the forest, Commander Smith merging them with the shadows as they closed in on the encampment.

Ahead, soft laughter and muffled voices drifted through the trees. The mercenaries lounged in comfort, away from the gentle rain and oblivious to the storm that surrounded them.

One or two gunshots were heard as some men fired rounds at the sky for no reason at all.

Commander Smith crouched low, signaling for his team to halt as they reached the edge of the campground.

Through the underbrush, he spotted the dim glow of battery-powered lanterns inside the cabins. The men inside had no idea what was coming.

Two team members circled around to the back of the Quonset hut and waited. Two guards were talking, then separated. In a coordinated strike, both mercenaries were dragged unconscious into the forest, secured, blindfolded, gagged, and left incapacitated without any weapons.

The team leaders moved with precision, setting flashbangs and smoke grenades near cabin doors. The countdown began. In a matter of moments, chaos would erupt. The mercenaries were expected to stumble from their cots, dazed, blind, disoriented, confused, and straight into the hands of the waiting strike force.

Commander Smith motioned. The team scattered like shadows, rigging tripwires at the base of the cabin stairs. Silent, invisible traps to drop the mercenaries before they even knew what hit them.

As the team shifted into position, the breeze picked up, carrying the sharp scent of pine and rain. Thick, dark, bubbling cumulus clouds blotted out the sky, draping the forest in just enough shadow to cover their advance.

The water team drifted silently across the lake, their black rubber crafts cutting through the water without a ripple, without a sound. They reached the shore, slipped out of the water silently, and took up their positions, cutting off any water exit.

They studied the cabins nearest to the water's edge and the tower lookouts high in the trees. Covered explosives were placed against the cabin walls. The men backed into the forest at the water's edge.

The mercenaries, still laughing and talking inside their cabins, remained blissfully unaware of the imminent danger. Others were rolling in pain, holding their abdomens, unable to speak, just moan.

A couple of guards wandered lazily around the perimeter of the campground, swapping stories and lighting cigarettes. One of them flicked out a match after lighting his smoke, stomping it like a park ranger as if forest fire were a big concern.

"Why do you always stomp on the match?" the guard asked, flicking the cigarette ash from his fingertips.

"It's a safety thing. Don't wanna set the woods on fire," the other replied casually.

They had no clue they were being watched or that the clock had already run out.

One of the patrol guards trailed behind, not paying attention, and drifted too close to the edge of the forest. A dark shape flowed behind him, quiet as death.

Before he could turn to react, an arm hooked around his neck, cutting off his breath. He jerked once, then slumped. The officer eased his body to the ground, limp and quiet. He didn't struggle. With his wrists bound tight, the officer gagged him, then silently dragged him out of sight into the brush.

Inside the campground, the strike force crept closer. The cabins sat in near total darkness, lit only by the occasional flicker of stray lanterns.

Borden's team tracked two rebels stationed on a rope bridge strung between two gigantic maples, their makeshift rope bridge swaying in the breeze. They would be the first taken out once the signal dropped.

The water team was in position near the cabins, their eyes and rifles focused on the guards high above. The tension in the air was profound. Nervous trigger fingers, waiting for the unexpected. Borden's heart hammered, but his hands remained steady and calm.

Almost time.

Across the campground, a guard called out, his voice edged with annoyance and irritation.

"Hey, where'd you go?"

There was no answer. He called again, louder. Still no response. The other guard shrugged, assuming his friend had fallen asleep or headed to the latrine. He muttered something under his breath and continued his patrol, completely unaware.

The wind stirred the leaves overhead as Borden and his team slid forward, mounting steps and standing beside the entrances to the cabins.

Chapter 69

Commander Smith gave a deliberate slash of his hand, sending the teams into action.

Flash-bangs tossed into the dark cabins. Tiny arcs of sparkling light cutting through the air before detonating with deafening, teeth-rattling blasts. Each explosion swallowed the room in chaos, screams muffled by the detonation, disorienting and blinding everyone.

For a split second, the world paused, then chaos erupted at a fever pitch. More flash-bangs flew through the open cabin doors, and windows. Each detonating with the same skull-splitting force.

Gunfire erupted as the strike force tossed smoke grenades through windows and doors, unleashing thick, choking plumes that spread like wildfire, consuming the cabins and spilling the occupants into the campground.

The mercenaries staggered from the haze, rubbing their ears, hacking, and coughing violently. Their shouts were barely audible over the roar of the noise, gunfire, and blood-curdling screams.

A few fired blindly into the cloud of smoke, bullets ricocheting off trees and pinging against metal.

They couldn't see.

Couldn't think.

They had no idea what was already waiting inside the camp.

Borden, Cross, and their team slid in like predators, their eyes cold, guns drawn. This was what they had trained for. Every move executed with flawless precision.

A mercenary, still dazed and struggling to regain his footing, stood in the square. Borden saw him first. Without hesitation, he drove the butt of his rifle into the man's gut, folding him in half before he crumpled to the ground. In one motion, Borden flipped him, zip-tied, done. The man wheezed on the ground, wrists locked behind his back, gasping for air.

Cross, using the smoke as cover, was right behind him, her movements swift and meticulous.

She climbed to the cabin porch, slipped around a corner, and came face-to-face with a mercenary.

Startled, he tried to raise his gun, but he was too slow. Her knee crushed his groin, doubling him sideways in agony. The butt of her rifle cracked against the back of his skull with a sickening crunch. His face smacked against the wall with a wet thud. He dropped without a sound. Cross dragged him off the porch, and zip-tied him.

She didn't pause, her eyes already scanning for the next target.

A man bolted from the same cabin, gun swinging wildly as he searched for a target. As he fired at Cross, she rolled and came up firing. Her shot dropped him face down, sprawled over the wooden steps, still forever.

The guards in the tree tower reacted, targeting Cross. Two officers fired at the muzzle flares. One guard slumped, grasped the railing, then tumbled headfirst fifty feet down. The second guard didn't stand a chance, caught in a burst of friendly fire from a panicked mercenary.

As men spilled from their cabins, the strike force hurled smoke bombs and flash-bangs into the camp square near the fire pit. Thick smoke swallowed the square. The confused cartel force fired blind, thinking they might hit their target.

A shot rang out, and one guard fell backward slumped lifeless against the cabin doorframe and slowly slid down.

Another raised his weapon. Cross was faster. Her bullet caught him mid-step, flinging him off the porch, face down in the mud.

"Clear the square!" Commander Smith barked, in a powerful and commanding voice.

With that the square became an intense battleground.

More men burst from adjacent cabins, or climbed through windows, weapons blazing wildly at the forest and in the direction of the square.

Bullets splintered the armory cabin's door and boarded windows. Rounds hammering the wooden structure like rain.

Smith ordered the portable floodlights. Harsh white beams bathed the square, cutting through the smoke and shadows. The cartel force shot at the lights, shattering bulbs, and scattering thin crippling shards of glass.

Confused they fired at the silent forest. The police returned fire with ruthless precision, tightening the noose.

Gunfire from the armory cabin blasted toward the forest. Rebels crouched behind wooden barrels, their rapid-fire rifles trained on twitching shadows. They fired wildly, hitting their comrades and nothing else. Borden signaled to his team, and they flanked the cabin, moving with silent fluency and efficiency.

A mercenary popped up from behind a crate, his rifle raised. Smith saw it coming and fired several shots, both hitting him squarely in the chest. He dropped without a sound.

"They're falling back!" a voice shouted.

The chopper blade slowly began to spin as the pilot engaged the engine. Friedman recognized the sound and fired. Multiple shots punched through the windshield. The pilot slumped over his control's arms hanging at his side.

The rotor steadily gained speed. It sliced the air with a rising whine.

Borden spotted another figure sprinting toward the helipad. The swoosh from the rotor blades roared louder. Dust and grit whipped into a choking dirt cloud. It was a second pilot, struggling to see. He yanked the dead aviator from the seat and scrambled inside.

Borden locked on his target.

"They're trying to lift off!" Cross yelled over the roar.

"Not today," Borden growled, already on the move.

Cross sprinted forward, weaving through the chaos. She hurdled over the cold fire pit missing a couple of lifeless bodies, her eyes locked on the fuel truck near the helicopter. She reached the truck just as a guard raised his rifle. Friedman's shot dropped him before he could aim.

Without pausing, Cross cranked open the fuel truck's valve.

The pungent stench of raw gasoline hit her as it spilled from the container onto the ground and pooled beneath the chopper.

"Get clear!" she shouted, striking a flare and dashing toward cover. She twisted and hurled the flare high in the direction of the chopper.

The flare arched overhead, casting an eerie red glow through the smoke. Cross sprinted, dove over a fallen tree, and hit the dirt, scratching her arm on sharp branches. She ignored the pain and crawled to cover hugging a large fallen tree.

The flare plummeted, igniting the pool of fuel with a violent hiss.

The explosion rocked the campground and echoed down the lake. The fireball lit up the night sky then disappeared behind a cloud of black smoke.

The debris field rained down on everyone. A strong fragrance of gasoline and gunpowder stung the air.

The helicopter bucked and dropped hard. Its rotors snapped, spinning off at high speed. The bird slammed into the dirt.

The dead pilot hung over the controls, his charred body strapped in place, his arms, and head flailing.

One broken blade whistled as it spun itself into the square, killing two rebels. Another splashed into the lake.

The inferno spread, engulfing the fuel truck inside the Quonset hut. Another blast tore through both, launching twisted corrugated metal into the sky.

Sick men laced with stomach cramps continued to hobble from their bunks, clutching their weapons, only to fall victim to gunfire.

The campsite had erupted into unbelievable pandemonium. The mercenaries who could, scattered in all directions.

Chapter 70

A few mercenaries, struggling to breathe and coughing aimlessly, fired into the haze. Others screamed for help. The fire was spreading, and several tried to break for the forest.

But the strike force was relentless.

They moved methodically taking down threats with precision.

Above, in the last active tree tower, the rebel guards fought back with automatic weapons. A strike team officer scaled a maple tree to the platform with the agility of a cat. He carried his knife clenched between his teeth.

At the top, the guard lunged toward the officer. Both men collided, rebounding across the platform. The guard slashed wildly, forcing the officer to holster his knife and retreat. The rebel chased after him, slashing the air with desperate swings.

The officer braced, reversed his grip, and prepared to disarm the attacker. They scuffled across the platform.

As the guard lunged with his blade, the officer twisted, redirecting the thrust force, and drove the knife into the man's own thigh. The man screamed in agony as the officer's punch sent him backward, crashing over the railing.

There was an abrupt end to his screams when he landed hard on the truck's roof and windshield with a sickening final thud.

The last tower was now neutralized.

Below, the mercenaries realized they were outmatched. Yet one man made a desperate dash for the second gas tanker.

He hauled his dead comrade off the shattered windshield, climbed inside, and slammed it into gear.

Pressing on the accelerator, the high beams bounced as the truck cut through the smoke. It was gaining speed moving toward officers scrambling to get out of the way. He gunned the engine, clearly intending to ram the police and turn the tanker into a bomb.

"Take him out!" someone shouted.

Borden didn't wait. He raised his Glock and fired, several bullets piercing the windshield and striking the driver in the head. The man slumped forward. The tanker swerved hard and slammed into a stack of crates.

For a split second, everything went still.

Then the world exploded.

The tanker erupted in a massive fireball. Shockwaves rippled through the ground, rattling the camp. Flames shot skyward, and smaller explosions burst across the site. Flaming debris rained down like meteors as officers dove for cover.

A deafening crack followed. The chopper's underground fuel storage ignited, triggering another blast that set several mercenaries on fire as they sprinted for the lake.

Screams faded into bedlam. The flames stretched toward the planets as the wreckage of the helicopter and fuel tanks burned into twisted metal.

Borden staggered to his feet, ears ringing, clothes covered in ash. He quickly reloaded. Smoke and fire choked the air. He spit out soot and pulled twigs from his hair. Around him, cartel fighters knelt in surrender. The battle was over.

"Secure them!" Commander Smith ordered.

Cross moved in, barking orders for prisoners to lie face down with their hands behind their backs. Her weapon stayed at the ready. Officers swarmed the cartel men, zip-tying wrists and dragging them toward transport trucks on the dirt road leading out of the camp.

Some mercenaries were too dazed to resist. Others were too sick, weak, or wounded to fight.

Above, the neutralized tower was again occupied. The remaining tree tower wobbled as a guard fired blindly down into the smoke. A strike team officer climbed from a neighboring tree and disarmed him with one brutal punch to the neck. The man was lowered by rope and zip-tied alongside the others.

At the far end of the campground, the main lodge stood eerily silent. Most floodlights had gone dark. Only two still flickered overhead.

Borden scanned the area, uneasy.

"Check the big cabin," he said.

Two officers stormed the building, kicked in the door, and entered with weapons raised.

Inside, at the far end of the boardroom, stood Scar-Face, the interrogator. The air reeked of smoke and gunpowder.

He grabbed an AK-47 from the wall and opened fire, forcing the officers to dive behind an overturned table.

"We're pinned down!" one officer shouted into his comms. He shoved a wooden chair past the edge of the table. It was shredded by bullets.

A third officer entered through the kitchen to help.

The interrogator grabbed the newcomer and barked at the others to stop shooting or he would kill his hostage. The gunfire halted. He ordered the remaining two to toss their weapons onto the table.

Borden circled the lodge and slipped through the rear entrance. He crept through the kitchen and paused at the entrance to the boardroom.

The interrogator held the officer in a choke hold, the barrel of the AK pressed to his temple.

"Drop it!" Borden cried out.

He aimed his Glock.

"You shoot, he dies. Then you. And by the time they reach their weapons, I'll kill them too," the interrogator warned, inching toward the veranda door.

No one moved.

Then Borden shifted, drawing the man's attention. That was enough.

The hostage dropped his weight, throwing the interrogator off balance as he aimed his gun a Borden.

Borden fired: once, twice.

The interrogator jolted backward, crashing into the wall, his arms outstretched then slid to the floor. The AK clattered beside him.

"Why don't you assist your fellow officers with the round-up outside," Borden said. "And send someone in here to collect this garbage."

"Yes, sir!" the officer replied.

Outside, the fires sputtered as firefighters arrived, pumping water from the nearby lake. EMS swept through the site, treating the wounded and stabilizing survivors.

Borden stepped into the smoke and wreckage. His boots crunched broken glass. The twisted remains of the helicopter still burned, casting a sick glow and radiating uncomfortable heat over the field.

The police had won, but the cost was burned into the dirt and cabins.

"Status?" Borden asked.

"Six or seven injuries on our side, all non-life-threatening," Cross replied. "Twenty-eight cartel fatalities. Twenty-four more wounded. Some were too sick to even leave their bunks. Whatever they ate crippled them. The weapons and ammo survived. We also recovered blueprints, smuggling routes, and maps of the Mexican railway from the main cabin.

Looks like they were planning something big."

"Does your count include the trash in the big cabin?"

"It does," Cross said. "What happened in there?"

"Pretty sure it was lead poisoning coming from the kitchen."

Cross did a double take. "Good work, everyone. Let's clean this up," said Borden.

The strike force worked through the night. By dawn, the camp was quiet now, apart from the murmur of voices and distant hum of police helicopters. The cartel's reign had ended here, in fire, smoke, ash, and blood.

The gentle rain continued to help extinguish the last of the flames.

Chapter 71

By first light, the scene had transformed from a battle-field to a smoldering wreck. The air still carried the bitter scent of gasoline, gunpowder, and scorched earth. Rain pattered lightly on twisted metal and blackened timber, hissing against hot surfaces.

Fire crews still moved methodically through the debris, dousing lingering flames. The smoke hung low, over the camp causing coughing and unwanted choking. Overhead, the sun barely broke through the dense overcast sky, casting the entire campground in a pale gray wash.

Borden met with Brad Smith shaking his hand.

"Thank you for your leadership and planning, Commander. This never would have gone down as cleanly without you."

Smith gave a tired nod. "We got the job done. You and your team performed well. The cleanup is yours now, but I'll have my crew send the full after-action report to your office. It will take a few hours."

They exchanged one last look of mutual respect, and Smith walked toward his truck, where members of his tactical team were already packing gear.

Cross moved beside Borden, wiping a streak of ash from her cheek with the back of her glove. Her clothes were soaked, stained, and torn at the elbow.

She winced as she looked down. "Pretty sure I gashed my arm during one of the explosions. Didn't notice it until just now."

"Let's get EMS to check it before we head back," Borden said.

They watched as officers loaded captured weapons into transport crates and tagged evidence for forensic teams to log.

Cartel members, most zip-tied and slumped against trucks or tree stumps, remained silent. Some stared blankly at the destruction, too stunned to speak. Others sat with heads down, complaining about cramps in their abdomen.

The helicopter was nothing but a collapsed skeleton, surrounded by scorched ground. The fuel tanker beside it had been reduced to twisted fragments. The Quonset hut behind the square had partially caved in. In one corner, a pair of evidence techs examined what appeared to be a hidden compartment filled with high-grade explosives and more rifles.

"This place was a fortress," Cross muttered. "And they still got flattened."

Borden glanced toward the lake. A handful of surviving cartel members sat with blankets draped around their shoulders, coughing, eyes red from smoke. They had been pulled from the water by officers during the final sweep.

A tech walked over with a small metal lockbox. "We found this under one of the beds in the main lodge," he said. "Thought you'd want to see it before we open it."

Borden took the box and examined it. The combination dial was scorched but still functional. He handed it off to another officer.

"Get it to evidence. Open it once we're back at headquarters."

Cross squinted up at the sky. "Looks like the storm's finally going to clear. Blue patches forming in the west."

"We'll take it," Borden said. "Let's start pulling out. We'll finish the debrief back in the city."

They began walking back toward the line of vehicles waiting along the dirt road.

EMS teams continued treating the injured while fire crews kept watch for flare-ups. It would take hours to secure and process the site, but the immediate threat was gone.

Borden stopped and turned to Cross. "You did good."

"You too," she said. "But we're not done. Not even close."

He nodded. "No. We just turned the page."

They reached the last truck in the convoy. Borden opened the passenger door for her, but she hesitated.

"You still owe me breakfast at Emily's," Cross said, her face half-smudged with ash, but smiling anyway.

Borden smirked. "I was hoping you forgot."

"Never."

"Fair enough. First, how's your arm? I'll understand if you can hold a fork."

They climbed into the truck and pulled away from the smoking wreckage behind them.

The road back to the city was long, but the victory felt satisfying after a hard-fought fight.

Chapter 72

Winthrop moved quickly, his footsteps echoing through the nearly empty hallways of his Toronto office. It was late, the city outside dark and quiet, but inside, his heart pounded like a drum.

He was ready. His bags were packed, his flight arranged, and the carefully crafted lie of needing an extended vacation would buy time with his superiors in the bureaucracy. He would vanish somewhere in the south before anyone could connect him to the Cartel's crumbling Canadian empire, or so he thought.

But there was one problem. He hadn't found the money.

His hand trembled as he reached for the handle to his private office. He was frazzled and needed time, just a little more.

He had to think clearly.

He struggled to focus.

He needed to remember the combination to the safe where he had stashed some of the funds, and then he would vanish. He already had millions offshore in a secret account no one knew about. He just needed to go.

Winthrop's mind raced, jumping between panic and escape. A nagging feeling told him someone had been watching, lurking in the shadows of his own guilty conscience.

The room inside was well lit, revealing no hidden corners, no place for shadows to deceive him.

But he still felt it, a presence.

He ignored the creeping sense of unease, his eyes locked on the safe behind the painting. His hands fumbled as he hunted through his pockets for the combination. Frustration simmered just beneath the surface, threatening to explode. "Where did I put that thing?" he muttered, too distracted by his desperation to notice the subtle shift in the air behind him.

The unmistakable click of a cocking gun froze him mid-motion. Was this real or a dream? he wondered.

Winthrop's breath hitched in his throat. He turned slowly, his heart hammering. Sean stood at the doorway, a pistol aimed directly at him. His expression was calm, unnervingly composed.

"Going somewhere, Winthrop?" Sean's voice was steady, stripped of any emotion.

Winthrop's mouth went dry as his mind scrambled for a way out. "Who are you? What... what are you doing here?" he stammered, trying to hide the terror tugging at his trembling heart.

Sean stepped forward, eyes cold. "You thought you could take the money and run, didn't you?" he said, his words drenched with quiet accusation.

Winthrop swallowed hard, his gaze zipping to the door, then back to Sean. "Tina sent me. She was afraid you'd take off with all the money," Sean said, his voice cold as ice.

The walls felt like they were closing in around him. Winthrop was close to a meltdown and desperate for a show of mercy.

"I wasn't going to run," Winthrop lied, his voice cracking. "I just... I needed more time. I was about to split it with her. I swear."

Sean's lips curled into a cold smile. "The safe's already empty," he said, watching the color drain from Winthrop's face.

Desperation clawed at Winthrop's chest. "I can get it back," he blurted out, trying to negotiate as he grasped for a lifeline. "We can still work together, with Tina. You don't have to do this."

But Sean wasn't listening.

He had already received his orders. The silence that followed was deafening, broken only by the faint creak of the floorboards as Sean stepped closer.

Without saying a word, Sean squeezed the trigger.

The gunshot echoed through the room, reverberating in Winthrop's chest like a shock wave from an earthquake. His body jolted violently as the bullet ripped through him, hurling him crashing against the wall. His hands instinctively flew to his chest, desperate to stop the blood now seeping through his fingers.

His wide eyes locked onto Sean, disbelief etched into his features.

For a moment, Winthrop's lips moved, but no words came. The reality of his betrayal and failure hit him all at once, and as his life ebbed away, so did his last sliver of hope.

Sean watched as Winthrop's body slid to the floor, blood pooling around him, his face blank, unreadable.

Sean didn't bother to holster his gun. His focus was on searching for and recovering the missing money.

There was no remorse, no hesitation, just the cold efficiency of a man who had completed his task.

To him, this was a loose end, nothing more. Winthrop was collateral, and this was effective damage control.

Outside, Detective Cross crept through the hall, her heart spiking at the sound of the gunshot hidden behind a suppressor.

She had been tailing Winthrop and wondered if he was the one who fired the gun. If not, then who?

Cross had received a tip just hours earlier from an experienced and credible undercover agent that Winthrop was preparing to disappear on what he called an extended vacation. The same undercover agent told her some Cartel money was missing, and Cross knew that wherever Winthrop was going, it would be expensive and probably wasn't just a holiday.

She reached the office door, her gun drawn, nerves on high alert. She didn't know what to expect, but something felt off. She could feel it in her bones.

She took a breath and pushed the door ajar just as another gunshot rang out. Her heart leapt into her throat, and she burst in, weapon raised.

What she saw stopped her cold. Pure disbelief. She stared in shock.

Winthrop was slumped against the wall, blood pooling around his lifeless frame. And someone stood over him, gun still in hand, his expression filled with unexpected surprise.

"Drop the gun Sean!" Cross barked. "What have you done?" she shouted, disbelief and shock fighting for control of her thoughts and emotions.

"I'm working undercover and reporting to Danielle Spade over at CSIS. You're Cross, right? We've met before, but I changed my appearance when I went undercover. I am your inside man. I'm the one who has been feeding your department with tips on the activities of the Mexican Cartel."

"Gun down. Now," Cross ordered, her voice steady but firm.

"Cross, I'm embedded within the Cartel," Sean said, turning and locking eyes with hers. For the first time, the truth cracked through, hitting her like a gut punch.

Sean wasn't here to help. No, her instincts screamed, he wasn't part of the solution; he was the problem. But there was something else, something she didn't understand yet.

"Cross..." Sean began, his voice softer, but she wasn't listening.

"Listen to me, Cross. I'm undercover. I work for CSIS. They have me embedded with the Cartel. Danielle Spade is my handler. You can check. We're on the same side, Cross."

"Drop it. Now."

Sean lowered his gun slowly and let go of it about six inches off the floor.

"Kick it over here," Cross ordered.

"Cross, we're on the same team. I'm the one who funneled intel to CSIS to guide you and Borden. That's how we got this far," Sean said, his voice escalating slightly. "You need to listen to me, Cross."

She couldn't see the second gun tucked under the back of his jacket, his hand inching toward it. He knew Cross was just another loose end, one more problem to erase.

He decided her time had run out.

When he killed her, he would stage the scene to look like it was a shootout with Winthrop.

Sean slid his hand behind his back and drew out his second gun, drawing it upwards and leveling it at Cross.

Her heart thundered as she raised her gun, but before she could pull the trigger, a shot cracked through the room from the doorway.

Sean staggered, his body jerking as blood stained his shirt and his eyes filled with surprise.

Cross spun, her eyes wide, as Borden stepped through his gun still trained on Sean.

Hitting the floor hard, Sean was gasping for breath as his blood began to pool beneath him. His fingers twitched toward the second gun, but he was too slow. Borden stepped forward, lowering his weapon.

"Don't," Borden said, cold as ice. Sean's hand stopped, his chest rising and falling with shallow, labored breaths.

"He's a double agent, working both sides," Borden said, turning to Cross. "Spade called me just over an hour ago, and I rushed here as fast as I could. Looks like it's a good thing I did."

Cross stood frozen, her mind struggling to make sense of what she had just witnessed. "He almost had me convinced he was one of ours," she murmured, lowering her weapon to her side. Her hands trembled.

"Why?" she finally asked, her voice barely above a whisper. "Why did he do it..."

"He was a double agent," Borden repeated, his voice thick with exhaustion. "He was working for CSIS. We've known for a while now, but we needed him to lead us to Winthrop, then hopefully to Tina and Juan. It was a covert operation arranged by Spade and Crawford."

Cross shook her head, disbelief still clouding her thoughts. "He... he killed Winthrop."

Borden nodded. "Winthrop was the last link. Sean was tying up loose ends, preparing an exit for Juan and Tina Estrada."

Sean's breathing slowed. His eyes found Cross, something like regret flickering behind them. But it was too late. His hand stilled. Then his body went limp.

Cross stood frozen. "Sean had been undercover all along, playing both sides, deceiving everyone. For what purpose, I can't really say," said Borden.

Chapter 73

Detective Cross stood in front of the house, silently staring at what had once been her prison. Her mind felt numb. The sight of the house was an unforgettable reminder of a recent past she was desperate to forget.

She blinked against the sting of memories. Her gaze drifted to the windows that once confined her, the driveway leading to the backyard, and the garden shed beyond. For a moment, it was too much. The weight of the investigation, the relentless pursuit of justice, and now, being back here where she'd been held captive.

It was not a pleasant feeling. One she didn't welcome.

The faint vibration of her phone brought her back to the present. Another incoming message lit up her screen. She didn't need to read it right now. She wouldn't allow her emotions to cloud her judgment. Not now, not ever. It was time.

Cross took a deep breath, slowly exhaled. For her, this was difficult. Then tapped send, booking another appointment downtown on Bay Street.

Her hand trembled slightly as she slipped the phone into her pocket. Even knowing it was the right thing to do.

The constables who accompanied her moved quickly, collecting evidence, weapons, and bags of drugs stacked high on the counters. Each ready for shipping.

Large metal boxes filled with drugs were stacked against the dirty bedroom wall. The people working inside the house had been quickly subdued. They were cuffed and paraded outside by uniformed officers to a waiting police transport.

Cross lingered at the basement door, her thoughts pulling her back in time. Focus, she thought, yanking herself back from the edge.

This was no time for doubt. In the end, she'd won, and that was all that really mattered. Her job here was done.

She walked to her car.

Miles away, Detectives Kim, now back full-time, and Friedman had begun their own search. The GPS had guided them out of the city and into the quiet, rolling countryside.

The transition from urban sprawl to open fields and farmhouses felt surreal. Kim glanced at Friedman, whose forehead was furrowed with concern.

"Are you sure this is the right place?" Friedman asked, eyeing a mailbox loosely fastened atop a rusted post leaning sharply to the left. "I feel like we're lost in the middle of nowhere."

Kim shrugged. "This is the address Cross gave us." He brought the car to a stop near the black steel gate, its rusted hinges lending it a menacing appearance. Beyond the gate, a long, winding dirt driveway, partially overgrown with weeds, led up a hill toward a house barely visible through the trees.

"Wow, this place looks like it belongs in an Alfred Hitchcock movie," Friedman said.

"I didn't know you watched movies," Kim murmured.

"I don't. Well, maybe once in a while."

A car sat parked more than halfway up the drive, seemingly abandoned.

"Locked gate out here, and someone's home?" Friedman said, eyeing the scene with suspicion. "How does anyone get deliveries out here? You think Amazon even comes this far?"

"Oh man, you've been in the city too long," Kim said.

Kim was already out of the car, climbing over the gate with ease. Friedman followed, and the two detectives moved cautiously up the driveway, gravel crunching beneath their feet. They paused at the car and looked inside.

Nothing!

No keys. No personal items.

"Hasn't moved in a while. Nothing strange about that," Kim muttered, though his voice betrayed his unease.

They continued their silent approach, moving along the side of the house and around back, circling cautiously.

At the front door, Kim knocked. "Toronto Police Services," he called out, his voice carrying through the still air.

No response.

He knocked again, harder this time. The silence inside was deafening. He exchanged a glance with Friedman, whose eyes narrowed. Without a word, they reached for the doorknob.

The door creaked open with a low, grinding sound.

"Hello?" Friedman called out.

No response.

With guns drawn, they stepped inside. The air was stale, with a musty odor hanging like a London fog.

Kim's heart raced as he scanned the room. Every corner, every shadow. Calculating the potential for danger.

"What's that smell?" Kim asked.

"Man, it reeks in here," Friedman muttered.

"Kitchen clear," Kim said quietly, nodding for Friedman to check the other rooms.

"Dining room's clear," Friedman said softly.

"Basement's clear. Just cold and damp," Kim added.

They regrouped at the foot of the stairs, tension mounting. Kim pointed to the top of the stairs, signaling they needed to sweep the second floor.

"Anyone home?" Friedman called up the stairs, his voice echoing through the silence. No reply.

The odor thickened as they climbed. They moved slowly, guns raised, scanning each doorway and room as they crept down the short, dingy hall.

Each door creaked open to reveal an empty bedroom, the air still and heavy with a putrefied odor.

They reached the second-to-last door.

Kim took a breath, hand on the knob. He turned it slowly and pushed the door open.

A body lay motionless on the bed. Madler's face was ashen, his half-open eyes fixed lifelessly on the ceiling. A single bullet hole pierced his forehead. Dried blood soaked the pillow and sheets beneath him.

Kim swallowed hard and kept his voice steady and professional as he called in. "Cross, we've found Madler. He's stone-cold dead."

The silence on the other end stretched longer than expected. "Say again?" Cross's voice crackled through the static.

"Madler's dead. Looks like he's been here a while."

A pause. "I'll arrange for forensics and the coroner," Cross said at last. "I'll inform Borden. Take your time and search the place thoroughly."

Kim glanced at Friedman, who was already moving to search the room. "Copy that."

Back at police HQ, Cross relayed the discovery to Borden, her voice calm despite the shock. "Kim and Friedman found Madler. He's dead," she said, pacing in her office. "They're sweeping the house for evidence."

Borden's voice came sharp on the other end. "We both know who's responsible for this. Tina. She leaves a trail of bodies everywhere she goes."

Cross bit her lip, her mind racing. "Yes, I agree with you. I've already issued a BOLO noting her and Juan as likely armed and dangerous."

"Good. We need to catch up to her and Juan before they slip away again."

"They won't get far," Cross said, her voice low and resolute.

Back at the farmhouse, Kim and Friedman moved methodically through each room. They opened drawers, checked closets, and combed every corner of the farmhouse for clues.

In the kitchen, they found nothing unusual. Just remnants of a quiet, uneventful life.

Frustrated, Kim suggested they start again. Back upstairs, they started in Madler's room. Friedman recognized a box from his military days. He opened a footlocker wedged up against the bed. They hadn't paid much attention to it when they first found Madler, as their focus was on him. Friedman opened it and spotted something in the box. "Kim, check this out."

He held up a small, timeworn notebook, its leather cover cracked with age.

Its pages were crammed with scrawled notes. Names, addresses, and dates. It was a road map, straight to the heart of the cartel's operations. And at the top of the list, one name stood out: Tina Estrada.

"Looks like we've got more than just a corpse," Kim muttered. His pulse quickened as the realization hit. This could be the break they'd been waiting for. At first glance, it was a treasure trove of intel.

Detective Kim snapped a photo of the page and sent it to Cross. "We've got something. This could lead us straight to Tina," Kim said.

Chapter 74

The phone vibrated just as Tina slipped into the penthouse, her mind already occupied with plans. She was annoyed by the interruption.

The number showing on the screen was unfamiliar, but her instincts told her it wasn't a casual call. She slid her finger across the screen and brought the phone to her ear.

"Who is this? How did you get this number?" she snapped, her nerves razor thin.

A long pause followed on the other end, just long enough to send a chill down her spine. Then, a voice, calm, steady, and void of any emotion, spoke. "Sean's dead."

Tina's blood froze. Her grip tightened around the phone as her heart pounded in her chest.

"What did you say?"

"You heard me. Sean's dead. Figured you should know. Considerate professional courtesy. "

The room felt small, closing in around her, the air thick with disbelief. Her stomach turned sour. Nausea surged up her throat, and she instantly felt sick.

Sean, her trusted right hand, the one person she believed would always protect her, gone. The one who kept her safe, the one person on whom she could rely. Dead?

She shook her head, refusing to believe it. "Who are you? How do you know that?"

The voice remained detached, as though discussing the weather. "Let's just say I didn't handle it. He was working for CSIS."

Tina's world instantly tilted on its axis.

Sean, working undercover. A cop?

The betrayal was a sucker punch, hard and unexpected. It had to be a lie. Her pulse thundered in her ears, fury bubbling up from deep within her gut. "You're lying," she hissed, though doubt was creeping in.

"Afraid not," the voice continued, still devoid of emotion. "He's been feeding them intel for months, maybe since day one. I figured you'd want to know. Consider it professional courtesy."

Tina nearly crushed the phone in her fist, fury flooding through her veins.

She'd been played and never saw it coming. "Why tell me now?" she demanded, pacing the room as her breath came in shallow bursts.

"Because Toronto's about to become extremely hot for people like you. Get out now. Come back when things cool off, which they will soon."

The line went dead.

Tina stood frozen in time, the loneliness and silence pressing in on her. Her thoughts swirled as she tried to grasp the magnitude of this betrayal. She wanted to scream. Cry. Break something.

Sean, of all people, had been feeding information to CSIS.

How long had this been going on?

How much did they know?

She hurled the phone across the room. It shattered against the wall and fell in tiny pieces, landing on the table and floor. A string of curses spilled from her lips.

She dropped onto the sofa, her fists clenched, with silent screams echoing in her chest.

Her natural instincts kicked in, and she realized there was no time to drown in shock.

Her mind snapped into survival mode. The clock was ticking, and she needed to act fast. She grabbed her backup phone and tapped a number she hadn't used in weeks.

"Drop the shipment early," she snapped as soon as the line connected. "Take it west to the warehouse in Vancouver. Get it done now. Send a text to this number when it's rerouted and when the shipment arrives."

There was no hesitation on the other end. "It'll be done."

She ended the call and immediately hit speed dial.

Juan answered. Her heart still raced, but the cold, calculating side of her was now in control.

"We are leaving now," she said as soon as he picked up.

Juan didn't ask questions. "Where?"

"Private jet. Meet me at the private lounge."

"Got it. I'm on my way."

Tina hung up, shoving the phone into her bag. She paused to collect herself, her hands shaking as she went over the plan in her head.

They'd escape to Mexico, regroup, and figure out their next move from there. The Cartel still had a firm grip on the operation, but Sean's betrayal had put everything at risk. There was no telling how much the police already knew.

She grabbed a small black duffle bag and ran to her safe.

Inside were stacks of cash, gold bars, and coins. She stuffed them in her bag, then grabbed the passports, everything she'd prepared for a moment like this. Her fingers brushed the cold steel of the gun she always carried.

Tonight, she might need to use it.

The city pulsed with tension as Tina moved swiftly through the streets to a waiting limousine. Her replacement driver maneuvered the sleek black sedan through Toronto traffic, taking back roads and avoiding major intersections, keeping her under the radar.

Tina was anxious. Every passing moment felt like a countdown to disaster.

She stared out the window, her mind flooded with thoughts of Sean's deception and what she missed seeing in his actions and comments.

How had he managed to fool her for so long?

How much had he compromised?

Her grip on the armrest tightened, her jaw clenched. Her anger over Sean's betrayal consumed her, clouding her focus.

The limousine came to a stop at the terminal gate. The driver, a man Tina had paid handsomely for discretion, turned around and gave a slight nod.

"You're all set. The runway's clear. But there's been some chatter about police activity near the airport. Might be nothing, but..."

Tina's fingers tightened on the door handle. "I've got to go."

Juan was already there, pacing along the side of the building. He wasn't sure about the sudden rush to leave the country, but he trusted Tina with his life.

He stopped pacing and leaned against the building with his arms folded and his head bowed. He could see the lights of the aircraft flickering in the dim evening light, the engine humming softly in the background, waiting for its two passengers.

"Tina!" Juan called, striding over as she stepped out of the car. Her eyes were wide with urgency. "What is going on?"

"No time," she snapped, brushing past him and heading for the jet. "We need to get out of here. Sean's dead. He was working for CSIS."

Juan froze, the color draining from his face. "Sean? Are you serious?"

"Do I look like I'm joking?" she barked.

"How much do the police know, Tina?" Juan shouted.

"We don't have time for this. Later. We need to leave before the cops find us."

"And where are we going, Tina?"

Juan muttered a curse, then said, "It's over, Tina."

"No way, Juan. We can still get out of here and come back another day. Trust me," Tina snapped. "Listen to me Juan, this isn't over. Now let's get moving before it is too late."

Chapter 75

Tina sat alone in the private airport lounge, her legs crossed tightly, one hand on the strap of her duffle bag. Inside were bundles of cash, gold coins, and uncut diamonds. It was her insurance policy, her escape plan, and payback for Arturo, all stuffed into one inconspicuous black bag.

Juan had just returned from the restroom. He rubbed his hands on his jeans, his nervousness showing a slight tremor in his hands. He gazed outside, then whispered to Tina, "No sign of police. No cameras in the hallway. We are clean."

Tina didn't answer.

Across the room, in a glass hallway, a uniformed airport security officer was speaking quietly with a police officer in plain clothes. She studied their gestures and facial expressions. As they spoke, the guard glanced toward the lounge, made brief eye contact with her, then turned and walked away while speaking into his two-way radio.

Her heart sank.

"I've been made. We need to move," Tina whispered. "They're here."

Juan frowned. "What do you mean?"

"There was a cop talking to a security guard and continually glancing my way. I'm sure they recognized me."

A soft ding chimed over the lounge speakers.

"Boarding call for Flight 479 to Mexico City. Passengers, please make your way through the private terminal gate and be sure you have all your belongings and passport."

Juan stood, fidgeting with his jacket zipper. "Tina," he whispered, "I forgot my passport."

"What?"

Two other passengers, a man and a woman in business attire, rose near the far side of the lounge and casually made their way toward the exit.

Tina's instincts flared. "Now," she hissed.

She reached into her bag and pulled the compact pistol she'd carried since Mexico City. She moved quickly, grabbing the woman from behind and jamming the muzzle against her ribs.

"Don't scream," Tina said, teeth clenched. "Walk."

The woman froze. Juan stepped in, placing a firm grip on the woman's elbow, guiding her toward the door as if she were a guest at a gala.

Tina and Juan slipped out through the lounge doors with their hostage between them, walking straight toward the runway where the jet waited, engines purring. The tarmac lights shimmered across the asphalt. The storm had passed, leaving everything slick and glowing.

As they stepped outside, a voice barked from behind a service cart.

"Freeze!"

Detective Gibson was disguised as a baggage handler and leveled his sidearm. "Drop the weapon!"

Tina spun toward her and yanked the hostage closer. "Back off!"

From behind a stack of crates, Borden stepped into view, gun raised, eyes locked on Tina. Cross appeared at his flank, with Kim and Friedman on the far side. Tactical officers emerged from behind the hangars. It was a trap.

"Let her go, Tina," Borden said calmly. "It's over."

Tina's voice cracked. "Take one more step and I'll put a hole in her."

Borden didn't flinch. "We've shut down your entire operation. The houses are gone. The camp is gone. Winthrop's dead."

That stopped Tina cold.

"What did you say?"

"He's dead. Shot himself. You're all that's left."

Juan's hand hovered near his jacket, shaking. "I'm not going to prison," he said to Tina. "I won't."

"Juan, no."

It was too late. He drew his weapon.

Pop.

A single shot rang out from beyond the tree line, so quiet it sounded like a snapped branch. Juan's gun flew from his hand and skittered across the asphalt. The handle busted into small fragments. He screamed, falling to his knees, clutching at his wrist. The hostage cried out and stumbled forward.

Tina's eyes darted toward the horizon, scanning the distant perimeter. She knew that shot hadn't come from the police. That was a professional shooter, someone using a suppressor.

"Who fired?" Cross barked. "Was that one of ours?"

"No one moved," Borden said, eyes narrowing. "We're not alone."

Tina stood frozen, still holding her weapon, though her arms had begun to tremble.

"Tina," Cross said, stepping closer. "Don't do this."

Tina didn't answer.

"You're surrounded. Your plan is done. There's no jet, no backup, no Sean. Just you. Let the woman go."

For the first time, Tina's facade cracked. Her lip quivered. Her hand dropped slightly.

Borden motioned to his team to hold.

Tina's gun hit the ground with a soft clack. She released the hostage, who scrambled into Gibson's arms.

Tina's knees buckled. Cross stepped forward slowly, cuffs in hand.

From the roof of a maintenance building far beyond the perimeter, the sniper had packed up his rifle. A sleek suppressor was unscrewed and slid into a velvet case. No fingerprints. No shell casings left behind.

He vanished into the shadows. He was never there.

Back on the tarmac, Borden stared across the airfield, unsettled.

"That wasn't us," he said to Cross. "So, who was it?"

Cross looked toward the horizon and whispered, "Whoever they are, they're an excellent shooter from back there somewhere. Get somebody out there and find where that shot came from and look for the shooter and any evidence. I want answers,"

Chapter 76

Borden crouched beside Juan, now face down on the tarmac, groaning through clenched teeth. His right hand was soaked in blood from a cut attributed to the handle, but the wound was clean, just one shot, deliberate and precise.

Friedman crouched beside him. "Through and through. Took out the gun but missed the artery. Whoever did that wasn't trying to kill him."

Kim stepped forward, scanning the horizon. "That wasn't one of ours. We had no snipers positioned. Who took that shot?"

Borden stood, his eyes scanning the distant rooftops. "Whoever it was, they were surgical. Took the threat out without hitting Tina or the hostage. That wasn't luck."

Cross was already placing handcuffs on Tina. The adrenaline was fading from Tina's face and replaced by blank resignation. Her gaze stayed fixed on Juan, as if trying to decide whether to scream at him or run to him. But she didn't move.

"We need to move them now," Cross said. "Let's get the hostage out, get Tina secured, and roll medics for Juan."

Gibson nodded. "On it."

The woman Tina had grabbed from the lounge was still shaking and wrapped in a police jacket and being escorted to an unmarked car with her husband. She felt safe now.

Borden approached Tina. Her hands were behind her back, wrists bound tight in stainless steel. Her duffle bag had been opened. Cash, gold, and diamonds glittered in the lamplight.

"Was it worth it?" Borden asked.

Tina said nothing.

"You had a chance to run clean. You had lawyers, diplomats, jet access, a dozen offshore accounts. You could've disappeared months ago."

Still nothing. Just the faintest twitch in her jaw.

Cross stepped in. "She doesn't care about the money anymore. Not after what she just found out."

Tina turned her head slightly. "He was all I had left."

Cross didn't flinch. "Then you chose wrong."

"It was a game, Tina," Borden said, his voice low but firm. "But in the end, an assault on justice never wins. You are under arrest."

The weight of his words sank into her like a stone. The empire she had built, the lives she had taken, the power she had wielded, the luxury she enjoyed, all of it was gone now. Stripped away by bad choices and a single gunshot. For the first time in her adult life, Tina Estrada had nowhere to run. No more plans. No more tricks. She was broken.

Two uniformed officers led Tina toward a transport van parked just off to the side of the lounge area. The steel door clanged shut behind her. She heard the screeching of the bolt as it slid into a locked position. She didn't bother to look back.

Nearby, paramedics had stabilized Juan and were loading him into an ambulance. His face was pale, lips pressed tight. He didn't resist.

"Keep him conscious," Borden instructed. "We need to talk to him before the painkillers hit."

Friedman came over. "Tarmac's clear. No sign of a shooter. Nothing on the rooftops, no heat signatures, no footprints. Whoever it was, they're long gone."

Gibson added, "No brass either. They must have collected the shell casing."

Cross looked to Borden. "Are you thinking what I'm thinking?"

Borden nodded slowly. "I believe I am."

Kim frowned. "You mean someone operating outside of us? A third party?"

"Maybe a contractor. Maybe a cartel defector," Borden said. "But they didn't kill Juan. They saved a life tonight. Took out a gun, not a heart."

"Still," Cross said, "they were here. They were watching. And they were close. How is that even possible?"

Borden's eyes moved back to the plane, now dark and sealed again. "Let's get a team on airport video footage going back forty-eight hours. I want every face logged."

Cross nodded. "You want me to notify CSIS?"

Borden considered. "No. Not yet. Let's hold that card. I want to know who that shooter was before anyone else does."

The team broke off. The air was cooling now, the early edge of morning creeping in. The storm was long gone but what it left behind hadn't settled.

Inside the transport van, Tina sat alone, her hands cuffed, her forehead pressed to the window. She stared out at the empty runway as it faded behind her. No words. No tears.

The van rolled toward the city. Tina closed her eyes and breathed slowly, the faintest smirk curling at the corner of her mouth.

Somewhere out there, someone had just taken a shot for her.

And someone else, someone she'd never seen, had her back.

Chapter 77

The atmosphere inside the command trailer was strained with unanswered questions. Detective Cross sat at a desk, eyes locked on the still image of Juan's weapon tumbling across the wet asphalt.

The bullet had struck with such precision and left no trace of the shooter. No muzzle flash. No sound anyone could identify. Just a clean disarmament that happened in the blink of an eye.

Borden leaned against the wall, arms crossed, deep in thought. "Who took that shot?" he asked, not expecting an answer. "It wasn't one of ours. Our snipers were never given the order to fire."

"It wasn't police," Cross replied, eyes narrowed. "And it wasn't a warning shot either. That was calculated.

Professional.

Someone took the gun out of play without hitting Juan directly. That takes more than skill."

Gibson entered with a printout, shaking his head. "We pulled footage from every angle. Nothing. No thermal signatures. No distant lens glare. Whoever took that shot did it from way outside our surveillance perimeter."

"You're telling me a sniper walked into a high-security operation, fired one shot, and walked away without triggering a single alarm?" That fence is at least 200 yards away. Borden's tone was flat. "Impossible shot."

"Look for a ladder. Check the roof for shell casings. Look for smudge prints on the roof. Look for any sign of a vehicle including a motorbike. Do you have any available officer out there?

"Apparently not," said Cross. "And the precision of that hit? That's someone who wanted Juan alive. Why?"

Friedman paced near the whiteboard, where photos of Tina, Juan, and their network still covered the surface. He tapped the side of his head. "Maybe it's a third player. Someone who wanted the take-down to happen but really wanted Juan in custody. Is he too valuable to kill? Maybe he knows something they need?"

Kim flipped open a fresh file. "It could be cartel. But it doesn't feel like cartel work. They don't spare people."

"Ghost," Cross whispered. The room went quiet.

Borden looked up. "What?"

"Ghost. That's what the shot felt like. Controlled. Silent. Vanishing. We've been hearing whispers about someone like this for years," Cross said.

"Rumors," Borden said.

"No profile. No name. Just a string of jobs with one thing in common. No one ever sees the shooter. Never any evidence. No one ever sees or hears him or her."

"You think The Ghost is real?" Kim asked. "I thought that was just street talk. Like an urban legend."

"Maybe I do," Cross said. "But Juan was disarmed by a single shot from what felt like a half a mile out. And not even a scratch on Juan. Whoever did that isn't simply good, they're operating at a level we're not ready for and have never seen before."

Gibson looked up from his laptop. "I'll cross-reference every known sniper profile and see if any have a history that fits. Military, intelligence, mercenaries. Someone has to know something."

"No one will talk," Borden said quietly. "Not about this. If The Ghost exists, he's not a hired gun. He's a ghost for a reason."

Cross stared at the grainy still frame again. The moment the bullet hit, the way Juan's body recoiled, the exact angle of the impact. It was like watching someone disappear in real time.

"There's no shell casing," she muttered. "No echo. It wasn't suppressed in the traditional sense. That means advanced tech or distance so great it bypassed all detection."

"And no heat signature," Friedman added. "We don't even know what direction it came from for sure."

Kim leaned forward. "So, what now? We've got Tina and Juan in custody. The camps are shut down. The operation's over. But now we have a bigger problem?"

Cross looked up, her voice steady. "We close the book on this chapter. But we keep a file open. Quietly. Off record. If The Ghost is real, this won't be the last time we hear from him."

Borden nodded once. "No press on this. No leaks. We say Juan dropped the gun. That's it."

"And if The Ghost surfaces again?" Kim asked.

"Then we pray he's still on our side," Borden replied."

"Borden I have a crazy thought, said Cross."

"You have had a lot of those lately. What's on your mind?"

"Do you think it is possible our ghost makes his own bullets?"

"I never considered that. Why do you ask that Cross?"

"Because there are never any casings at a crime scene. So, what if genius made his own rifle in the style of a Remington .223 or Winchester 308. Suppose he built an internal casing of some kind that held the gun powder and bullet? The bullet is fired and there is an internal suppressor. The cartels would want that weapon as would military around the globe."

"It can't be done," said Borden.

"Really?" said Cross. "Do you remember Steve Jobs when he said at an Apple conference, 'one more thing', and then held up the first iPhone that changed the world and communications forever?"

Outside, the clouds parted slowly, the last light of the evening brushing the horizon. In the distance, past the airport perimeter, past the fences and cameras, a single child size footprint marked a patch of sandy gravel where no one was supposed to be. Then the wind blew it away.

Chapter 78

After they finished eating, the group made their way back to the station to prepare for business as usual.

The city's neon lights flickered in the distance, reflected in puddles on the wet streets. Borden, leading the way, turned to Cross as they reached his office.

"Come in for a minute," he said quietly.

Cross followed him, shutting the door behind her. She dropped into the chair opposite Borden's desk, exhaustion settling into her bones. Borden sat down, looking across the desk at her with a seriousness that caught her off guard.

"How are you holding up?" he asked.

Cross hesitated, then sighed. "I'm... better. Still sore. Still not sleeping much, but I'll get there."

Borden nodded, his gaze softening. "Good. I'm not here to pry, but I know what you went through, and I know it's hard to admit when you need help. I've been there."

Cross studied him, waiting.

"You can be tough and still need a lifeline," Borden continued, his voice almost too calm. "There's no shame in talking to someone. You're a good cop, and you've got a lot of years ahead of you. I don't want you burning out because of pride, and I for sure don't want you second-guessing yourself and making a mistake."

Cross offered a faint smile. "I'll think about it."

"And you'll let me know if you need anything," Borden added.

She nodded. They both knew this conversation wasn't over, but for now, it was enough.

"Didn't say anything at our time with the team, but Danielle Spade called. She told me the Mexican government arrested Valdez, the president of the railway company. So, we may not need satellite to track drugs shipped via the trains anymore."

"Well, that is really good news. Your sister would be proud of you, Cross, just as your colleagues are," Borden said.

Borden shifted in his chair, a frown pulling at his mouth. "The ambassador's butler still doesn't add up either. It's too clean. No witnesses, no trail. Just like the ambassador's murder."

"The butler?" Cross asked, raising the question.

"Coroner ruled it an accident," Borden said with a sigh. "A freak fall after learning his employer had been shot."

Cross stared at him. "You really believe that?"

Borden shrugged. "I don't, but we're out of leads. Unless you think a professional assassin is still out there..."

Cross leaned back, her mind racing. "Maybe we've been looking at this wrong. Someone hired that killer, someone powerful enough to keep it buried. Maybe this wasn't just about drugs. It was political or something else."

Somewhere in Mexico, a phone number was dialed.

The man who answered it was calm and methodical. His voice was quiet but confident, the kind of voice that exuded control. "Yes?"

A low chuckle echoed from the other end of the line. "I called to thank you for ensuring my re-election."

"That's why you hired me. I get things done," came the reply, smooth and detached. "And I always pay attention to the small details, so you don't have to."

The sound of papers rustled on the other end. "Your bonus fee has been transferred."

"Not necessary, but appreciated," the voice replied. "I enjoy working for you. Congratulations on your re-election. Until next time."

The man on the other end hesitated, his tone lowering. "But the election hasn't been held yet."

"I know," the assassin said, a smile in his voice. "But I've already taken care of that for you."

The line went dead, the air thick with the finality of the exchange.

Back in Toronto, Borden stared out the window of his office, the weight of unfinished business pressing against his chest. Somewhere out there, the person who had orchestrated it all, who had hired the assassin, was still pulling the strings.

Or maybe there wasn't anyone there at all.

Chapter 79

Two days later, the courtroom buzzed with media chatter and low murmurs as Tina Estrada was escorted to the defense table. Her wrists were shackled, her expression stone cold. She didn't glance at the reporters packed into the gallery, didn't acknowledge the cameras or whispers. Her mind was elsewhere.

Next to her, Juan sat hunched, his shoulder still bandaged beneath his suit. He hadn't spoken since the arraignment began.

Across the aisle, Borden and Cross stood quietly behind the Crown's table. Both had been pulled in for witness prep and briefing sessions since the take-down. Neither had slept much. Tina's arraignment was just the beginning, but both knew the real weight was still coming.

The clerk called the case, and the judge entered, an older woman with silver hair and no tolerance for games. She reviewed the charges without fanfare: drug trafficking, money laundering, conspiracy, attempted flight from justice, and dozens more lined up in waiting.

The defense requested bail.

The Crown shut it down.

Tina didn't flinch when the judge denied her release and ordered her held in protective custody until trial. But Cross noticed her left eye twitch, just for a second.

Outside the courthouse, reporters surged toward Borden as he emerged.

"Detective Borden! Any comment on the capture of Tina Estrada?"

"Was this coordinated with CSIS?"

"Do you know who fired the shot at the airport?"

Borden stopped on the steps and gave a measured reply. "Tina Estrada is in custody and will face trial. We believe justice will be served. That's all I can say."

He turned and walked past them, ignoring the flashes and questions.

Across town, a different kind of investigation had begun.

Detective Kim sat in the back corner of a darkened room inside the Special Investigations Bureau. On the screen in front of him: freeze frames from The Ghost's possible sniper nest.

Satellite overlays. Thermal grid maps. Audio snippets from the airport.

Nothing that led anywhere.

"I've been through all of it," he muttered, rubbing his temples.

Friedman leaned in. "Whoever this guy is, he's not sloppy. No shell casings. No prints. No digital footprint. Either he's a ghost or he's better trained than anyone we've dealt with."

Kim clicked through another set of timestamped photos. "He doesn't want to be found. That makes him dangerous. But also... maybe useful."

Friedman raised an eyebrow. "You think he's helping us?"

"I think he helped Tina not kill that woman. I think he took a risk to disarm Juan and didn't try to kill anyone. That's calculated restraint."

Friedman leaned back. "Maybe we've got a vigilante."

"Or someone deeper in the game than we realize," Kim said.

No one in the unit had a name. But around the office, "The Ghost" had started to circulate.

It wasn't official. Not yet. But it was growing.

Back at police headquarters, Borden stood at his office window, watching the traffic roll past. Cross entered without knocking.

"We've locked down two more cartel houses in Brampton," she said. "CSIS found routing data on encrypted servers that Tina never wiped. Looks like she was sloppy in the end."

Borden nodded. "She thought she had time. She didn't."

"She still thinks she'll walk. She's playing it cool. Juan's falling apart, though. He keeps asking for deals."

Borden half-smiled. "They always do. Let him sweat."

Cross lowered her voice. "You think we'll hear from The Ghost again?"

Borden didn't answer right away. He stared out the window, watching a lone figure on a motorcycle weave through traffic, helmet dark, jacket plain.

"I don't know," he said finally. "But I think we'll know when we do."

She nodded. "Until then, we've got enough fires to put out."

Borden turned from the window. "Let's start with Winthrop's case. The minister's death can't be buried under headlines about Tina."

"Already on it," she said. "Preliminary results suggest his death was personal. We're pulling his phone logs. There may be more to it than we thought."

Outside, the city moved on, oblivious to how close it had come to chaos.

But somewhere out there, The Ghost was still watching.

Waiting.

And not even the police knew what side he was really on.

Chapter 80

It had been almost two months since Tina and Juan Estrada were convicted in a Canadian court and began serving eighteen years in federal prison.

Carole Ruth closed the file and handed it back to the clerk from the Department of International Transfers of Offenders, saying, "Everything is in order. Now, get them out of here and save the taxpayers a pile of money,"

The clothes Tina and Juan had worn when arrested no longer fit well. Both had lost weight in prison.

Shackled, they were led to the prison yard and boarded a transport wagon that arrived at a special non-public gate near the back of Pearson International Airport, not far from the lounge Tina had enjoyed months earlier.

From there, they departed on their final trip back to Mexico to serve out the remainder of their sentence, as agreed upon by Corrections Canada and the Mexican authorities.

Hours later, Tina and Juan were escorted through a doorway in a chain-link fence towering six feet above them. There were no clouds in the sky as they arrived at a high-security compound and were put to work in the sweltering heat for most of the day, separated by another chain-link corridor.

Inmates stared at them. They were the newbies. No one approached them. No one spoke to them. They just took a two-second peek, avoiding eye contact. The inmates knew to stay away and watch what happened next.

A few days later, a visitor showed up at the prison requesting a five-minute meeting with the warden. He produced an official document allowing for a highly unusual request to speak to Tina and Juan together in private.

The permission letter was signed by the President of Mexico.

The interviews took place an hour later. Neither Tina nor Juan had an opportunity to speak prior to being led to a tiny, secure interview room. They were not prepared for what would happen next.

They sat at opposite ends of the table, and the messenger sat at the center. For a few moments, no one spoke.

The messenger asked if they were being treated well under the circumstances. Then he asked Juan, "How's your shoulder or hand coming along? Not sure where your injury was," he said. "Has it healed well?"

Juan responded in the affirmative.

"The leadership here in Mexico was disappointed to learn about Sean. We know you depended on him for many of his specialized services, and learning that he was a spy... well, let's say he got his reward. We're not interested in dwelling on the past but looking more to the future. Arturo wanted you to know he is grateful for the millions you forwarded, and whether you'd be interested in helping him out with some special assignments?"

Tina responded, "Of course," followed by Juan, who agreed.

"That's wonderful. Arturo will be pleased," said the messenger. "Please, tell no one of this meeting. If anyone asks, it was an uncle who came to see you. I'll contact you shortly."

Two days later, Juan and Tina each received a parcel containing new clothes, shoes, and toiletries.

The warden asked to see them, and they arrived at his office separately. They sat quietly, like schoolchildren waiting outside the principal's office.

The door opened, and a guard escorted another trembling prisoner, desperately trying to hold back tears, from the warden's office across the room and into the hall. The secretary looked over at Tina and Juan and told them both to enter and sit down.

The warden greeted them and reached for a folder on his desk.

The warden said to Tina, "I understand you are considered a friend of our President and our former Ambassador to Canada. Yes, that is correct. I also understand you were on a compact list of possible candidates to be our next Ambassador to Canada. Is that right?"

"Yes, sir."

Juan looked over at Tina. He was hearing this for the first time and his mouth was wide open, staring at his sister.

"Well, it seems someone really likes you. I have two letters, one signed by the President of Mexico, the other by the Prime Minister of Canada. They both say the same thing, actually. As of this day, you have been granted a full and unconditional pardon for any and all crimes you may have committed willingly or unknowingly in the past in both countries.

Any criminal records will be expunged, and there will no longer be any record anywhere of any convictions in either country."

Tina's jaw dropped as she looked at Juan, then back at the warden.

"The same pardon has been given to your brother Juan Estrada."

Tina and Juan stared at each other.

"You will both be escorted to a private lounge, where you will change into new civilian clothes. Once you are ready, a guard will guide both of you to the front gate, where you will be released from our custody and your passports will be returned to you.

I believe there is a limousine waiting for you. I wish you both well in your future business and hope I never see you here again."

When the prison door opened, the prisoners working in the yard stopped what they were doing and watched as the entourage moved toward the chain-link wall. Two or three inmates tipped their hats and gave a wide smile.

The prison chain-link wall contained a smaller door that opened, allowing both Juan and Tina to slip through into the sunlight wearing designer sunglasses. They both stood there for a moment, turned around, and looked at the prison and the inmates standing quietly in the yard watching their every step.

There, in front of them, was a shining new black limousine with a chauffeur standing beside the open back door.

Tina looked at Juan, her voice fierce with resolve, "I told you, I had a plan, and it wasn't over. Now do you believe me?"

Tina slid herself across the plush leather seat in the back of the limousine. Juan followed and the driver carefully closed the door behind him.

Tina's gaze turned from the prison to the window beside her. Her eyes dilated in horror at the sight of a sidewinder missile heading directly toward her. A split second later a huge fireball erupted into the sky. Pieces of molten metal rained down on the pavement in sparks of black, yellow, and orange. Then silence.

Acknowledgements

I would like to acknowledge the contributions of family and friends who have supported me on this book-writing journey.

My daughter Emily Santorelli and her husband Matthew, along with my son Peter McKinnon and his wife Janice, gifted me so much love and encouragement to finish this project. Thank you for believing in me.

Detective Dave Elford has been an amazing resource to me throughout this project. A detective story would be incomplete without the insights of a true detective to bring realism and understanding to what these fine men and women in police services go through every day to protect us. Thank you, Dave, for all your help. You are a true friend.

I am grateful to my nephews, Michael and Matthew Walton, for their help and encouragement as I worked on this book. I love you guys; you're the best of the best, and I thank you and your EMS colleagues for your dedication to saving lives and helping people every day.

I would never have been able to design the stunning book cover or get this story through the publisher without the help of Ken Steven. Ken, you are indispensable, and I appreciate your creative talent.

Joan Vilma Mannering, I thank you for your encouragement during our many phone calls and your support and love during the writing of this story. Thank you so much. I will love you and Walt forever.

And a huge thank you to my wife, Donna. You allowed me the time and space I needed to create this work. I love you.

One More Thing

Thank you for joining Detectives Mark Borden and Janet Cross on their wild journey.

Did you enjoy hanging out with Borden and Cross in their adventure as much as they did to have you along?

If you have a moment, would you consider leaving a review on Amazon? Your words can help other readers discover *Assault on Justice* and it'll go a long way toward keeping Borden and Cross chasing the truth in their next adventure.

Here's how to leave a review:

1. Go to your local Amazon site. In the search bar, type: *Assault on Justice.*
2. Click on the book cover to go to the book's page.
3. Scroll down until you see the "Write a Review."
4. Share a few thoughts, even a sentence or two makes a big difference.

Thank you. I'm sure they appreciate your support.
Monty McKinnon

About The Author

Monty McKinnon retired to a tranquil life of writing books and building custom-made acoustic guitars after a successful career in finance. His YouTube channel, with nearly 30,000 subscribers (@montymckinnon), features more than 300 videos on the art of guitar construction. His first fiction novel, *Chasing After Justice*, with Detectives Borden and Cross, is available on Amazon. His two previous non-fiction books, *Well, That's The Way I See It*, and *Priorities*, are also available on Amazon. Monty and his wife, Donna, live in Newmarket, just north of Toronto, Canada.